Sheep Pen Cañon

Sheep Pen Cañon

James D. Crownover

FIVE STAR
A part of Gale, Cengage Learning

GALE
CENGAGE Learning

Farmington Hills, Mich • San Francisco • New York • Waterville, Maine
Meriden, Conn • Mason, Ohio • Chicago

All scripture quotations, unless otherwise noted, are taken from the King James Bible.
Five Star Publishing, a part of Gale, a Cengage Company

LIBRARY OF CONGRESS CATALOGING-IN-PUBLICATION DATA

Names: Crownover, James D., author.
Title: Sheep Pen Cañon / James D. Crownover.
Description: First edition. | Farmington Hills, Michigan : Five Star, a part of Gale, Cengage Learning, 2019.
Identifiers: LCCN 2018025279 (print) | LCCN 2018026603 (ebook) | ISBN 9781432847234 (ebook) | ISBN 9781432847227 (ebook) | ISBN 9781432847210 (hardcover)
Subjects: | GSAFD: Western stories.
Classification: LCC PS3603.R765 (ebook) | LCC PS3603.R765 S54 2019 (print) | DDC 813/.6—dc23
LC record available at https://lccn.loc.gov/2018025279

First Edition. First Printing: January 2019
Find us on Facebook—https://www.facebook.com/FiveStarCengage
Visit our website—http://www.gale.cengage.com/fivestar/
Contact Five Star Publishing at FiveStar@cengage.com

Printed in Mexico
1 2 3 4 5 6 7 23 22 21 20 19

To Ethel and Jane,
My Greatest Fans

ACKNOWLEDGMENTS

A special thanks goes to Asa Jones, cowboy and manager of the Kenton Museum in Kenton, Oklahoma.

The enthusiastic help of the ladies at the Cimarron Heritage Center Museum in Boise City, Oklahoma, was invaluable.

Introduction

If you recall the final events of Lee Sowell's story in *The Ox That Gored,* you might find this introduction to *Sheep Pen Cañon* repetitive. However, there will be those who have picked up this latter book without first reading the former; and there will be those who have read the former who would like their memories refreshed as they continue reading the record of Lee Sowell, U.S. Deputy Marshal, at large.

In the last chapter of *The Ox That Gored,* Lee and his posse had just delivered a gang of train robbers to Marshal Carroll at Fort Smith. When he picked up his mail, Lee found the following letter:

August 2, 1888
Dear Deputy Sowell:

I write this appealing for your considerable assistance in a matter of great importance to me. I have recently filed on a section of land in the Cimarrón Valley, New Mexico Territory, below Black Mesa. My problem is that I have no cattle for the range and no manpower to develop the land so I can prove up my claim. Is there any way you could assist me? I confess to a dearth of ready cash, but there are other compensations you may find more to your satisfaction. I am a good cook and have experience handling stock. At this time, I am having a bunkhouse built on a hill not far from Sheep Pen Cañon and that lovely stretch of the river we enjoyed on our visit there.

In anticipation of your assent to my rescue, I have taken the liberty of filing for a section adjoining mine in your name. There is an abundance of grass here, as you know, and if I had a mixed herd of a hundred head or so, I would soon have a fine herd of cattle. Another herd of the same size would serve your needs also.

Please reply as soon as possible, care of General Delivery, Florence, Oklahoma. I am most in need of your assistance.

Sincerely, and with Love,
Katherine Ingram

Lee had grinned, and thought: *No dust gathers on her saddle.* This fit right into the plans he had; for only moments later did Judge Parker swear Gamlin Stein in as a new deputy U.S. marshal. "Turnin' loose of the deputy work," Lee tells us, "an' lettin' Gam and Harm go it alone is a lot like settin' your kid on a horse th' first time. You feel responsible and want to trot alongside t' catch th' kid if he should fall, but in th' end, he's gotta ride on his own, an' so will these boys. The time for gradual letting go had passed, an' it was best I get out of th' way—and that's just what I did.

"I offered my resignation but th' marshal would have none of it. Instead, I will be a deputy, at large. It took a couple of days t' settle up business in town. Early one morning, I rounded up my stock an' struck out for Liberty Springs, Arkansas."

There, you are. Now, dear reader, that you are informed or refreshed, slip off your shoes, unbutton your collar, and unbuckle your belt. Sit back and read more of the adventures of Lee Sowell and his friends in No Man's Land.

—James D. Crownover

Chapter 1
The Witness

September 1888

"Lee Sowell!" The bailiff announced from the courtroom door. It took me a moment to get those blasted crutches under my arms, and I wobbled to the door. Judge Parker hardly looked up as I moved down that center aisle. Some yokel ogler had moved his chair out in the aisle a little, and I had to squeeze by while he sat there grinning at me. As I sidled through, my crutch tipped his spit can over on his foot and it rattled down the aisle ahead of me. The man jumped and cursed as his own spittle soaked into his sock. "No tobacco allowed in the courtroom," I hissed. I hoped that can had been full. Judge glanced up from under a cocked eyebrow. He nearly smiled.

The court clerk stood, Bible in hand, as I fumbled through the gate. He lowered the Bible so I could reach it with the crutch pinned under my arm. "Do you swear to tell the truth, the whole truth, and nothing but the truth, so help you God?"

"I do."

"Be seated, please." He motioned to the witness stand chair. It was a tight squeeze, getting in the chair behind the low divider. One of my crutches clattered to the floor. I shoved the chair back against the wall and cocked it so my stiff leg could stick out the gateway.

Ross Scanlon, the prosecuting attorney, shuffled his notes and stood. "Mr. Sowell, would you please state for the court your name and occupation?"

"Yes, sir. My name is Lee Sowell, Deputy U.S. Marshal—at large," I added.

Scanlon almost frowned, but I wasn't about to let that jake-leg lawyer of Newman's challenge my right to be where I was that day. "Explain what 'at large' means."

"It means I can be anywhere in the U.S. and enforce the laws, make arrests, and assist other law enforcement officers in pursuit of their legal duties."

"Where were you July 31, 1888?"

I made some show of drawing my diary from my pocket and opening it to the right page. It carried a lot more weight with the jury if they knew I had notes and a diary to go by. "I was on the Atchison, Topeka and Santa Fe Railroad, shipping cattle to Granada, Colorado."

"You had to stop in Dodge City?"

"Yes, we had to stop there to offload the cattle and feed and water them. We got there the early morning of August first. There was a telegram there for me from Deputy Gamlin Stein."

Ol' Ross frowned. He didn't like me running ahead of his questions like that, but I didn't care for his speed. My leg hurt and my head hurt, and I wanted out of there as fast as possible. "Tell us what was in the telegram . . ."

July 1888

I unfolded the telegram and read: "Train robbed at Woodward stop Robbers headed north to the Outlet stop. Gamlin Stein."

Tex studied the telegram. "Well, Gam, we'll just send these cows on their way an' run right down an' grab those robbers for you."

"Telegram sent the twenty-eighth from Woodward, so I figger they're in th' Strip by now. Wouldn't be much out of th' way to jog down an' ease through th' Outlet, let these cows graze along while we look around."

"Sounds good to me, Lee, let's go." Tex grinned at the

thought of a little action other than herdin' cows.

We fed and watered the cattle, and I made arrangements to leave them in the railroad pens until we were ready to leave. "We need an outfit. Go find us a wagon while I run up to Rath's and order supplies."

I was at Rath's quite a while, orderin' up things we would need on our trip, things I thought Kat would need and some nice things for her cabin. Tex came stompin' in to help and order some things he needed. It took some time to get the gear wrapped for the trip, and when I stepped out on the front dock with a load for the wagon, there dozed Pet and Tobe hitched to a chuck wagon; our saddle horses stood hip-shot, tied behind. The old wagon had seen better days, but it was well built and seemed sound, with iron axles, a big grub box, and a possum belly full of firewood.

"Where in th' world did you git a chuck wagon, Tex?"

He grinned. "That livery 'most give it to me, said it made him want t' cry seein' it ever' day an' knowin' they wouldn't be comin' up th' trail anymore."

It was true; those glory days of trail drivin' were over. The town was quiet, with half th' saloons and stores closed and boarded up and the rough entertainment people gone to the hell-town at track's end. Dodge was taking on the look of a tame county seat town.

The Grangers were even having a fair out on the end of Front Street. We parked in the wagon yard, our wares tied snug under a wagon sheet, and wandered out on the grounds. The farmers and wives were showing off their produce, vying for ribbons and prizes for the best pumpkins, plum jam, quilts, sheep and cattle, pies, and other products of the farm.

A race was in progress with youngsters on squat little ponies beating around the track and the crowd cheering them on. A paint pony nosed out the second place buckskin ridden by a barefoot boy. The winner was a girl no more than nine years old, her blond pigtails and bright ribbons flying behind. As she trotted around her victory lap, the rest of the field, all boys, walked their horses. Instead of turning at the curve of the track, they continued down Front Street, disgusted that a *girl* had beat them.

There were booths and tents set up down the fairway, and the aroma of good things cooking filled the air. All kinds of dishes were offered by ruddy, blondish, and buxom German farmwives.

These were a sturdy people who began their trek to the high plains in 1763, when Catherine the Great, German-born ruler of Russia, offered land, tax breaks, cultural autonomy, and no military conscription to Germans who would settle in the empty high plains along the Volga River, where the hardworking German serfs prospered. A hundred ten years later, Czar Alexander II revoked Catherine's promises, thereby making for a mass exodus of the German Russians to America. Whole villages packed up and moved to the high plains of the United States, where they found a treeless plain that looked a lot like the home they had just left.

Without these good *Russlanddeutschen,* it is probable wheat would have never been planted on the dry plains, for sewed in the linings and pockets of their clothes were seeds of a winter-hardened wheat named turkey red. Incidental to the wheat seed were a few seeds of the thistle plant they named *perekati-pole,* meaning *roll across the field.* Americans christened it *tumbleweed.* With hard work and determination, the Germans re-established their farms and villages on the plains, sometimes giving them the same name they had on the Volga steppes. They were succeeding in making a life on the prairie, where a few years ago only buffalo fed on the rich grasses and, more recently, thousands of cattle grazed.

Tex, being familiar with German food and somewhat conversant in the language, ordered us up heaping plates of sauerkraut with sausage, and dark rye bread with sour cream butter, served with a mug of stout beer. We sat on the ground beside one of the tents and ate.

"Without a doubt, Tex, that's the best kraut I have ever eaten. Think I'll have another plate."

"Better save room for one of those strudels," he mumbled through a big bite of bread and nodded toward a booth across the way.

"You're right about that," I said, "I'll get us a couple while you finish up." The lady in the strudel booth anticipated my desires, and by the time I got there, she had two rolls of sweet-tart cherry strudel on a plate. Returning to Tex, I discovered our sauerkraut plates refilled and the boy grinning up at me. "Thought we would have room for more after all."

I loosened my belt before I sat back down. A pretty *fräulein* refilled our mugs and smiled sweetly at Tex. Down by the racetrack someone began calling, and there was a stir among the people. Our beer maid hurried off and Tex jumped up to follow. "You can have my strudel, Lee."

I groaned. Such food to a batching deputy was heaven, and I could think of only one thing that would make a young man give it up. Sure enough, Tex soon passed by with the crowd hurrying to the caller. He was carrying a fancy wrapped box with the *fräulein* on his arm. *Well you can go on, squire Tex. I'm gonna finish my meal.*

By the time I finished and waddled down to the doings at the racetrack, the box auction was over, and Tex again had that box in his lap and the smiling girl on his arm.

I sat down and asked, "What's goin' on, Tex?"

"The barker is entertaining the crowd before we break up and eat pie. That boy he has up there talking to him is Malvina's little brother." He looked to be about twelve years old. *Fräulein* Malvina leaned forward and smiled at me. Tex introduced me to Malvina in German and I smiled at her.

The barker was asking the boy humorous questions, and the crowd was enjoying his answers. Tex would translate for me the things he understood, which didn't seem to be too much. Then the man asked the question that proved to be the last one. Malvina's hand flew to her mouth and she uttered an exclamation of distress.

"He asked the boy what his sister wouldn't eat before she went to a dance," Tex whispered.

Instead of saying "onions," as everyone expected, the boy grinned and looked at his sister. "Beans!" There was a stunned silence for a moment; Malvina covered her face with her apron and the crowd roared with laughter. Brother stood there grinning, obviously enjoying the moments he had left before sisterly judgment descended upon him.

Tex put a sympathetic arm around the crimson-faced girl and said something to her. "We're going to find a quiet place and eat some pie. You want a piece?"

I groaned at the thought. "I couldn't take another bite. I'm gonna go unhitch the horses and put them in the corral, then I'm gonna roll up in my bed under the wagon and sleep off my overindulgence."

"I reckon I'll be along later." Tex grinned and followed the girl's retreat.

Chapter 2
The Long Branch Fight

"My posse man, Tom Shipley, recognized one of the Newman bunch going into the Long Branch Saloon and woke me late on the night of August first."

"Who was this man?" lawyer Scanlon asked.

"He was Sanders Bain, Pard Newman's cousin."

"Can you identify the man for us?"

"Yes. He's the third man from the left at the defendant's table."

"Objection!"

Judge Parker looked at the defense attorney, "On what grounds?"

"The man the witness identified is not Sanders Bain, your honor."

I picked up my diary and thumbed back a few pages. "August 2, 1888. The man who identified himself as Sanders Bain in the Long Branch Saloon stands five feet, seven inches, weighs 135 pounds, has brown eyes and black hair. There is an S-shaped scar running from his left ear down his cheek, the left earlobe missing. The first finger on his right hand is missing, and he has a through-and-through bullet wound on the outside of his right leg about midway between his knee and his hip."

There followed a delay in the testimony while the defendant was examined and found to be the man described in my notes. That established, Ross turned back to me. "What did you do when your posse man saw Mr. Bain?"

"We entered the Long Branch and, after confirming his identity, arrested him . . ."

★ ★ ★ ★ ★

"You sure that was Sanders, Tex?"

"It was him right down to his limp."

I reached behind the wagon seat and got my shotgun. Even at close range, two barrels of .00 lead beat five or six .45 shells in most men's eyes—and I was surer of getting a hit with that scattergun. "Let's go see."

Tex checked his loads, adding a shell to his empty chamber. "Ready." I gave him another handgun.

"You go around back and cover the back door. I'll give you a minute to get there." The boy nodded and trotted off, disappearing into the alley at the corner of the block.

"Hey there, neighbor," a man hailed as I crossed the street, "where you headed with that scattergun?"

It was a short feller with a badge on his chest and his hand on the pistol in his belt. I noticed he let me get a good distance away before hollering at me. "I'm a U.S. marshal, Officer, fixin' t' arrest a train robber. Wanta come along?"

"Where's yore badge?" The hand stayed on the gun butt.

"I ain't got it, an' I ain't waitin' another minit t' explain myself to a Doubtin' Thomas city deputy. If you ain't comin' with me, foller along an' make sure I don't get back-shot." I turned toward the saloon.

"It's illegal t' carry a gun in th' city."

"Not for U.S. marshals goin' t' arrest a felon," I said over my shoulder; there had been enough delay. Tex could be inside stirrin' up more trouble than he could handle alone. I hit the boardwalk in a trot just as war broke out inside and a man was backin' out th' batwings. I lowered my shoulder and hit the near door hard, propelling the shooter back inside. As he fell, he rolled and fired blind. There was a cry behind me as I kicked the gunsel's gun out of his hand and touched him above his ear with my gun barrel. A shot from my right sang past and crashed into the mirror behind the bar. I ducked and fired at a dim figure dodging behind an overturned table. The room was long and narrow, and the back end was invisible in the dark. "Tex, you all right?"

"Where you been? You almost got me killed," he replied from somewhere in the gloom. A gun flash lit the pall of smoke in the room, and I fired back with my other barrel and scooted around behind the bar. The bartender was lying on the floor waving both empty hands at me.

"I didn't tell you to start a war without me," I yelled. The barkeep's sawed-off counter gun lay on the floor, and I grabbed it up. "What's th' load?" I whispered.

"Two aught, both barrels."

Through a hole blasted in the panel below the counter, I spied a man crouched behind the piano. To my right was the man from behind the table, creeping my way, silhouetted in the window. Gathering myself, I jumped up and fired at the man in the window as my barrel swung around and fired at the piano man. The second boom of the shotgun covered the sound of a pistol, and a sharp pain seared across my upper arm. Glass shattered behind me. "How many?" I asked the barkeep as I reloaded my gun. *I'm cuttin' these barrels down first chance I git,* I thought. Barkeep held up three fingers. There were two men lying on the floor near the door, and the man by the piano was groaning. "Piano man, you still got fight?" I asked.

"Damn right," he retorted.

I peeked through that hole again and saw the man climb up the piano until he stood and started my way. I had to turn the double barrels sideways to get them through the hole. My finger was tightening on the front trigger when I heard a soft sigh and a gun clatter to the floor. A peek revealed the man lying on the floor, fight obviously gone.

I stood and looked. The three bodies were still, but the first man was softly groaning and would soon come around. I hurried out and collected guns and knives. Barkeep lit a lantern and I blinked at the sudden light. "It's over, Tex, you can get up here, now."

"Think I'll stay right here a minit," he replied. That wasn't good.

"Stand aside, men." Another policeman pushed his way through the door, his gun leveled at my navel. "Who the devil are you?"

"I'm a deputy U.S. marshal, and I'll thank you to point that cannon somewhere else. These men are train robbers, guard them. I have a man hurt in the back." I grabbed a lit lantern and hurried into that blasted back gloom. "Where are you, Tex?"

"Over here." He lay behind a row of beer barrels, his bandanna tied around his right leg below the knee. There was blood on his overalls. "It's just a graze, but my leg's so cramped up I can't walk on it."

I pushed up his pant leg and looked at the wound. "Didn't leave a groove, looks more like a tunnel. I'll help you up, an' we'll get you to a doc." I lifted him up and hung his arm over my shoulder. We three-legged it to the front of the room where a crowd was slowly gathering around the walls.

"You're gittin' me wet, Lee, your dang arm's wet with blood, an' it's all over my shirt."

"Sorry. Got a scratch myself."

The deputy was sitting in a chair, facing two men propped up against the front of the bar, one with blood caked above his ear, and the other with shot peppered down his side. He didn't look to be bleeding much. The deputy motioned to the piano man. "He ain't goin' nowhere."

Wouldn't you know the last man standing would be the only man dead?

"Doc's outside tendin' to Sam. He should be in soon."

"Sam the other deputy?" I asked. "He hit bad?"

"Naw, just caught one with his collarbone."

"Move over there, folks. This is not some fairground show. There's work to be done in here, *git out of the way.*" A black doctor's kit pushed between two men followed by a stout man, one of his suspenders hanging, his top pants' button undone, and house slippers on his feet. "I'm damned if a man can't get a night's rest without some bunch shootin' up each other and whining for a doctor. Who's hurt worse?"

"I guess that man layin' over there, Doc, but he's beyond repair," the deputy drawled.

"Well, can you tell me who's next, Joe Don?"

"Take care of this leg first, Doc," I said. "I'll check out the rest for you."

Doctor Daniel Stepp peered up at me over his glasses. "Thank you, feller. Who might you be?"

"I *might* be King Cotton, but folks call me Deputy Lee Sowell."

He ignored the comment and turned his attention to Tex. "Hop him up on that bar, King, and let me get to that leg."

A man from the crowd came over, and we sat Tex up on the bar so his legs dangled over the edge. Doc pulled up a chair, rummaged through his bag, and pulled out a pair of scissors. He began slitting the new pant leg and Tex groaned.

"Hush there, young man. You can get that *fräulein* you were squiring tonight to sew them back up—if you can get her away from the beans." He chuckled at his joke.

"Hmmm, not too bad." He squeezed a little blood out of the two wounds. "Missed the bone." Peeking around at the bartender, he said, "George, hand me a bottle of whiskey—*not that rotgut.*" He waved the proffered bottle away. "The good stuff." He took a scrap of white silk out of his bag and soaked it with the whiskey after taking a swallow himself. With the rag draped over the end of a long silver rod, he pushed the rag through the wound. Tex was holding the edge of the bar with both hands, and the knuckles went white as his face. His jaw was clamped and sweat beaded on his forehead.

"Just be glad that wasn't a smaller caliber, son. That would have really hurt," Doc said as he dabbed at the fresh blood. "We'll bandage that up good, and in a week or two you'll be good as new."

"Ne-ext!" Doc announced. I haven't heard as good a call in a barbershop.

"A *week or two*!" I almost groaned out loud. "This feller has .00 from his shoulder blade to his hip, Doc."

"Let's see. You bleeding bad anywhere, feller?" The man didn't answer. "Doesn't look like it. I'll have to take him to the office and work on him. A little chloroform wouldn't hurt there. What about this man?" The doctor pulled the man's chin around so he could see the side of his head. "Gotta have a couple of stitches." He stood and shrugged up his other gallus. "Bunch of you men take these two to my—"

"Doc, these men are train robbers fresh off a job and dangerous. Can you work on them just as well at the jail?"

Doc gave me a sharp glance. "S'pose I could. Office beds are full anyway. Joe Don, haul 'em to jail, and I'll be there directly." He glanced at the crowd. "Mack, there's a pair of crutches behind my office door. Scoot over there and fetch them for this boy. Deputy, *put him in a bed,* and elevate that leg some. Keep him warm, and if he runs *any* fever, let me know right away, day or night."

I was dying inside. "Day or night" meant time spent when we needed to be moving.

Doc grabbed my arm. "Wait a minute, Deputy Cotton, let me look at that other arm. That's a fair amount of blood you're ventin' there."

I had hardly noticed except to shake blood off my fingertips occasionally. When I looked, my whole sleeve was soaked in blood. Before I could stop him, Doc had slit my shirtsleeve to the shoulder. "Dadblast it, Doc, last thing a man needs out here is a short-sleeved shirt."

He grinned up at me. "Got half interest in Rath's store, an' every little bit of business helps. Looks like you got about six stitches coming there. When you get the boy in bed, come to the jail, and I'll fix you up." He ripped the sleeve the rest of the way off and tied it tight around the wound. "That'll keep you from dripping all over the floor until I get to it." He hurried out the door, calling to someone in the street.

The man named Mack brought in a pair of crutches, and we stood Tex on the floor and fitted the things to him. He took a step or two while I steadied him with my good hand under his belt.

"Ain't a spare room in town, much less a bed," Mack said, " 'Less'n you kick someone out."

"We'll make do somehow," I said. This bed business was a luxury for deputies and posses. Most likely, Tex would be just as comfortable on a bed of hay in the wagon. We pushed through the crowd still pressing in to see the damage, and as we emerged, a stout man in farmer's clothes approached. In a thick German accent, he said, "We have place for young man to stay." He led us to two women standing in the shadows across the street. It was Malvina and an older woman, who must be her mother. The girl came forward, anxiety showing in her manner, and spoke softly to Tex. The mother took up her station on the opposite side of Tex and began to steer him down the street toward the wagon yard. Papa and I—the ignored—fell in behind.

"Lee, you there?" Tex inquired.

"Right behind you."

"They insist on taking me to their home. Say there isn't a bed available in the whole town."

"They live close to here?"

"It's a place called Gray Center about twenty-five miles west of here."

"Think you can stand the trip?"

"I ain't all that bad off, just awful tired. I left a lot of blood in th' saloon."

"I got held up by a nosy deputy wantin' t' disarm me."

"They showed fight as soon as they saw me. The one you buffaloed is Sanders Bain."

"The city marshal has them down at the jail. I have to go see to them. Ask if there is a place at Gray Center I can leave our cattle while I go help Gam. These Newmans has got my dander up."

There followed a broken conversation amongst the four of them with the result that the papa, who was Emil Melton, tapped my arm and nodded that there would be room to keep the cattle there as long as needed. I left Tex in the care of the Meltons and hurried to the jail. This was gonna be a busy day. Doc had the shotgun victim laid out naked on a table, sleeping in a chloroform fog while he mined for lead. The man's body had circles drawn around the holes already probed, and it looked like Doc was almost finished with him. I talked to the marshal, and he agreed to hold the two long enough for the Arkansas court to send someone with papers and get the prisoners. It took eight stitches to sew up my arm. I thanked Doc again for ripping up my shirt and paid him for services rendered to me and Tex. Payment for the two prisoners and burial of the third came from Bain's pocket over his protests.

Chapter 3
Ingalls Inn

Prosecuting Attorney Scanlon looked at his notes a moment, then turned to me. "There was a delay in pursuing the train robbers at this point, wasn't there?"

"Yes, the train robbers had attacked and wounded my posse man, Tom Shipley—"

"You also call this Tom Shipley 'Tex,' don't you?"

I frowned at the interruption. "Yes, we do."

"Go ahead, Deputy Sowell."

"I had to get medical attention for Mr. Shipley and secure accommodations for him while he recovered from his wound. It became necessary for me to find a replacement for him before proceeding. While I was accomplishing these things, a fight broke out between the towns of Cimarrón and Ingalls, in Kansas, over the location of the Gray County seat. The citizens appealed to me to stop the war."

At the Dodge City train depot, I sent a telegram to the marshal at Fort Smith, then inquired about the disposition of my cattle. There was a siding at Ingalls, only six miles north of Gray Center, and the stationmaster said he could get a local to haul the eight carloads there as soon as they were loaded and traffic allowed. The cattle were loaded by late afternoon, and we unloaded them at Ingalls just after sunset.

There I sat with two hundred head of cattle, team and horses, and a wagonload of supplies. I hooked up Pet and Tobe and drove south on Main Street. The liveryman was just settling under the light of his lantern swinging from the hay lift when I drove up. "This th' way to Gray Center?"

The chair plopped down on its four legs. "Shore is, feller. Was you twelve feet tall, you could see th' lights from here."

My arm was throbbing and my head hurt. "Suppose a man could get a bite t' eat sommers and sleep in that wagon yard without interference?"

"This place is quiet as a cemetery in winter after 'bout eight o'clock. Nothin' gonna bother you till th' rooster crows. Pull 'er 'round th' corner, an' I'll put th' stock up while you go 'cross there to th' boardin' house an' eat."

He pointed to a well-lit two-story house across the street and didn't have to say anything twice. I stomped dust off my feet on the steps and clumped across the painted porch. A tall, portly lady met me at the screen door. "Wash pan's around the corner, cowboy. Kick your boots off here and I'll go set you a place."

I dumped used wash water on rosebushes by the back steps and poured a pan of fresh water. To my surprise, it was warm, and there was a bar of Pears soap in the soap dish. I washed my bare arm to the bandage and a little bit above. The stitches had leaked, and the bandage had a red spot I couldn't hide. The rosebush on the opposite side of the steps got a watering, and I went back to the front door, kicked off my boots beside a couple other pairs, and went in.

It was a large open room, the living room to my right and a dining room with benches next to the long table-sides to my left. A door at the back of the room led to the kitchen.

"Latch that screen, if you would," the lady requested. Two barefoot men sat on the near bench, their backs to me. I walked around the end of the table and took the proffered seat in front of a platter loaded with a steaming steak, mashed potatoes, and some kind of wilted greens with chunks of bacon in it.

"Looks like you met with an accident," the lady said. "I'm

Mrs. Sarah Ashmore, and that's Rockin' R Bill. This feller is Jimbo Jackson."

Jimbo Jackson had garters on his sleeves and still wore the shaded visor of a telegraph operator. My guess was he was a railroad boomer, one of those itinerants who roamed the railroads, picking up jobs as they needed them.

Rockin' R Bill grinned at me over his coffee cup. One of his front teeth was missing, and by that I knew he was the real article. I nodded. "Name's Lee Sowell," and set to finding the flower designs on my china plate. Mrs. Ashmore brought me a thick slice of hot bread and motioned to the butter bowl on the table.

"My, that was good, Miz Sarah. Reckon some come-after would just about top me off," Bill said. A young girl from the kitchen whisked away the two empty plates and refilled coffee cups all around.

"When Mr. Sowell finishes his meal, we will all sit down for a slice of your come-after, Bill, and we'll have a little conversation with it," Miz Sarah said.

It didn't take long for me to finish, and the boomer said, "Miz Sarah, that man needs a second helping of taters an' greens. We got all night to wait for him to finish." Almost before he was through talking, the young girl entered with fresh helpings of both and another slice of bread. "Thank you," I said and finished my second helpings. Dishes were clattering in the kitchen, and I grinned at the two men across from me. "If I'd'a known I was gonna have t' eat barefoot, I'd'a worn socks without holes."

"I carry a dress pair in my pocket just for this purpose." Jimbo Jackson grinned.

Lorna Hardy, the young girl, brought in five small plates and set them before us, one in the vacant space to my right, and one at the head of the table. Miz Sarah entered with a pie high with meringue and sat at the head of the table while her helper sat between us and opposite Rockin' R Bill. Five slices emptied the pie pan. "Here's your come-after, Bill. Now you be the first to tell us the events of your day."

The young man looked longingly at his coconut cream pie and said, "Me an' that lineback dun took turns bustin' each other all mornin', an' this afternoon I rode th' other two hosses I broke and shook some o' th' kinks out'n 'em." He cut the point off his pie and savored his first bite.

"That's not all you did, is it?" the lady of the house asked.

"Oh-h-h . . . no, ma'am, I split some kindlin' for you and filled th' coal bin."

"And that's all? Seems I saw sparks flying from the well house."

My neighbor blushed mightily and pulled her feet under her bench. Bill grinned. "Don't know a thing about that, ma'am." It was obvious Bill had been turned loose from the Rockin' R Ranch for the winter, and he was getting along by breaking a string of horses and working for his board. Most likely, he slept outside or in some barn loft to keep his expenses down. Our attention turned to Jimbo Jackson, who sat next to Bill. "The wires have been hot all day, Miz Sarah, about the shooting at the Long Branch in Dodge City. Some U.S. marshal shot it out with three men of the Newman gang that held up that train down in Indian Territory last week. One of them is dead, and the other two are in jail, injured. The deputy and his posse-man took hits, and so did City Deputy Hitson. Seems they'll all be well." He looked at me. "I have a good idea our guest knows more about that happening than all of us combined."

All looked at me, expecting a reply that didn't come before I savored another bite of that pie. "I am a deputy U.S. marshal, and it was me and my posse that arrested the train robbers." I told them about the fight. "The Emil Meltons have taken my young partner to Gray Center to recuperate, and I will leave my herd of cattle there while I help deputies capture the rest of the Newman gang down in the Outlet."

Miss Lorna snorted. "It's that Malvina."

Miz Sarah smiled. "Jealousy does not become you, young lady. Mr. Lee, how is your arm? Were you hit hard?"

"No, ma'am, it was just a graze, but Doc put stitches in it." It seemed that my full stomach and over thirty-six hours without sleep all came together on me at once, and I could hardly hold my eyes open. "I should call it a day, if you will excuse me." I made to rise and had to sit back down.

"How rude of us!" Miz Sarah exclaimed. "You've been up since yesterday morning, had a battle—got shot—moved your cattle here, and you're worn out. You are going to bed right here. Lorna, the room at the head of the stairs is ready. Go turn down the covers and light us a light. You two men get him up there; I have some laudanum in the kitchen."

Over my protest, Rockin' R Bill said he would sleep under the wagon and it would be safe. Miz Sarah would have nothing else but that I sleep in the bed. I didn't have the strength to resist and soon found myself medicated and chin deep in a featherbed.

I awoke midmorning with an urgent need and sneaked out the back door, down the outside stair to the privy path. Bill, at the woodpile, advised, "Don't git off that path, Lee, sand spurs'll git you." I managed to stay the "straight and narrow."

Bill stood leaning on the axe handle as I returned. "Where's your socks?"

"Didn't have time t' look 'em up," I replied, pulling a sand spur out of my heel.

"Go on an' wash up; I'll git 'em for you."

"Thanks, I will." I felt a little dizzy and carefully walked to the back steps. It felt good to wash and even better to sit down on the steps and stop my head from spinning. Bill came padding around the porch from the front door with my socks.

"Wouldn't let me cut through th' kitchen," he grunted as he sat down beside me.

"Can you help me herd those cows down to Gray Center?"

"What for you takin' them to Gray Center? They ain't nothin' there but four or five German families. They're farmers an' have plowed and planted winter wheat. You'd have t' go a ways for grass—most likely have t' pay for the privilege to graze." He looked off up the road to the tracks. We could hear my cattle bawling. They were getting hungry and thirsty. "Ain't no water there, either 'cept them German wells, and that'd be expensive too. River water's free and so's th' grass growin' along it."

"You thinkin' that ol' Dutchy Melton saw money when he looked at me?" I asked.

"More'n likely he seen a way t' get paid fer your man stayin' there an' sparkin' his daughter. Mallie's gittin' on t' marryin' age, an' th' ol' man's thinkin' that's one less mouth t' feed. Them Germans is tighter'n Dick's hatband, always lookin' t' make money out'a somethin'." Bill shook his head and chuckled. "He don't stop t' think Miz Evaline might like havin' Mallie 'round t' help with her chores."

"Be careful. Ya might talk yourself into a job."

Rockin' R Bill grinned, "Why, for shore I'm tryin'. Couldn't think of a better way t' spend a Kansas winter than babyin' a herd o' Whiteface an' Durham cows."

I'm not so gullible that I take every man's word for things, but Bill's pitch made some sense. Bein' a cowhand out of work and having free water and grass at hand, not to mention good strong corrals t' keep those cows in at night, made it all mighty attractive. "You got in mind what you would charge for your services keepin' that herd?"

"We-e-ell, ranch foremen 'round here get a hundred a month—"

"I ain't got a ranch, an' two hundred head o' pampered cattle don't make much of a herd, an' you won't have th' headache of ramroddin' a bunch of wild cowhands. Since I can't provide found, I'll pay you fifty a month t' graze an' water th' cows, and keep them overnight in th' pens."

Bill ruminated on that a minute. "Miz Sarah sets th' finest table in th' state, but she's more expensive than other places, too . . . I'm thinkin' more like sixty a month would cover expenses an' give me a little salary."

Now, it was my turn to think. "Tell you what, Bill, I'll give you two choices: I'll pay Miz Sarah for two meals a day an' a greasy-sack lunch an' pay you forty a month t' take care of that bunch of cows; or I'll pay you fifty a month, an' you make your own arrangements for your eats."

Bill Wylie grinned. "Make it fifty-five an' I'll take you up on th' deal."

"Dadblast it, you're hard t' deal with. Where I come from, fifty-five pays a foreman. Fifty'd pay a chuck wagon cook."

"This ain't Indian Territory, an' I ain't no common cowhand. Was you not t' come back till spring, you'd find all your cows an' they'd be fat, too."

That got me t' thinkin': *was I not t' come back till spring—or—was I not t' come back* . . . which was a distinct possibility in my profession . . . "Bill, this might not be so straightforward an' simple as we might think; if I don't come back until spring, or not at all, those cows would need to go to their owner out in New Mexico west of No Man's Land a ways. Would you be willing to get them to him? His name's Kat Ingram."

No, I didn't say her. *Th' reason's obvious, ain't it? Not knowin' Bill all that well, he might get th' idea a woman might not be comin' t' find out what happened to her cattle like a man would, if Bill was to steal the herd. He'd think different if he knew Kat like I did.*

"I don't know, Lee; what's that involve?"

"We got two homesteads on th' Cimarrón a few miles west of Florence. You could ship the herd to the end of tracks, an' you would only have to drive them less than a hundred miles to the owner's place. You'd have that chuck wagon with enough grub for th' trail, only there's a bunch of stuff in there for th' lady of th' ranch. I can assure you employment for the summer and maybe longer. There's also th' chance you might want t' homestead a place of your own out there.

"I can make arrangements for the train transportation and for keeping the herd in the pens for the winter. We'll pay you fifty a month and two more hands forty a month, payable upon delivery of the cattle to the ranch."

Now, *Bill* was rubbin' his chin. "Gonna hafta think on this some, Lee."

While Bill was "thinkin' on it," we walked over to the station, and I made arrangements with the stationmaster to make the cattle cars available upon request by Bill or myself. He made out two orders, and we each signed one.

"This'll be my first shipment of that many cattle to the end of tracks, but since you will have a wagon with it, I can give you immigrant's rate, which is considerably less than cattle rate going the other direction," the stationmaster said. He did some figgerin' on a piece of paper. "Deducting the rate you paid from Ingalls to Granada, Colorado, and applying that to the rate from Ingalls to the end of track, turns out this railroad owes you some money. I'll have to have this confirmed by the division at Dodge. They will probably let me know this afternoon."

"Well, Bill, that gives me time to take Tex's horse to Gray Center and see how he's getting along. You'll have time to decide if you'll take me up on my proposition."

"Sounds good, Lee." With that, we both went about our business.

We hadn't ridden the horses since they got on the train, and we were almost to Gray Center before either one got their kinks out. I didn't have any trouble finding the Melton place. Tex was sitting out under a grape arbor with Malvina, his leg propped up on a nail keg. He didn't look happy. Mallie took the horses to the barn and went to the house to get us a glass of tea.

When she was out of earshot, Tex whispered, "Lee, you gotta get me outta here. They got me married off an' diggin' taters, pickin' beans an' wheat an' kids poppin out like popcorn. *I ain't ready fer that!*"

Tex liked his women, but in smaller doses than he was gettin'. I struggled to keep a straight face. "You ain't ready t' ride, and I ain't ready t' drag you off into th' Strip an' amputate that leg in some dry camp a hunnert miles from anywhere."

"I mean it, Lee. If you don't git me outta here, I'll go by myself."

"How's your leg?"

"It's healin' good. I can almost walk without these crutches."

"The dom leg's much hurt, Herr Lee. You mus' not heed what this man says." Malvina sat a tray with a pitcher of tea and three glasses on the table.

"How does it look to you, Malvina?"

"It . . . seeps?" she said, groping for the right English word.

We spent the afternoon sipping tea and talking, Tex acting as interpreter for Malvina and me. Mrs. Melton summoned from the house, and Malvina hurried to help with supper.

"What are we gonna do, Lee?" Tex whispered.

When did this become our *problem*? I thought. "Tex, you got shot night before last, and you can't travel any without doing yourself real damage. I've been thinkin', an' maybe I have a plan. I've hired a man to take care of the cattle and maybe drive them to Sheep Pen Cañon later. We were thinkin' about a spring drive from the end of tracks, but if you help him, you could probably make the trip yet this fall—if you heal up soon enough."

"I'll be ready next week—"

"No you won't, and you know it. How silly—no *stupid*—would it be to let a little through-and-through bullet hole in the leg kill you, or leave you lame for life, because you wouldn't give it time to heal? If you want that, I won't be any part of it. I'm takin' both horses back with me, and the last day of this month, Bill Wylie will bring your horse down. If Mrs. Sarah Ashmore at the Ingalls Inn says you are well enough to travel, you can drive the chuck wagon. *You cannot ride a horse to Sheep Pen Cañon.* Those are my conditions. Take them, or we part company right here—and I'll still take your horse back to Ingalls."

Tex looked a little surprised, but he knew I meant every word, so he nodded. Emil drove up the team he had been plowing with, and I went over to help him with them. While he put up the harnesses, I drew water for the horses and he came out with oats for them. The barn was neat and clean and arranged quite differently from a ranch barn. When we got back to the arbor, the table was set for a feed. We sat down to eat, and I'll have to say that food was substantial and bountiful. I pitied the horse that had to take me back to town.

Tex was real quiet. When I got ready to leave, he said, "I'll be ready when Wylie comes the end of the month, Lee."

"Good," I said and rode out. A little ways out, I switched to Tex's horse. It wasn't long before we could see the lights of Ingalls, but we rode a long ways before we got there. That darned flatland.

Chapter 4
The Gray County War

There was just a hint of pink on the western horizon when I rode into town. Thorny had just lit his lantern and pulled it up on the hay lift rope. It hadn't stopped swinging before he sat propped two-legged in his chair.

"Don't get up, Thorny. I'll take care of these horses." Of course, that didn't stop the man from getting up and helping. Thorny Kingsley was an old stove-up vaquero with the soft, south Texas drawl lingering in his speech. Back in 1838 or '39, a mother delivered her baby boy under the shelter of a wagon sheet somewhere around old Washington, Arkansas. The family was on their way from South Carolina to the Lone Star Nation to start a new life where land was plentiful and people scarce. The proud mother held her infant to her breast, and as he took his first nourishment in this world, she named him Thorndyke Kingsley, Thorndyke being her maiden name.

The boy struggled under the weight of that name until he was ten or so, when he shortened it to Thorny. After that, no one called him Thorndyke without challenge. The boy grew strong and wiry, convincing those who clung to the old name that the new name was healthier for them to use. "No one uses that name on me, 'cept Ma, and gits away with it." He must have said it a hundred times.

His pa died when the boy was eleven, and when he was twelve, Thorny hired out as a vaquero to help his family get on. In 1854, he was one of the first men (at fifteen) Colonel Dick

King hired for his new ranch on the Rio San Catrudos. For the next thirteen years, he never slept under a roof, being busy herding cattle and horses, chasing Juan Cortina and his thieves from south of the Rio Grande. "Didn't need t' go off and fight Yankees. We had our own war right there at home," he would say. He poured us two cups of coffee and set our chairs for just the right angle of two-legged repose against the barn wall.

"Everything is awful new around here, Thorny. How old is this town?" I asked after my first sip.

"Weren't nothin' here a year ago last May, then ol' Hop Bitters Soule hit on th' idée o' makin' his own town here near th' head of his canal. He's built 'most ever' building in town, an' sometimes stays in Miz Sarah's when he comes down from Dodge. He's set his sights on makin' this th' county seat of Gray County. Soule's built a railroad to Montezuma t' git their vote. They stuffed th' ballot boxes enough that th' State Soopreme Court's ruled that Ingalls has won th' sheriff and county clerk positions.

"Asa's hired th' Mastersons, Tom an' Jim, an' Bill Tilghman an' some more o' th' Dodge Peace Commission t' watch things. We call them 'the Killers.' They ain't been doin' nothin' but struttin' around scarin' people. I hear somethin' big's gonna happen tomorrow, but ever'one's close-mouthed about it."

"Neither here nor there for me," I said, "I don't get mixed up in those political doin's."

"Same here, Lee. Let 'em fight it out among their selves." After a few minutes, Thorny asked, "Ya hear 'bout th' Stevens County War?"

"Can't say as I have."

"Got pretty bloody. They may still be killin' people up there. Gov'ner's had t' send in th' militia twict, now. Two fellers named Price and Wood went down there to establish a town, an' Price rode into Hugoton to look things over. Th' census taker, a man named Calvert, invited him t' join th' town, sayin' it didn't make no difference if he was a visitor. Price got into th' spirit of things by namin' himself, partner Wood, and many others, includin' imaginary folks to put on the census list. Some o' those single friends of his got saddled with a bunch of kids, an' when they were through, they counted twenty-somethin' sets of twins!" Thorny laughed.

"Well, Price an' Wood bought a piece of land north an' a little east of Hugoton and laid out a town; named it Woodsdale, and th' fight was on. In the county elections, John Cross of Woodsdale was elected sheriff. Sam Robinson got mad and moved to Hugoton, where they made him town marshal. A bad man named Short was made Woodsdale town marshal, and he was given a warrant for Robinson's arrest. When he went to arrest Robinson in Hugoton, they had a shootout, both emptyin' their six-guns and not hittin' anyone. Short left empty-handed."

I got up and poured us both fresh coffee.

"Short heard that Robinson had gone down into th' Neutral Strip, and he got up a posse t' go after him, ignorin' th' fact that he didn't have any jurisdiction outside o' town an' there was no law in th' Strip. Short sent word to Woodsdale for more help. Robinson got away, and Short and his posse was chased out of th' Strip by a bunch from Hugoton." Thorny paused to cut a fresh chew of Mickey Twist, and then continued. "Sheriff Cross invited volunteers to go see what had become of Short, and four men agreed t' go with him. Meanwhile, Robinson had run into another of the Hugoton gangs, and they turned around.

"Cross an' his posse wore their horses out and found old man Haas and his boys cuttin' hay at Mustang Lake, and decided t' spend th' night with them. They had just laid down under one of the haystacks when th' Hugoton bunch surrounded them and ordered 'em out. Cross's party was not armed and got caught flat-footed. Robinson murdered Cross and a feller named Bob Hubbard. J.B. Chamberlain shot Herbert Tonney. A man named Eaton was sleeping in a wagon and got up and ran, Robinson and others chasing him. Robinson came back braggin' he had shot Eaton. They couldn't find the fifth man, Wilcox, for a while. When they did, they stood him up by the other dead, and Robinson shot him. Wilcox groaned until someone put another bullet into him.

"The Hugoton bunch give out that they had a battle an' killed th' Short posse, but Herbert Tonney wasn't dead an' told th' truth of it."

I sat there thinking about what the man had said. What a sordid tale, men choosin' up sides an' killin' each other over nothin' more than whose town would be the county seat. It was enough to make me sick—sick of the killing and sick of havin' to deal with it all. The dinner bell rang at the boarding house, and I said good night and ambled over to the porch. Jimbo Jackson and another railroad man were already washing up. I poured fresh water in th' pan and tried to wash thoughts of those murders out of my mind. We had a pleasant meal, and I settled into that soft bed early.

Persistent knocking on my door jarred me out of my sleep. I was still pulling my pants up when I opened the door and saw Miz Sarah standing there, lantern in her hand, her hair down and a robe thrown around her shoulders. "Something terrible is going to happen in Cimarrón, Deputy Sowell. The Killers are headed there to grab the county clerk's papers. You have to do something!"

I groaned and turned back to find my shirt and gun belt. As I sat on the bed putting my socks on, Miz Sarah explained what was happening. "Mr. Soules has offered a thousand dollars for anyone who brings him the county papers, so the Dodge Peace Commission has taken a wagon down there to get them. Oh, I'm afraid there will be blood spilt."

"Well, if it's spilt over which damn town gets to be the county seat, it's useless excess blood anyway," I growled. "Nothing's more stupid than that, unless it's some moneybag offerin' a reward for someone else doin' his dirty work. Where's my boots?" I grabbed my shotgun and checked its loads as I ran down the stairs. My boots were just inside the front door, and I stomped them on across the porch. Thorny came out of the barn holdin' a lantern high and leading my fresh horse, already saddled. Sleepy-eyed Lorna Hardy stood aside, then trudged back across the street to the house.

"Are you coming, Thorny?" I asked as I mounted.

"Nope. I don't play politics." His voice faded behind me. "They ain't been gone long."

We settled into a long lope. I wasn't set on establishin' a speed record on the six miles to Cimarrón. The trouble would be there when we got there.

It was a while after I heard the first boom of a Sharps .50 before I heard the pop-pop-pop of smaller guns. As we neared, the sound became continuous. The racket of a wagon coming along the road almost drowned out the intermittent boom of the .50. I stopped well off the tracks of the road and waited for the wagon. It flew by without pause, the driver whipping the mules, and a dozen men hanging on in the bed. A ways past me, the wagon swerved off the road and bogged in deep sand. In an instant half a dozen men were out, pushing and lifting the wagon through the sand.

I moved still farther from the road and hollered out. "This is a U.S. marshal. Hold still there." Just as I figgered, a half dozen guns sent bullets singing down the road. I circled well out in the field and came in ahead of the wagon, while the Killers concentrated on who might be coming up behind them. The driver continued whipping the mules mercilessly, even though they could not move the wagon. He didn't even see me before I backhanded my quirt across his back. He raised that whip to strike me back, and I blew it in two with my shotgun and dove for the ground. Only a couple of shots flew through where I had been sitting on the horse. "The next shooter's gonna get a face full of buckshot," I promised. "I am Deputy U.S. Marshal Sowell. *Stand down.*"

That quieted them some and I was able to talk with them. "What is going on here?"

"There's a bunch of Cimarrón men after us, bent on killing th' lot of us," someone answered.

"Are they ridin' close b'hind, or are they comin' afoot, 'cause I haven't seen hide nor hair of 'em. Why are they chasin' you?"

" 'Cause we got th' courthouse papers Mr. Soule sent us to get." A tall man who was assuming spokesmanship pushed through the men.

"I suppose I am to be impressed that *Mr. Soule* sent you on this mission and bow and scrape and let you go on your way." My anger was rising even higher.

"You well should; how do we know you're a deputy, anyway?" The man approached—too close—and as he reached for the shotgun barrel, I laid the quirt across his face. The lash wrapped around his neck and I pulled, spinning him half around. He fell to his knees choking. I pulled his pistol and kicked his backside and he fell facedown, choking for breath.

"You'll have t' take my word for it, bein's it's too dark t' read my commission, an' I'm th' one holdin' this scattergun."

Cooler heads were beginning to prevail. It wasn't like I hadn't been around town and these men hadn't seen and known who I am. "Deputy, some of us are shot up, and it won't be long until those Cimarrón men come pounding after us. We need to get these men treated."

"You're goin' th' wrong way. Th' doctors are at Dodge City."

"We get to Ingalls, Mr. Soule's got a train there, an' we can get to Dodge faster," one man said.

"And you can collect that thousand dollars. Won't be much divided among th' bunch of you. Is it really worth it?"

There were only groans from the wagon to answer. That infernal Sharps boomed again. "What are they still shooting at?" I asked.

"We had to leave three of our men there," the driver snarled, still smarting from my blow.

"Hey, and that'll be three less t' split th' reward with, won't it?"

"It ain't that way a'tall, Deputy. Those men were upstairs in th' courthouse when those Cimarróns hauled hell outta th' shuck, an' we couldn't wait any longer." The man almost whined.

"It looks like I have more work t' do an' don't have time t' fiddle for you boys. Take yourselves to Ingalls and tell Asa Soule that if he's still there when I get back, I'm gonna arrest him and every man with him. Driver, you're fired. Get down and stand over there. Someone else drive that don't mistreat th' stock."

It took only a moment to push the wagon back up on th' road, with it mostly empty. "Now load up this piece of work." I indicated the man still wheezing for air. "And *walk* those mules to town. No one will be coming after you. Be sure and turn them back to Thorny, an' don't leave them standin' sommers." The fired driver made to get on the wagon and I said, "Hold on there, friend, you're not ridin'."

We watched the wagon drive away and I mounted my horse, "Now, mister, start walkin' towards Cimarrón."

"You ain't gonna take me back there, are you? They'll kill me!"

"Well, they should, what with you riding into their town in th' middle of the night and shootin' up th' place. No, I'm not gonna take you to town, though it would be fair. There's three fellers would like t' talk to you about runnin' off an' leavin' them. We're goin' this way until I'm sure you can't catch up with that wagon, and then I'll cut you loose. You can either walk back to Ingalls or go up to the tracks and hope they'll stop t' pick you up . . . wouldn't count too much on that, though."

We walked on toward town. The closer we got, the more nervous the man got. When he was on th' edge of bolting, I let him go. He trotted into the dark.

Light was spreading over the sky as I approached the edge of town. There was still shooting down the street, and I could see men scattered about behind various covers watching the windows of the upper floor of the building serving as a temporary courthouse until a proper temple to their "civilization" could be built.

A couple dozen men bristling with guns rode from a side street and loped my way. I turned sideways in the road and held up my badge against the sunrise with the prayer they could see it and take heed. They slowed and stopped about fifty feet away. "I can stay you fellers a lot of trouble," I lied. "My posse has taken the thieves into custody, and they'll be makin' a trip to see th' judge. What's goin' on in town?"

One of the men answered, "We got three of those fellers surrounded in th' courthouse, an' they ain't gettin' away from us alive."

Another man spoke from the crowd, "They done killed I.W. English, and four more are wounded, mister. The only way they're gittin' outta town is horizontal, law or no law."

The first man, who seemed to be the leader, handed his rifle to his neighbor and, holding his hands high, palms open, kneed his horse toward me. He came up close and spoke, "I'm Ott Suggs, city marshal here. Are you a sheriff or something?"

I showed him my badge, "I'm a deputy U.S. marshal out of Fort Smith. What's goin' on in town?"

"We got the Masterson boys and one other man trapped in the upper floor of the courthouse. The intention is to stretch rope with them if they live long enough. I ain't got much influence with these men right now, Deputy. Mr. English was only an onlooker, not even carrying a gun, and the four wounded are upstanding, normally peaceful men. These people are only defending their property and town against an invasion of professionals on Asa Soule's payroll."

"You don't think there's any way we could talk them into stopping this and get the men out of town safe?"

"They're very determined," the marshal said. He seemed to be genuine and concerned about the situation.

"Bat's up there?"

"No, it's Tom and Jim. Bat's in Leadville, I believe."

"Know th' other boy's name?"

"Brown."

"Neal Brown?"

"Yeah, I think so."

I sat back and thought. Tom and Jim Masterson together couldn't add up to one Bat, but being Bat's brothers carried a lot of weight. Tight as the brothers were, you could bet the longer this lasted, the more likely Bat—and his friends—would become involved. "I've got an idea how t' save them, Marshal, if you can keep them alive long enough. I'll have to go back to Ingalls to do it."

"Not much I can do thataway, but I'll try my best."

I turned to the waiting crowd. "Men, I know you have a right t' go after that gang of Killers, but that would surely cause more bloodshed. Believe me, one drop of your blood isn't worth all th' blood in that whole gang. They are gone and won't come back to Cimarrón so long as I have anything to do with it. We can get those three in the courthouse down without any more Cimarrón citizens getting hurt if you let me. Go back and be sure they don't escape before I come back with word for you."

"I think it's a good idea to let the deputy handle matters here, gentlemen. If what he does doesn't work, we'll still have those three to dispose of ourselves," Marshal Suggs said as the others gathered around us. I was glad the raid occurred in the night, when these men were sober and had clear minds.

"How do we know he's gonna keep his word?" someone asked.

"If what I am planning doesn't work, you will still have the hostages," I replied.

Someone in the back of the crowd hollered, "Hey, here comes a train draggin' that Soule's castle ahind it."

All attention was directed to the railroad across the Arkansas River and the engine approaching, with the Soule Hop Bitters car its only customer. Almost as one, the crowd turned and galloped across the dry riverbed to the tracks.

Seeing the gang surrounding the tracks, the engineer put on steam, and the train accelerated toward the would-be posse. As it passed, men on both sides of the tracks opened fire. Every window in that luxury car was blown out by the time the train was out of range. The train had to run another gauntlet of lead going through town when those around the courthouse realized what was happening. It stopped in Dodge City long enough to disgorge the wounded and a couple who elected to stay there, then disappeared into the dawn.

As soon as the posse left me, I turned and hotfooted it to the Ingalls station. Jimbo Jackson was at his key, listening to the traffic and relaying messages. He glanced up at my approach and said, "Got an unscheduled headed east from Dodge. We're trying to clear the tracks and get it aside."

There was a pause in the traffic and I asked, "Jimbo, can you send a message and make it look like it came from somewhere else?"

"Sure I can—if I want to get fired and never touch a key for the railroads again. Anyway, all th' key men would know I sent the message by my hand."

By that, Jimbo meant that each telegraph man can be identified by his key work, and the Cimarrón operator would know who sent the message. "You can send a message to a town and they can then send it legally, can't they?"

"Yeah, that would be legal as far as the telegraph is concerned."

"Good, I want you to send this message to the operator in Leadville and have him send it to Cimarrón": *To the citizens of Cimarrón, Kansas, stop If you harm my brothers in any way I will visit you with the biggest army of gunmen ever assembled stop Bat Masterson.*

Jimbo read the message and grinned. "They got the Masterson boys?"

"Tom and Jim are holed up with Neal Brown on the second floor of the courthouse dodgin' lead from the good citizens of Cimarrón," I replied.

"Be glad to send it, but you probably didn't know that Bat's in Denver."

"Will the Denver boys relay it just th' same?"

"Yeah, sure they will. Hotfinger's on the key this morning, an' he'll enjoy doin' us th' favor. I'll have t' collect for both the messages, and I'll disconnect the eastbound line so Cimarrón won't see it."

"No problem. Send it as fast as you can. We may be able to avoid some bloodshed an' neck-stretchin'."

Jimbo was tapping before I finished, and we waited for a reply. It came from Denver in the form of a telegraph to the mayor of Cimarrón, Kansas: *To the Mayor of Cimarrón, Kansas stop Have assembled a posse to rescue my brothers from your grip stop Serious consequences to the town if my brothers are harmed stop*

Bat Masterson.

"That Hotfinger must be a poet," I growled.

Jimbo laughed. "Cost you more money, too."

Half an hour later, the keys lit up with a message from the Cimarrón "mayor": *To Bat Masterson stop Ceasefire holding, brothers safe stop Mayor of Cimarrón.*

Jimbo Jackson laughed. "Didn't want t' give his name, did he?"

"Will Hotfinger deliver that message?"

"He's required to, but it will likely get lost on the way to Masterson."

Lorna Hardy peeked around the corner and said, "Mr. Lee, Miz Sarah said to tell you the eggs are in the skillet and the biscuits are still warm."

"Jimbo, send a telegram to the sheriff at Dodge to arrest and hold any Peace Commission boys who stopped off there. The charge will be murder in Gray County. Alright, Miss Lorna. May I escort you to the kitchen?"

The girl blushed prettily and nodded. We walked down the street. My horse turned himself into the livery where Thorny took up the reins and led him on back. We turned, and I offered the girl my arm as we climbed the steps and walked around to the kitchen door and washstand. The screen door squeaked as I was drying on the fresh roller towel. When I looked up, Miz Sarah was standing, holding the door open. "Shed your boots here, Lee, and we'll eat at the kitchen table."

There were only two eggs on my plate, eyes open just like I prefer them, but the stack of flapjacks and tin of "Genuine Vermont Maple Syrup" balanced the meal out nicely. I pushed back from the empty plates as Miz Sarah poured a second cup of coffee and Lorna whisked the dishes away. "Now, Lee, tell us what happened."

I told the ladies my goings-on since they had roused me in

the night. They both laughed when I told about the telegrams.

"Those Cimarrón boys won't take it kindly if they ever find out their wait was so you could fool *them,*" Lorna said. She was busy rolling out dough for pies as she listened, flour to her wrists and a wisp of hair in her eyes.

I declined a second refill of my cup and excused myself. My arm ached, and Sarah caught me rubbing it. "Some laudanum will do away with that pain, Lee."

"That would be nice if I was gonna sit in th' porch swing and doze, but I have to be busy for a while. I might be able to take you up on that this evenin'."

"Any time you need it. Thank you for looking after things—and not shooting the messenger." She smiled.

I hurried over to the telegraph office. "How's it goin', Jimbo?"

"Fine. We got the train switched to th' side at Bucklin Junction in time for the western express to get through. Nothin' more 'bout Bat an' his army."

"Is there any law at Bucklin that would arrest any of those boys that might jump off there?"

"Perfessor said no one got off, but they was all 'bout froze. They hooked on a boxcar to ride in out of th' wind. Soule wanted an express through to Kansas City, but the railroad refused. Looks like he's gonna be on a slow train through Kansas for the next day or two."

"Send a message for all law enforcement agents along the line to arrest any man who gets off that train. The charge is murder in Gray County, Kansas. I'm goin' down to Cimarrón an' see what's happening there—I'll pay the charges."

"As good as done, Lee. Be careful." He turned and was tapping the key as I left.

Chapter 5
Three Caged Birds

Bass Reeves told me once: "A lawman goin' into a fight learns not t' waste his time thinkin' about whut's gonna *happen when he rides into hell. He spends his time thinkin' o' all th' things that* could *happen an' what he's gonna do if it does. If he does a thorough job of it, he's mos' likely t' ride out th' other side alive."*

There had been a lot of activity in Ingalls, but I paid little attention to it in the pursuit of my own business. I rode down the Cimarrón Road on a fresh horse. At the edge of town, an overturned wagon blocked the road and men were in the fields either side digging holes. A man squatting in the shade of the wagon stood and, with rifle in the crook of his arm, held up his hand. "Halt there, mister."

I turned sideways so the muzzle of the shotgun across my lap pointed at the man. He took a couple of steps sideways. "What's going on here?" I asked.

The man spat a brown stream to the side and said, "We're expectin' visitors from Cimarrón, an' we're plannin' a welcomin' party for 'em. Sheriff says no one is to leave town unless he says so."

I pulled my vest back so the badge showed. "See this? A U.S. marshal's badge trumps a sheriff's tin. Set that rifle down an' walk around the end of that wagon a bit—that's good. Now watch me as I ride down that road *without* the sheriff's permission." I grinned at the man to show I wasn't mad. "Now, I'll probably be comin' back this way sometime today or tomorrow, and I want you to spread th' word that my right to ride this road will not be challenged; can you do that?"

"I think I can, Deputy, you have a nice day, now."

"I wonder if the devil said that to Judas as he descended into hell."

The man spat again, wiped his mouth on his sleeve, and grinned. "Don't know; *I* never heard him say it."

"Let's hope neither one of us ever does, friend."

Even at a distance of four miles or so, I could see the dust rising from rifle pit diggers at the edge of Cimarrón, and most likely some old scout had already spotted the dust my horse raised as we loped along. I could detour south around the blockade and come in behind their defenses, but on this infernal flatland, that would mean a ride of fifteen miles or so just to keep out of sight. The easiest thing would be to ride right down the road, but I might not get close enough to identify myself before they started shooting. If that old buffalo hunter unlimbered his .50 caliber on me, I'd be dead before th' sound of the shot got to me.

Even though the river was dry, the sand would be damp enough to hide the sound of the horse walking and not raise any dust. My only problem would be the guards they would have there somewhere. Overall, that looked about the best route to take, an ol' Hoss agreed.

We picked a gentle slope to go down. The bank on the south side was over my head, which was a little worrisome since I could not see if anyone was lurking there. I pinned my badge on my vest where it could be seen and maybe give me pass—or be a bright target.

When we neared the town, I reined Hoss in and we went slower, stopping often to listen and look. The slant of his ears told me there was someone or something near. It could be men, a stray horse, or ol' bossy down by the bank grazing. The horse stopped and, raising his head, sniffed the air. It wasn't a horse or he would have spoken. It was not likely to be anything other than a two-legged critter. I slid off, left him ground-tied, and climbed up the bank in some button willows. There was nothing showing downstream, so I left the river a ways, then walked parallel to it to see if someone left a trail. They did, and it was fresh, though in the sand it was hard to tell how many there were.

Near the river, I began picking up the sound of voices talking low. ". . . tell you, Pete, I can shoot th' wart off a flea's ear an' never hurt him, might near as far away as you could see him."

"Shore you could, an' if'n it were a he-flea, you could geld him with one shot an' he'd never bleed."

"Likely, if he was turned just so."

"Then why-so you ain't got one o' those Killers in th' courthouse?"

"Too busy shootin' up those fellers on th' ground; winged two of 'em, I know of."

"Shore you did, an' my mama's Calamity Jane."

They were lyin' on the bank about ten feet apart, one looking up the river, and the other on his back contemplating the sky. Beyond them, there were tracks in the riverbed. Someone had crossed to the other bank. I could see the willows move and made out the barrel of a gun. I would have to keep low out of his sight to get to the two on this side.

Closer to them, I said, "Howdy, boys. Fish bitin'?"

Stargazer rolled over, "That you, Ira? 'Bout time you got here."

"I ain't Ira, this is U.S. Deputy Sowell, and one of you needs to run down and bring my horse up here. Someone's gonna have to lead me into town so's I don't get shot—and so no one will suspect you got sneaked up on unawares." This job was so much fun sometimes.

The lookout asked, red-faced, "How'd you git here?"

"Easy enough with two tenderfoots like you. Hop down there an' go get my horse. Be sure you don't scratch up my saddle comin' through th' brush. Stargazer, tell your man across th' river ever'thing's alright here, so's I don't get dry-gulched."

He stood and waved his bandanna to the bushes across the way, and a bush waved back. "It's safe, mister. He won't shoot now."

I stood up. "Good. Soon's my horse gets here, you an' me are gonna walk into town to the courthouse, side-by-side."

"Yes, sir."

The lookout came up leading my horse, still looking mad. "Dammit, Bob, if you was doin' your job like you should of, we wouldn't o' been caught like this."

"Don't worry, Pete, I won't tell anyone. At least you were doing a good job. Bob's gonna escort me to th' courthouse, an' you can shoot him when he comes back, if you want to."

"I'm gonna give that some thought," Pete said, starin' at Stargazer Bob. "Maybe just callin' him Stargazer from now on would be 'most as good."

"We better git goin'," Stargazer mumbled.

There had been an occasional shot coming from town. By that we surmised there was at least one hostage holdin' out. Hopefully there were three. The guards had made themselves comfortable and settled in to watch. The occasional shot was coming from the ground. Probably the treed men were running low on ammunition. There wasn't a shard of glass left in the upper windows, and what curtains left were in rags.

"Stargazer, take my horse over to that livery and tell th' man he'll need a bait of oats. I expect to be here all day, so he can put him in a stall."

Stargazer mumbled something at the corner and took Hoss to the barn.

There was a man in a chair propped back on the wall around the corner and out of sight of the courthouse. He nodded and grinned, "Still got 'em holed up, Deputy; it's just a matter of time, now. Nothin' else, we'll starve 'em out."

"They ain't likely t' starve before Bat Masterson gets here with his army, feller. Where's Ott Suggs?"

"Most likely down to th' station, listenin' t' those wires with our mayor. They worry too much about what Bat's gonna do. Bring 'em on, I say."

"Sure you do. They ain't a bullet made with your name on it, is there?" I turned and took the back streets to the train station where sat the marshal with Mayor John Matison and several others.

"Bat Masterson's threatened to bring an army of his friends down to rescue his brothers," the marshal said to me.

"So I heard. What's your plan?"

"Bring 'em on, I say," a portly man with an ancient muzzle-loading shotgun said.

"Anyone who thinks a bunch of merchants and clerks can stand up against the likes of Bat Masterson, the Earps, and Doc Holliday is a damned fool—and yes, I know Doc is dead." The man blinked and backed up a step or two, shuffling from foot to foot. I kept him in sight as we talked. "Are they coming, Mayor?"

"We haven't heard." By his demeanor, he was taking the threat of invasion seriously; hopefully, cooler heads would prevail.

"Mayor, the law has taken six of the invaders, and there is a notice to every town along the tracks from here to Kansas City to arrest any man who leaves that train and hold him for transportation back here. There is no need for vigilante law; the courts can handle things."

"Too many of us knew and liked I.W. to let his murder go unpunished. There is no sure thing any court out here will be able to do justice."

"You have to give them the opportunity, Mayor; otherwise, they will never be strong enough to keep the law. If they fail, vigilante justice can still act after the trial."

"You don't have to convince me, but you'll have a hard time convincing those out there"—he indicated the men guarding the courthouse—"that the law can bring us justice out of this."

"We can take care of our criminals without the government interfering." The man with the ancient gun was regaining his courage.

"Law and order only 'interferes' with lawbreakers. It doesn't bother lawful men." I looked at the idiot. "You and that antique you're carryin' can't take care of a cross-eyed cowboy with a repeater rifle. Do you think they're gonna hop off th' train and march down the street t' rescue those men? They will come in here at night upwind, and set a small fire in one of these tender-dry houses. While you all are fighting that fire, the courthouse will be evacuated without anyone firing a shot. The only shooting liable to be done is those Killers will be layin' out in th' brush takin' shots at the bucket brigade lit up by the burning town. Come daylight, you'll be starin' at the ashes of this town, and the hostages will be gone.

"Maybe you'll rise up and burn down Ingalls in revenge, and then some place like Montezuma or Ensign, even Gray Center, will become the county seat. Who wins in that?

"Mayor, it will take Bat a little time to gather his 'posse' and get here. You may have ten to twenty hours to talk these men into standing down an' letting me arrest the hostages. I'll take them to Fort Dodge to be held while the powers that be sort out when and where a trial can be held. Will you call a cease-fire so I can go in and talk to the hostages?"

My talk had taken effect. A few minutes after I stepped out of the room, Mayor Matison sent runners out declaring a fifteen-minute cease-fire. He walked with me to the courthouse and we entered the ground floor of the building. The room was littered with trash and broken glass. *Where did all this splintered wood came from?* Then it hit me; I looked at the splintered ceiling and realized the townsmen had been firing through the second story floor.

At the stairway, I called, "Jim, Tom, Neal, this is U.S. Deputy Lee Sowell. Hold your fire. I'm coming up." I stomped up the stairs and just before my head would have shown, stopped again. "The mayor has declared a cease-fire so I could talk to you. Do you agree?"

"Come on up, Lee. We won't shoot," one of them replied, and I climbed on up, my hands high. For a moment, I didn't see anything but an empty room littered with the remnants of glass and furniture. The floor bulged where bullets had penetrated. "We're over here, Deputy."

They had forted up on top of a pile of cabinets and overturned desks to protect them from shots coming through the floor. Three disheveled and grimy faces appeared over the top of the pile. "Didn't bring us any water, did you?" Tom Masterson asked with a little grin.

"If I brought you water from that bunch out there, would you drink it?"

"Probably not," Neal Brown snarled.

"Otherwise, how are you doing; anyone hurt?"

"Not much, only th' usual scratches and cuts from flying glass and brick and such," Jim said. "Excuse us if we don't come out to greet you. One of those boys out there might forget there was a hold on shootin' should they see one of us."

"We're just layin' around for th' next stage t' come in. We missed th' last one when th' mules—or driver—bolted ahead of schedule," Tom explained.

I looked around at the room full of bullet holes. If this building were a ship on water, it would turn upside down just from the weight of all that lead embedded in the walls and ceiling. "Word is that Bat is gatherin' a posse t' rescue you."

"Blast his nosy hide, why's he think he's gotta interfere ever' time we get into an enterprise? You go tell him we'll holler if things get tight here. Otherwise, tend to his own cards," Jim growled.

"Any chance th' boys'll come back down th' tracks t' pick us up?" Neal asked.

"Don't look like it, Neal. Last we heard, they dropped th' wounded off at Dodge City, and they're highballin' it across Kansas for th' border."

"I knew it! That bunch of cold-footed sissies! I hope they catch them, every one!" Neal's anger was understandable; the surprise was that he expected anything more from a bunch of bullies.

"I'm negotiating with the town to get you three out of here unharmed. If it all works out, I'll arrest you and take you to Fort Dodge to be held until other arrangements can be made. Otherwise, you can expect to get lead poisoning or spend the rest of your life stretching rope from some telegraph pole or rafter not far from here. If you shoot anyone else out there before I can finish my negotiations, th' deal will be off."

"Don't worry, Lee; we ain't got a dozen shells between us, an' we're savin' them for our next turkey hunt," Tom assured me.

"Just be sure those turkeys have feathers an' aren't within gunshot of this building. We'll all be lucky if we get out of this without shedding more blood."

"If you get things worked out, just wave the white flag, an' we'll start packin'," said Jim.

"Time's up," the mayor advised from below, and I left the boys in order to be out of the many lines of fire before our allotted time expired. Mayor John Matison was trottin' across the street without waiting for me, and I walked after him. Someone rang the fire bell, and a half dozen rifles added confirmation. The truce was over.

We met in the back room of the mercantile store across the street from the courthouse. "Mayor, the three men will agree to be removed from the courthouse if I can assure them safe passage out of town. I can't do that, but you can. It seems the best thing to do to end this standoff and more bloodshed."

"It's the best chance we have of preventing Bat and his boys from visitin'," the marshal added.

Mr. Mayor shook his head. "I don't know. Seems the boys are pretty set on showin' these three what shootin' up a town and killing its citizens can get them."

There you go again, counting votes afore next election. "This isn't the time to take a straw vote, Mayor; it's time to convince those people out there that this is the safest and right thing to do."

The mayor rubbed his stubbled chin and thought a moment. "You are right, Deputy. I'll talk to them." And for the next hour and a half he did. The man put up a convincing argument, but it took a lot of time. I watched with increasing anxiety as the sun sank toward the far mountains. It was dark by the time Mayor Matison had completed his mission. "The men have all agreed to let you arrest the Mastersons and get them out of town, Marshal."

"That's good, but it's too dark to safely remove the men now. We will have to wait for daylight. I will make arrangements with the railroad to have the local here in the morning and take them to Fort Dodge. Ott, will you be my deputy and help me escort those men to the fort?"

"Be glad to, Lee."

"Good; now where can a man find a good meal around here?"

"Rest Haven Saloon sets a pretty good board—and th' beer's cold." Suggs grinned.

"I'm buyin' first round," Mayor Matison volunteered. He led us out the back door of the mercantile and a block later, into the back door of the saloon. He paused at the food bar and selected a couple of sandwiches, then headed to a table, calling, "Pitcher of beer, Charlie, and three glasses."

It took me a few moments longer to fill my plate and follow the mayor. Charlie was pouring the beer when I sat down. It wasn't Mrs. Ashmore's table, but it would do, and the beer *was* cold.

I washed down the sandwiches, and the mayor offered to pour me another glass. "Another beer, and I'd go to sleep right here an' not wake up till next week." I left the two officials talking Cimarrón politics and made my way to the courthouse without getting shot at by either side.

There seemed to be an unspoken mutual agreement that hostilities would cease during the hours of darkness, and that was good enough for me. A candle sputtered on a table set up in the middle of the bottom floor and a couple men lay sleeping. I found an unbroken chair and propped it against the wall of the stairwell. It was so quiet I could hear snoring coming from the occupants of the floor above. I dozed off and dreamed. Bass Reeves was talkin' to me: *"Lee, you'll learn that a deputy don't sleep when he's in th' field. He may lay down and close his eyes, but they's always a part of him that doesn't sleep; knows ever' thing goin' on 'round him an' sounds th' alarm when—"* Somethin' ain't right. My eyes popped open.

It was as black as the insides of a dog, only the door and windows framing a lighter sky. Something *wasn't* right; what was it? The upstairs snoring hadn't stopped; nothing moved in the room. All I could hear was the blood pulsing in my ears.

Then there came the softest rustle of clothing. Someone on the stair behind my ear had lifted his foot to the next step. As he shifted his weight, the stair creaked. In almost instant sequence, a gun cocked upstairs, that soft snoring stopped, and two more guns above cocked. How many times had that sound been the last thing a man had heard before a roar had sent him into eternity?

The figure stood frozen on the stair, framed in the light of an upstairs window. The body leaned slightly and the foot slid from the tread. It didn't squeak. It seemed like it took ten minutes for that person to back down the three steps to the floor. I stared with bated breath, straining to see that silent journey across the debris to the door. It took a long time. The silhouetted figure at the door revealed a smallish person, hair in a bun at the nape of the neck, and the silhouette as it passed the window was most definitely feminine. *That was a woman! In pants!*

Well, one thing was sure, I was not going to move before the light of day. Too many people around here with heavy trigger fingers.

The distant whistle of a train woke me just at sunrise. The two guards woke and arose, and we went out to greet the day. Looking around, I could see several men at their posts awaiting the events of the day. Mayor Matison appeared across the street and came toward me. Ott Suggs stepped up on the porch from the side.

I called to the mayor, "Have the men pull back, and we will bring the prisoners down."

While he was directing the men, Marshal Suggs and I met the three men coming down the stairs. Suggs produced the manacles. We took their guns and cuffed their hands in front. The mayor stepped through the door. "I will go with you to the train. It's ready."

I turned to the three prisoners; "I have cuffed your hands in front so that if something should go wrong out there, you can protect yourselves by reaching the guns the three of us will have under our coats. We'll have our guns on you, so any unnecessary reaching for the hidden guns would prove very painful to you. Tom, walk to the right beside me. Neal, you will be to the left of the mayor right behind us, and Jim, you walk to the right of Ott behind them. Stay close, walk a steady pace—and stay calm."

We walked out on the porch and faced a dozen men lined along the walk across the street. Out in the street, we turned toward the tracks and the men across the street paralleled our path. Not a word was spoken. Tom Masterson was pale. If he had any moisture in his body, it would have been running down his face like mine was. That hundred yards may have been the longest walk I ever took. It was a great relief to seat the prisoners behind the steel walls of the coal tender and listen to the engine gather speed as we left the town and its defenders.

The rest of the trip was so routine it was boring. We turned the prisoners over to the army jail and rode the engine back to Dodge. Ott Suggs and I parted company at the depot, and I never saw the man again. There were some supplies to pick up. Since the local didn't come through before late afternoon, I had time for a haircut and bath. I bought some shirts for myself and another pair of bibless overalls to replace the ones Tex got cut up.

I met Doc Stepp with his black bag on the boardwalk. "Hello yourself, young man," he said to my greeting as he was hurrying on to a patient somewhere. A half dozen steps beyond, he stopped and said, "Hey, you're th' one with the groove in your arm, aren't you? Let's see it." He was back and rolling my sleeve up before I could protest. "Got six stitches, didn't you?"

"Eight."

"Never mind." He poked around on the arm, and I fought the urge to flinch. "Looks good, no inflammation. You'll have a nice scar to tell your grandchildren about. Wait three weeks before you take those stitches out. Gotta go." And "go" he went.

Someone chuckled behind me. "That Doc shore does hit it hard an' make good medicine, don't he?"

I turned to see Deputy Joe Don Jones standing in the doorway, pickin' his teeth with a folding knife.

"How you doin', Deputy, had any excitement lately?"

"Not since you left town—an' I like it thataway."

"Seems awful dull around here. Want t' go down to No Man's Land and chase train robbers with me?"

"Won't do no good t' catch 'em there. Ain't no law coverin' 'em."

"Somethin' always turns up t' make things right. I need a driver and deputy. Might pay more than this city marshal business, and there's a price on th' feller we'd be chasin'."

Joe Don put away his folder. "You serious 'bout me goin' with you?"

"Serious as a parson on Sunday—only I need t' know your real name. They's too many Joneses livin' 'round here."

"Jones is th' real thing with me; I'm one of Dirty Face Ed's little brothers."

Dirty Face Ed Jones was well known in these parts, having established with his partner, Joe Plummer, the Jones and Plummer Trail from Dodge to Fort Elliott in the Texas Panhandle. He was nicknamed Dirty Face because of the scars left by black powder from a gun going off too close to his face. "Them's good bloodlines. What do you say, want a little variety in your life?"

"I'll think on it."

"You got until th' westbound local leaves this afternoon. I'll buy your ticket." We didn't discuss pay, but I was sure it would be more than he got from the city. I wandered down to the station and bought two tickets, one to Ingalls and one to Cimarrón, where Hoss was lollin' around th' livery barn. I heard the train whistle just as Joe Don rode up on a black horse with white stockings on his forelegs. He was leading a roman-nosed grulla.

"They both kicked up a fuss t' come along, an' I couldn't say no," was his only explanation. He loaded them into the cattle car while I paid their fare.

Joe Don's elbow in my ribs woke me as we slowed for the station at Cimarrón. "Leave the horses at the livery and ask at Miz Sarah's for a room for the night. We'll be headin' south tomorrow."

Hoss was rested and ready to go, so I pointed him on th' road west an' told him t' wake me when we got there.

The call, "Halt where you are," woke me to find Hoss stopped twenty feet short of that overturned wagon. "This is Deputy Sowell, and I'm comin' through." It was still light enough that the ones behind the wagon could see me draw my shotgun out of the scabbard.

"Come on through, Deputy."

"Damn right, I am," I muttered. None of the holes lining either side of the road were occupied. Maybe things were cooling off some. We threw Hoss in with the two Jones horses in the livery pen, and I trudged over to the boarding house, hopeful it wasn't too late for supper. There were several pairs of boots at the front door as I passed to the washstand. My arm was stiff and hurting, and I didn't feel like being around people, so I rapped on the back screen door when I found it latched. Lorna Hardy came to the door, a steaming pot in her hand.

"Reckon I can eat in the kitchen tonight?"

She hesitated only a moment and unlatched the door. "Sure, Lee." She hurried back to the stove and I removed my boots and padded to the kitchen table. "Mr. Jones is telling us what happened at Cimarrón. You must be tired after all that."

"Be careful what he says, Lorna. He wasn't there."

She dished up a plate of steaming rice and poured a thick beef stew over it. There were biscuits and butter. While I ate, she brought a tin of molasses for dessert. "Mr. Jones says he's gonna be your deputy when you go after those train robbers."

"Yes, Tex isn't able to go, and he and Bill are going to bring the cattle to Sheep Pen when he's able to travel."

Lorna looked very sad. "Bill says he may not come back."

"I don't know about that, but he'd be a fool t' leave all the things he loves here behind." A little flush of pink rose from her collar and touched her cheek. It made her prettier. "Maybe he won't."

"Do I still have a bed upstairs?"

"Yes. Mrs. Sarah has kept it for you."

"Well, I thank you for the supper and good night, Pretty Miss; I'm sneakin' up th' back stair t' bed. Joe Don Jones is on his own." And I padded up the back stair and down the hall. The last thing I remember is opening the door to that room.

Chapter 6
No Man's Land

"When did you start for No Man's Land?" Lawyer Scanlon asked.

I looked at my diary. "It was the morning of Thursday, September 5, 1888, that I was finally able to start for No Man's Land. We determined to strike the Beaver River somewhere above Beaver City and track down the river to town."

"What was your purpose in doing that?"

"I wanted to try to get the outlaws between us and Deputy Gamlin's posse if possible. While we were in Beaver City, we found that the gang had bypassed the town."

When I came out from settling up with Mrs. Ashmore, Joe Don Jones had our horses ready and waiting, our bedrolls and "kitchen" tied to the packhorse. He stood between the horses, head down, pretending to do something with the pack ropes.

Lorna was standing by the door with a broom in her hand. When I stopped to say goodbye, she gave me a big hug. "You be good, Miss Lorna, and I'll take care of Rockin' R Bill for you."

"You can try, but he'll get into more trouble accidently than th' two o' you can handle." She smiled and blinked away a tear.

I paused at the top of the steps and looked around. It was a good habit to get into. The street was empty except for Thorny Kingsley in his accustomed place propping up the livery wall, and a man standing on the station platform looking our way. I was aware of Joe Don mounting. He turned south without looking up at me or saying anything. It didn't take a genius to understand he wasn't in a visiting mood with the stranger now striding our way. The man stopped in front of me, and looking at the receding figure of my posse man, asked, "That wouldn't be Joseph Donaldson going there, would it?"

"Don't know him by that name, myself. He goes by th' handle o' Cimarrón around here." The man should know better than to go bandying names around indiscriminate like that. I showed him my badge. "He's my cook, and we're heading south to chase train robbers."

The man cursed under his breath. "I could swear that's him . . ." He stared at the receding figure, seeming to make his mind up about something. "Been with you long?"

"Long enough." I was getting tired of this impertinence and mounted up. Turning toward the livery, I rode over to where Thorny sat. "Here's a couple of dollars down on holding all your rental horses until in the morning," I said low.

Thorny nodded and winked. "Shore thing, Lee. Good huntin'."

The stranger was talking to Lorna through the screen door as I left. How Joe Don got a quarter mile ahead of me without loping, I'll never know. He stayed that way all the way to Gray Center.

Tex looked a little better this time, and his attitude was better. Maybe being th' center of attention by two women was comfortin' to him. Looked like he was well-fed. His wound was healing nicely, and I was pretty sure he would be ready to go by the end of the month. We didn't stay long. Joe Don hardly got off his horse, kept looking back toward Ingalls. I gave Tex some money and said my goodbyes to the ladies. My cook started out before I had my foot in th' stirrup. "Hold up there, Joe Don," I snarled. "You act like th' cat that landed on th' stove—an' quit lookin' back. Ain't no one follerin' us."

He took one more look behind and said, "Alright, Lee."

"Seems to me 'Joe Don' is an awful long handle t' use."

He grinned. "I was named after my grandpap. They called him Joe Don and me JD."

"Well, that's what I'm gonna use. Elsewise, one of us could be dead afore I get all of 'Joe Don' out in a tight place."

We went south to the Liberal road. After we crossed the Cimarrón, we left the road and rode the edge of the breaks down into the Strip. It was easy riding along the flats. That night we rode down to the river to water, then camped in one of the draws out of the wind.

"How we gonna find those robbers in all this country, Lee?" JD asked as we watched the prairie coal fire die down.

"This country ain't as big as you might think, looking at it. A man has to be close to water t' live out here, and there aren't that many watering places. Also, Pard Newman likes his comforts, an' he isn't likely to spend all his time around a camp. We came in west of Beaver partly to see if anyone had passed through, and mostly to come into the town from the west. With Deputy Stein following them from the east, we might catch our trainmen between us—if we're lucky."

"I don't like dependin' on luck t' get me through somethin'."

"Me nuther, JD. Let's do ever'thing we can t' avoid chance, then Lady Luck will only have t' help us out once in a while. It's little things left undone that git you in trouble, so take care of them and those big things will tend t' take care of themselves."

He chuckled. "Hickok was so fussy about things, we called him the Old Woman, but he never got caught flat-footed before the day he sat on the wrong side of the table."

"Wasn't th' cards at all, was it?"

"Nope; th' little things got him."

Where the Cimarrón turned east, we were forced to ride south to avoid some rough country around a creek that flowed north into the river. This took us up on the divide between the

Cimarrón and Beaver Creek. The creek had a wide bottom that made travel easy, so we rode along the north edge of it, keeping our eyes out for any human activity. There were plenty of signs of cattle, and we passed a soddy with the roof caved in and two dugouts that had been abandoned. Late in the afternoon of the fourth day after leaving Ingalls, we saw signs of increased activity and knew we were closing in on the town of Beaver. We found a dugout in a draw on the south side of the creek and set up our camp there. No one had been there for some time, and the grass up the draw was ungrazed. Our horses would have to pass the dugout to escape the draw, the sides being too steep for them to climb, so we strung a rope across the mouth of the draw and had us a horse pasture.

"What's your plan now, Lee?" JD asked as he cut our last onion into the beans.

"Are you familiar with Beaver?"

"Nope; never been there."

"I can't take th' chance that one of th' Newman gang might know me, so I am gonna do some night-spying. Since you are not known to them, you could ride in and look around without getting into trouble. After we eat, we'll ride in and look around."

JD nodded. "Good. This drinkin' nothin' but water has got to me. It'll be good t' git somethin' with some taste to it."

"Stay away from th' whiskey, an' don't expect th' beer t' be cold," I said.

Beaver City was laid out on Jim Lane's road ranch that served the travelers on the Jones and Plummer Trail where it crossed Beaver River. The country had not been surveyed, so Jim couldn't file a legal claim. Under these circumstances, his claim was honored under the rules of squatter's rights. A bunch of Wichita men formed the Beaver Townsite Company with the intention of establishing a "boom town" on the Beaver River in

No Man's Land. After looking over the land, they decided that Jim Lane's ranch was the best site for the town. Consequently, William Waddle, the local agent for the company; and Ernest Reiman, the surveyor, attempted to run Mr. Lane off his land, which they could not do. They came to the agreement that they could commence with their survey in exchange for two blocks of lots reserved for Jim Lane. This was done, and the company commenced to advertise their new town across the country. Things went fine up to the day it was discovered they could not produce deeds to the lots. Therefore, people took possession of them by squatter's rights and the Beaver Townsite Company got nothing to show for their trouble. Lady Justice smiled.

The town attracted honest, hardworking people intent on establishing themselves in a place where opportunity smiled on them and they could own a piece of the land. D.R. Healey built the first livery stable. The second most important building, the saloon, was built by Jim Donnelly.

Two men calling themselves O.P. Bennett and Frank Thompson appeared and set up their enterprise of "Road Trotting," which consisted of intimidating settlers into paying them for the privilege of remaining on their claims. Eventually, their lawlessness prompted action to stop their activities. A posse was formed, and the two men lured into a building and shot to rags.

An inquest was held and reported the following findings:

"We, the jury appointed to view the remains of O.P. Bennett and Frank Thompson, find that they came to their deaths from the gunshot wounds received at the hands of many law-abiding citizens, thereby inflicting, as near as possible, the extreme penalty of the law as it should be done in such cases. The deceased were bad citizens, one having run a house of prostitution and the other living in open adultery in our town. Each was accused of stealing and receiving stolen property, some of which was found in their possession after they were killed. They had each been firing into houses, holding a dozen or

more claims and driving honest settlers out of the country, and their untimely ending is the result of their own many wrongs."

The verdict was signed by seven of the early Beaver City citizens.

One of those posse members was Billy Olive, the eighteen-year-old son of the recently deceased Texas rawhider, Print Olive. Billy seemed intent on following in his father's footprints. He lived in a dugout with his common-law wife, a "belle" of the streets, who apparently had a roving eye. She was attracted to handsome bartender Bill Henderson.

In a fit of drunken hilarity, Olive commandeered the saloon where Henderson worked and proceeded to destroy it. He then put his gun against the head of the terrified Henderson and pulled the trigger. It snapped on an empty cartridge. Henderson ran, secured a rifle, and shot Olive dead. No inquest was held, and Billy Olive's body was sent to his mother in Nebraska.

No Man's Land, where there was no law, attracted the dregs of society looking to escape the consequences of their crimes in lands where law held sway. These three deaths made it apparent that the honest folk of Beaver City had to organize to protect themselves from the lawless element. They coordinated a provisional government and elected officials. Addison Mundel, who had built the first wooden business house, was appointed city marshal.

The city council and good marshal had established a stable government and a relatively quiet town by the time JD and I arrived a couple of years later. While JD nosed around the several saloons, I located Marshal Mundel at his business and had a private talk with him. He had not been made aware of the train robbery until recently, had not noticed any new suspicious characters hanging around, and none of the old suspicious characters were throwing around any money.

Later, when JD and I got together at our camp in the hills

west of town, we surmised that the gang had not reached Beaver and were most likely somewhere east of Beaver City, between Gamlin's posse and us. "If they aren't, they most likely have bypassed Beaver and are headed on west," I said.

"I would head for Beer City or Tyrone instead of Beaver City," JD allowed. "They don't have a marshal and city gov'ment t' mess with."

"I would too, but we can't be sure of that before we meet up with Gam and his posse."

"Why would Stein chase those men into No Man's Land, knowing he can't arrest them here?" JD asked.

"He can't arrest them for the law, but he could arrest them for the railroad and collect a large reward."

"So-o we would get a reward if we caught them first?" There was a light in JD's eyes.

"We could, but that isn't th' reason we're chasin' them."

"Why then?"

I looked at JD and aimed to make a sharp reply; then realized he didn't understand my motives. "Because, JD, Gamlin Stein and Harmon Lake used to be my posse. They're outnumbered agin' a bunch of desperate characters that would as soon kill them as kill a skunk. I don't want my friends shot up, if they ain't already."

He nodded. "I can understand that, Lee, but it makes me feel I been drawn into a deal I might not have any business bein' in."

"That wasn't my intentions. If you feel strong thataway, I'll pay you for your time an' you're free t' go."

He lifted his hat by the brim with his forefinger and thumb, scratched his head with the other three fingers, and grinned. "Guess I'll stay around an' see what happens."

I grinned. "Good. Anyone traveling this time of year is gonna stay close to water, an' th' only reliable place is along th' Beaver.

That'll bring them right up to town. It is probable the robbers will need supplies and fresh horses. Even if the bunch don't come into town, they'll send someone for what they need—"

"An' we'll be th' welcomin' party when they do."

"Even so, it may be that they'll bypass town altogether. We're gonna do a lot of ridin' t' make sure we don't miss 'em."

JD groaned and I chuckled. "City deputies don't do much riding?"

"No, an' my rear end got plenty of that comin' down here."

"Tender ass an' flat feet, huh? If we have t' go all th' way to Carrizos after these fellers, you're gonna be doin' a lot more ridin', so you need t' get toughened to it. Addison is keeping watch in town an' has warned the townsmen of who may show up. We are gonna patrol the river and up in th' breaks some. It's th' best we can do for now."

"Them sharps in town were droolin' over th' prospects of fresh meat with jangle in their pockets, an' I got invited to a table ever'where I went. Think I'll go in an' teach them a little about cards," JD said with a grin.

"Go ahead, but be on those river bottoms lookin' for sign about sunup. I'll take the hills on this side of the river. If you find anything, come back to camp. I'll pass through about noon."

In a few minutes, JD left for town, and I turned in for the night well away from the fire and hidden under a cedar tree.

The Big Dipper told me it was well past midnight when I awoke and saw the glow of our fire someone had stoked up. I approached camp with my gun in my hand—thank you, Bass—and discovered JD dozing on his saddle, his hat down over his eyes and a cup in his hand, teetering toward an accident.

"Been waiting long, JD?" I asked softly. The cup jerked upright, sloshing coffee on his overalls.

"Don' know how long it's been, Lee. I was afraid of lead poisonin' if I stomped around lookin' for you; must have dozed off."

"Anything happen in town?" I hadn't expected to see him before sometime in the afternoon of the morrow.

"Yeah . . . there was a new man in town. Loves t' play poker, kind of small, like a cowhand, bowed legs, wears a flat-topped hat, talks a lot."

"Does he have a limp?"

"Yeah. Says he got shot in th' knee in some mix-up a few years ago."

"Charlie Siringo."

"Who?"

"Charlie Siringo, the Pinkerton man."

"They're on it already?"

I grinned. "Probably one or four of them were on that train when it was robbed. Don't worry about Charlie. His philosophy is *'Let Them Come to Me'*; we won't see much of him outside a saloon or far from a deck of cards."

"Bet he's after the reward," JD grumbled.

"You should know Pinkertons don't accept rewards. They buy sheriffs' goodwill with them."

"Naw, I haven't had much ado with them."

"Just as soon not see Charlie; dang, ever' time I turn around, somethin's keepin' me from bein' seen in town."

JD laughed. "You're as famous as a bunch of outlaws."

"We don't want Charlie t' git wind deputy marshals are after Pard. He'll tell th' world, an' th' world will be askin' us what business we have in No Man's Land. I'm gonna get a little more shut-eye b'fore morning. You goin' back?"

"Not tonight; I'm gonna go t' sleep too." He unspooled his bed, kicked off his boots, and laid his hat by. "See you in th' morning."

I brushed cedar needles off my pillow, picked them out of my socks, and lay back down. Siringo wouldn't be any trouble; in fact, he might help.

I wore out Hoss riding the breaks looking for sign that wasn't there. When I rode in to camp that evening, Joe Don was there roasting two thick steaks. "Three men an' a wagon drove into town midafternoon."

"Gamlin an' his tumbleweed," I said.

"Yep, they're provisionin' up an' will leave in th' mornin'. Gam says th' gang's ahead of them, still headed west."

"You talk to him? See any sign of the robbers?"

"Naw, I didn't talk to them, just listened to th' talk. There weren't any signs the Newman bunch came down the river flats either."

"Are you still saddled up?"

"No, why?"

"We got riding t' do, JD; go saddle up while I finish th' steaks. We'll eat on th' road."

I finished the steaks while JD brought his horse in and saddled him. "Where we going?"

"To catch a little birdie if he hasn't flown already. Take these steaks while I saddle. Hoss is gonna be mad."

JD was gnawing one of the steaks when I rode back. He handed mine to me, and we rode to the edge of the brush. "If we're lucky, th' self-appointed spy hasn't left town to inform that Newman bunch where Gamlin an' his boys are. We need to intercept him and keep Pard in th' dark as much as possible. In fact, whether we catch this bird or not, you and I should follow those robbers and keep them from setting up an ambush for the tumbleweed boys. Loan me your rope and go back and pack up camp." I looked the bottoms over. "You see where the banks narrow up there a ways?"

"Yeah."

"I'm gonna string our ropes across that narrow place just

above horse-head height and see what we can net. When you come back, ride down the middle of the bottoms till we meet up. Hopefully we'll have our little birdie caged by then."

"I think he'd prob'ly leave town after full dark," JD added.

"Right; let's get crackin'."

He turned back to the camp, and I trotted on upstream to the narrows. It didn't take long to string the rope from a fallen log to the base of a cedar bush on the other side. As best I could determine, it was just the right height except at the ends. I hoped there was enough slack so we wouldn't hurt anyone too bad. If they were running, they could get themselves killed.

Joe Don appeared with the packhorse in tow in no time, and I reminded myself to check that load before we went very far. We tied the packhorse and JD's horse to the log and I rode to the other end of the rope and tied Hoss to a bush. We wouldn't need the horses if things went right; our quarry would be on the ground.

A watcher is blessed when he doesn't have to watch a long time. That night we were blessed, for not three quarters of an hour later, someone came along. He was jog-trotting, and I was running to him before he hit the rope. There was a grunt and satisfying thump when the man fell. Luckily, both of his feet came out of the stirrups. I had my knee on his chest and his gun in my hand before he could catch his breath. "Don't move, partner. You might be hurt worser than you think."

JD trotted up and I said, "Pard was right—Jim—that deputy sent a spy to find us out." Our prisoner was hacking and coughing. He tried to speak but couldn't. I struck a match. The light showed a man in his thirties or so, with rope burn from the base of his neck to his chin. His mouth was bleeding and chips of tooth clung to his lips. When the light burned my fingers, I dropped it. "Go fetch a canteen for this feller. Seems he's bit his tongue or somethin'."

We sat him up. He rolled over on his hands and knees and spat. "Looks like you might have lost a tooth there, feller," I said.

He said, "Um-um," and something more that was unintelligible and sat back down with a groan.

"Where are you?" the newly christened Jim inquired, so I struck a match, and he appeared with the uncorked canteen.

The man took it and washed his mouth out before taking a swallow or two. After a couple of attempts, he was able to croak out, "I ain't spy." He took another drink of water. "I come to warn Pard . . . there's a marshal on his tail . . ." He took another drink ". . . and they are comin' hard tomorrer . . . with that city marshal."

"Feller has t' think fast t' come up with that tale," Jim observed.

"Don't matter what he says. Pard said t' do him in, an' I'm in agreement with him."

"You're gonna kill me just 'cause some feller said to, an' me bringin' him information about his enemies?" The man's voice was getting stronger, but he was still hoarse. Jim gave him another drink.

I thought a moment. "Don't see where we got any choice, feller. If you know Pard, you know he don't take ignorin' his orders lightly." We lifted the man to his feet. He seemed to have some pain or stiffness in his back.

"Why do we have t' kill him if he was comin' t' help us?" I couldn't see his face in the dark, but the tone in his voice told me that this was no longer the play-acting "Jim." This was JD Jones the lawman, who wasn't at all sure of my real intentions. I was still mostly an unknown person to him; and it was reassuring to me to know that he would not go along with wrongdoing regardless of who the "doer" was.

I started to object. "But we don't know—"

"I rode with Pard and th' boys down in th' Nation," our captive interrupted. "He'll know me," the man croaked.

"I ain't never seen you b'fore tonight, feller, an' I been ridin' with Pard some time." I shook him erect. "What's your name?"

"Tobe, Tobe Jennings."

"Never heard of yuh."

"He's th' one Lute said held off that Lighthorse posse while the rest of them swam th' Canadian," JD said.

"Yeah, that was me," Tobe lied. "Nearly got caught for it, an' never got my cut o' th' takin's."

I snorted. "Pard's still got it in an envelope with your name on it. Saw it just th' other day. Come on, let's git this over with."

"Now hold on, Le-impy. I don't mind robbin' fat-cat banks an' trains, but I don't hold to shootin' unarmed men just 'cause someone said to. This feller says he's out here t' help us, an' I believe him."

Limpy! I'll wring his neck, I thought. "An' you ain't been here long enough t' know Pard expects us to do as he says or they'll be con-se-quences."

JD cocked his gun. I wondered if he really thought I was serious. I had no doubt he was. "Th' con-se-quences here is you or me is gonna be dead afore that feller is."

"You got th' drop on me. Do as you please," I said.

He grabbed Tobe and pushed him toward his horse. "Consider that you have dee-livered your message to us an' now your job is done. Th' only safe direction you can ride is north, an' don't ever show your face south o' th' Kansas line again. It wouldn't be good for your health."

The man caught up to his horse, and when he was mounted, turned. "I th—"

"Shut up and ride afore *both* of us changes our mind," JD said.

The man trotted to the riverbank, and we heard his horse cat-hoppin' up the slope.

Chapter 7
The Dry Cutoff

"So you failed to trap the robbers; what did you do then?"

"We met Deputy Stein and his posse and decided he would continue his pursuit of the gang and posse man Jones, and I would cut off a big bend in the river by a forced ride overnight in another attempt to get ahead of them. We suspicioned they would attempt to ambush the Stein posse, and we would have to spoil their plans."

"Limpy? *Limpy?* Is that all you could think of?"

Joe Don couldn't hide his grin. "Well, I almost said 'Lee,' an' I knew that wouldn't do; th' rest was just inspiration, I guess."

"Nex' pretend name you get's gonna be 'Jack' an' your last name'll be 'Ass.' " We left that rope up all night and slept on each end of it, but didn't catch any more "birds." Sign along the bottoms showed no one else had come along before we got there. If we were lucky, the Newman gang didn't know how close Gam was.

About five miles up the river, we found their campsite. The ashes were still warm. Instead of going back to the breaks and the flats above, the gang stayed in the riverbed, not bothering to hide their tracks. The best we could determine, there were six horses. Two of them were heavily loaded. We took them to be the packhorses. Their progress was slow, most likely because their horses were nearly played out. We tried to match their pace. At noon, we found a shady spot and rested. The river made a great dip southwest before turning back northwest, and

I drew me a map and studied it.

"JD, do you know anything about this country?"

He lifted his hat off his face and studied the question a moment. "It's awful dry, an' no one lives out here, an' th' only ones likin' it are Injuns, buffalos, an' coyotes—aside from th' usual compliment of poisonous crawlers and plants."

"A lot o' good you are. I knowed that after thirty minutes in this country."

"Sorry." The hat lowered over his eyes.

I stood and rubbed out the map with my foot. "You get all th' rest you can, buddy. We're gonna do some night-riding." His only response was a grunt. I moved the horses to a new spot of grass and left them eagerly grazing.

Just before sunset, I roused up, kicked the snoring Joe Don's feet, and took the horses to the only stagnant pool they would drink from.

A voice came from the brush: "Can you believe we spent the afternoon stalking robbers in their camp and it turns out to be Lee Sowell and Tex?"

"If that's Tex, he's grown some an' bought socks." Harm spoke from the bushes a few yards away.

"Tex don't wear socks, an' you know it," I replied. "Hope you got somethin' good t' eat. I've been havin' t' eat my own cooking."

Harmon Lake stepped out of the brush, a big grin on his face. Gamlin scrambled around and slid down the bank to the riverbed. JD's horse shied a little and Hoss lifted his dripping nose, snorted, and resumed drinking.

"Hey, Lee!" Joe Don implored. He was sitting up, his hands on his head, and Bud Lake was holding his rifle on him.

"Better hold him there, Bud," I instructed. "He's a dangerous man."

JD made an angry response intended for Bud's ears only, and

Bud laughed and relaxed. Harm shook my extended hand and Gam slapped me on the shoulder—the wrong shoulder. "What's wrong, Lee? You hurt?"

"Got stung last week up in Dodge City; come on over and meet Joe Don."

Harm looked concerned. "Where's Tex?"

"Tex is laid up in Gray Center, Kansas, with a hole in his leg an' a sweet little German girl nursing him back to health and matrimony."

"Tex gettin' married?" Gam asked, doubt and suspicion in his voice.

"He's scared to death that's where it's headin'." I couldn't help laughing.

Bud leaned his gun against a bush and shook my hand.

"How'd you git here, Bud?"

"Nick drew th' short straw," he said, a big grin on his face.

I introduced them to Joe Don before Harm and Bud went back downstream to retrieve their horses. "We left our Tumbleweed wagon at Beaver," Gam explained. "Addison Mundel or one of his men will start this way with it in a day or two."

I stoked the fire up and set the coffee on. "We have some venison, and Harm will cook rice for supper," Gam said.

"We were about to cut across the bend and try to get ahead of that bunch. Then we would have them between us. Sooner or later, they're gonna set up a nice little ambush for you, and we are planning t' spoil it," I explained.

"Can you wait for supper?"

"No. They are at least half a day ahead of us, and we are going to have to hustle ourselves to get ahead of them. How about you bringing up our packhorse? We can make better time that way."

"What do you plan to do with them?" Joe Don asked. "You can't arrest them out here, there ain't no law."

"Probably the best we can do is recover their loot an' maybe put enough lead in them to discourage them from comin' back to the territory." Gam dug his cup out of his possibles.

I filled cups around. "Doubt they'll get too discouraged."

"Bud or Harm could go with you, Lee."

"Thanks, Gam, but your horses have been on th' go all day, and ours are rested. You're gonna have your hands full if they ambush you before we can get to them."

Joe Don was watching Harm prepare steaks and looking awful wishful. Harm grinned and tossed him the first cut. JD wasted no time hangin' it over the fire. I saddled the horses and brought them around. We mounted up and Harm handed JD his sizzling steak on a stick. "If we catch up with Newman and he has set up an ambush for you, we'll hang a red union shirt high up somewhere beside the trail so you can see it."

"That's good, Lee, happy hunting." Gam shook my hand, and JD and I were off. It was almost a mile up the river before we found a wash that wasn't too steep to climb to the plain above. After that we made good time on a southwest track. Just as dawn was beginning to show, we came to a trail that led down to the Beaver.

"Looks pretty well traveled, JD."

"Yeah, there's a little settlement south of here where the Hardesty range is. I imagine their closest market is those pens south of th' border at Tyrone." There was considerable traffic across the bottoms where a herd had been driven up the trail. We couldn't find any indication that a bunch of horses had passed through along the river.

"Looks like we headed them, JD. Let's make camp and rest a little. I'm starvin'."

Back up the draw the trail ran through was a campsite by a seep that emptied into a buried barrel. Some deadwood had been dragged up, and it didn't take long to get a fire going and coffee and jerky frying. It was quite a ways around the bench to grass that hadn't been grazed.

We were just finishing our meal when two cowhands rode up. "Step down, boys. I'll put more water in th' coffee," JD invited.

"Don't bother with more water. Just give me a spoon an' I'll eat th' dregs," the shorter man declared. The second man was tall and skinny with a prominent Adam's apple that bobbed up and down a lot when he talked. His name was Strawberry, and the short, stocky man was called Reel, short for Reelfoot. The two were Hardesty men out riding bog, and both were amply endowed with caked and drying mud from removing cattle stuck in the boggy and quicky river.

"Which direction are you fellers going?" I asked.

"We came down Agua Fria to Beaver, and we'll go down to a line shack on Palo Duro Creek for th' night," Reel said.

"Then we'll turn around and come back up, most likely pulling th' same dam cows outta th' same spots they was in before," Strawberry snarled.

"And probably getting th' same sharp-horned 'thank you' you got before." JD chuckled.

I had made sure the men had seen my badge. We didn't say anything about what we were doing, and they had showed th' customary courtesy of not askin'. "How far is it to Texas from here?"

Reel thought a moment, " 'Bout ten mile as th' crow flies."

"Best way from here is t' bear southeast till you hit th' Palo Duro and go up that creek. Th' line is about five miles south of where Huckleberry Creek comes in from the right. Where th' creek comes out of Texas is th' county line 'atween Ochiltree and Hansford counties. There's a monument on the state line at the corner," Strawberry advised.

"Straw knows a lot about that monument and state line." Reelfoot grinned.

We rested a while. When the two vaqueros prepared to leave, I asked, "Mind if we ride along with you a ways?"

Strawberry nodded. "Might could use some help with some of those mavericks."

We saddled up and followed them down to the river. Soon we came across a steer bogged in the mud. "Your turn, Reel," Strawberry declared.

With a grunt, Reelfoot threw his rope over the steer's horns and dismounted as Strawberry's rope settled over the horns. The cow shook his horns as Reel approached. It didn't take too long to loosen the hooves, and we watched as the two horses pulled the animal to solid ground, Reelfoot's horse performing without a rider. The cowhand waded out of the mud, slinging wads of the stuff off his hands as he came.

No telling how far away the Newman gang was, and I didn't want these two tangled up with them. "Fellers, there is a gang of train robbers coming up the river. We don't know how far away they are, but I don't want t' take th' chance o' them tangling with you. It would be best if you would not go down the river any further than here until they are out of the way."

Strawberry nodded. "Imagine we could work back to the Fria and have plenty t' do."

"If we don't hear from you by this time tomorrow, we'll be comin' on down th' river," Reelfoot said.

"That's reasonable. Just be careful if these men are still about. After we stir them up, if we don't get them, they'll be mean as red wasps in August."

"Don't worry about us. We'll be wary—and we got stingers too." Reel patted his rifle stock. With a wave, they turned back up the river, and we went on our way.

Those wide-open bottoms were worrisome. We tried to take advantage of whatever cover we could find. It wasn't much, and both of us strained to see any sign of the gang.

It was the sound of an axe chopping wood that gave them away. We hid the horses in the brush. Joe Don went down the left side of the river, and I hotfooted it across into the brush on the right side. Somewhere around the bend a tree fell, and my guess that it fell across the bottoms was right. Newman was planning on Gam still driving the wagon and had blocked the bottoms so the wagon would have to drive through the boggy streambed. It would slow them down, if not bog them completely; a good place for an ambush. It was just past a sharp bend in the river, and Gam would have no warning before he was on top of the blockade and well within rifle range.

I jerked my red union top off and tied a knot in the end of one sleeve. With a fist-sized rock in the sleeve, it made a pretty good sling. There was a tall slim cottonwood tree and on the fourth try, the shirt stayed high in the tree. I prayed Gam would see it in time and Newman and company didn't.

One man was in the limbs of the fallen tree and the other three must be back downstream to catch the posse in crossfire without cover. A stirring of the brush in a gully just ahead warned me, and I crept up to the rim and looked down on six horses. A man slept under a bush down toward the river. They must not be anticipating a long wait, for the animals were still saddled and the packhorses loaded.

I had been trying to figure how we could make a legal arrest of these men, and the opportunity was there staring me in the face! If I could steal those horses with the loot on them and lure the gang into chasing us, we might be able to get to the state line before they caught up.

I slipped up the rim of the gully and down the side above the horses. It was easy enough to untie them and string the packhorses behind me. When all was ready, I slapped leather to the horses in front, and we galloped down the gully. Their guard jumped up at my yell, and the lead horses ran over him, sending him tumbling. Out on the bottom, we ran straight across the river, shooting and yelling.

Joe Don appeared, running like a scared rabbit, and caught up to one of the horses. Shots and yells were coming from the barrier. We laid low on the horses and ran up the bottom. Soon we were out of range and around a bend. We slowed down and JD hollered, "Have you gone daft, Lee? What are we going to do now?"

"We are going to Texas and draw a bunch of train robbers after us."

"They gonna chase us afoot?"

"No, we'll give them a little transportation; take that ganted horse there and snag his line in a bush. We'll leave our horses for them to find. Four men and three horses will slow them enough that we can stay ahead of 'em."

"Bet they leave someone behind, and then we'll have a race."

"You're probably right . . . maybe we ought to go on with all the horses and cut our odds to two men . . . no, leave the horse. We need t' catch as many of them as we can."

JD tangled the ganted horse's picket line in the brush and hurried to catch up.

"We'll go right up Palo Duro all th' way to the line," I told him.

"How can you be sure we're being followed?"

"I'll show you." And I reached over to one of the packs and spilled a Dutch oven to the ground. About a mile farther, another pan fell from the packs. Just before turning up Palo Duro, a flour sack sprang a leak and strung flour around th' corner to Palo Duro Creek bottoms. I sent JD on with the horses and waited at the mouth of the creek to be certain we were followed. Half an hour later, three horses appeared, one lagging behind with two riders. It was time to ride on. At least they weren't killing the horses t' catch us. Pard was being smart.

We needed to lighten the packs. When I caught up with him, I saw that JD had moved two of the heavy sacks to the two empty saddles, easing the packhorse loads considerably. We rode on in the late afternoon. I hollered ahead to JD just after we passed Huckleberry Creek. "Six more miles or less—" A fountain of sand spurted up in front of my horse, followed by the boom of a Sharps rifle. "Oh crap, JD, they got a buffalo gun. Step it up a little."

We were able to put a little more distance between us while the rifleman mounted up. The gap was too far for Winchesters, and that was good. The gathering gloom would take away any accuracy that Sharps rifleman might have. Their best chance was to follow until their horses—or ours—gave out. I hoped the gang had not thought of the Texas line.

Even with a lighter load, one of the packhorses was faltering.

"Cut him loose, JD, and leave him here."

He started to remove the sack of money, then stopped. "We'll see it again even if we leave it here, won't we?"

"One way or th' other, we sure will." The faithful horse made to follow us, so I cut the pack loose and hazed him into the brush. He stumbled a few steps and stopped, looking back. "Go on, now. You done your job well; take a rest." It wasn't likely the robbers would take the time to catch the horse, and now they would be carrying that heavy bag instead of us.

Joe Don kept up the pace and we didn't hear the Sharps again for a couple more miles. The shot was wider this time, the boom just as loud. Looking back, I saw only three men and three horses. *Don't think about Texas, Pard.*

They were gaining on us, pushing their horses to catch up before losing us in the dark. The Sharps no longer boomed, but there was an occasional rifle shot, still too far away for accuracy.

"We made it," JD shouted, pointing to the survey monument off to our right. He cut across a loop in the creek and trotted the horses into the mouth of the cañon the creek flowed out of. A mile farther, I dropped off my horse and slapped his rump. Behind a chest-high boulder, I checked my loads and waited. It was scary how quick they rode up. If we had gone another mile, they would have caught us on the run. I put a shot in the dirt in front of the lead horse, and he skidded to a stop.

"Put your hands up—" No use finishing that sentence. I was talking to empty saddles. A shot hit my rock and whined away. I fired at the flash just to let him know I knew where he was. Where was JD? Gravel clinked to my right, and I threw a shot that way. Another shot hit my rock and splattered my face with grit. They were surrounding me, and fast. I turned to retreat to another rock when something slammed into my head and my right leg. Everything went black. I don't even remember hitting the ground.

Chapter 8
Joe Don Jones Takes Over

We hadn't even stopped running when Lee opened up on the gang. I jumped off with my rifle and started back to help him out, when thought of the loot turned me back. The bags were hidden away in a hurry. When I rounded the corner, a bullet passed my head with a whine. The line of fire was no place to be. The nearest safe place to go was up the side of the hill. It was getting darker, nothing visible but shapes and shadows. *Sun stand thou still upon the Palo Duro.* If Joshua could command it against the Amorites, so might I against the Newmans—maybe. Three flashes at the mouth of the cañon all converged on one location where Lee must be. A shadow rose from behind the boulder, and Lee took one step before a volley of shots from those three places felled him.

"Got th' s.o.b., Pard." A man rose from the ground to my left, and I took careful aim. He fell with a grunt.

"Hell's bells, that's the other one." There was movement to the right of Lee's position. Gathering my feet under me, I snapped a shot and jumped up the hill. The gang's shots indicated they expected me to go downhill. Working my way forward some, I strained to find the third man, but he was a crafty one and didn't move.

Another shot whined off the rocks behind me. *That pesky feller's gittin' plumb careless.* With my back against a rock and my knees propping my gun up, I aimed and counted, ten, eleven, twelve, thirteen . . . another shot came, and I counted again . . .

eleven, twelve . . . I squeezed the trigger and rolled away in a frantic hurry.

"Ah-h-h . . ." The groan faded away, and the man fired no more. Three quick shots spattered on my backrest, but I was too busy moving to see where they came from. A game of cat-and-mouse began.

"And the sun stood still, and the moon stayed, until the people had avenged themselves upon their enemies."

I couldn't tell if the sun stood still, because it was hidden behind the mountains, and it was going to get black as pitch—and soon. Not a sound came from Lee. That was worrisome. Another worry was that the man or men left could head up the cañon now that there was no one to stop them. I had to get to the bottom of the cañon and see to Lee. Now the dark became my friend. I stood and very carefully crept down the hill, holding on to the cedars.

The scrape of a boot warned me, and a match flared where Lee should be. A man was standing with his pistol pointed to the ground. I fired, and the match fell to the ground. There was a soft groan. Throwing all caution away, I hurried through the maze of rocks. "Lee, are you hurt?" The answer was the click of a gun on a spent shell. "You might as well put that gun down, feller. It'll do you no good."

"Guess you're right," he answered, but I heard the cylinder open, and he grunted to remove bullets from his belt as I ran forward. My leg struck a boulder, shin high, and I fell against the pistol held in the man's hand. A shot went off almost in my ear, and burning powder stung my face. I grabbed the warm barrel in my left hand and swung my pistol overhand at where I thought his head would be. Sparks flew where gun hit rock, and I swung again. This time it hit home, and the man's hand holding the gun relaxed. He lay still, and I lay there a moment to let the shaking stop.

Now it was my turn to strike a match. I found myself sitting against the outlaw where I had fallen on his legs. He was out cold, a trickle of blood creeping down his cheek from his temple. I got just a glimpse of Lee lying on his side, his gun in his hand. Blood stained the sand dark around his head, and his pant legs were dark with moisture. *Oh, dear Lord.* I had heard a man's bladder let go when he died, and it sure looked like that had happened to Lee Sowell.

Shots fired; I dropped the light, huddled behind Lee's shelter rock and thought. It could be any of the three robbers out there, two injured and the one left behind; then again, it could be Gamlin and his posse.

"That you, Gam?" Silence. "Gam, it's me, Joe Don. Are you there?"

After a moment, a muffled voice answered, "I'm here, Joe Don, where are you?"

The voice wasn't familiar. "Who drew th' long straw?"

There was no answer to that. Slowly my nerves calmed. My prisoner stirred. I rolled him over and put Lee's manacles on behind his back.

Lee groaned and stirred, "Be still, Lee. They're still out there." He cocked his pistol, "Lee, *be still.*"

Bang! He fired in the wrong direction, back toward our horses. In the flash, I could see he was firing over the legs of our prisoner. I heard him dig his heels in and crawfish away from the line of fire. Lee's next attempt to shoot clicked on a fired shell. He groaned and passed out again. At least he was still alive, but if he didn't get treatment soon, he would most likely bleed to death.

The faint creak of saddle leather and a hoof striking a rock warned me that Gamlin was approaching, "Stop, Gam! You're walking into an ambush," I yelled. Almost simultaneous shots flared at me from either side. Then it was dark again—the darkest night in my memory.

Aside from the ringing in my ears, those two shots were the last sounds heard in that cañon the rest of the night. I crawled to Lee and found the gun where it had fallen from his hand. He groaned when I rolled him over and felt around his head until my fingers found a long gash in his scalp. It wasn't bleeding much. Ripping up his shirt made enough cloth to wrap his head good enough to stop any bleeding.

It occurred to me that the stain on his pants might be blood. A careful search down his left leg from top to bottom found nothing wrong with it. His pants were dry below the knee, and I switched to the right leg. It was wet nearly to his ankle, and just above the knee on the inside was a bullet hole in the cloth. It had not passed on through; the bullet must still be in him. The bleeding had almost stopped, but when I slit his pant leg with my knife, the wound bled again. More shirt material tied in place with his pant leg made a compress over the wound. There were no more wounds, so I made him as comfortable as he could be on that ground and sat beside him. He didn't move. An occasional check to see if he was still breathing reassured me.

That was the longest night in my life. A new moon gave no light. The only thing good about it all is that I didn't get a bit sleepy. So many things were hanging undone. We needed water in the worst way; the horses were scattered all over the place, still saddled, and some pack-loaded. Two or more outlaws were out there in the rocks somewhere, waiting to shoot us up. Gam and his posse were there somewhere, and the light of day might expose them to fire from the outlaws. Their horses were most likely untended. The only thing positive about the situation was that the loot was perfectly safe where it was, and nobody would find it without me. The morning star peeked over the eastern horizon. It was high in the east before a faint light showed the approach of Ol' Sol. I drug Lee into the cover of the boulder, then took survey of the things around us.

A plowed-up trail showed where my prisoner had scooted into the brush on the far side of the wash. He wouldn't be too hard to find. Downstream, there were horses tied on both sides of the wash where Gam and his men had found shelter. Somewhere between us were two or three outlaws hidden in the rocks, watching for anything to move. There was nothing to do but wait and watch. It grew light enough to see that my bandaging job on Lee had stopped the bleeding, but he was still a mess, dried blood caked in and sand everywhere, and he had to be cold, naked from the waist up. I took my shirt off and covered him, then realized what a good target my red union suit made; so I took it off and traded it for that shirt.

Something stirred the brush up on the ridge across from us. All I could do was watch, not knowing if it was friend or foe. Heat waves began shimmering down the wash, making it look like the dry bed had water in it. A stir in the brush to the right caught my attention, and a rifle barrel appeared with a rag tied around it. Then a man stood and stumbled out on the sand, one arm hanging limp and bloody.

"Got to have water," he croaked. Laying down his weapons, he stumbled up the creek toward the last pool in the cañon. After he had gone a ways, another flag appeared, and a second man with a bloody shirt walked into the open from the left side of the wash. With his hands high, he too walked toward the pool. As he passed, I asked, "Is there anyone else out there, feller?"

"Find out for yourself," he growled. A shot in the sand just in front of his feet brought him to a stop.

"Kinda exposed there to be so rambunctious, ain't you?"

He stood very still for a moment. "You gonna kill me?"

"Only if you don't answer my question. *Is there another man out there somewhere?*"

"Yeah, an' he ain't shot up like we are. I hope he shoots you to rags." He resumed his journey to water.

"Gam, there's another man between us somewhere. Be careful."

The stirring of the brush on the hill opposite resumed. From the amount of brush disturbed, it had to be my escaped prisoner. I put a shot above him and one below and yelled, "If you move again, I'll fill you full of lead."

There was a sudden flurry of shots downstream, and in a few seconds a man emerged with his hands high and Harmon Lake right behind him. That made all four men. I trotted after the two wounded men. There weren't any weapons up there, but there were horses saddled and ready to ride if they wanted them. The second man was just reaching the water, but the first man was trying to mount a horse from the right side because of his useless left arm. The horse was objecting.

"Hold on there," I hollered, and the struggle ended. The horse trotted away, and the man sank to the ground. The third canteen I found shook like it had water in it, and I hurried back to Lee.

Harm had stopped there and looked up at my approach. "Looks like Lee got th' worst of it."

"Worse than any of th' rest." Gamlin knelt beside us and helped sit Lee up a little. While he held him, I wet a piece of shirt and rubbed his lips clean. He responded to the moisture, and I held the canteen to his lips. He only took a sip or two. Bud appeared with a bedroll. When we got Lee on it, we carried him to the pool and under the shade of some willows at the edge of the creek.

Gam sent Bud and Harmon after my escaped prisoner, who turned out be Pard Newman. He was scraped up and dirty as a pig from crawling across the ground on his heels and butt;

never had been able to stand up on his own. It was a real relief to hear Gam's wagon come rattling up the creek with a cupboard full of food and a secure place to keep our prisoners. Marshal Mundel had sent it with a boy named Ike as driver. Tagging along behind came the packhorse we had released, recovered some from his labors.

Now that we had the medicine kit from the wagon, we gave the wounded proper attention. The bone in Lee's leg was broken, so we put splints on it. Harmon sewed the gash in his head together. We spent the rest of the day catching up horses, treating wounds, and making a decent camp. It was certain we would not be moving before Lee was better.

Two riders coming up the creek about sundown caused some concern. In a moment, I saw that they were the two Hardesty hands, Strawberry and Reelfoot.

"We come to see if you boys needed any help rounding up those train robbers," Strawberry said as he squatted by the coffee pot.

"You are about twenty-four hours too late," I replied.

"Whoowee." Reelfoot wiped imaginary sweat from his brow. "I feared we wus gonna be here on time."

"Reel has an aversion to flying lead," Strawberry said over his steaming cup.

"Breaks me out somethin' awful," Reelfoot asserted.

Pard had been particularly obnoxious about his arrest, maintaining it was not legal in the Strip. After telling him once where we were, we ignored him and went about our business. Now he implored the two cowhands: "Say, fellers, tell these ignorant deputies there ain't no law in No Man's Land and they can't arrest people here."

Reelfoot got up and walked over to where Pard was shackled. "Is you under *arrest*?" he asked, unbelieving.

"Arrested me right here this morning."

"Well, I'll be glad to tell these ignoramuses it ain't legal t' arrest a man in th' Strip—"

"Good, you tell 'em an' get me th' key to these shackles, I got business elsewhere."

"—*and* I'll tell you that you are sittin' on good ol' Texas soil, about a mile south of th' border." Reel grinned.

"It ain't so," Pard whined.

"Lived here too long t' know otherwise," Reel replied. "B'sides, Straw's allergic to Texas, an' he's been sneezin' ever' since we crossed th' line."

"He still won't believe you," Harm said.

"He can't afford to believe that. It's his only salvation." Gam grinned at the prisoner, "You might as well admit it, Pard. You been outsmarted."

Pard's reply was not worthy of print.

Lee drifted in and out of consciousness all night long. He was restless, and one of us stayed with him and the other two wounded the whole time. We kept him drinking water, and his temperature didn't seem high. The man with the broken arm was Lin Huie. We splinted the arm and secured it in place so he couldn't move it around. Our third injured man identified himself as Loftis McCoy. A bullet had hit him in the side and cracked or broken two ribs. We sewed him up and bound his ribs tight. Regretfully, Pard Newman was unharmed in the fight; neither was Moon Adams. As is usually th' case, those two gave us the most trouble.

It was the next morning after the two vaqueros had left to continue their bogging route before anyone mentioned the loot from the robbery. "Say, JD, where is th' loot from that train?" Bud asked.

"Been meanin' t' ask th' same question, myself," Gam added.

"Three bags are buried in a very safe place. We left one where that packhorse give out, expectin' someone t' pick it up. You didn't see it?"

"Nope, but we wasn't p'tic'lary lookin' for it at th' time," Bud said.

"We saw where you cut th' pack off that horse, but it was empty," Harm added.

"Pard, did you-all pick up that bag of loot when you come by?" Gam queried.

"That ain't loot, it's *our money.* We were haulin' it to th' bank when you fellers stole it. I don't remember any of us pickin' it up, do you, Moon?"

"Nope, pretty sure none of us did," Moon replied. The two wounded bandits merely shook their heads. They were feeling pretty rough.

"You don't suppose all of us missed seein' th' bag, an' those two cowhands found it, do you?" I asked.

"I'd give a fifty-fifty chance that they found it and kept it. More likely, they would have pulled out a handful apiece for 'reward' money an' brought th' rest to us," Gam opined.

I had been watching our prisoners from beneath the brim of my hat and saw a grinning Pard elbow Moon. "Most likely, that feller Newman took the bag and has it squirreled away somewhere between here and where we left it." The grin faded only a little bit, but I saw.

"Two distinct possibilities," Gam said. "We're gonna be here a few days; might as well take a look. Harm, you and JD saddle up, and we'll go tracking. Bud can stay here with our patients an' prisoners."

Dry, sandy soil doesn't keep tracks long in this windy country, and that is what we found when we tried to track yesterday's activities along Palo Duro Creek. We were pretty sure we found the depression where that bag had hit the ground, and there were some kind of tracks around it, but we couldn't tell what they were. The only sure thing we learned was that the bag was gone. There were too many trails through the sand to follow, and we were reduced to riding the edge of the brush and following any traces that left the creek bed. Nothing turned up. Some of us rode that trail every day of the week we were there, all for nothing.

The more we questioned the prisoners, the more I was convinced that Moon Adams had something to do with the money's disappearance, but we didn't learn anything from them.

Our two wounded prisoners recovered quickly, but Lee was a worry. At the end of eight days, he sometimes had a clear mind, always had a severe headache, and his leg gave him a lot of pain. Gam was nervous about sitting there longer. When Reelfoot and Strawberry rode up that afternoon, they had a conference with Gamlin, after which the two rode off and Gam called us together.

"I've made arrangements for Lee to stay at Hardesty Ranch until he is better. Any trip in the wagon in this land would be too much for him. Reel and Berry have gone to the ranch to get a wagon and figure they should be back about noon tomorrow. When they get here, be ready to move. We'll go south to Tascosa and take the train from there to Paris, then on to Fort Smith."

Lee griped about that a little. "I can make it just fine, and you'll need me to testify at any trial they have. There's gonna be a big fight about where these yahoos got arrested, and we don't want them turned loose on th' lie they were arrested in the Strip."

"I'll give you th' same argyment you gave Tex." I quoted chapter and verse about how, in this case, "I ain't gonna haul you across this country and have to amputate your leg in some dry camp, then bury you out there somewhere."

"I never said that, JD."

"Shore you did, an' I got witnesses to it. Th' trip to

Hardesty's will be hard enough for you, but it's a way better than a hundred an' fifty miles cross-country."

"JD," Gam shouted, "we need that loot."

"I'll get it," I replied. "We gotta move that tumbleweed wagon." I unpacked the shovel while Harm harnessed the mules and hitched them to the wagon.

"You mean we been sittin' on top of our money all this time?" Pard growled. I just grinned at him. Harm and I had agreed he would pull the wagon out of sight of camp while we retrieved the bags. As they pulled away, I began digging where ol' Tumbleweed had been standing. We could still hear Moon Adams cussing after they were out of sight.

When I sat down and started taking off my boots, Bud laughed. "Knowed where you put those bags." He slipped off his boots and rolled his pant legs up.

The creek was surprisingly deep, and we only found one bag in shallow water. I had to strip and dive after the others, then couldn't lift them and swim out. We tied a rope to the bags, and the boys pulled them to shallow water where we could pick them up. The bonds and bank drafts were ruined, and what little paper money there was, wasn't much better. "Those can all be replaced without loss," Gam said, so we tied the bags closed. They were all stowed away out of sight before Harm brought the wagon back to an unusually quiet camp.

"Where's our money? We want to see it," Moon demanded. He noted my long, serious face. "What's wrong, couldn't you find it?"

Gam acted mad. "The idiot has forgotten where he buried it." He stomped off into the brush.

I moved over closer to the wagon and said in a low voice; "I know where I buried it, Moon, and I parked the wagon over it, but it's gone. Someone stole it."

"How could that be?" Pard asked. "We been here near th'

whole time it was buried, an' I can assure you no one's been diggin' under this wagon. You just parked it in th' wrong place."

"Yeah," Moon agreed. "Go dig over there, an' if it isn't there, dig on th' other side of th' wagon."

"I'm give out, an' my hands are blistered something fierce. These others is so mad at me, they won't dig. It may come to leavin' here without th' money."

Pard grinned. "I can just see this bunch doin' that. We'll be here till you find it, so you might just as well start diggin'."

"These hands ain't diggin' any more today. You can hang your hat on that," I said.

"Say, Bud," Pard implored. "how 'bout lendin' a hand on this shovel? Sister JD is give out, an' his lily-white hands is blistered."

Bud looked up from his packing, "Dig it yourself, Pard. You claim it's your money; well, act like it. I ain't your servant."

"I'll dig," Moon volunteered.

"Gam, alright if Moon does some of th' diggin'?" I asked.

"Shore, but you keep an eye on him. If he runs, shoot him."

The man could hardly sit still long enough for me to unchain him. He grabbed the shovel and surveyed the territory.

"Start there at the end of th' wagon," Pard advised. "They done dug where the wagon was parked."

Moon Adams set to work with gusto, and the sand flew for several minutes before he paused. "Say, JD, just how deep did you bury that loot?"

"Oh, not over a foot, foot and a half. Didn't have an awful lot of time since you were throwin' lead at us."

He stretched his back, rubbed his hands on his pants, and dug more, this time shallower. By the time his ditch exceeded twenty feet, the dirt was flying a lot slower and rest times became longer. Rubbing his hands on his pants, he begged, "Anyone got a pair of gloves they'll loan me?" The only answer was to give advice on where to dig next.

Pard Newman had watched the project with interest, then amusement when he caught on to what was going on. He began giving instructions now and then. Their conversation got so hot that Moon threw down the shovel and yelled, "You're so smart, git down here an' dig for yourself, I quit."

"It's time you took a break, anyway, Moon. Hop back up there on th' wagon an' I'll put you back on th' pickit line." I hoped I could get that done before he caught on.

He and Pard sat and discussed where the loot might be buried and where to dig next. We rejected the occasional request from one or the other to "stick the shovel down" here or there. After lunch, Bud brought out one of the packs and plopped it down by the rest of the gear with a distinctive silver clink.

Moon jerked upright from his rest. "What was that? I heard th' sound of coin."

"Naw," Harm said. "It was th' spoons in th' wreck pan you heard."

"Wasn't neither. I know that sound, an' it was coins janglin'. Where'd it come from?"

Bud was in the process of bringing up a second pack, and when he dropped it beside the other, it too made that silver ring. Now, I wouldn't say Moon was slow, but he's like all of us when we set our mind on something and harness up with blinders on. It just never occurred to him we were playing a trick.

Pard started easing away from his buddy as the truth began to dawn on Moon. "Why, you dirty dogs, you had that . . . well, I'll be . . . what a lousy trick . . . You knew too, Pard?"

"No, no, not at first, Moon," Pard protested. "But I figgered it out . . . honest, I wasn't in on it."

"He caught on b'fore we had a chance t' get th' shovel in his hands," Harm said and handed Moon a dollop of lard to rub on his hands.

"You had th' silver all along, didn't you?"

"We have three bags, and we'll get th' fourth if you tell us where it's hidden," Gam said.

"Well, if I knowed, I wouldn't tell you," Moon swore. " 'Specially after that trick."

"Then I guess we'll just have to leave it out here for someone else t' find," Gam said. "We're leavin' soon as those boys come for Lee."

Berry showed up within the half hour with a wagon bed full of hay. We soon had Lee tucked into it. I rounded up our stock and followed the wagon.

Last I saw of the posse, they were makin' dust south for Tascosa, Texas.

Chapter 9
Hardesty Ranch

Jack Hardesty was a stern man given to sharp talk. His strong convictions were typical of many cowmen of that day, not countenancing profanity or associating with men who took the Lord's name in vain. His convictions greatly influenced the type of men he hired. They were generally men of good moral standing.

Four of the Kentucky-born Hardesty brothers didn't catch the gold fever until 1859. By then, the fields of Colorado were no longer green, or golden, if you please, and the boys moved on to Montana, where their fortunes improved greatly. Gold they found there made them all wealthy men. R.L. (Jack) and his brother, John F. Hardesty, invested their money in land and the ranching business. They had holdings in Texas, New Mexico, Kansas, and Oklahoma.

In 1879, Jack, with the honorary title of colonel, and John established their Half Circle S Ranch along Coldwater Creek forty miles southwest of Beaver City and about eight miles north of Texas. They located their headquarters under the breaks of little Chiquita Creek, where they built a substantial ranch house and outbuildings. Trail herds from Texas threatened his Hereford cattle with the Texas fever. Colonel Jack and his neighbor, Ludwig Kramer, organized an army of cowhands and owners and confronted the herds at the Texas line. Threat of war was averted, and the herds were directed to a trail south of Beaver City, saving the Strip from the dreaded disease.

When Jack got the Half Circle S organized and running to his satisfaction, he turned the operation over to John Durfee and moved to Dodge City, where he could better manage his many holdings. His visits to the ranch were most often with a party of guests who spent their time hunting and fishing. Eventually, a small community grew up around the ranch, and the colonel enjoyed giving parties at the ranch for his neighbors.

It was to this ranch that Lee Sowell rode in the wagon bed of hay, his head aching, and his leg taking note of every bump along the way. The place was dark when we drove into the yard. Lee insisted we not wake anyone. He would just sleep in the wagon, now that it was no longer in motion and he could relax. We turned the stock into the pasture, and Strawberry retired to his bunk while I crawled into the wagon beside Lee.

The ranch began to stir before sunrise. I left the sleeping deputy for a regular bunkhouse breakfast with real eggs and a stack of flapjacks to th' rafters. The cook was one of the first Chinese cooks I had seen, and he could really cook.

John Durfee came in while we were having a second cup. "Why are you boys sitting here while that injured man is layin' out there in that wagon?" he asked.

"That's Lee Sowell, the deputy," Strawberry explained, "an' he wouldn't hear of us wakin' camp in th' middle of th' night; said he could sleep just as well right there till mornin'."

"I've sent for Juana. You better get out there an' be ready t' take orders," Durfee said with a little smile. Breakfast broke up at that, and there was a general movement to the door. Reelfoot explained. "Juana's th' housekeeper in th' big house. The only one she don't outrank is Durfee, an' he don't cross her."

I thought the woman looking down into the wagon must be over six feet tall. Men were hurrying here and there to the tune of her orders. She was in the process of wagging her finger in his face and scolding Strawberry. ". . . leaving this poor man out here in the cold all night long. You should be flogged, Straw Berry and for a penny, I would do it myself!"

Two men with harnessed mules coming from the corral saved Berry's hide. "Bring the wagon up close to the veranda and do it gently."

She turned and someone gave her a hand as she stepped down from the steps on the side of the wagon—and disappeared! Still giving orders, she reappeared marching to the house at a pace few men could match—and she wasn't over five feet tall.

Lee heard my voice and called, "Joe Don." I peeked over the side.

Lee's eyes were wide. "Who was that, JD? You're not gonna let her take me over, are you? All I need is a bunkhouse bed an' peace and quiet."

"Lee, it looks like you're out of my hands, an' there ain't no one here big enough t' rescue you."

"Joe Don, don't let that woman get ahold o' me. Get me outta here. We can make camp somewhere it's quiet an' I can sleep."

"It's too late, Lee, we're trapped. You gotta make th' most of it." The wagon moved with a jerk and eased around in a big arc, coming up so close to the high veranda, the hubs rubbed against the wall. Juana stood at the edge of the porch, seeming to tower over the wagon, "You, you, you . . . and you." She pointed at four of us. "Get in the wagon on that side and help these men get that poor man up here—and be careful about it."

Taking hold of the sides of the bedroll, the eight of us lifted Lee and laid him on the porch. The little woman shooed us away with a wave of her hand and knelt beside the patient, examining him from head to foot. She asked a hundred questions, never pausing for an answer. "Rosalba, we will have to wash this man before he can come in the house. Go get ready . . . and get my scissors and razor." A silent shadow behind the screen door departed. Juana waved at us, awaiting her beck and call. "Take him around the back to the patio, and be careful about it." With that, she disappeared into the house, issuing orders to Rosalba and other unseen occupants.

"Joe Don, if you leave me in that woman's clutches, I swear . . ."

"Ain't nothin' nobody can do for you now, Deputy," Berry said with a wide grin. "You cain't blame JD for a thing. He's a victim, same es you."

Lee groaned. We deposited him on the patio, where several buckets of steaming water were being poured into a large tub. Juana appeared, loaded down with towels and clothes, followed by a boy with a chair. It only took us a moment or two to get Lee seated in the chair minus his overalls and shirt. There he squirmed in his union suit bottoms and nothing else while Juana shooed us away. "Get to work, the day is half over, and you haven't turned a hand. We can take care of things here from now on."

"JD, go to Carrizos and get Kat Ingram back here." There was desperation in Lee's voice I had not heard before in our short acquaintance.

"Who's Kat Ingram?" Berry asked as we returned to the bunkhouse.

"He's Lee's partner in a ranch they're startin' over west of No Man's Land."

"Cain't go far west from there an' stay in th' Strip," one of the others said.

"I think it's up th' Cimarrón a ways in New Mexico Territory," I said. "Looks like I'm on my way there."

"You may as well go. You ain't gonna see that man for a while," another hand said. Nods and grins all around confirmed his statement.

It didn't take long for the men to disperse to their chores. They left me to my own devices. I saddled up, then gathered our horses from the horse pasture so I could go over them and see what they needed. A couple of Lee's needed shoeing, but my two seemed fit and in good shape for travel. I turned the horses back and talked to the smithy about shoeing Lee's two.

With nothing else to do, I rode around the place. A cross up on the brow of the flats drew my attention, so I rode over to see. It was a fresh grave. On the cross were the names of the occupants, a man and woman by the name of Cruze. The date of death was December 1887, not a year ago. It seemed unusual that a couple would die at the same time. I guessed there was a story here.

Later, I could see the men below gathering around the bunkhouse and I rode into the yard just as Cookie rang the iron. We were all sitting around the porch after supper when the silhouette of the cross against the red sunset reminded me to ask about it.

"That's Joe Cruze an' his wife up there," Reel said. "They got caught out on th' prairie in a blizzard. Joe had th' saloon here at th' settlement," he continued, "an' he and his wife agreed to spread th' word about Colonel's Christmas Eve party. They were on their way to Beaver City when a blizzard caught them."

"Best we can tell," one of the others said, "their horses broke away from the buggy and left them. One of the horses didn't get far, but the other showed up at the gate of the Kramer Ranch with his harness still on. They immediately started a search and soon found the dead horse and empty buggy. Searching more, they came upon the bodies of the two, wrapped in each other's arms, the wife's head on Joe's chest.

"We got them back here and had a time getting the bodies thawed enough to lay them out for buryin'. While smithy put together a double coffin, th' captain of th' buryin' committee—

who shall remain unnamed, though we on th' committee knows him well—took us up there on th' hill to dig that grave. He marked off a spot, handed out blister handles, an' tole us t' dig while he went to town t' organize our relief . . ."

While that spokesman relit his pipe, another took up the tale. "We commenced t' dig, an' someone hollered at our chairman, 'How deep?' "

" 'Just dig until I say stop,' he shouted back, so we began t' dig."

His pipe lit, narrator Number One took up the tale. "Meanwhile, our captain went into the saloon t' recruit a relief crew an' got caught up in a poker game, forgetting all about us up there in th' cold diggin' that grave—"

"—Till late in th' afternoon when as he says, 'He came to hisself' and rushed back up there with a hastily assembled crew. We had dug that hole so deep we could hardly throw th' dirt out. We were lyin' on our bellies watchin' th' diggin' an' about t' go to town an' get a bucket and rope t' haul out dirt when he rode up," narrator Number Two put in.

With a warning eye on Two, Number One continued: "Inspectin' that ten-foot-deep hole, he declared, 'That's deep enough, boys. Yuh done a good job. Drinks is on me, an' you boys on th' relief crew don't have a thang t' do.' Then he turned and rode pell-mell back to town. If there had been a gun amongst us, he'da never made it.

"We had a reg'lar funeral. Th' colonel gave a good sermon, an' th' hull town turned out, for the couple was pretty popular here."

A third or fourth commentator added, "It wasn't a very cheerful Christmas last year, but we made up for it July th' fourth."

We had watched a buggy roll into the yard while the story was being rehashed for probably th' hundredth time. The driver got out and talked to John Durfee for a few minutes.

Their conversation finished, John and his visitor walked over to us. "Boys, our postmaster got a letter today you-all should hear." Moving around under the porch lantern so he could see, the postmaster read us the letter. Here's what it said:

To the Hardesty Postmaster;
Dear Sir:

I take my pen in hand to ask you if you know of a man in your community by the name of Joe Cruse—[spelled with an *s* in the letter, John explained]—my husband. He is supposed to be there seeking work and I haven't heard from him in a long time. Would you please notify him that his wife and children are in dire straits with hardly a thing to eat and only rags for our clothes? We need his help with winter coming on.

Please relay this message to Joe if he is there and if not, please reply to me at the address given below.

Sincerely, Mrs. Joe Cruse

There followed an Illinois address where the poor woman could be reached.

It was a moment or two while this soaked into our minds and someone said, "Well, I'll be damned."

Another voice rose above the murmur of the crowd. "We ought t' dig that man up an' hang 'im."

"I been there, Zeb; he's ten feet deep, an' I ain't goin' back."

"B'sides, he'll be stinkin'," someone in th' crowd said.

"He stunk when he was alive an' we didn't know it," someone else added.

"Too bad we didn't git thet letter when he was alive. We could have really hung him then."

"It's a real shame," John said, "and we don't know who that woman buried with him was at all."

"If she's got family, they may never know what happened to her."

"We oughtter take up a collection t' send to that poor woman."

Durfee had been thinking and said, "Wait a minute, fellers, Colonel Jack is holdin' th' proceeds from th' sale of Joe's property, including the saloon, while he tries t' locate next of kin. I'll write him what we have found out here, and he will be sure to get that money to Joe's family. Colonel's good with words, an' he can break th' sad news to th' widow when he sends her that money. It won't be necessary t' mention the other woman, and the widow can keep good thoughts about her deceased husband."

That plan met with the approval of the crowd. When John and the postmaster left, the boys turned to advising me where, when, and how to make the trip to Florence. They finally agreed that I should follow the Beaver up to where Corrumpa and Cienquilla creeks come together to form Beaver River. Florence is a little west of north from there, about twenty-five miles, the first half of which is very dry across th' Llano Estacado. There should be water at old Fort Nichols. If not, South Carrizo Creek just north of the fort would have water along it.

The route they planned was exactly the route I had already chosen, so I was in good shape. Sunrise the next morning found me following my shadow up Beaver River. Just for the change of it, I made a leisurely trip, camping up on Corrumpa before making the last leg into Florence.

The post office had moved south of the Cimarrón after I left there a couple years ago and changed its name from Carrizos to Florence. George Marrs's lunch counter moved with it, and I took full advantage of the opportunity to enjoy the saloon's hospitality. Tomorrow was soon enough to meet Mr. Kat Ingram.

Chapter 10
Kat Ingram

I found my friends Red, Sol, and Spider in Marrs's saloon trying to talk Pete into a poker game. "I'm flush out o' silver an' matchsticks, fellers. An' asides, I'm lookin' at you three an' not likin' th' odds o' comin' out anything less than naked. I got a better chance survivin' a rattler bite."

"Aw, come on, Pete, you ain't got nothin'—" Spider began, then spied me. "Sa-a-ay, ain't that a Joe Don Jones I see standin' by th' bar pickin' his teeth?"

Chairs scraped as others turned and looked. "Nah, yore weak eyes is foolin' you agin, Spider, that feller's all dusty from ridin' th' plains, an' you knows yourself Joe Don don't do that kind o' labor," Red said and turned his chair back to the table.

"Red," Sol said in a stage whisper, "I smell fresh meat, an' his pockets is jinglin' with th' common medium."

"Why, I believes yo're right, Sol. I jist now got a whiff of it myself." Red turned back to me. "Welcome to Florence, stranger. Care for a friendly game?"

"Think I'll stick with that feller Pete an' his rattlesnake friend," I replied. "It looks safer there to me."

"Smarter'n he looks," Pete observed. He pulled another chair up to the table, "Have a seat, stranger, an' tell us what brings you t' this part of th' world."

Their grins were as warm as a handshake, and I sat down among friends. "I'm on my way to Sheep Pen Cañon Ranch t' fetch Mr. Ingram to Hardesty t' rescue Lee Sowell from Juana, the Half Circle S housekeeper. This Ingram must be *some bad* if Lee thinks he can outdo Juana."

The boys grinned and nodded. "That's one match-up I'd care t' see," Sol observed.

"My money's on Juana," said Pete, the snake charmer.

"Now, you know that ol' Ingram feller can be somethin' for-mid-able when he needs t' be." Pete rubbed his chin in thought. "I think my money'll be on Kat."

"Looks like we have a difference of opinion here," Red the Moderator said. "I'll be honored t' hold your money, gentlemen."

"Yeah, for just es long es it takes you t' git t' Trinidad," Pete charged.

When negotiations on the conditions and amount of the bet were settled, I had to relate our adventure with the Newman gang and how Lee got shot up and made prisoner of Juana of Half Circle S fame. ". . . so Lee sent me out here to fetch this Kat Ingram back to the ranch with some idea he can be rescued," I concluded.

"This meetin' sure looks to be a historic moment in th' story of No Man's Land, an' I think our eddication would be incomplete if we were not witness to it," Pete said to the nods of the others.

"Joe Don, our friend, we propose to escort you and Mr. Ingram from here to Hardesty for this historic occasion," Red declared. "First thing in th' mornin' we will show you to Sheep Pen Ranch and help convince Kat to accompany us to Hardesty, if need be; though I think he will be anxious t' go once he hears of Lee's predicament."

To that, I agreed and ordered a nightcap before we retired to their open-air accommodations for the night.

The source of Marrs's supply of fresh eggs was a closely kept secret that tied us to his prices for them. It was left to me to spend my common medium for five breakfasts. I began to wonder which would last longer, my money or my time in Florence. Well-fed and happy, we proceeded up the Cimarrón to Sheep Pen Ranch.

The ranch house was a half-mile off the trail on a knoll overlooking the valley. As we approached, a lady came out the door and sat in a rocker on the porch, a rifle across her knees, a prudent precaution for that place and time. My companions hung back as we approached the yard fence. I removed my hat and spoke to the lady, "Good morning, ma'am. I am Joe Don Jones and I have a message from Deputy Lee Sowell."

"Well, light and come on in, you and your friends. Hello there, Red, Sol, Pete, and Spider." The boys returned her greeting, hats in hand. She smiled. "I must say, young man, that you are quite brave to associate with such adventurers as these."

A young girl emerged from the house with a tray of glasses and pitcher of tea, and we sat around the porch passing the time of day and sipping the sweet amber drink. As the young girl poured our second helping of tea, Miss Ingram said to her, "Mollie, Mr. Jones has a message from Mr. Sowell for us."

"Oh, we've been so anxious about him. We expected him to be here two weeks ago or more." By her response, I took it that the girl had special feelings for Lee. Just like the rascal not to mention that.

I smiled. "My message is for Mr. Kat Ingram. Is he around?"

Miss Mollie looked puzzled. Miss Ingram glanced at Red, who was taking a long drink of tea; then she smiled and looked at me. "There is no *Mr.* Kat Ingram, Mr. Jones. My name is Katherine Ingram and everyone, including these four scalawags, calls me Kat."

"I-I-I didn't know," I stammered. My face felt hot, and Spider snickered.

Red slapped his leg and crowed, "You got him, Kat! Look at that face."

"*I* didn't 'get' him, Red. It was *you four* that led him on," Kat replied. "Don't be too embarrassed, Mr. Jones. This happens occasionally, and I am used to it. We are also used to the pranks these fellows pull."

"Yes, ma'am. I should have known also." I stowed a note in my head to seek revenge at my earliest opportunity.

"Enough shenanigans. What is the message from Lee?"

"He is at Hardesty and wishes you to come to him . . ."

" 'Rescue' is the more appropriate word, Kat," Sol said. "He is under the care of Juana."

"Care? Is there something wrong with him?" Miss Ingram's concern showed on her features, and Miss Mollie's hand shook so she sloshed tea from the pitcher. She set it down, her face pale.

I tried to break the news gradually. "He is recovering from injuries he got when we helped Deputy Gamlin Stein capture the Newman gang of train robbers. I left him under the good care of Señora Juana."

Miss Kat had regained her composure. "How is he injured?"

"He got a grazing shot to the head that had to be sewn up, and a bullet broke his upper leg. His desire is for you to come rescue him from Señora Juana."

"Huh," she puffed. "It's just like that grouch to complain about good treatment and nursing. I'll go down there and *help* that angel Juana, and Lee Sowell hasn't seen the half of it! Mr. Jones—"

"We address him as Joe Don or JD, Kat. *Mr.* Jones is his dad back east," Sol said.

I nodded. "Joe Don or JD would be just fine, ma'am."

"And you may call us Kat and Mollie. We don't stand on formality out here."

"Yes, ma'am. Thank you."

"We must get ready to leave in the morning, Mollie." Then to us: "Sol, see that the hands know we are leaving, and arrange for Tomas and Colita to take charge of the house. Red, you and Spider go round up the mules. Pete, haul out the buggy and see that it is ready to travel. You'll need to soak the wheels, then grease them good. I want a lot of hay in the bed. Mollie, see to the provisions, and I will pack for both of us. Now hurry, all of you. I want to leave before sunup."

Just like that, Kat Ingram took charge. By sunset, all chores were done and the buggy loaded and ready to drive out of the shed.

Not a soul was stirrin' when we rode through Florence, and we didn't stop until we were out of the breaks where we left South Carrizo Creek. We swung around the head of Swede Creek and crossed the Santa Fe Trail on the plain. The trains had killed the freight traffic, but settlers and pilgrims were still using it. Traffic had slowed enough so that the grass grew tall again.

Instead of going on south, we turned southeast. It was a long, dusty ride to the breaks of the Beaver. Getting down those steep banks to the river was a chore for the buggy. A rope on each back corner of the bed and snubbed to saddle horns kept the buggy upright. Even so, the ladies chose to walk down the hill. We watered at the river and found a nice arroyo to camp in for the night.

I couldn't see how that buggy could ever get down the river bottom in that sand. To my surprise, we climbed out to the flats on the south side of the river and continued southeast. Late afternoon brought us to the Agua Fria or Coldwater Creek, and we rode downstream on the flat above the creek. Dark caught us still a few miles from Hardesty. Kat reluctantly agreed we would have to stop for the night.

We arrived at the ranch before noon the next morning. John Durfee was crossing to the bunkhouse when we rattled into the yard. He greeted the ladies courteously, helping Mollie down while Red offered his hand to Kat.

"We've come to offer Juana our assistance in caring for her patient, John," Kat said.

Before John could reply, Juana answered from the porch, "Come right on in, ladies. The patient is here. Someone needs to sit on him while I change his bandages and remove stitches from his arm." She greeted Kat warmly as she would with one well-known. Kat introduced Mollie as they entered the house.

Chapter 11
The Odyssey of Rockin' R Bill and Tex Shipley (Tex's Tale)

The month of September 1888, was one of the longest months of my life. I had a bullet go through my lower leg in a fight with some of the Newman gang in the Long Branch Saloon at Dodge City and spent a month at the Melton farm at Gray Center, Kansas. Now, don't get me wrong; I'm grateful for the care Mrs. Melton and Malvina gave me—especially Malvina—but a man needs other men around and a little respite from female attentions.

Sunday afternoon, the last day of September, two strangers in a buggy drove into the Melton farmyard. The man introduced himself as Bill Wylie—the Rockin' R Bill who Lee had told me about. The young lady was Miss Lorna Hardy. She and Mallie disappeared into the house, chattering happily.

Even though there was a chilly wind blowing, we sat on the edge of the porch and smoked. "Think you're ready t' herd some cows?" Bill asked.

"I'm packed an' ready." Packing was easy, since I only had one spare outfit, which stayed in my possibles bag when clean—and in that house, nothing stayed dirty long.

"I got you a room at Miz Sarah's tonight. She's ready to declare you fit or unfit for th' trail. I've ordered cars, and the railroad will take us to End of Tracks. From there it's only about a hundred miles or so to Sheep Pen Cañon."

"Where's End of Tracks?"

"Stationmaster at Ingalls says it's somewhere past Granada,

Colorado," Bill replied.

"We may want to find out for sure where it is in relation to Sheep Pen—might be we'll want to get off short of there."

"You're right. The shorter th' drive, th' better this time of year." *The shorter th' drive, th' better* any*time of year,* I thought.

Lorna came to the door. "Bill, I need to be back in time to fix supper."

"Well, it's time to be rollin', then." He tapped out his pipe and stood.

Mallie brought my bag out while I said my goodbyes to Mr. and Mrs. Melton. The old man was grinnin', probably glad t' be rid of me, but his handshake was firm and his invitation to come back sincere. Mrs. Melton gave me a big hug and wiped her eye with the corner of her apron. I threw my crutches in the back of the buggy and turned to tell Malvina goodbye. She grabbed me and kissed me on the lips right in front of everybody. She was near tears, and I felt a lump in my throat—a little one. "You write me a letter, now," she said in a little quivery voice.

"I will if you write me. Send it to General Delivery, Carrizos."

"They renamed it 'Florence', Tex," Lorna said.

"It may take us a month t' get there, so don't worry." Somehow I got into the spring seat beside Lorna. It was snug with th' three of us, but no one complained.

Staying in one place for a whole month was awful confining for a man used to sleeping out 'most every night—and usually never two nights in a row in the same place. That ride back to Ingalls was sure a tonic. I didn't realize how tired I was until we stopped and I eased down off that buggy. The trip up those stairs to the boarding house porch seemed to take forever without my crutches.

"You can keep your moccasins on, Tex," Lorna said as she

held the screen door open.

I understood what she meant when I saw the row of boots lined up on the porch. The "No Boots in the House" rule was in effect at the Melton house as well. It was a good rule in this land of dust or mud, sand spurs, and fresh droppings. Mrs. Ashmore was a tall, handsome woman and made sure I was comfortable in the sitting room before returning to the kitchen. Several men sat around the boarding house table talking while they waited for supper.

"We got word that Lee and Gamlin captured the Newman gang after a fight," Bill said. "Lee got shot in th' process."

"How bad?" I asked.

"Broke his thigh bone an' creased his head pretty good. We heard he was having more trouble with the head wound than the leg. Juana, the woman in charge at the Hardesty household, is taking care of him. He couldn't be in better hands, I'm thinkin'."

"You know those folks down there?"

"Yeah. Got some friends work for the colonel. They say it's hard t' say who's in charge when th' Old Man is gone, th' manager or Juana. She must be some force t' deal with."

I laughed. "Bet Lee's 'bout t' pitch a fit."

Mrs. Ashmore stood at the head of the table. "Dinner is served, gentlemen."

Bill and I joined the others at the table. "Tex, you sit here at the head. A chair will be much easier to get into than that bench." Mrs. Ashmore smiled and held the chair for me. When I was seated, she said, "Mr. Jackson will you say grace for us?"

A feller halfway down the table with garters on his sleeves said the blessing. I took it he was some kind of clerk. When Bill introduced him, he said he was the telegraph operator for the railroad. Miz Sarah's board was much more varied than the Melton fare had been, and I appreciated that it wasn't as heavy.

That rich food is good for a working man, but when you're sitting around doing nothing, it weighs awful heavy on your system.

Bill made a lot of talk about the "come-after," and I didn't know what he was talking about until Lorna appeared with two pies, one apple and the other cherry. I managed to get a sliver of both and they were good—melt-in-your-mouth good.

The crowd gradually drifted away. Bill excused himself and went to the kitchen to help Lorna with the dishes. "Now, Thomas," Miz Sarah said to me, "let us have a look at that leg of yours."

She propped my foot on a low footstool and carefully rolled my pant leg above my knee. We had a little bandage on the wounds just to keep my overalls from rubbing against them. She looked at the wounds and poked around on my leg some. It sure was sore, but I tried not to let her know how it hurt. She sat on the end of the bench and said, "It looks to be healing good. Get up and walk to the sitting room and back."

I limped the circle she described and sat back down. "You know Lee—Mr. Sowell—gave me authority to decide when you are ready to travel." She paused a moment, and I knew she was at the crossroads of a decision.

"Miz Sarah, I know it would be pushing things some for me to travel now, but it's October, and th' weather won't hold much longer. I promise you I will take care of myself and not do anything that will do harm to my leg."

"You will have some scarring inside, but if you reopen that wound, the scarring will be twice as bad—if it ever heals at all. I will think about this overnight and let you know my decision in the morning."

"Yes, ma'am." It was all I dared say.

"Your room is the first one on the left at the top of the stair. It is ready whenever you are, but you are welcome to join us in the kitchen and visit while we clean up."

"Thank you, ma'am. I believe I will sit in the kitchen a while b'fore bedtime."

"Good." She rose and hurried to the kitchen, and I limped along behind.

There was a small kitchen table in the back of the room. I pulled out a chair and sat and talked to the three as they worked. It was obvious that Lorna and Rockin' R Bill were sweet on each other. Bill helped in the kitchen in order to be with her. Lorna washed, Bill dried, and Miz Sarah stored the dishes. When that was done, the two women began preparing for the next day's meals. They pushed Bill out of the way, and he joined me at the table. It wasn't long before I felt the need to rest. I excused myself so I could climb those stairs unobserved. I made it by climbing with my left leg and bringing my right up behind. It hurt when I put my weight on my right leg to step up with my good leg. The sheets were sunshine fresh and I drifted into a dreamless sleep.

Bill was not present at breakfast. When I asked, Lorna said, "He's gone to order the cars." She said it with a sad sigh. That meant good news for me, but I didn't show it out of consideration of the girl. Later, Mrs. Ashworth said, "If you were not pressed for time, I would have you wait a week, or even two. You have to promise to take care of your leg and *never* ride a horse. That would set you back all over again, and no telling what you would do 'way out there on the plain without any help."

"You could lose your leg or get gangrene and die, Tex," Lorna added.

Miz Sarah gave me a large piece of white cloth and a bottle of denatured alcohol. "Wash the wound with alcohol morning and night, and change the bandage for a clean one every night. If you keep it clean, you shouldn't risk infection."

"Yes, ma'am, I will. Thank you."

Bill clumped across the veranda and called through the screen, "Can't get th' cars afore day after tomorrow or th' next day. Gotta go take th' cattle to graze. You comfortable, Tex?"

"Just fine, Bill. You go ahead. Miss Lorna said she would entertain me."

"She better . . ." he started, then stopped. Even through the screen, we could see the blush creeping up his neck, and we laughed as he quickly turned away.

That night after supper—Mrs. Ashworth proclaimed it was dinner—we got together and made some plans. I was to go through the chuck wagon again, make sure we had everything ready to go, and change our destination back to Granada, Colorado. Rockin' R would see to the cattle and horses. We had known we would need another man to help with the herd and Bill said, "I've found someone who will go with us and help. He's th' nighthawk from the Rockin' R and says he's ready to see some new country. You might think he's a little young, but I know his experience, and he'll do us good."

"Bring him by and let me talk to him," I said.

"Wanna talk to him tonight? I could start him in th' mornin' an' let him get used to th' cattle some."

"Sure." Bill left. I went out and sat on the porch and smoked. Soon he returned with a boy almost as tall as he was, and thin as a rail. "Tex, this is Bud Pack. He's ready t' go with us to No Man's Land."

Bud shook my hand with a firm grip and a friendly grin. "Glad to make your acquaintance, sir." His voice was deep, but cracked like voices do when they are changing.

"How old are you, Bud?" I asked.

"Fifteen, sir."

I'd judge you to be about thirteen, I thought. His clothes were well worn and a little ragged. Our talk satisfied me that he would be capable to do the things we needed him for. "If you think thirty a month and found will suit you, you can start tomorrow morning, helping Bill with the cattle. I will set you up with our account at the general store. When you get in tomorrow night, go over there and buy yourself an outfit of clothes. How are your boots?"

"They'll be good. I bought them last spring."

"Make sure what you get is warm and tough. We'll get some winter weather before we get to the ranch."

"Yes, sir." The boy couldn't stop grinning as he shook my hand again. He bounced off the steps into the darkness.

The station agent was put out some at changing our destination a second time, but he finally got it done. "I can't get the cars until day after tomorrow, and the engine will be here the next morning."

"We'll load the stock the morning the engine gets here. I don't want them stuck in the cars all night, and I want them watered before we load them."

That didn't seem to set well with him, but we were the paying customers, not here for the convenience of the railroad. He figured a six-hour run for the hundred and forty miles to Granada, not counting any sidetrack time for through traffic. I had him wire Granada to make sure there was room in the stock pens for our cattle overnight, and there was. With the addition of Bud, we were short on our cavvyard. I asked the stationmaster, "Know of anyone around here with some cow-horses for sale."

"No, we get very few of those here. Mostly, we get th' heavy draft stock for these farms. Granada gets a good traffic in cattle. I'll bet you can find all the cow-horses you need around there."

"Thanks for the information, I guess we'll wait until we get there and see what turns up."

Our talk about winter weather stuck with me. At the store, in addition to making arrangements for Bud's outfit, I bought extra supplies of food stock and blankets. It would be bad enough to be caught out on the range in a storm, but ten times as bad if we ran out of food.

Stepping out of the store, I realized how tired I was, and it wasn't even noon. If this was the way things would be, I was going to be in real trouble when we hit the trail. I made it to a rocking chair on the hotel's veranda. There I sat and dozed until the crowd began gathering for dinner—the noon meal, that is. The next two days crept by. I made use of them by walking to build up some strength. Bud and Bill had the cattle loaded by midmorning the third day, and the train rolled out for Granada before noon.

We were lucky not to have to be sidetracked. By dark the stock were unloaded and contented with fresh water and hay. We found an outfit, the Triangle T, that had just shipped their herd, so Bill bought almost their entire cavvyard. The ranch's brand was a triangle on top of a T, and the outfit was nicknamed the Spade Ranch.

We also picked up three of their hands who were anxious to return to the home range right away for one reason or another. Mostly, those reasons wore skirts. Now we were set. That night was sure a long one.

The cattle were featureless blobs against the dark when we turned them out and across the tracks just east of town. I hooked Pet and Tobe to the wagon, and we drove south ahead of the herd to pick a place for the noon rest. After crossing Granada Creek three miles south of town, there was nothing but featureless prairie. I made camp about midway between there and Durkee Creek. The chuck wagon was the tallest feature in that land. I was glad for the wood stored in the possum belly. I soon had a fire going in my fire pit. First order was to get the coffee on. Second was a pot of beans that would be ready the next day. Today it would be steak and sourdough biscuits.

The Rockies far to the west were the only things to break the flat monotony of the prairie. Already, they were turning white with the winter snows. The herd was only a dust column. Gradually individual animals and riders emerged from the cloud of dust. When I could hear the cattle bawling, I got ready for the feed.

When I threw my hat in the air, Bill and Bud stayed with the herd and sent the three Triangle T men to eat. The three were Bill French, Jacedo Nuñez, and Bull Young. Because there were two Bills in the outfit, we christened Bill French "Spade Bill" or just "Spade." Jacedo became Cedo, and what else can you call a man named Bull? They were all three wiry and thin, though Bull was nearly six feet tall. Their clothes were trail-worn, but they had fresh haircuts and new sombreros. I suspicioned new clothes right down to new boots were stored away in their bedrolls, waiting to be worn when they rode in to some nester's or sheepherder's yard to visit his daughter.

There isn't much to say about the next days of prairie travel. We navigated by the Twin Buttes far to the west of our track. Otherwise, it was all dust and searching for water until we reached a community the settlers named Springfield, Colorado.

Chapter 12
Pulga and Ladrón

The town of Springfield was laid out in 1887 by the Windsor Town Company in th' hope it would boom. It was nothing but a dusty street with a few dugouts and a wall tent that fancied itself a general store when we saw it.

The store was run by Frank Pierce Tipton, late of Springfield, Missouri; hence, the name of the new settlement. In addition to selling his scant stock, he sold lots for the Windsor Company. We stopped the herd a little ways out of town when we saw all the stakes and flagging that covered the ground. More than one rancher has been charged for restoring a survey in those boomer towns when their cattle disturbed those precious stakes.

We found Mr. Tipton sitting on his plank-on-two-barrels counter, swinging his legs and watching our progress. "Howdy, boys. Where you headed?" Only a newcomer from back east would ask that question.

"Goin' south," Bull returned.

Tipton ignored the short reply and offered, "What can we do for you today?" as if the only reason we were there was to shop his store.

"We could use some air-tights if you got any," I answered.

"Sure do. We got canned tomatoes, peaches, pears, sardines, and beans."

"They puteeng beans in thee cans, now?" Cedo asked. "Iss fantasia."

"That's right, Cedo, them little cans don't hold enough t' git a man to th' next meal," Rockin' R Bill observed.

"I don't have any beer, but I do have whiskey made right here in town by a Missouri woods craftsman." Tipton set up four shot glasses and poured from an olla.

Bull held his glass up and swirled the liquid. "Clear as water." He turned the glass up and drank it down in one swallow.

"Yessiree," Tipton said while Bull caught his breath. "Real likker don't have color. Ain't got a plug o'tobacco or horse piss or anything else t' make it purty, just pure alcohol."

"Shore beats that Taos Lightnin'," Bull croaked.

Being forewarned, the rest of us sipped the liquid. Even small sips left a fire in our throats. We were all silent while we cautiously "took our medicine."

Tipton held up the olla. "More, gentlemen?"

"I learned not t' pour kerosene on a fire a long time ago," I said. "What do I owe you, friend?"

"Dime a can. Five cents, th' drink."

I bought a can of peaches and a can of tomatoes for each man and paid for a drink apiece, including Bud Pack and Spade French, who were watching the stock. "You don't dare give those two boys more than one drink of that whiskey," I warned Tipton. "That older feller starts seein' queer animals, an' is liable t' go shootin' 'em. Shot a man's ear off in Dodge. Th' boy's too young t' dip any deeper."

"I'll be sure to avoid that," Tipton promised. "Yuh only got two watchin' your stock? This country's got more horse thieves than fleas; you'll be lucky t' get out of here with anything but foot-leather."

"Thanks," I replied. The warning was not news to us. We had slept light our whole trip.

Cedo had been digging into his pocket and laid a dime on the counter, "I weell take one of thee bean cans," he said to

Tipton. He took the can, hefted it for its weight, and looked at the label.

I read it to him. "It says, 'Pork and Beans, made from the finest beans and pork, processed in our Elmira, New York, kitchens.' "

"Wee will try these beans; eet may bee that they are better than the dry ones, Señor Tex."

"It would save us a lot of cookin', wouldn't it?"

"*Sí,* but eet costs much. Wee geet much more dry beans for our moneys." Cedo sat the can on the chuck table and waited for supper to roll around.

"It looks nice, dosen't it?" Bull observed.

At supper, Cedo took his can and poked a small hole in the top to let the pressure out and sat it beside the fire. He turned it occasionally. When steam came out of the hole, he opened the can with his knife. "Ah-h-h, ees babee beans," he exclaimed and poured the contents onto his plate.

The beans were the small, white, navy bean variety with two or three cubes of pork fat swimming in the considerable broth. Cedo spooned a bite and concentrated as he chewed. "Thees iss too sweet to bee good beans; maybee they intended for candy after thee meal." He passed the plate around, and we each took a small bite.

"Think you are right, Cedo. We better stick to the good ol' *frijoles* for real food," Rockin' R Bill opined.

"Makes you want t' taste th' real thing, don't it?" Spade commented.

After two or three tentative bites, Cedo set the plate aside and poured a fresh cup of coffee. It was one of the very few times at a chuck wagon that I saw any leftovers, and those thrown out on the prairie. Cedo didn't say another word about canned beans, and *frijoles* remained our primary food.

That very night, even though we had double guards, thieves

stampeded the cattle, then ran off our cavvyard and my mules. That left the working hands with only one horse apiece tied to the wagon wheels. Bud and Spade were riding guard. They stayed with the stampeding horses until some well-placed shots discouraged them. They met the others as they returned toward camp.

I was mad as a nest of stirred-up hornets, sitting there in the middle of nowhere, my wagon worthless without those mules, and me unable to ride.

Fortunately, this is the place Rockin' R Bill showed his mettle and took over the search. Spade Bill told me how it happened.

Rockin' R Bill Takes Over

The five of us gathered in a knot. After a minute or two, Cedo said, "Theese *pulga* need to learn what we do with thee *ladrón de pradera.*"

"Huh? What's he sayin?" Bud asked.

"He said, 'These fleas need to learn what we do with thieves of the range,' " professor Bull translated.

Rockin' R Bill spoke up. "Bud, give your horse to me. Bull, let Spade have yours. Cedo, keep your horse. You and Bud and Bull stay here until you get more horses. Bull, ride Cedo's horse into town at first light and see if you can borrow some horses. When you are mounted, follow our trail. Spade and I are going after our horses first, you three look to the herd. If you catch up with it before we get back, don't give these range fleas any slack. A long shot with a rifle is as much as they deserve. If they run, stay with the herd, and find good ground and water for them."

It took the boys a moment or two to strip saddles and gear and swap horses around; then we were off. The two spare horses we took with us could make up for the advantage the thieves had with the cavvyard as their spares. If they changed horses a second time, we would lose the race and never catch up with them. When it was light enough, I took the left edge of the trail, and Spade took the right. Somewhere along the way, the horses would leave the cattle for their own destination. We hoped that would happen after sunrise so we could find their trail. Far ahead, we saw the dust of the driven cattle. They didn't stop at sunrise, and we began to find calves that dropped out from fatigue. Some of the cows had gotten away and returned to their calves.

When our mounts began to lag, we stopped and changed horses. Both of us were angry at the abuse the cattle were enduring. "Spade, I'm ready to stop that herd," I said as I mounted.

"Me, too. Leave these horses, and let's ride for the cattle. I suspect the cavvyard turned off in the dark."

The herd wasn't more than three miles ahead and we set sail, checking our guns as we rode. When we were within a mile of the cattle, I drew my rifle from the boot and rode with it across my lap. Even this far behind the herd, the dust was heavy. The thieves could not see us coming, as thick as the dust was around them.

Spade rode close to me and I said, "Most of these boys will be behind the herd to keep them running. Let's start on this side and sweep the tail end of the herd clean of drivers. That will stop the run, and we can take care of the thieves when we can see them."

"Driving the men out in the open is a good idea," Spade said, "but I ain't takin' any chances. First man shows fight is gonna be dodgin' my lead."

"Good enough. Let's ride." I pulled my bandanna over my nose, and we circled out to the right of the herd where we could see a little better. There was one man in the lead. When we saw one of the drivers in the dust, we charged him. He was concentrating on the cattle, and we were within twenty feet of him before he saw us. My horse hit his on the shoulder, and horse and rider went down.

Spade didn't slow, but just kept running. I ran to catch up. Another figure appeared to our left, and when he raised his gun to shoot at the unsuspecting Spade, I shot him out of his saddle. The next rider we saw was racing ahead of us. He shouted at the fourth man as he rode by. When we emerged from the dust, both were riding as hard as they could away from the herd. I slid to a stop and jumped to the ground. The lead man whirled and fired three quick shots our way while I was taking careful aim and fired at the man still running. It was a hundred fifty, two-hundred-yard shot, and I had my doubts, but the man threw up his hands and tumbled off his horse. When I turned my sights to the shooter, his saddle was empty, his horse trotting off.

"Got 'em," Spade exclaimed.

Gradually, the herd came to a halt. We searched for the lead man, but he was already gone, a small figure running northwest more than half a mile away. The man I had run over was limping, trying desperately to catch his horse. Spade started toward him. "Get his horse, Spade, and then scatter this herd afore they lay down. If they bunch up, they'll overheat and die."

"Looks like you got a good lick, there," Spade called to the man afoot. "Drop your gun right there and move out of the way. I'll get your horse. You ain't goin' anywhere fast."

The man pulled his six-shooter and hesitated. I saw Spade raise his rifle to his cheek. "Don't make me kill you, feller."

He dropped the gun and limped away. Spade leaned over, picked up the gun, rode to his horse, and led him away as we scattered the herd. Already several cows heavy with milk were backtracking, going to find their calves. The heat from the cattle was so intense, all three horses were sweating, and every thread I wore was wet. We all were going to need water, and soon. We managed to get the herd mostly scattered before they lay down. A cool wind was blowing. With luck, we wouldn't lose any cattle to overheating.

I rode upwind out of the herd and dismounted. Both of our horses were sagging, their heads low. I wanted to take their saddles off, but hesitated to do so. Spade rode up and dismounted. "I think we can undress them. We're alone except for that one."

We stripped the saddles and rubbed the horses down with their blankets. Leaving them ground-tied with the reins, we walked to the last thief. He had his boot off. His foot was already blue and swelling.

"Looks like you broke a blood vessel or two there," I said.

"I think *you* broke it," he growled. "If I had a gun—"

"You had one in your hand and dropped it," I growled back. "That was your last chance, and you didn't take it—"

"It don't matter whether you took it or not. We're all gonna be dead if we don't find water—and soon," Spade interrupted. "Where's th' nearest water, feller?"

"That's Lone Rock Draw we crossed back there. If you foller it down a ways"—he pointed east—"there'll be plenty water."

"Bill, how's your horse?"

"Looks to be a little better than yours, Spade. I don't know if he'll be getting lame after that collision, but it might be good to walk him some so that shoulder won't lock up on him. Why don't you walk him east there and find us water? I'll keep this feller company. If the herd gets cooled off some, we'll follow."

Spade gathered up all the canteens we could find and rode over to where the other two thieves had fallen. Their horses didn't offer any resistance, so he led them back to where Rockin' R Bill and his prisoner sat. One of the horses looked to be in a little better shape than mine, and he mentioned it to me. "He may be, but that brand on his hip may get you a dose of lead or a temporary rope-stretching job should the right people find you on it."

Spade decided to take his own horse and rode east.

Looking up our back trail, I couldn't see any dust from our followers. Because of that, I hoped they had seen where the cavvyard had turned off and followed it. I could see cattle all along our back trail. Some were cows, and some had already found their calves. It was gonna take some work to gather the herd, and we still might lose some to thirst if we didn't move. These tired horses didn't help the situation at all.

Spade Searches for Water

The draw was dry where we intersected with it, and didn't look much better as we moved on. Three miles or so downstream, the draw ran into another stream, and we began to find water. My horse perked up. I let him drink at the second pool we found while I backtracked and filled the canteens at the first little pool. Riding back up the right-hand draw, the horse and I found several long pools of water that looked like they would be enough for the herd. After a couple of miles, we climbed out of the draw and angled for where we thought the herd was. It only took a small correction to ride directly to them. The cattle had begun to stand up, and Bill was getting nervous about trying to hold them together without knowing where to drive them.

They had the four horses bunched. One stood with his right foreleg slack, and I figured he was the one Rockin' collided with. His horse showed little sign of injury, and I became hopeful he wasn't hurt bad.

"There's water enough in the draw Lone Rock runs in to. It's less than five miles away," I said. "If we head them in the direction I came, they'll find it."

Bill looked relieved.

"That's Sandy Arroyo," our prisoner said. His foot had really swollen. He and Bill both drank from the canteens. We fixed one of the horses for our prisoner and tied the horse's lead rope to my saddle horn. When Rockin' R whistled his "Let's Go" signal to the herd and began walking slowly toward the arroyo, they understood and followed. I stayed behind and urged the slower cattle to rise and follow. Lead Steer pushed his way to the front just behind Bill, and we were on our way. When the leaders smelled water, Bill rode back and we scattered the herd so they wouldn't get to the water in a bunch. After they drank, we hazed them out on the prairie where they grazed some, then lay down again.

"Bet they don't give us any trouble for a couple o' days," I said.

"I wouldn't take that bet," Rockin' R agreed. "One of us needs to backtrack and pick up those cows and calves left behind. They'll be scattered everywhere looking for water, if we don't hurry."

"My horse is fagged out, and these others are on th' quarantined list. How's yours?"

"Tired." Rockin' R looked at our prisoner. "Where did these horses come from?"

"Down in the Territory near McAlister."

"How long have you had them?" I asked.

He scratched his chin and thought. "Maybe three months." Then he added, "There ain't no chance the former owner's gonna follow us. He's under a pile of rocks."

"Well, here's th' deal," I said. "One of us is gonna ride that horse there. He looks the freshest. If that rider comes to grief riding that horse, you're gonna become th' fruit of a cottonwood limb. Now, tell us how safe it will be to ride that horse."

"We rode those horses all this time and had no trouble. I don't see how you could be in any danger riding it."

We found a shady spot on the brink of Sandy Arroyo,

unsaddled the horses, and let them graze, except for one.

"Spade, stay here, an' I'll go round up th' strays." Rockin' R threw his saddle on the horse and rode out to the trail.

We must note here that, true to western custom in these matters, the prisoner or his disposition was never mentioned again. The wayfarer who passes that remote portion of Sandy Arroyo will note the four rock-covered graves on the bank above the stream.

Chapter 13
A House Raising

The sound of Rockin' R and Spade's horses running after the herd had hardly died when Bull grabbed the reins from Cedo and mounted up.

"Where are you goin' Bull?" Bud asked.

"T' git us some horses. An' no, I ain't waitin' fer daylight, an' no, I ain't gonna ask t' borry 'em . . ." The rest of what he said faded into the breeze of his departure. Cedo and Bud trudged back to the wagon lugging the spare saddles.

Tex was sitting there in his own stew. "What's goin' on?" he asked. Impatience and frustration dripped from his every word.

"Thee Bull ees gone to geet us horses, and Spade and Rockin' R Beels are chasing thee horse stealers," Cedo replied.

Bud dippered water from the barrel and drank. "Don't think Bull had in mind rentin' any horses. It'll be more like appropriation, so you better be cautious if anyone comes out from town lookin' mad."

"Don't worry about me. I'm mad enough t' bite nails in two, an' a good dustup would do me good," Tex growled.

There was just enough light for the three men to see the returning Bull. The two horses he led were heavy draft horses, not the kind to chase after cattle. "Not a cow pony in the town," he complained. "Hurry and saddle up. We can still catch up with that herd."

Cedo stood very still for a moment, his hand resting on his pistol. "You forgeet you are riding my horse, Bull."

"Sorry, Cedo. I was in too much of a hurry. Guess I'll put my saddle on one of these big boys. Hope my cinches are long enough." Bull got down and handed Cedo the reins.

In a few moments they were mounted and ready to ride. "Hope I don't git nosebleed 'way up here," Bud complained.

Off they trotted, and it wasn't a hundred yards before Cedo and his pony were leading the way. As the light grew, they moved to either side of the trail, trying to determine where the horse herd left the cattle. Naturally, Cedo was the first to see the trail of the cavvyard where they turned northwest.

"There they go," he shouted and continued along the cattle trail.

"Hold up there, Cedo," Bull shouted back. When they had gathered, he said, "It doesn't look to me like it would have been daylight when the horses turned. I doubt Spade and Bill saw it. Let's look around and see which way they went."

Cedo and Bull dismounted and searched through the horse tracks for a familiar print, while Bud searched across the cattle trail. In a few minutes, he exclaimed, "Here's their tracks; they stayed with the cattle."

"You're sure?" Bull asked.

"Yeah, I'm sure, unless some o' them cows stole th' horses' shoes an' wore 'em," he said as he followed the horse tracks.

"Smartass," Bull grunted as he mounted and followed. After two hours of trailing, Cedo stopped and waited for the two to catch up. "They are heading for thee brreaks of Two Butte Creek."

"Most likely already there," Bud said. "We ain't prepared to make a long search, and I'll bet we would be outnumbered if we caught up with 'em."

"Yeah, an' I' ain't anxious t' walk into an ambush in those gullies," Bull said. "What d'yuh suggest we do?"

"Thee mulas cannot stay with horses long, an' I beelieve they will fall out soon. Wee should follow some more and see eef wee can get them."

"Good idea. Lead on, Cedo." They turned back to the trail, searching for the shod tracks of old Pet and Tobe. Soon they emerged from the crowd, and it was plain they were falling behind. At the crossing of Bear Creek, the mules left the trail of the horses and moved down the creek, obviously searching for water. At a wet spot in the sandy bottom, the searchers found two holes the mules had pawed. They were full of water.

"Got their drink," Bud observed.

They continued following those mule tracks on down the creek. The mules' pace was more leisurely. They stopped here and there to graze a bit, drinking in the occasional pool. The searchers picked up their pace. "They had a big head start, but we should be getting in sight of them soon," Bull said. He turned his horse up the bank to the prairie for a look. "Well, I'll be danged if we ain't been hornswoggled by a couple o' mules," he cried.

The two in the gully rode to the top, "What ees eet thee mulas do?" Cedo asked.

Bull pointed southeast and there, glowing in the red of the setting sun, was the white canvas of the Springfield General Store.

"You mean we been jobbed by a couple of mules an' followed them in a circle back to th' wagon?" Bud swore. "Hell's bells, I think I'll shoot 'em both."

"Y'er too close to th' wagon, an' you'd hafta shoot Tex if yuh shot those mules."

"*Sí,* this ees r-right, Bud." Cedo was grinning. "I theenk ees time for supper." He spurred his horse toward Springfield, and the wagon and two vaqueros followed.

It's necessary for us to backtrack to the top of the morning to relate the things that passed with Tex on this day.

Tex sat on the wagon tongue and watched the receding figures with mounting frustration. *Damn that Newman gang, and damn that Long Branch fight,* he thought. He rubbed the soreness in his leg above the wound without being aware of it. Even riding in the wagon was painful—so much so that he suspicioned the saddle might be easier. No, it wouldn't. If he kept that foot out of the stirrup, he couldn't ride properly and he would wear out the horse and himself.

Best not to think about that. He looked around for anything that might occupy him. It was going to be a long day. He stoked the fire and added coffee to the pot, then looked through a mess of beans, picking out little pebbles that had posed as beans when they were shelled. Soon they were bubbling away, and Tex added a chunk of salt pork for flavor. *Now, all that's left for me to do is sit and watch it boil.*

Sunrise found him rolling up bedrolls and tossing them onto the wagon. *Probably only to get them out and spread them again when the boys come back,* he thought.

Some movement toward the settlement caught his eye about midmorning. Two men were approaching on foot; one carrying a long gun. Tex picked up his rifle and levered a shell into the chamber, then sat down to await their arrival. They stopped a reasonable distance from camp and Tex greeted, "Hello, gentlemen, come on in, the coffee's hot."

The two hesitated, took a step forward, and stopped. "We are looking for two horses that were stolen from our corral last night," the man with the shotgun replied.

"You haven't seen them, have you?" the second man asked. Tex didn't like his tone.

"No, we haven't seen them. Yuh think they may have come this way?"

"We were wondering."

"Well, you're welcome to cut our cavvyard to see if they're there. They might even be in with th' cattle, but I wouldn't wander there afoot."

"Where are your horses?" There was that tone again.

Tex feigned a look around. "Oh, I forgot. Someone ran off our horses and th' whole damn herd last night. The others are all out lookin' for 'em. Could be those horses of yours got stolen at the same time.

"You folks need to realize that when you start a town out here without some kind of law, outlaws an' other kinds o' human trash join you. They hide b'hind your honesty an' most o' th' time bully you. A good vigilance committee would rid your town of such vermin." Tex was aware, as were his two visitors, that the thieves who stole the herds had watched their arrival from one of the dugouts in town. "Come on in and have a cup of coffee," Tex invited again.

The two hesitated, then the one with the shotgun said, "No thank you. We will follow the herd."

"You'll never catch them afoot, and there are five men on horseback chasing the herds. If your horses are with them, they will bring them back—if they catch them."

The sick feeling in the pit of Tex's stomach was telling him how rare it was that owners ever caught up with stolen horses. The chance of catching the stolen cattle was only a little better. The two visitors conferred a moment, turned without further comment, and retraced their steps.

"You folks can clean up with a good vigilance committee," Tex yelled after them.

Even this late in the season, the sun could be awful warm. After lunch, Tex spread his blanket in the shade of the wagon and slept until the sun peeked at him under the wagon bed. As he sat up, the approach of three riders driving two horses caught his eye. They were coming from the northwest. *Not very likely to be any of our bunch,* he thought.

The gait of the driven animals soon told him they were mules. He watched with rising interest. *It* is *them, but why are they coming from the north?* He dug out two picket pins and the sledge and set the pins in the ground. At his whistle, Pet perked up and lumbered toward him. Tobe never came to the whistle, but he was never far from Pet. Cedo, Bull, and Bud rode to the wagon and stripped their horses. They were sitting by the fire with cups steaming when Tex returned. "How did you get north of us?"

"Those infernal mules led us in a big circle," Bull growled.

"*Sí,* they escaped from the cavvyard and went down thee creek, which took them just north of town," Cedo explained.

"We ain't done nothing but ride a big circle," Bud complained.

"I thought you were goin' after the cattle, weren't you?" Tex asked.

"We were, but the Bills missed it when the horses broke off in the dark, and they followed the cattle. We figgered t' follow the horses, but they had too big a jump on us. When we found where the mules left, we followed them—"

"Back to here in a big circle," Bud repeated, shaking his head.

Tex eyed the two tired workhorses. "Some fellers in town lookin' for horses a lot like those."

"Would it be those two walkin' out here?" Bud asked.

"Why, I bet it would," Tex said. "That's a shotgun he's carryin'."

Bud got up, sauntered behind the wagon, and poked his head over the tailgate. Cedo eased over to the wagon tongue, and Tex stood up to greet the visitors. Bull didn't move. "Come on in and have a cup with us," Tex invited for the third time that day.

"We come t' git our horses." The man with the gun nodded

toward the two tied to the wagon wheels.

"Are those yours?" Bull asked as he rose. "I'll tell you, they were sure lifesavers today. We found them with those two mules there; couldn't keep up with the herd, I guess. Since our own two horses were give out, we just saddled them up and turned th' others loose. We'd of still been trudgin' across that prairie without them."

"You should pay us for the use of them," Shotgun said.

"We paid you by bringin' them back to you." Bull didn't smile when he said it.

"Nevertheless—"

"We'll pay you a dollar a head, if you'll pay us a dime a head for all th' horses we lost today." Tex was getting mad. "Better yet, why don't you show us which of those dugouts were not slept in last night, an' we'll prepare a nice welcome for those yahoos who stole our stock."

"We can't do that," the unarmed man said. "They'd have our hi—" Shotgun nudged him in the ribs and he hushed.

"Never mind, gentlemen. We can find that out for ourselves," Tex said.

"We just have one more little chore t' do, an' I'll personally bring those horses to you; but if you're carryin' that scattergun when I come by, I'm gonna stand out of its range and shoot your liver out." There was no doubt in anyone's mind that Bull would do it, and with a grin on his face.

"We want those horses now," Shotgun demanded.

Now it was the unarmed man's turn to punch ribs. "That will be all right with us, gentlemen. We would like to have the horses before dark—if that's convenient," he added.

"If that's your condition, we will have to act now. I'm sorry to say we won't have time to visit with you any longer. Good evening, gentlemen." Tex threw his dregs into the fire and rose.

The two men backed up a step, turned around, and walked stiffly away.

"They'd wet their pants if I made a rebel yell." Bud grinned.

"Just don't do it while that scattergun's in range," Tex warned.

"Come on, boys. We gotta find a vacant dugout." Bull mounted the horse he had been riding. Soon, the other two were following him. Tex watched with no little longing to be with them. He saw them stop to talk to the two men a moment, then ride on to the settlement.

Bull stopped at the first dugout and roped the ridge beam. As he began to ride away, a woman came boiling out of the house, and Tex could hear her screaming. Bull stopped, and there was some conversation. Tex saw her point to a dugout set away from the rest, and Bull shook loose his rope.

That's th' one I would have picked, Tex thought.

People came out of their houses and gathered in little groups, watching the three vaqueros.

The boys rode over to the dugout, and Bud ducked inside. There seemed to be some conversation among the three. After a moment, Bud trotted out and, without mounting, hurried his horse away from the building with the other two.

The sudden explosion rolling across the plain made Tex jump. He watched the dirt roof lift a good three feet into the air, dust and smoke boiling out from under it, and then settle into the hole that was once the dugout. He heard screams from the women, then shouts and laughter. A group of barefoot boys, dancing and yelling for joy, ran toward the ruins. A little curl of smoke and dust showed where the house had been.

Cedo rode for the wagon. Bull and Bud rode to the crowd. In a moment, they turned toward the wagon, a young boy riding behind each man. Cedo rode up with a big grin on his face. "Thee outlaws left sticks of dynamite too close to the stove, would you believe eet?"

Soon saddles were stripped from the horses, and Tex gave the two boys biscuits. They rode off munching their treats, bare heels kicking big bellies.

"That was some show, boys." They turned to see Spade sitting his horse and grinning. "Is there anything here for a working man to eat?" he asked.

Tex reached into the wagon and tossed him a can of tomatoes, "Beans in th' pot, coffee's hot."

"I could use some of that myself," Bud said. Soon all four of them were shoveling in beans and drinking tomatoes from cans. Between bites, Spade said, "Rockin's holdin' th' cattle down south there an' hopin' we'll bring him a wagonload of chow and a bedroll."

By the time the four were through eating, Tex had the camp cleaned and the wagon ready to go. They hooked up the mules and said a not-too-fond goodbye to the budding Springfield. It was pitch black before they got to Rockin' R, guided by his fire.

Chapter 14
Blue Norther (Tex's Tale)

No one questioned why we didn't move the next day—in fact, no one felt like moving, especially the cattle and horses. We now had nine horses and two mules to move two hundred head of cattle to Sheep Pen Ranch.

"I wouldn't start out this way with untried cattle, but these cows are pretty much trail broke, an' we just might get them there with th' horses we have," Rockin' R observed.

"How far do you think it is to the ranch?" I asked.

Spade rubbed his chin. "Reckon it's less than sixty mile, don't you, Bud?"

"Couldn't be more than that," Bud opined.

"With this outfit, that's no less than six, maybe seven days," I figgered.

"Eef thee weather, she hold," Cedo added.

"Rockin', I'm thinkin' that as long as she don't bend north, we should follow Sand Arroyo so long as she has water in her. That would get us within about thirty miles of Carrizo Creek. There's no water in that stretch," I said. "It's all flat-iron flat up to the breaks of Carrizo, and then you're in butte country with that black caprock."

"Bud, you and Spade and Cedo know this country better than we do. Is that a good plan?"

"*Si*, Rockin', iss good theenken'. I would guess wee may be farther up Sand than we theenk, an' it may not bee as far as you expect to thee buttes."

"Yeah. I don't remember the upper end of Sand being that far from Carrizo or the buttes, but it may be farther from the end of *water* in Sand Arroyo to the Carrizo," Spade said.

"There ain't no guarantee Carrizo'll have water, either," I said. "The good part of that is that we won't be too far from the Cimarrón, and she'll have water."

"So tomorrow we will head up Sand Arroyo. When we run out of water, we head southwest to Carrizo Creek and down Carrizo to th' Cimarrón River and Florence Settlement." Rockin' R stood up. "And with that settled, I will take first watch. The rest of you can wrangle out when your turn is. Just know that I will be rollin' up in my bed in two hours, and one of you better be on duty." He mounted up with terms of endearment ringing in his ears.

Night-riding is one part of a drive I didn't miss. I was glad to retire to my blankets while the boys wrangled out the night schedule.

The last night-rider had just relieved Bud when I got up and began fixing breakfast. Bud didn't bother to lie back down. When he threw his roll in th' wagon, he came around and offered his assistance. I put him to making coffee while I rolled out biscuits. There wasn't much to do then but watch the fire and wait for the time to start the steaks. The cattle were up and on their way before Cedo and I had broken camp. Rockin' was going to try to herd the cattle with four men in order to keep the horses as fresh as possible. The extra man would ride with me.

Our plan was to push the herd at a brisk pace all morning, and then slow them after noon and let them graze. We drove about fifteen miles, in my estimation. At sundown, we hoped to water them, then bed them down in a good place.

I was up in the wagon digging out vittles for breakfast when I noticed the top of a butte to the southwest. Not far from it was the tip of one of those sugarloaf hills typical of the butte country. "Fellers, I can see the buttes from here," I exclaimed.

"Yer dreamin'," Spade said. He jumped up on the wagon seat and stared in the direction I pointed. "Well I'll be danged if it ain't. How far away d'yuh think that is?"

"I'd say not more than twenty miles. I can judge better when th' sun comes up," I replied.

There was much speculation about where we were, and how far to th' Cimarrón, and when we would get there that night. We all were anxious to see the sunrise on those far buttes so we could better judge their distance.

I had just thrown the steaks in the big skillet when Bud proclaimed, "I don't think it's twenty mile to that butte, Tex. Come up here an' look."

I had to squeeze in between th' two Bills to get in the wagon. There was no room for me on the seat, so I hung on to a tent stay and teetered on the edge of the sideboard. The discussion over the distance was lively. I said, "No matter how far it is, we need to aim a good deal west of there to hit the Carrizo."

"What makes you think that, Captain Fremont?" Spade asked.

"Do you see any other buttes east of those we're lookin' at?"

"No."

"Then those must be the first ones on the far east of the range. Carrizo Creek is almost midrange of that line of buttes, and if we go where I think we should go, it won't be long until we see the tip of Mesa de Maya either straight on or a little south of our line."

"Mesa de what?" Rockin' R asked.

"Black Mesa," came three replies.

"Well, why didn't you say so?"

"Son, you are entering the land of *poco tiempo,* and you need to learn th' Spanish side of our English language," Bud instructed.

"Sí, sí." Cedo grinned.

I stepped down and flipped the steaks. They would be well done on one side. We were ready to go in record time, our unspoken intention to be under the shadow of those mesas by sunset.

The mules and horses were skittish, and the cattle actually started walking on their own. All the boys had to do was to turn them from south to southwest.

There was a long run across the flat and monotonous plain. I sat and dozed as those tired mules trudged on. Bud was riding shotgun this morning and had taken the reins. He nudged me awake and said, "Here, Tex. I'm goin' back an' crawl into my roll."

"Why you lazy—"

"Oh, don't worry, I'll be back in time for you to get your roll."

"Have you gone daft? What are you talkin' about?"

"Look up there at that beautiful blue sky." He pointed northwest at a sky so blue, it was almost black at the horizon.

My heart jumped. "Blue norther!"

"Them's my sentiments 'xackly. Be right back."

I stopped the wagon and gave a yell to the herders, pointing to the sky. In a moment, five vaqueros were donning every piece of clothing they had, tying down their sombreros with their bandannas or a scarf, and wrapping up in every blanket they had—except for the one they draped over their horses and under their saddles. I took my tarp and threw it over Tobe, tying it fore, aft, and under. Spade had another tarp on Pet, and Cedo was changing their bridles to the blinder bridles. That would give their eyes some protection. Rockin' R and Spade tied all four of the spare horses to the back of the wagon while Bud saddled the fifth. I had been depending on him to be my windbreak. Now I was on my own up there on that wagon. I jerked the spring seat out and laid it in the back; then I made me a nest in the bottom of the bed and stacked bags of flour and beans tight all around me. I did all this on the move, for those mules would not stand still. The hard part of it all was going to be to keep all the stock from drifting with the storm and not maintaining the southwest course.

The animals had sensed the weather change before we had, if we had only been alert enough to pay attention to them. Their pace had now become brisk, and it was hard to keep the mules from running. A cool breeze came from the northwest and gradually became stronger, turning into a cold, roaring blast. The sky was clear and the sun dimmed only slightly by a little blowing dust. It gave no warmth. Down, down plunged the temperature, until I thought the bottom had fallen out of it. Cold crept into my fingers through my gloves and two pairs of socks. Even though I was sitting on several layers of clothing and tarps, my buttocks and legs were numb, and I worried I'd freeze. Ice built up on my beard and mustache. When I rubbed them, the hairs broke off like icicles.

This was the moment when the mules took over and turned south for the breaks of the Cimarrón, the cattle following. Down a wide ridge into a draw we plunged and, at the bottom, into the riverbed. Fortunately, the bank was washed at this point, and we got into the bed in one piece. I don't expect anyone who hasn't experienced a blue norther to believe it, but the river was frozen over deep enough that it held the weight of mules, wagons, and cattle. It was as far as we could go, the far bank being vertical. That was fortunate, for we were quite protected from the howling wind. The mules stopped and stood with tails to the wind, their heads low.

It must have taken me a long time to rise from my nest and climb down with numbed feet and hands. I fumbled with the rope holding the horses to the wagon and led them to the lee side of the mules. They huddled together for what warmth they could get. Pet allowed me to tie a blanket around his head and cover his ears, but Tobe would have nothing of it, and I had to leave him to his own devices.

The cattle couldn't find a way out of the bed, milled a little, and bunched tightly together. There were several deer and a couple of elk among them. There was an overhang on the high north bank of the river that offered some protection from the wind. We all crowded against it and worried that the press of the cattle might crush us. The wagon was so packed in by the herd that we couldn't move it. If it had been possible to get the bed off and tip it up against the bank, we would have had a shelter from both storm and animal. Our only refuge was under the wagon, so we bunched up there with all the cover we could get.

Maybe it was something within the cattle conscience, or just the pressure of the cold air, but the herd continued to mill at a slow pace, the ones on the outside constantly pushing their way into the herd, forcing the warmer cattle outside where the cold drove them to seek the relative warmth of the interior of the herd. This slow dancing mill continued throughout the night. More deer, elk, and antelope joined the herd. It amazed us that the little antelope avoided being trampled by the larger animals.

Our suffering was intense, fingers and toes numb and unfeeling, the possibility of frozen extremities a reality. No one was allowed to sleep. Though talking was impossible, we moved and jostled one another to make sure our neighbors were awake. Had we been standing, I'm sure our actions would have looked much like the cattle milling.

Near daylight, the wind died off, leaving us with the bitter cold. Without the wind, the animals began to warm. They slowed their milling and spread out a little. We climbed up on the wagon and looked around.

"Time to get these animals out of this river and back up on solid ground before the ice thaws," Spade Bill said. The three men from this region of the world knew a lot about surviving a norther, so we took their advice. Our horses had participated in the mill and were scattered in the herd.

Seeing a horse at the edge of the herd and near our entrance gully, Bud stepped down from the wagon and walked across the backs of the cattle to him. Once in the saddle, he rode into the herd a little ways and began hazing the cattle up the draw to the ridge. Once that had begun, the mill became a trail herd and, on their own, exited the riverbed. As the herd thinned, the other men found their mounts and rode to help.

Four of the five saddled horses survived, but Rockin' R's horse died and was trampled by the mill. His saddle was ruined. Bill came back to the wagon and helped me prepare to move. We didn't attempt to organize the bedrolls, just threw them into the wagon and followed the herd.

The cattle spread out over the plain while the wild animals drifted off in various directions. There was a large deadfall to the right of the gully. I drove over there, and we went about building a big fire along the trunk of the tree. Two pots of coffee were soon warming in the coals. I chopped off chunks of frozen meat with my kindling hatchet and plopped them into the skillet. The sourdough had frozen, and there was no chance biscuits would rise, so I made fry bread.

Cedo and Bud took care of the mules while I cooked. "Tobe's ears have a black rim around them; I suspect by summer his ears will be somewhat smaller," Bud reported.

Cedo grinned. "But thee Pet, he no geet thee blackness. May bee Tobe notice that and let you bandage his ears, too."

"You forget we are talking about *mules* here, Cedo."

The scalding coffee made good hand warmers, and there was more holding of cups than drinking for a while.

"I think my toes'd break off if I took my boots off," Bud said.

"Pour some of this coffee in your boot an' warm 'em up first," Spade suggested.

"Eet does a good job on thee insides, forr surre," Cedo said.

Spade stood at the edge of the riverbank surveying the riverbed where we had spent the night. I walked over and joined him. The bed was torn and stirred in a great circle of concentric rings where the cattle had walked. There was so much dirt on top of the ice, it looked like the river was dry. There must have been a dozen dead cattle scattered about, and every calf too small to stay in the mill was dead, scattered around the perimeter of the mill. Two of our spare horses lay dead.

"That won't be the end of it, Tex. There will be a lot of those cattle out there on the flat will lose their hooves and have to be put down. Our best course is to stay here a couple of days and see how things shake out with them."

"Folks living close by might be glad to harvest some of the beef off the ones we have to kill," I said.

"They just might have a lot of meat off their own cows," Spade said.

"Yeah. 'Bout all we're gonna get out of this mess is a bunch of hides."

"We should pull the ones down there up here, where we can skin them."

"We should not leave them there to foul the water for other people downstream," I said. "Let's eat, then we'll get busy."

"Good by me. Tex, let's go." And Spade turned back to the fire.

By some miracle, we had found the only gradual slope down to the Cimarrón within miles. If the cattle had turned south at any other place, they would have walked over a bank. Most of the banks were vertical and there were others so steep the cattle would have rolled to the bottom. When we had a chance to look around, Cedo said we were just southwest of Razor Blade Mesa.

"That puts us about twenty-five miles downstream from Florence, as the crow flies," Bud estimated.

"We have eleven cows and sixteen calves down there to skin. No tellin' how many of these up here will have to be put down," Rockin' R said.

"I theenk maybe two of thee horses down there can be skinned also," Cedo added.

While we ate, a light south breeze arose, and the air seemed to warm up some. I found four big knives in the chuck box and set about sharpening them while the others dragged carcasses up the hill. We found out right quick that it was no good trying to skin an animal frozen stiff, so that project was put off. *Hopefully forever,* I wished—and it turned out my wish came true.

Chapter 15
Meanwhile, Back at the Ranch (Lee Sowell Returns)

Attorney Scanlon continued, "So you were able to get ahead of the gang of outlaws and foil their ambush?"

"Yes, but we could not arrest the men legally in No Man's Land, so I took their packhorses loaded with the money and lured them over the state line into Texas, where we were able to arrest the gang after a gunfight."

Prosecutor Scanlon addressed the jury. "The successful prosecution of this case rests on the determination if this was a legal arrest made outside the boundary of No Man's Land." Then turning to me, he asked, "Are you sure *you were south of the Texas state line when you made the arrests?"*

"I am positive. We passed a tall monument on the state line where the county line between Hansford and Ochiltree counties in Texas met the state line. We were about a mile south of the line on Palo Duro Creek when we arrested them. In addition, two residents of the area confirmed that we were in Texas."

"You were wounded in this gunfight and not able to continue with your duties, is that right?"

"Yes. I was unable to make the actual arrests and spent some time at a nearby ranch recovering from two wounds I received that day."

Lawyer Scanlon addressed Judge Parker. "I have no more questions, Your Honor."

The hard part of my testimony was about to begin, and I didn't feel at all good about it.

★ ★ ★ ★ ★

That woman took me over like I was a piece of property. First thing I knew she had me in a tub of water so hot I thought it would slip the hair like a scalded hog. I never got such a scrubbing, but before long I got to feeling better. Just when I began to enjoy my bath, a huge man came in and, with his hands under my arms, lifted me like a baby out of the tub and stood me on the tile floor of the patio. There I stood on one foot, naked to the world, and this giant of a man took a bucket of lukewarm water and poured it over my head.

"Sit," he said, and he lowered me onto a stool that had been set behind me. He placed another stool under my still-splinted leg.

Someone dropped a towel onto my lap from behind, and I covered my nakedness as best I could. The towel-dropper was a girl, and she began rubbing my back with a towel. I cautiously dried my chest with a corner of my towel while managing to keep myself covered.

The woman came chattering across the patio with a large mug in her hand. She thrust it at me and demanded, "Drink—all of it." I drank and soon felt the soothing effects of the laudanum overtaking my body. No pain, no anxiety, just sleep, blessed sleep.

I awoke warm and fresh, in a small room with an open window, its sill full of flowering pots. That same young girl sat in a chair beside me, her hands folded in her lap, watching me intently. When I tried to smile, she arose and called down the hall, "He awakes."

In a moment, we heard soft footsteps coming from somewhere in the recesses of the house. Juana paused at the door, that large man towering behind her. Somehow they looked familiar, but I did not know them. The little woman surveyed the room with a nod of satisfaction. "Good. We have cleaned you up, sewn your head wound together, and splinted your leg properly," she said in perfect English with that little Spanish lilt that makes their speech so enchanting. "Did you sleep well?"

"Yes."

She nodded and smiled a little. "And what shall we call you?"

"What?"

She came over and looked intently into my eyes. "What is your name?"

"My name is . . . my name . . ."

"I think we will call you Lee," she said, and that sounded somewhat familiar. "Do you know where you are?"

I had not thought about where I might be, "I must be in Liberty . . . Liberty Springs."

But that doesn't seem right, I thought. *This was not my mother and sister, and our house was made of logs, not adobe—adobe? What's that?* I stared at the woman leaning over me. "I don't know where I am. What is wrong with my head and my leg?"

She took my hand and patted it softly, "You have been shot. One bullet grazed your head, and a second broke your leg. Now you are in Colonel Hardesty's house in No Man's Land. The blow to your head has made you forgetful, but your memory will come back to you as you heal. You should sleep."

It was as if I *had* to sleep, and I slept. I awoke as if in a dream. It was dark, and a small candle flickered on a table beside my bed. A man who seemed familiar dozed in the chair, and I slept again.

I slept a lot, it seems. Sometimes they would wake me and feed me soups and broths and such. One day I awoke and there was a beautiful woman standing over me. "Who are you?" I asked.

"I am Katherine," she answered, "but you can call me Kat."

I closed my eyes. *I know a Kat.* And I opened my eyes, "Hello Kat."

"Hello, Lee," she said, and a tear rolled down her cheek.

Things slowly came back to me after that. I could remember things that had happened and move my head without much pain and colored lights going off inside it. They soon had me sitting up. A few days later I walked with the aid of crutches and it seemed a dozen people were hovering around me. I became restless, my mind wanting to do more than my body was able to do. When I pushed, my body pushed back, so I had to try to be content with where I was. It seemed everything had to be gradual, gradual.

"Anyone seen Lee since he disappeared into that house?" JD asked.

John Durfee laughed. "Yes, I get to see him every day and tell him why I won't take him to the bunkhouse. Juana has taken good care of him, and if he doesn't get well soon, he won't be able to button his pants."

There was a stir at the ranch house door. Kat held the door as Juana rolled Lee out in a chair with wheels. "You have a wheelchair here?" Sol exclaimed.

"Colonel Jack has th' makin's of a hospital in there an' we've made good use of it, too," John explained.

The crowd walked over to the edge of the porch to say their "howdys." Lee looked pale, but the spark was back in his eyes.

"Howdy, Joe Don. What did you arrest these scamps for this time?"

"They held up th' general store o' Florence an' robbed it of all its stick matches. I caught 'em red-handed with th' goods—well they had th' loot long enough that Pete had their whole stock."

Lee nodded. "Not surprised. Not surprised at all."

"He suckered us outta th' Strip by sayin' you was gonna read your will an' it mentioned us," Spider added.

"Learned that from th' master deceiver," Sol grumbled.

JD noticed that Kat stood smiling, her hand on Lee's shoulder. *No; it would be more proper if I said Kat beamed. It's Lee and Kat, not Mollie! I should have caught on sooner,* he thought. Remembering the special attention Pete and company had paid to the girl, *I must say it is a nice thought that she is still eligible for a man to court.*

Juana summoned from the house, and the two women left us to ourselves. "I'm ready to go to Sheep Pen Cañon, fellers. When can we start?"

Pete elbowed Sol, "He still don't know, do he?"

"Know what?" Lee demanded.

Pete shrugged and looked at JD. "He still don't know he's done lost control of th' whole sit-ti-ation when he come into th' clutches of a woman."

"Some folks is jist slow t' catch on," Red observed.

"We'll probably be able t' leave about a minute after Doctor Juana says you're fit t' travel," JD said. It felt good to know someone besides Lee Sowell was in charge, an' JD could remind him of that fact.

The mail hack came rattling into the yard and the postmaster got out. "Lee, I have a registered letter here you have to sign for." He handed Lee a form and pencil and when Lee had signed it, the postmaster handed him the envelope. Lee looked at it and groaned. "Don't even have t' open it t' know."

"What is it, Lee?" Sol asked.

"It's a subpoena from Fort Smith," JD said, and Lee nodded.

"All I need t' know from it is th' date I'm expected t' be there." He opened the envelope and read a moment. "November 15, 1888."

Pete laughed. "Judge Parker may be the only one in th' world who outranks those women in there."

The grin on Lee's face betrayed the thought that he had seen his deliverance. *Behold, thy redemption draweth nigh.*

They had to postpone the Newman trial to December seventeenth, because Gamlin was somewhere in the Territory, and Lee was unable to travel.

It turned out that Kat was quite a trader. She bought a hundred head of improved mixed stock from John Durfee and sent them packing for Sheep Pen Ranch with Pete as trail boss and Sol, Red, Spider, and Blackie, the red-headed member of the hay crew, as trail hands. They left shortly after the first blue norther of the season, and word came back that they had made it whole. They were to stay on the ranch and watch the cattle.

When I thought I was able, Joe Don, Mollie, Kat, and I struck out for the end of tracks at Tyrone. I soon regretted my decision. Even the train ride east to Joplin and south to Fort Smith was very tiring. I was glad to get there and get a few days of rest before the trial. It started on a Monday morning.

Deputy Gamlin, with Bud and Harmon Lake, were already there. We got together for a little celebration—with the ladies; not in some saloon. They were going to stay around after the trial at my request.

The primary lawyer for the Newman gang was S.W. Harman. I liked him. We had many a conversation about law enforcement in Indian Territory and what we deputies went through. Later on, he wrote one of the first books about the work of the court and Judge Parker. It was titled *Hell on the Border.* He was a good lawyer and a gentleman—outside the courtroom. There was a raft of other lawyers helping Harman, but I don't remember who they were.

S.W. stood, looked at some papers in his hand, and walked over to me. "Deputy Sowell, are you comfortable?"

"As much as I can be."

"In your deposition you say that you lured the Newman gang

into Texas by taking their gold and running for the state line. Is that correct?"

"Yes, it is."

"And why did you steal their money?"

"It wasn't their money. It was stolen from the Atchison, Topeka and Santa Fe Railroad in a train robbery near Woodward."

"How can you be sure the money you took was from that robbery?"

"The coins were still in the bank bags and the bonds with them were issued by a Kansas City bank and identified by that bank as being in the shipment on that train."

"Woodward, Oklahoma?"

"Yes."

"But you found these men in what is known as No Man's Land. How do you know they were the ones who robbed the train?"

"Deputy Stein had trailed the robbers' tracks from Woodward. When he caught up with them, these men were at the end of those tracks. They had loo . . . personal items taken from the train's passengers."

"When you took the money, you stole the horses they were packed on, didn't you?"

"The packhorses were stolen property, and I confiscated them."

"Now explain for the court what you did with the money and animals."

I squirmed around so I could see the jury and Judge Parker better. "The money was taken in No Man's Land, where there is no law, and no United States court has jurisdiction over the area. If we were to capture these men legally, they would have to be where the courts of the United States had jurisdiction, such as Kansas, Colorado, or Texas. Texas was the nearest state, and I proposed to lure them there by taking the money into that state, where the arrests would be legal."

S.W. addressed the jury. "And now, gentlemen, we come to the critical question of whether the arrests were indeed legally made in the State of Texas.

"Deputy Sowell, how do you know that the men were in Texas when you arrested them?"

"I was informed by two men who live in the area that there was a monument on the Texas state line at the common north corner of Texas counties Ochiltree and Hansford. They described the stone as being about three feet high and having an X inscribed on the top. We were at that time on Palo Duro Creek, and that creek crosses the state line at the monument. All we had to do was follow the creek and look for the monument. When we found the monument and creek as described, we continued up the creek about a mile, where we found a place we could safely defend."

"Did the men come to you?" S.W. asked.

"Yes. I ordered them to surrender, and they chose to resist."

S.W. addressed the jury. "We have heard Pard Newman testify that they resisted because they were in No Man's Land, and any arrests made by officers of the United States was illegal." Then he asked me, "Who fired the first shot?"

"It was getting dark. The first shot came from the direction of the prisoners and struck the rock I was standing behind. I do not know which man fired at me."

"Did you return fire?"

"Yes."

The lawyer addressed the jury. "You have heard testimony that this encounter was made approximately one mile inside the State of Texas. Mr. Newman has testified that when they left the area the next morning after their arrest, they passed a monument about a mile *south* of the site of their arrest, making the arrests within the boundaries of No Man's Land and, therefore, illegal. I must ask you again, Deputy Sowell: *was the encounter you had with the men on trial here inside the State of Texas?*"

"Yes. It was at the least one mile inside the state line."

"I have no further questions, Your Honor."

Judge Parker turned to me. "You may step down, Deputy Sowell."

The bailiff retrieved my fallen crutch and assisted my exit from the witness box without accident. I found a seat next to Kat in the audience. She squeezed my hand and held it a moment.

Ross Scanlon stood and addressed Judge Parker. "Prosecution wishes to call Mr. Thomas Wood."

The bailiff went to the door, and in a moment he escorted a man to the witness stand and swore him in.

Ross addressed the man. "Please state for the court your name and occupation."

"I am Thomas Wood, surveyor for the U.S. Government."

"It is my understanding that you have very recently investigated the location of the monument on the Texas state line that marks the common north corner of Hansford and Ochiltree counties," Ross stated.

"That is correct."

"Can you tell us what you found?"

"Yes, sir." The surveyor pulled a small book from his pocket and turned to the appropriate page. "At your request, I went to the site of the monument. On 10 November 1888, my crew and I located the monument—"

"And you also located the site of the gun battle Deputies Sowell and Stein had with the so-called Newman gang," Ross interrupted.

"Yes I did, and—"

Ross interrupted again, "Tell us where the fight *and arrest of the defendants* took place in relation to the monument you found."

Thomas Wood looked frustrated. "The fight took place approximately one mile north of the monument we found."

There was a stir among the crowd and the Newman boys grinned and whispered. Judge Parker frowned and raised his gavel. It was enough to return order to the room. Joe Don grinned at me, and I winked.

"Let me ask you again, where was the fight in relation to the monument?"

Wood replied, "The fight was approximately one mile north of the monument as we found it."

" 'As you found it.' Please explain what you mean by that."

"When we set a survey point, we reference it to permanent features found nearby, so that if that survey point is lost or disturbed, it can be reset without resorting to a long survey process. In this case, none of the reference points for this survey point were present. In addition, the monument itself was not set as deeply into the ground as required."

Ross nodded, "I am guessing by that, you suspected the monument was not where it was supposed to be."

"That is correct. We then set about finding the original place for the monument. It took us some time to find it and once we established the point by measuring off the reference points, we dug down four feet and found the stone that marked the exact point where the county line struck the state line."

"You mean that the monument didn't establish the point you are talking about?"

"Monuments are too easily disturbed or tampered with, so we set the primary point below it in the hope that it doesn't get disturbed."

"So you found the true point on the Texas state line by finding the reference points and exposing the true survey point buried four feet in the ground, is this correct?"

Yes it is."

"Now, Mr. Wood, this is very important: Where is the site of the battle the deputies had with the Newman gang in relation to the true Texas state line?"

The surveyor referred to his survey notes. "The northern extreme of the fight area is eighty-one chains south of the state line and twenty chains west of the Ochiltree-Hansford county line."

"Please translate that into feet or miles for us."

"The point is 5,346 feet south of the Texas line and 1,320 feet west of the county line."

Prosecutor Scanlon asked, "What is your expert conclusion about the location of the fight and arrest of the defendants?"

"They were arrested more than one mile south of the state line within the state of Texas."

There was much consternation at the defendants' table and much whispering between defendants and lawyers and between lawyers and lawyers. Though they tried, they could not shake the testimony of Mr. Thomas Wood. He had obviously been on the witness stand before, and he was just as obviously angry that someone would disturb and move the survey monument.

With positive proof that the arrests had been legal, the trial continued on to its conclusion, with the result that every defendant was found guilty and given sentences to be served in a federal penitentiary in Ohio.

Pard Newman failed to see the error of his ways and was ushered from the courtroom vowing vengeance on everyone involved.

Chapter 16
Judge Parker Presides

Kat and I had talked it over and decided that, since we were going to be partners, we should make it legal and official. Therefore, she and Mollie got busy while we were concluding business at the marshal's office and made all kinds of arrangements, including a big dinner for both posses and other friends in one of the finer restaurants in town. The ladies even bought new outfits for themselves and took me to get a new suit with all the trimmings.

When time came, I donned my fine feathers and called for the ladies at the hotel. I hobbled to the restaurant just down the block, a fine-looking lady on each arm. There were heads turning along the street and a couple of hoots at me from my friends we happened to meet. I took note and jotted their names down in my mind.

The host showed us to our private dining room and hurried off to the kitchen to finish making arrangements for our meal. We were the first ones of our bunch there. Kat was nervous that there had been too much celebration after the trial and no one would show up.

"Don't worry, Kat, they'll be here," I said. *And they better be sober too.*

Well, they did show up, all of them at once, and the servants rushed around and began to serve our meals. It was a great contrast from our evenings on the trail, with all the camp chores to be done and one eye out for any intrusions from belligerents.

We had a long evening of "fellowship and food."

I had a speech prepared for the evening. At nine o'clock I stood and called for everyone's attention. "Ladies and gentlemen, as you know, Katherine and I have formed a partnership in a ranching operation in New Mexico Territory. We decided that while we are here and you are with us, we would like you to witness the signing of our contract." I moved to the front of the room where Kat was waiting. As I passed his table, I asked, "Gam, will you join us as a witness?"

Kat nodded at Mollie, and she rose to stand beside us. When we were in place, the door opened and Bass Reeves walked in. To my great surprise, he was followed by Judge Isaac Parker. I looked at Kat. She wore that "gotcha" smile.

A pin dropping on the floor would have made an awful noise in that room as Judge Parker approached, stood in front of Kat and I, and then addressed the audience. "I chanced to meet Parson Reeves as he was coming here tonight. Upon learning the purpose of his mission, I reviewed the provisions of his contract and found them most thorough and binding. However, the good parson, being the practical man he is, urged me to include the provisions and restrictions of the civil law into this agreement, to which I readily agreed. Join us here as we proceed with the ceremony."

There was scattered applause and laughter as the crowd arose and gathered around us. When we turned, the judge stood beside Bass. It was one of those rare times that Bass removed his hat. I noticed a little gray sprinkled in his hair. "Dearly beloved, we are gathered here . . ."

I knew the words by heart. After all, I had memorized them at Bass's insistence—and had maybe used them myself a time or two—but I don't recall the rest of the recital of those words that night. My mind was so full of thoughts of my fortune at finding the one who was as willing to spend her life with me as

I was with her.

"Hear now the words of our Lord from Matthew chapter nineteen, verse four: *Have ye not read, that he which made them at the beginning made them male and female, and said, For this cause shall a man leave father and mother, and shall cleave to his wife: and they twain shall be one flesh? Wherefore they are no more twain, but one flesh. What therefore God hath joined together, let not man put asunder.*"

Judge Parker then said, "Katherine Ingram and Robert E. Lee Sowell, you may now sign the two forms of your contract."

There on the table lay a beautiful marriage certificate from the church and the civil marriage form. It was quiet while we signed both documents. When we finished and turned to face Judge Parker and Bass, they said in unison, "Now, we pronounce you man and wife. You may kiss your wife, Lee."

And that I did.

Judge Parker kissed the bride and shook my hand while the audience hooted and applauded. I shook Bass Reeves's hand and then gave him a big hug, "*Parson* Reeves?" I whispered.

"You better believe it." He grinned.

There followed some of the most enjoyable days of my life. Kat set about rounding out the things she needed to make our cabin a home, and I helped as best I could. We had our picture made and copies sent to friends and families, and we just spent time together.

I knew this would be the closest I would be to the home folks for some time, so we packed a few things and set out for Liberty Springs, Arkansas, where Kat would get a view of a culture entirely foreign to any she had ever seen.

We took the Little Rock and Fort Smith Railroad to Morrilton and spent the night. Next morning, I rented two horses, and we were soon on our way to Clinton, where we spent the night before riding up Archey Valley.

Our homestead was on the mountaintop tucked under Reves Knob. Ma was surprised and excited to see us, especially Katherine. "About time you settled down and had a family, Bobby, and I see you have chosen your partner wisely."

Pa had been gone for some time, and brother Wesley had taken over the farm. He had built a cabin around the shoulder of Reves, and the path between the two houses was well worn. While Ma and Kat got acquainted, I trotted around to Wes's house. The yard was full of youngsters who ran for the house at sighting me. Only a three-year-old stood his ground, his bare bottom peeking from under his gown, which hadn't grown with him. When I passed, he hurled a rock at me with surprising accuracy.

"Lee Sowell, you quit throwing rocks at visitors and git in here before I tan your bottom." Wes had married Sarah Clutts, and they had a house full of kids. Little Lee was their last because, as Ma said, "They ran out of names for them and had t' start over with yours."

Sarah shaded her eyes against the sun and stared until she recognized me, then squealed and ran to greet me. "Bobby Sowell, what are you doing, sneaking up on us like this? Let me see you . . . Why you look fit, but a little pale. Why are you using that cane? Have you been shot agin? I swear, if they keep peckin' at you, there won't be nothin' left t' bury. Hollis, run down to the cornfield and get your pa. Tell him we got company. Zoe, bring a chair out here for your uncle afore he falls. Land's sake, Bobby, cain't you say nothin'?" She caught her breath and laughed. "I'll bet it's 'cause I cain't stop rattlin' on. Oh my, my." She fanned her pink face with her apron tail and laughed again.

Two kids brought out two ladder-backed, cane-bottom chairs from the house, and we sat under the giant burr oak tree in the yard and visited and waited for Wes to appear. He gave the mule to Morgan, the eldest, and came on over to us. "Well, hello there, Bobby. When did you slide in?" he said and gave me a hug. Seeing my cane, he grinned. "Wanna wrestle? Think I might be able to take you now."

"I'll have t' forfeit, Wes. This leg has to mend first. Kat would have my hide if I broke it agin."

"Kat? Who's Kat, Lee? O-o-oh, you done got a woman, ain't you?" Sarah fairly bubbled with excitement.

"I came over to see you an' let you know Ma is cookin' supper for us all at th' house. She asked if you had any buttermilk and if you could make a pan of bread."

"I certainly can do that, and I just picked a mess of turnip greens. I'll bring them, too." Sarah got up and hurried to the house, issuing orders to various children. "Mittie, go pick your apron full of poke. Git th' tender leaves. Hollis, haul in some of that wood and put a stick in th' stove—*Lee,* put that rock down right now."

"Lee, do what your mama says." Wes spoke softly. The boy dropped the rock and toddled to his pa's knee on the other side of me and stared, his finger in his mouth. Wes patted his head. We visited awhile, watching the shadow of Reves creep east across the hills. Wes stood and said, "I've gotta clean up some if we're gonna gather t' eat. Tell Ma we'll be there soon's th' bread is done. Lee, you can go with Bobby to Grandma's if you want."

Lee took his finger out of his mouth and picked up a rock before he toddled off to Grandma's. "Rock's for any snakes he might see," Wes explained. "I swear, that boy was born with a rock in his hand. Mighty good with them, too."

"I know," I said, rubbing my leg. I turned and followed the child.

"Don't worry about him," Wes called. "He's been usin' that trail since he could walk—maybe a little b'fore that."

By the time home was in sight, I was far behind Lee. I watched him go to the door, wipe his feet, and put down the rock before he entered. Presently, I heard him squalling. When I got to the house, he was standing in the basin being dried off, a fresh gown ready. Kat laid the towel down and threw the gown over her victim's head. This one came to mid-thigh, covering his bottom. He made to jump down, but she grabbed him. "Hold on, Lee. I haven't combed your hair."

The comb encountered several "rats" that had to be untangled while the boy squirmed. When she was through, the boy looked brand-new. "Now, don't you go getting dirty before supper," Ma admonished.

Kat looked at her mud-streaked apron and laughed. "That boy had half the mountain on him."

"He tries to go to bed like that. It almost drove Sarah to distraction before she thought to put him in a pillowcase. It only postponed the battle; the scamp is growing out of it. She could use one of those twelve-foot-long bags they pick cotton in next," Ma supposed. We laughed at that image.

The table was set for six places, and Kat looked at me with a question in her eyes. "Sarah says that since Morgan does a man's work, he should sit at first table with the rest of the adults," I explained, hoping she was familiar with the old custom of adults eating before the children.

"And well he should," she said, by way of assuring me she remembered the custom.

The house looked just like I remembered it, except that Ma had a four-hole cookstove sitting on the hearth with the pipe going up the fireplace flue. It was just the right height for her to use without stooping, and she had all four stove lids occupied.

We sat at the table Pa had made, on the benches Pa had made, and ate the supper Ma had made (with Sarah's help), and it was really good to be back home. Little Lee sat on his pa's lap and ate all he could reach, as much from his mother's plate as from his pa's. When it came time for the children to eat, he insisted on his place being set and continued to eat.

"Is that boy hollow, Sarah?" I asked.

"It sure seems that way, Bobby." She sighed. "I haven't seen him full but once or twice."

Wes and I sat on the porch and watched the children play as we smoked our pipes. The women joined us when the dishes were done, and we sat and talked until dark. Lee climbed the steps and stumbled to his ma, crawled up in her lap, and fell asleep. "He's got two speeds, full gallop and off." She laughed.

Wes stood and summoned the kids. "Time to go home. Lee, you oughta go see Uncle Jake and Uncle Drewery b'fore you leave."

"Think they'll be at home, Ma?" Drew and Jake Moss were Ma's brothers. They were older and lived back in the hills as far away from all neighbors as possible.

"Yes, and they'd be tickled t' see you, son," Ma said.

"We'll hang around here tomorrow and probably drop off over there the day after," I said.

Wes picked up the sleeping boy and led his wife down the steps and across the yard. "Come over and see my corn, Lee. We got a good stand this year."

"You need someone t' do some shuckin'," I said.

Wes laughed and said, "Good night."

Ma insisted we take the downstairs bed, but I insisted on sleeping in the loft in my old bed. It was just like it had always been, and I went to sleep watching the stars outside the window. Late in the night, soft breathing next to my ear startled me into realizing that someone was in bed with me. It was Kat. It took me a moment to get my bearings and remember.

Ma was up early, and we dragged ourselves out of bed soon after. We spent the morning bringing in her many potted flowers for the winter. She had every leaky old pot and every coffee can she had emptied planted with flowers and bulbs; we stored them under the floor for the winter.

After noon, I wandered over to Wes's barn where he and the kids were shucking corn and tossing it into the corncrib. They were having fun with their work. Lee insisted on throwing the ears of corn into the crib. It kept him busy running from one to the other collecting the ears and fussing when someone threw one.

We worked until Sarah came down with the milk buckets, and she and Zoe milked. I walked home in the dusk to find Kat and Ma sitting on the porch rocking and waiting supper on me. "Better get an early start in the morning if you're gonna have any visitin' time with Drew and Jake," Ma said as we climbed the ladder to bed.

My uncles were Jake and Drewery Moss, and Aunt Sarah was Uncle Jake's wife. They were pioneers of the first order and I have spent many hours listening to their stories—none of which I would guarantee as being *totally* authentic.

The horizontal distance to my uncles' cabin wasn't all that far, but the vertical distance into the bottom of the head of the Little Red River's Middle Fork was quite long and steep. We would have done better riding mules for that trip. Kat seemed to enjoy the ride, though she must have been nervous a time or two. The leaves had already turned, but there was still plenty of color left in them. I love that fall time when the growing pressure is off everything, and nature seems to take a breath before fading into winter's sleep.

We would rest on the switchbacks of the trail, take in the view, and I could tell Kat about my uncles and Aunt Sarah. "You're gonna hear some of the language of the hills today, and you may have to listen hard to get it all," I said. "Uncle Jake and his wife, Aunt Sarah, live in one side of the cabin. Uncle Drew lives across the dog walk on the other side. We buried his wife, Aunt Elizabeth, in their front yard. Both families must have a hundred kids and grandkids scattered all over these hills."

The cabin hadn't changed much; that mountain lion hide was still nailed beside the dog walk, and a newer one I hadn't seen balanced it on the other side. Uncle Drew held down the bench on the porch, smoking his pipe while he rested from splitting their winter's supply of firewood.

"Hello there, Bob, how yuh doin'?" He greeted as if I had never left the hills, but only hadn't visited in a few days.

I helped Kat down and hitched her horse to the rail. Uncle Drew tapped his pipe out on his heel, stood to greet her, and offered his hand.

"How d'ye do, ma'am. My name's Drew Moss, welcome to our home."

A door opened in the dog walk and Aunt Sarah stepped out. "Thought I heerd voices out here. Is that you, Bobby Lee? My, my you haven't changed a bit—well maybe a little peaked—what's wrong with ye? Oh-h-h, where's my manners? You have a guest; I'm Sary Moss," she said, her hands folded together in her apron.

"This is my wife, Katherine, Aunt Sarah."

"Land's sake, Bobby, you fine'ly done hit. Welcome to our home, Katherine. Come on in here, an' we can git acquainted whiles I rustles up some dinner. Drew, whur's that Jake?"

They disappeared into the house, and I heard them talking in the kitchen. Uncle Drew sat back down and repacked his pipe. "How ye bin, Bobby? Don't recollect whin we seen you last. Air you still lawin' fer thet jedge down to th' fort?"

"I am, Uncle Drew, and we're on our way out to New Mexico t' do a little ranchin'."

"Gotcha a place, do ye?"

"Yes, we homesteaded a couple of places. I had to come back to testify in a case, and we bought some cattle."

"Went out there once. Too flat an' dry fer me, an' there weren't no trees."

"Where we are, there are a lot of cedar woods on the hillsides. Th' grass is plentiful, an' it should be good cattle land."

Drew Moss nodded and puffed on his pipe. "Guess we better rustle up thet Jake fer Sary. She be callin' dinner soon." He stepped off the porch and we walked around the house to the barn. "Jake, dinner's 'bout ready, an' we got company," he called into the darkened barn.

"Tho't I seen someone comin' down th' mountain while ago. Who be hit?"

"Hit's Bobby Lee, Uncle Jake," I replied. "How are you doin'?"

"How ye doin' yerse'f, Bobby? Ain't seen you since Moses was a pup." He emerged from the barn, wiping his hands on his pant legs. His grip was firm.

The dinner bell rang, so we went to the house and washed up. Aunt Sary's fare wasn't fancy, but it was substantial food—the kind needed on a farm. Kat seemed relaxed with these strangers, and the conversation didn't drag. After the dishes were done, the women came out on the porch and commandeered two of the rockers. Uncle Jake occupied the bench, and Uncle Drew and I sat on the edge of the porch. Uncle Drew whittled on a stick. "How er things on th' mountain, Bobby?"

"Seems to be pretty quiet. Wes and the kids are shucking corn fodder, and Lee is runnin' amok amongst 'em."

Uncle Jake grunted. "Same es here. We need some 'citement t' shake things up a bit."

"Yuh'll hev plenty of *ex*citement next month if we start trappin." Uncle Drew studied his carving critically an' resumed whittling. "Mayhap you'll run into another mountain lion an' hev t' lay 'round healin' all season while I does all th' work."

"In a pig's eye, you'll do all th' work! I done more with one arm than you could of done with three."

"Maybe you should 'splain' t' our guest," Uncle Drew rejoined, "jist whut we're talkin' 'bout here an' she kin be jedge o' who done th' workin'."

"I've heard the story 'bout a dozen times," I said with a laugh.

"Miz Katherine ain't heered none uv hit! Go 'head an' tell yore tale, an' I'll be here t' verify th' truth uv it an' wipe out any em-bell-ishmentations you might try t' throw in!" Uncle Drew warned with a cocked brow.

"Shore an' all yuh wants t' do is make sure I don't tell *too much* truth about whut part ye had in th' whole thang."

I grinned at Kat. "You're in for a tale, Kat. I just hope it doesn't result in any friction between brothers."

"Seems those two sticks has already been rubbin' agin each other," Aunt Sarah said with a smile.

There followed the tale of the time Uncle Jake rammed his fist down the throat of a mountain lion in an argument over ownership of a beehive full of honey. It took up the rest of the afternoon, with the three elders contributing their parts in the event. This was the first time I heard the story from the three of them at once and I enjoyed it as much as the first time I heard it.

It got quiet, the three having talked themselves out, and no sounds but crickets softly singing their evening song and the creak of a rocking chair. Fireflies began winking across the meadow.

"Goodness sakes, look at th' time. It's nearly dark, an' supper's not near ready. Drew, git youself to milkin'." She and Kat hurried about preparing supper while we did the evening chores.

I have always marveled at the fortitude and courage of those tough old pioneers who could laugh and make light of their calamities. They would carry on through some of the most trying times and dangers and overcome them with a shrug and a smile. They were made of sterner stuff and left a legacy of character their children could build on that has lasted for generations. We should never forget what they did for us.

We spent the night with them and watched the sun rise as we climbed the mountain back to Reves Knob. Little Lee met us, rocks in hands just in case. He wanted a ride to the house, so I made him throw down his rocks before riding in front of me and taking the reins.

All too soon for me, the visit came to an end. We left after the hugs and kisses and usual promises to get together again soon—a "soon" that never came. Kat and I retraced our trail back to the train and Fort Smith.

Chapter 17
The Kansas City Bottoms

We didn't have to worry about neglecting Miss Mollie West while we were gone. She was well entertained by the young squires in our bunch, and it was obvious JD did not count it a burden to escort her wherever she wished to go.

As December approached, we became anxious to return to our ranch before we were shut out by the high plains winter. The last week of November found us chugging north to Joplin, Missouri, a carload of furniture and supplies tagging along behind, with our horses and buggy in another car.

We had to lay over in Joplin for the AT&SF train west, so we took a cab to the Joplin Hotel. It was a brick structure, the best in town. When the ladies were established in their room, JD and I scooted across the street to the Club Saloon.

The building the saloon was in was brought here from Baxter Springs and was the first permanent building in what was then known as Murphysburg. After it had served as a grocery store for a while, Joe Ferguson bought it and established his Club Saloon in it. Being early in the afternoon, Joe had little business, so he shared a beer with us and told us about the town.

"Murphysburg grew up around and quite literally on top of the lead and zinc mines the area is famous for. In 1871, a fellow named John Cox filed a plan for a town on the northeast side of Joplin Creek. He named the town for preacher Harris G. Joplin, who had been in the area since about 1840. Eventually the two towns merged under the Joplin name, the northeast side being primarily residential and old Murphysburg on the southwest side of the creek being the business and entertainment district. When the Kansas City Southern Railway built through town, they went up the valley parallel to Joplin Creek. A bridge over the creek connected the two areas." Joe paused while he refilled our mugs.

"Club Saloon sits on the southwest corner of Fourth and Main, with the Joplin Hotel across the street on the northwest corner of the intersection. The Donehoo Drug Store occupies the northeast corner and the three-story House of Lords restaurant is just north of it on Main Street.

"They got the restaurant and bar on the bottom floor, gambling and gaming on the second, and the girls are on the third floor," Joe explained. "I ain't got no girls, but the games here are just as lively, if you come at th' right times.

"Louis Peter's lead and zinc mine is across the street on the southeast corner. Lead came first, but the jack, as they call zinc, is more valuable. The whole town is dotted with mines and slag piles," Joe said. "There are tunnels all under the town and occasionally a sinkhole appears and swallows things."

We finished our beers and returned to the hotel where we found our ladies waiting and ready to eat. Mollie had found an advertisement for the House of Lords Café. The bill boasted the café as *"The Place of Quality, Joplin's leading Restaurant, catering to those who care. The best of everything the markets afford await you here, prepared to your liking by expert cooks and invitingly served. Our service is exclusively a la carte, charging you only for what you get, which experience has demonstrated is the only satisfactory method. J.E. Moats, Manager, T.C. Nolan, Proprietor."*

"Looks like we're bound for the House of Lords, Joe Don, I gotta go comb my hair and put on a fresh shirt," I said.

JD took the hint, and we retired to our room to clean up while the girls waited.

The restaurant was just north of the hotel and across the street. We crossed at the corner, the ladies holding up their skirts to avoid the dust. A short walk brought us to the House of Lords. A uniformed greeter escorted us to our table and gave each of us a menu. Our waiter brought us four glasses of water with ice in it, and waited for our orders.

"The lady and I will have the baked Mackinaw trout with sauce du excelles, with the pommes Parisienne, and sliced tomatoes. We would like iced tea, please," I said, hoping my pronunciations were right.

Joe Don squirmed in his chair, "The lady would like the petit poulett boulil, a la crème, Boston cream fritters with port wine sauce, and iced tea. I will have the roast prime beef, demi glace, candied yams and green peas, with iced tea."

We got through that relatively unscathed, and I winked at Joe Don. "Think I had rather eat at Marrs," he whispered.

Mollie laughed. "No menus in French there."

We spent a pleasant evening. The food was good, and Rahn's Special Ice Cream was a "special" treat. As we were leaving, a little gray-haired lady, clutching her bags closely, met us. She was obviously in great distress. Kat stopped, laid a hand on her arm, and asked, "What is the matter, madam? May we be of some assistance?"

"Oh, my, my," she whispered, "I have stayed in town too long. Now I must go home in the dark across the Kansas City Bottoms, and the thieves and robbers are out. They are sure to rob me and take my things." She was near tears, "What shall I do?"

"Is there not a policeman on duty who will escort you safely to your home?" I asked.

"No, the police do not go into the bottoms. They are too busy patrolling the crowded streets around the saloons to protect them, and arrest their patrons to swell the city's funds.

No policeman patrols the outlying streets."

"Unbelievable," JD said.

"Ma'am, I am a deputy U.S. marshal. If you will wait here, I will escort these ladies to the hotel there, then come back and escort you home."

Relief and uncertainty crossed the lady's face. Kat reassured her. "He *is* a deputy. When he returns, he will show you his badge and then see that you are safe."

Maybe the old lady wasn't reassured, but her face showed she was hopeful, and she nodded. We hurried on to the hotel, where I picked up my badge and stuck a pistol under my coat. JD did the same. When I showed the lady my badge, she seemed reassured. She was too upset to ask JD for any proof of his position.

I hailed a taxi. When the little lady gave her address, he responded, "No. ma'am. I don't cross the Kansas City Bottoms after dark. No cabby does."

"I am a deputy U.S. marshal," I said, showing him my badge and gun. "I will see that you are safe if you take us across."

"I don't know, Marshal, that's a pretty rough area. I could lose everything with those thugs out."

"This is a government operation, and I will be responsible for any damage done to your property. Let's go."

"I-I-I don't know . . ." He shook his head. Still not sure, the driver turned and clucked to his horse. We drove up to the end of Main Street and turned toward the Joplin Creek Bridge. Our driver slapped the reins, and the horse broke into a trot, then a run with more encouragement. Dark figures stood in the road. Perceiving the driver's intent, to run them over, they dove aside. When we were on the bridge, the driver slowed his horse to a trot, then a walk. It wasn't far to the lady's house. We dropped her off and turned back to the bridge.

I stood and talked to the driver. "I want you to drive slowly so I can crack a few heads as we go back."

"You're not goin' t' arrest 'em?" JD asked.

"No. If I did, we'd have to take them to Kansas City or St. Joe, where a judge is. I ain't gonna take th' time for that. Sit over there on that side with your gun out, and I'll take this side. Anyone tries to board, buffalo him—or more, if you have to, but avoid any gunplay if possible."

Our driver had taken all this in, and I quickly swore him in as a posse member. "You have the authority to defend your property by any means necessary," I said, indicating his whip. He nodded and grinned. "Thinkin' I'm agonna enjoy this ride."

We took our seats, and the driver clucked his horse up. A dark figure stepped into the roadway before we were off the end of the bridge and grabbed the horse's lines. "Whoa there, boy," he said. "This here's a toll bridge, an' th' tender at th' other end said you hadn't paid."

A voice from behind the buggy startled us. "Gentlemen, continue on your journey. We will see you safely across the Bottoms."

I looked, and there must have been more than thirty men behind us, white bandannas around their necks.

One of the men said, "Allow me to explain, sirs; we are the Knights of the Open Road. Those Weary Willies and Ancient Sons of Leisure are giving us a bad name.

"The little lady you just escorted home is a kind soul and has always given us something from her meager larder when we asked. The vermin of the Kansas City Bottoms would mistreat her and rob her and the other kind ladies who are charitable to the down and out. Tonight, we will convince some of them that this is a good time to seek coach accommodations on an outgoing train. You may fire when ready, Gridley."

A man jumped onto the buggy from each side, reaching for the driver. I heard a smack and grunt from JD's side of the carriage as I came down on the crown of the feller on my side. He fell to the floor of the wagon. The driver's whip cracked like a shot three times, and the "gatekeeper" cried out and released the horse, who resumed his travels. As we passed, the gatekeeper jumped onto the step and tried to board the buggy. His momentum onto the step was met by JD's fist full in the face with a loud smack. He fell backward with a groan. Our passenger at my feet groaned and stirred. I helped him up. JD's boot to his backside ushered him overboard.

As we cleared the bridge, the Knights behind us swarmed along either side. Most were carrying clubs of assorted kinds and sizes, and some had a shirttail full of rocks and other missiles. For the most part, the crowd was quiet. Only a word here and there was spoken as we advanced. A whistle blew continuously, and there was a stir of dark figures ahead of us, some running away and others gathering in our pathway.

As we approached the opposing crowd, our "Gridley" whipped the horse into a run, and we parted the gang like a ship through water. JD and I hung out either side of the taxi, slashing and swinging as bodies passed or charged us. Someone tried to climb over the back of the buggy, and I gave him something to think about on the back of his head. The crack of that whip was almost continuous, and we heard shouts and cries all around us.

We were suddenly clear of the crowd. As soon as our driver could, he turned the horse around and prepared to charge the crowd again. "Hold, there, 'Captain Gridley.' The armies are too mixed to charge again; we might hurt some of our allies. I have another mission for you." I relieved him from posse duty, gave him instructions, and paid him generously for his service.

He grinned and said, "I wouldn't have missed it for a hundred dollars." Then he turned his faithful steed and proceeded on his errand while JD and I watched the conclusion of the battle.

Soon the enemy was vanquished, and the Knights of the White Bandanna stood bloodied, but victorious. Joe Don and I cheered. I waved my crutch and announced, "Men, there is a sandwich counter and keg of beer awaiting us at the Club Saloon. Shall we proceed?"

And we did proceed. Our cabby was out front of the club watering his horse, and he joined us at the keg. Joe Ferguson's customers were put off by the crowd of hoboes prior to hearing what they had done; then all gaming stopped and they pitched in for another keg for the heroes of the moment. Someone handed me a white bandanna. It was torn from linen, like a sheet, and I suspected some wife was a sheet short when she took in the clothes from the line. JD and Cabby were donning theirs, and we wore them proudly.

No one seemed seriously hurt. One of the knights set up in a corner and treated the wounded. By his expert care, I figured he was a doctor. *A doctor on the hobo road,* I mused. The man with the cultured voice who had addressed us from the dark was certainly an educated man. I wondered what tales of triumph and tragedy stood about in this room.

When it seemed all was going smoothly, I gave Joe another ten dollars to cover any added expenses, and JD and I slipped out for the hotel. I paused in surprise when I saw the crowd in the lobby. The clerk was talking to a man in police uniform. I noticed the captain's bars on his shoulders. Joe Don disappeared up the stairs to replace his torn and bloody clothing. Kat brought my coat to cover my ripped and soiled shirt, and the captain inquired from the desk, making our conversation public to all. "What is going on over at the Club Saloon, sir? They tell me an army of hoboes has taken over the place."

"Those men are not hoboes. They are the Knights of the Open Road." There was a stir of mirth from the crowd. "They are celebrating their victory over the vermin that infests the

Bottoms and robs and harasses your citizens who live on the east side. There will be quite a few of those Sons of Leisure leaving town between now and tomorrow morning."

"Hear, Hear" and "Amen" came from the few in the crowd familiar with the conditions between north Main Street and the Joplin Creek Bridge.

"I will have officers here soon to watch the club and post men there to see no one or nothing is harmed."

"It won't be a very rich crowd to mine, Captain. These men have no money for your coffers. What you should do is clean out the Kansas City Bottoms and eliminate the everyday hazards to the citizens of this city. I would be ashamed if I allowed such an area of lawlessness to exist in my city."

The captain turned red and blustered, "Who are you, and what makes you think you can say such things?"

"I am a deputy U.S. marshal, and I am well qualified to make the statements I have made. There is no police presence in the Bottoms. Crimes committed there go unpunished. Your police force is patrolling the crowded gaming and saloon district, arresting those who may have deep pockets, and neglecting your stated purpose, which is protecting the citizens of this community."

To this, the people applauded and cheered.

"Those Men of the White Bandanna in the Club Saloon have done your work for you tonight, and they did it to protect ladies who find themselves on the wrong side of the Bottoms when night falls. If any of your men harass one of them tonight, I will detain him, take him a few miles west of here, and arrest him. He will then have the privilege of going before Judge Isaac Parker and explaining his actions.

"You will not need a patrolman to keep the peace here tonight, and it would be just as well if your patrolmen stayed away."

Anything more I might have had to say was drowned by cheers from the crowd. The captain disappeared into the room behind the desk. The clerk had a big grin on his face.

A man called to his imaginary wife, "Go to bed, darlin'. I'm going to Club Saloon to celebrate." He exited with a half dozen men, the laughter of the crowd in their ears.

Kat took my arm, and several people interrupted our departure to shake my hand and congratulate me on my speech.

Mollie and Kat shared a room. JD and I had the adjoining room with a shared bathroom between. We entered the ladies' room to the sound of running water, and Mollie exited the bathroom. "The bath is running for you, Lee. It's good and hot. That will help your leg." I had healed enough that I could take the splints off for short rests. It didn't take me long to shed them and get in that tub. It was hot, almost as hot as Juana's baths. Kat came in and scrubbed my back. It sure felt good. "Think you can rub some . . ."

"Shush." She slapped me with the cloth. "We can catch up on that later."

I grinned, leaned back, and closed my eyes. Kat pulled the plug and left.

Chapter 18
Vigilance

1889

Riding trains is a special kind of torture. If the windows are open, soot and hot cinders decorate your face and clothes. Close them, and you smother. You always know what the temperature is outside, because that is the temperature in the car. Some like the clickety-clack of the wheels on the rail joints, but a broken leg feels every little bump, and those bumps tend to make its owner grouchy. At least that is what I blamed my rotten mood on. When Kat, Mollie, and JD had enough of me, they moved to the other end of the nearly empty car and ignored me. I couldn't blame them. I would have moved too, if it had helped.

Even at thirty-five or forty miles an hour, going back home was a long trip. I almost wished for train robbers to visit and break up the monotony, but no one robs a westbound train; it's the eastbounds that carry the silver and gold, mostly in the money belts and pockets of the passengers.

Our two cars were sidetracked at Liberal, Kansas. We unloaded our horses and buggy and drove them to the livery stable after the ladies and their baggage were safely deposited in the hotel. We stayed an extra day so Kat and Mollie could shop one last time before leaving the settled world. JD and I spent our time rounding up a span of mules and a good used wagon to carry our goods. One look at that carload of goods, and I went back and bought an overjet and another span of mules.

★ ★ ★ ★ ★

JD wiped the sweat dripping off his face with his shirttail. "Couldn't we find a hotter day t' unload this oven? I'm about t' freeze in here," he yelled from the emigrant car.

"Wind's blowin' open that other door," I hollered.

"I'd hafta dig t' git to it."

I trudged around the end of the car and opened the door. "How's that?"

"Better," came his muffled voice from the back of the car. I doubt he could tell any difference where he was working. It was nip and tuck to get everything on the wagon.

"They's places we'd lose half th' load if a rope give or that tarp ripped," JD observed.

"Give it a couple days t' shake down, an' it'll ride—if nothin' breaks." I wrung my shirt out and pulled at my soaked pants plastered to my rear end. The nice thing about this country is that you dried out quickly. By the time we stowed the wagon and animals at the livery and walked to Main Street, we were mostly dry.

"Hello there, boys, how about a ride to Beer City?" The speaker was in a hack with other ladies of the night, their parasols waving and bouncing with the gyrations of the buggy. Many of the soiled doves were from Dodge and other points east. They lived in Liberal and commuted to work at Tyrone or Beer City on the hacks that made regular runs.

"Don't see an empty seat," JD replied.

"Oh, it's all right, you can sit on my lap . . . Or *I* could sit on *yours,*" a fair Cyprian suggested. Either way would have been a load.

"Danged if I ain't tempted," JD muttered.

"To sit on her lap, or go get a beer?" I looked at the sun. The clock on the corner in front of the bank read three-twelve. "We got time for a beer before the girls are ready to eat. Let's go."

We trotted after the hack and plopped down on the tailgate. The buggy settled with our weight to the o-o-ohs of the ladies. Conversation was lively and provocative for a vigorous young bachelor like JD. I just wanted a long, cold drink.

The hack driver stopped where the road intersected Beer City's main street. "Coldest beer's over at th' Yellow Snake." He pointed to a saloon catty-corner from where we sat, and we hopped off to six invitations for future visitations from six ladies.

"We want to ride back with you, driver. Come by and we'll buy you a beer," I hailed.

He replied with a wave of his whip and trundled his charges down the street to their various destinations.

Beer City was located just south of Liberal, the Kansas prohibition laws, and Granger laws against introducing Texas cattle into the state. It was nicknamed White City, after the tents that first made up the establishments in the town. Calling it a town was a stretch; it was never platted, never had a church, post office, or school. The town prided itself as the only town where there was absolutely no law of any kind. You can imagine the kind of human flotsam and jetsam that were attracted to such a place—and they came in droves.

"Who would have ever thought you could get a *cold* beer in No Man's Land?" JD asked as he wiped foam from under his nose.

"Did you fall in?" I asked, looking at his half empty mug.

"You cowboys look like you need a rest and some recreation."

We turned to see a portly lady standing at the top of the stairs, a cigar in one hand, and the barrel of a shotgun in the other. She wore a housecoat with the top unbuttoned, revealing a much-wrinkled cleavage.

"They're broke, Nell," the barkeep answered.

She turned without another word and faded down the hall, the thump of her gunstock marking her progress. It stopped and a door slammed.

The bartender grinned. "Pussy Cat's like an old retired fire horse that hears th' bell an' cain't quit comin' to th' firehouse. Last herd's come an' gone, an' she's still fishin'."

"She take that shotgun t' bed with her?" I asked.

"Some say she does. I never had occasion t' find out, myself." He grinned and wiped the mahogany bar top.

Beer City existed long enough to establish some form of order to its society. At the back of the saloon was a heavy-gauge wire pen. Returning from a trip to the back alley, JD asked the barkeep, "What's that pen back there for? You keepin' a pet bear or lion?"

"No-o, that's our bullpen. You know, there's three kinds of drunk: social drunk, lion drunk, and hog drunk. A man gets hog drunk, we empty his pockets and put him in the bullpen where the pickpockets and thieves can't get to him. His money goes into the safe while he sleeps it off and is able to take care of himself. When he's sober, we bring him out, give him a 'hair o' th' dog that bit him' on the house, and his possessions. One of our enforcers escorts the man to where he's safe."

"Enforcer?" I questioned.

"Yeah, we have enforcers who curry out the riffraff and usher them to the door. They encourage them to leave town, and most of them do. Card sharps, pickpockets, and bunko men are not welcome in Beer City."

"What kind of feller do you hire to be an enforcer?" JD asked, thinking about his future employment possibilities.

"Mostly these young German farm boys who've toughened up wrestlin' horses an' plows all their lives. An Irish rail-hand gets premium wages. Pound-for-pound, he's the best."

"Why don't you hire a sheriff and deputies to cover the whole town?" I asked.

The bartender laughed. "They tend to get independent and

want t' do things their own way. We got a self-appointed sheriff once, ol' Lew 'Brushy' Bush, up from Texas with a herd. He made his living chargin' the businesses down here for his protection and rolling the drunks he caught—bad for business.

"Pussy Cat Nell, running the 'hotel' upstairs, got tired of it and she put a load of buckshot into him. Other 'customers' of his joined in, and when they were through, he had seventy-four bullet holes in his body. That way, nobody knows just who killed ol' Lew.

"Most of the bottled dynamite sold in Beer City and Tyrone and the rest of No Man's Land comes from a whiskey still, hidden in a No Man's Land cave. It's operated by a man who calls himself Judge L.M. Hubbard. Judge Hubbard preached a message named 'Organic Law,' whereby the Strip could govern itself, but it didn't work out. Several communities formed vigilance committees that attempt to enforce law and order."

Lee nodded and grinned. "I was sent into No Man's Land to try to locate a gang of robbers who used the area as a refuge. I worked on a ranch as a cowhand," he told his audience of two. "We were over east on the 101 Ranch in the spring roundup when Judge Hubbard and his vigilance committee rode out of the dark into our camp one evening without so much as a 'hello' or 'howdy.'

"Such an entry garners a lot of attention, and a lot of tin plates were laid aside and men rose, hands on gun butts.

" 'Welcome, men. Light down and have a bite to eat. Cookie has a pot of beans ready.' Henry Jones, boss of the 101, said, ignoring the bad manners of the visitors.

"The riders made not a move, and someone behind me said quietly, 'O-o-oh, dam.'

" 'Thank you, Henry,' the judge said, 'we may just do that, but first I have some things to say. As you know, the Organic Law has been disbanded and it is now up to us to govern as we can. The vigilance committee'—he waved his arms as if embracing the men around him—'has set some rules you should be made aware of. I have them here in written form, but feel it would be best to read them to you also: No rancher shall allow a stranger to eat or sleep at the ranch or its camps unless first getting the man's name, where he came from, and where he is going. Suspicious characters are to be turned over to the vigilance committee for questioning and determining what is to be done with them . . .'

"There were other regulations put forth, but I doubt many paid any attention to them; the first two were enough to raise tempers to the boiling point," Lee said. "Swearing under his breath, the man next to me began pulling his gun. I put my hand on his arm and whispered, 'Hold on a minute, let's see what happens.' It was an effort for him to relax and ease the gun back in its place.

" 'And now, Henry, we'll accept your generous invitation to sup with you.' The judge made to dismount, as did his committeemen.

" 'Hold on there, Judge, we have some questions for you,' Henry yelled.

"The judge settled back into his saddle, eyebrows raised at the ranchman's audacity to challenge him. I stepped forward. 'First of all, Judge, what is *your* name?'

The mighty judge sputtered. 'Why, Lee, you know my name is Judge L.M. Hubbard.'

" 'His name was Sutter in the States,' someone in the crowd on the ground hollered.

" 'Where are you from, *Sutter*?' Cap Leslie had eased into the crowd and leaned on the muzzle of his Sharps .50.

" 'Why I don't see where that's any of your—'

" 'Where are you going?' Henry Jones interrupted. The man next to me snickered.

" 'Sh-h-h,' his neighbor demanded.

" 'I'll be going on to another camp soon.' The judge reined his horse as if to leave, and a man grabbed his reins and led the horse to the side.

"Henry pointed to another man in the committee. 'What's your name, feller?'

"The man drew himself upright. 'My name's Isaac Sample.'

" 'That's right, you tell him, Bill. Don't let him call your bluff thataway,' someone yelled from our crowd.

" 'Where are you from, *Bill*?' the OX Segundo demanded.

" 'Why, I . . . I . . . I'm . . .' Isaac/Bill stammered.

"A man took his reins and led him over to where the judge sat, still sputtering and steaming. Three more men were subjected to the same questioning and failed the test in one way or another; mostly the first question, for it seemed someone in our well-traveled crowd had known them by a different name elsewhere.

"Henry turned to the remainder of the committee. 'Men, we haven't got all night to question each one of you. Since we can't, it's our sad duty under the rules of your vigilance committee to deny you our hospitality. You may go, but do not stop on the range of these ranches.' He named the eighteen ranches in the roundup, including the ranches the reps were from. 'For you to stop on any of these ranches would be in violation of these rules, and we would have to detain you.'

"You can take custody of these who have failed the test and examine and dispose of them as you see fit," I said.

" 'Hold on there, Lee,' Leslie warned. 'We can't let them have these prisoners with them armed. You men there, disarm the prisoners.'

"A dozen men surrounded the detainees and soon had them relieved of all weaponry. Someone produced a gunnysack. The guns were unloaded, and, along with the knives, were deposited in the sack. The boys tied it to one of the packhorses the committee had.

" 'It pains us greatly to deny you our hospitality, but we must obey the rules of the committee. I'm sure you understand,' Henry said.

"Almost as one, the vigilance committee turned to leave. We watched them fade into the gloom. Men returned to their cold plates to finish their meal. All was quiet for a few moments, then someone giggled like a little girl. Another snickered, and we all broke into uproarious laughter. It was a good hour before our composure was restored and we attempted to resume the routine of a roundup camp. Even though our sleep was shortened, we arose at Cookie's call in good humor. I don't know who was first in line, but when he reached his fork for a steak, Cookie hit his hand with the spatula.

" 'Hold on, there, feller,' he bawled loudly, 'what's yore name?' "

JD and the barkeeper laughed.

"That's a good tale, Lee, I've had some experience with both sides of vigilance 'justice,' " Joe Don said. "I was a member of one of the more responsible vigilance committees when we came upon another committee about to hang a horse thief caught with stolen horses.

" 'You're just in time t' see a horse thief get his due,' the rather bloodthirsty leader of committee number one hollered.

"The victim was a man well known and popular in the community—a man no one particularly wanted to see hanged. 'You've already had the trial, have you?' I asked.

" 'No trial necessary if he's caught with the goods.' Number One nodded toward the stolen horses.

" 'Every man ought to have a trial before you hang him,' I replied.

" 'No, *he* don't. Throw th' rope over that limb, boys.'

" 'Let's have a vote on that, both committees included,' I demanded. The nods of my posse members added weight to my demand.

" 'Very well, Joe Don, have your vote.' He grinned, noting our committee contained fewer men than his.

" 'All those in favor of having a trial raise your hand,' I instructed. Of course, my committee was unanimous for a trial, and ol' One was displeased that a good number of his posse was in favor of a trial as well.

" 'A trial it is, and since we captured the culprit, *I'll* be the judge,' One asserted.

"By drawing straws, three men from each committee were chosen as jury, and two 'lawyers' were appointed. The jury heard the case and retired to the shade of a cottonwood to deliberate their verdict. After a time of palaver, smoking, and kicking gravel, they returned to the 'courtroom.'

" 'Have you reached a verdict, gentlemen?' the confident judge asked.

" 'We have, Yer Honor.'

" 'What say you?'

" 'Not guilty if he'll give the horses back.'

" 'What?' roared the incredulous judge. 'You mean a man caught with the goods is not guilty? Of all the subversions of justice I have ever seen, this is the most blatant! You have witnessed this trial, and you know the proper verdict. Go back and deliberate some more. If you don't come up with the obvious verdict, I'll have you all whipped!'

"The duly chastised jury returned to the tree," Joe Don continued. "There was again much auguring, smoking, and kicking. Finally, it seemed the jury came to another verdict. They returned to the 'courtroom.'

" 'Have you reached a verdict, gentlemen?' the judge demanded.

" 'We have, Yer Honor.'

" 'What say you?' The judge was now smiling, the noose slapping softly against his leg.

"That jury stood in an arc, the judge being the center thereof, hands on gun butts.

" 'Not guilty—*and he can keep the horses.*'

"This time, the court was forced to accept the verdict, and the judge resigned and retired from all vigilante work.

"A few days later, the victim of the theft found his missing horses in his horse pasture," JD concluded.

"I heard all about it," Barkeep said to Lee, after he had a good chuckle. "Both posses an' th' defendant came tumblin' in here an' had a hilarious time celebratin' th' trial."

The hack driver shuffled in and we bought him a couple of beers. He delivered us to the hotel door and we hopped off to find ourselves standing at the feet of two lovely ladies waiting with lifted brows for their men to escort them to a restaurant. Both of us ran upstairs and changed into fresh shirts. That's all we had time to do.

Chapter 19
The Ghost of Bill Coe

Early the next morning we left Liberal, following the train tracks to Tyrone. In 1888, the Rock Island Line extended its line five miles into the Public Land Strip and built cattle pens. It remained there, the end of tracks, for fifteen years. The town that grew up around those cattle pens was named Tyrone. Thousands of heads of cattle were shipped from Tyrone every year. The last herd had come and gone, and the town was boarded up and practically empty. The loading pens looked forlorn and abandoned, except for one lone steer bawling in the last pen.

"O-o-oh, stop, Lee, stop! That poor cow is trapped in that pen without food or water." Mollie hopped out of the buggy and ran to the gate.

"It's a steer, Mollie," JD corrected from the wagon.

"Don't stand in the gate, Mollie, get behind it." I hollered.

The steer turned and stared at the new opening to his prison. He pawed the dirt and bellered a couple of times, then sniffed the air.

"Smell fresh air comin' through that new openin'?" JD asked the animal.

Deciding it was safe, the steer trotted out and dipped his horn at Mollie as he passed. The last we saw of him, he was on a high lope south.

I couldn't get far driving the buggy before the pain in my leg forced me to quit. Kat drove most of the time.

By pushing it, we could have made the ranch in a little over two days, but we paced ourselves to get there in three days. We only stopped at the post office in town to pick up any mail for folks out our way. Relocating south of the river made post office and town more convenient.

The buggy in the yard told us that Pete and the boys had arrived. The chuck wagon parked in the shed behind the buggy told us Tex and Rockin' R Bill had also made it. There was a light in the cabin, and the smoke curling out of the chimney foretold a warm welcoming.

The door of the bunkhouse opened, and a dark figure stepped out of the light into the shadows. "Hello the house. It's Lee and Kat and company," I hollered.

"Well, hello, Lee; 'bout time you showed up." Tex's voice came from the shadowed figure as the door filled with men coming to greet us. The ranch house door opened, and the diminutive figure of Colita appeared. Kat and Mollie had left the buggy and were hurrying to the house. The closing of the door cut off their mixture of English and Spanish chatter. I bungled out of the buggy and started unhitching the horses.

"JD, we'll unload that wagon in the morning; just leave it parked up close to the front door for the night."

"Yuh got seven good hands here, Lee. We'll empty that wagon in no time," Rockin' R Bill said. "Come on, boys."

"Careful how you untie those ropes," JD cautioned. "You could start an avalanche."

I opened my mouth to protest, and Pete, standing by me, said softly, "We got a night prowler, Lee. Best to get this stuff inside and secure."

"Prowler?"

"Yeah. He's got the sheepherders so scared, they've left the country, a reg'lar sheep stampede west. You won't find any o' th' few Mixicans left around here out after dark. They shut down tight, an' you won't see a light afore th' sun comes up."

"If you boys are set on unloading that wagon tonight," I called, "go in th' house an' make room to pile it in the floor; th' women will want to get into sortin' it tomorrow." I lowered my voice. "Tell me about this prowler, Pete." The boys were concerned about alarming the women, but I was sure Colita was filling them with all the details—and more—as we spoke.

"It started after you left. People started missing things like clothes off th' bushes after they washed, a ham out of th' smokehouse; mostly food and clothes." Pete continued, "When people started gettin' savvy to it, they began t' look around an' notice things—like a door left open, a huge barefoot print here and there, animals spooked, dogs scared. I didn't believe about th' rattlin' chains until I heard 'em outside th' bunkhouse one night. Me an' Ol' Scattergun went to take a look, an' when I started to open th' door, Tomas's hound shoved it open and set a world record gettin' under a bunk. Only thing we found was one huge footprint next morning and Cookie's fresh beef quarter missing."

"We think he took to th' river," Sol said from behind me, "an' natcherly, we lost him there. I be witness to th' chain rattlin', Lee."

"No one has seen anything at all?" I asked.

"Nothin' but footprints, an' few o' them," Pete answered.

"Got people spooked some," Red added. "Couple o' weeks ago, Pressley heard chains rattlin' an' took a sound shot in th' dark. Winged th' livery helper puttin' up mule harnesses."

"Not much goin' on 'round here after dark. Them saloonkeepers is beginnin' t' complain, but I noticed they don't empty th' slops afore daylight." Pete sniffed in disgust.

"Well, we at least know it isn't a ghost," I said.

"How's that, Lee?"

"Ghosts don't leave footprints, Sol."

"We figger they's a sign he leaves fer some reason or other, no more than we found of 'em," Sol replied in defense.

"What about those chains, Lee? Bill Coe was buried with his chains still on him," Pete added.

"An' I'll guarantee you they're rustin', still on his bones, and still under that tree down by Fountain Creek in Pueblo."

"It's plumb dangerous t' be outside after dark," Red said. "Shore cramps my soc-i-al activity."

"Well, we'll just have to catch this thief," I said.

"How d'yuh know it ain't a ghost?" Pete persisted.

"For one thing, Pete, ghosts don't eat, an' ghosts don't wear people clothes. For another, they's more than one of 'em."

"How'd yuh come t' that conclusion, Lee?" Sol asked.

"One person couldn't have eaten all that food he stole by himself, even if he's ten feet tall an' carries his chains around with him."

"O-o-oh, don't let that get around. We'll have *every* Mixican leavin', an' then who's gonna make my tamales?" Red groaned.

"That ghost stays around, they won't be any meat left t' put in 'em enyway," Tex interjected as he passed, laden with a big box for the house. "You boys just keep on with your palaverin'. It's much more important than gittin' this truck unloaded an' safe from that ghost."

The admonition took effect, and all hands hove to and unloaded the wagon. When all was in, the living room bulged with assorted boxes and furniture. The women had wisely left off all supervision of the pandemonium and departed the scene. When the unloading was done, we retired to the bunkhouse.

I sat at the table with the tablet and pencil and questioned the boys about this ghost that has been prowling the countryside. Using dates, where known, and places, I drew a map of the area, but in the end we couldn't find any discernible pattern to his visits.

"Shore takes a lot of th' fun out of it when you says it ain't a ghost, Lee," Bill said with a grin.

"I'm not sayin' I don't believe in 'em, but I never heard of a ghost needin' clothes and food," I replied.

"But what about those chains?" Red asked.

"They keep folks guessin', don't they? I suspect they are used to scare people and keep them cowerin' in their houses instead of fillin' a common thief's hind end with bird shot—or a .44 round," I said.

"Still say it's more fun thinkin' it's a ghost," Bill persisted.

"You can go right ahead believin' that, Bill, an' I'll go ahead and catch those scoundrels an' put 'em in jail," I said.

"It's a long ways to a jail from here, Lee, an' then, they leak like a sieve," Red informed me.

"Yeah, a ghost'll sift right through th' walls," Pete added.

"Well, I can see right now that you fellers are pretty good at resistin' logic, so I'll just leave you in your ignorance and toddle myself off to bed," I said.

"Blow out th' light when you leave—" Red began.

"An' leave th' latch string in, if you please," Sol interrupted.

"You can take care of those matters yourselves." And I left.

Kat was waiting for me in the living room. She was sorting some of the things from the wagon and looked a little sheepish when I caught her at it. "Your bath is waiting in the bedroom, Lee . . . or you could sleep in the bunkhouse if you want."

The choice was obvious. Of course, I opted for the danged bath. She came in while I was drying and looking for my nightshirt. "Put out the light, Lee. You won't need a nightshirt for a while." Seems like I'm always bein' told what t' do.

Winter weather began to interfere with our investigation of Bill Coe's Ghost, as the whole countryside named him. The first storm hit the week before Christmas, and it blew and snowed for three days. The cattle suffered, not being used to this climate. They drifted down into the timber on the Cimarrón, and we lost a couple of older cows.

We gathered them and headed them up Sheep Pen Cañon. I watched them spread out, looking for grass. "These cows are gonna have to have shelter if any of them live through th' winter."

"Best shelter in this country is the south side of some bluff where they can git out of th' wind," Blackie offered. We rode up the cañon and looked at several of the coves.

"Th' second one looks like the largest and best," I said, as we turned from the last box cañon on the west side of Sheep Pen. The mouth of the cove faced east, with vertical rock walls on the north and west. The south wall was not vertical, but still too steep for a cow to even contemplate climbing. "Even with that north wall, I would like to have more shelter for them—at least for the first few years."

"We could build a loafin' shed along that north wall; it would also give shade in th' summertime when th' sun's up north," Tex said.

"Looks like th' thing t' do," I agreed.

"I've built a few barns and sheds, Lee," Pete said.

"Think you could handle Tex and Rockin' R for helpers? Bein' vaqueros, you know they wouldn't be puttin' up any of that hated 'bob war' fence."

"I could probably handle them if you gave me authority t' shoot them if they didn't work out."

"Make sure your aim is good; we don't have time t' nurse sick people."

We spent the rest of th' day laying things out like we thought they should be.

"It's a long ways from the ranch house, Lee. Maybe you should build a line shack up there," JD said as we rode into headquarters after dark.

"I'll think on that, JD." I put up Hoss and headed for the house for supper.

"This project is beginning t' cost," I said to Kat as we lay in the bed, talking.

"I suppose any new enterprise such as starting a ranch from scratch will be expensive. And there are always those unexpected expenses," Kat said. She laid her head on my chest and puffed. "Your hair tickles."

"I ain't shavin' my chest." I stuffed the sheet under her face and she giggled.

The next morning, Red, Sol, and Blackie agreed to build the fence across the mouth of the cove. While they rode to the slopes of Black Mesa to cut posts, I drove the wagon to town to buy supplies. We loaded enough sheet iron to roof a ten-by-twelve shack, and I cleaned out Fairchild Drew's stock of barbed wire, to the disapproval of the ranchers warming around the stove. Even their shopping wives frowned.

"Don't worry, folks. I ain't fencing th' range, only a pen for my cattle t' weather storms in." I said it loud enough for all to hear. The men grinned.

It was a rare thing to get to eat at noon with the women at the house. When I drove on up the valley, Kat and Mollie rode with me. After much discussion by all, we opted to build the shack into the east end of the shed so it, too, could be shielded from the north winds and be handy to the pen. The fence would join the building where the shed began, leaving the shack outside the enclosure. It would have one door on the south side and one on the west side directly into the shed.

Our concentration on the ranch was interrupted by complaints that our "ghost" was back and prowling the nights, taking things he apparently needed. He seemed to know when someone butchered, and made his midnight appropriations accordingly. This ghost was very good. If it were not for those chains he carried, we might never have known the same person was doing all the mischief. Even then, I was convinced there was more than one person involved. Something had to be done. Either we ran the scoundrel out of the country, or we had to catch him.

The hands had a lot of work hauling material, cutting poles for the shed, and then building. I was satisfied they would be busy enough to stay out of my way while I pursued the ghost of Bill Coe. There had to be a way to trap him, but the casual attitude of my friends convinced me that I was primarily on my own in the project.

Chapter 20
A Call for Blue Earth

You would think I had a plan for capturing this ghost man—and you would be wrong. I had no idea what I was going to do. I could set a trap, but from all we could deduce, this person was exceptionally strong. It would take an army to capture him, and I didn't have an army.

The first thing we learned as deputies was that we never worked alone, yet here I was with that very intention. The second rule of law enforcement is that you need to know the territory, and I wasn't very familiar with this part of the country. That part of the job could be accomplished alone, so I began a systematic search of the countryside. With town as the center, I divided the area into four quarters and began my survey in the northwest quadrant, since I knew most of it except the top of Black Mesa and beyond.

The hands had made good progress on their projects. After spending the night with them, I rode on up Sheep Pen on the pretext of checking on the area and the cattle. The climb to the top of Black Mesa was steep but passable. There wasn't much up there but grass and that black lava cap. From that vantage point I could see the countryside for miles around, and it saved me a lot of riding. Me and Hoss stayed two days up there studying the country. Late the second day, we found an easy gulch to descend on the north side and were gratified to find water, having gone without since my canteen was drained.

We followed the creek and discovered the ruins of some kind

of shelter and corrals from some cattle operation. It hadn't been used in a long time, and I was surprised at the remoteness of the location. Poking around the shelter, I uncovered an anvil block and realized this had been a smithy—Bill Coe's blacksmith shop and cattle pens where he altered the brands of the cattle he stole.

"Well, ol' Hoss, we been drinkin' from Blacksmith Creek," I informed him.

He nodded his head as if to say, "I knew that all along."

"You didn't, either; you're as new to this country as I am." I heeled his ribs, and we moved on down the stream to North Carrizo Creek. We were familiar with Robbers Roost, so I turned up a cañon they named Road Cañon. At the top, we rode across the mesa and descended into Easley Cañon. In all our riding, I had not seen any sign of current habitation by men, or any natural place such as caves or overhangs where a man might hide. Easley Cañon was the same, but a cañon across the mesa from Easley that drained east was very narrow, with vertical and near-vertical rock walls. It certainly offered shelter, but was too narrow and rocky for Hoss. I determined to keep it in mind and return to explore it.

Albert Easley had homesteaded the cañon. Finding Coe's Roost in ruins, he had taken the rock and built his home and barn and a dam across the Carrizo. People said the house didn't look near as good as Coe's building, but then, Coe was a rock mason. Apparently, old Albert wasn't. His son, Miller Easley, now lived on the ranch.

Marrs told me that Miller had a twin brother named Bill. They were born not long after their older sister, Margaret, was born. When Albert went in to see his wife after the twins arrived, he exclaimed, "My gosh, Molly, three babies and not a tooth!"

We crossed the Cimarrón just south of Castle Rock, in my

imaginary southeast quadrant. Hoss took us up South Carrizo Creek and branched off up Willow Creek. Toward the top, we found rough going and rock bluffs, and there was no sign of recent human passing or occupation. Flint chips and rock art told of prehistoric activity. When Willow Creek petered out, we turned southeast to South Carrizo Creek and proceeded down it to the north. South Carrizo and North Carrizo creeks run into the Cimarrón several miles apart. How they were named is subject to speculation. Most likely, north and south were added to the names when it was discovered there were two creeks in the area named Carrizo. South Carrizo is a pleasant little spring-fed stream that meanders down a gently sloping broad valley ideal for grazing stock. It was still open range when Hoss and I rode through. At the breaks of the Cimarrón, the hills closed in on the valley to become about a hundred yards wide. It was flat with scattered cottonwood, walnut, and elm trees. There was a plum thicket and the promise of a goodly grape crop from vines high and low in the trees.

Hoss demanded we stop so he could graze some, so I unsaddled and picketed him on some likely looking grass and dozed while my coffee came to a boil. Hoss seemed determined to stay awhile, so I walked down the stream after lunch.

Up the slope of the west hill a ways was an outcropping of limestone rock. As I rounded the curve of the hill, there appeared a huge slab of the rock that had fallen over when it was undermined some time in the long past. Just beyond that, there was a little hollow under a part of the rock formation that hadn't broken off. The interesting thing about it was that someone had walled the hollow off by stacking a wall of unmortared rocks around the edge of the overhang.

The inside of the shelter was small, with only crawling space, and was maybe large enough for two to stretch out and sleep. It looked like a shelter possibly built by cowhands seeking a dry place to stay when they were range-riding. Back in a dry corner was a stack of folded blankets. I had passed a small fire pit on the way up the bank. As I turned to look down on it, my eyes focused on a footprint—a small, bare footprint like that a child or woman would make.

The folly of my blundering struck me like a blow. *Lee Sowell, you idiot, ridin' all over this country looking for a thief, and the first place you find sign, you bull right in on it, never thinking about what you have found. You idiot!* It would have felt better if someone had hit me then—hard.

Somehow, I had to erase all sign of my passing and get out of sight fast. Actually, fast was not possible if I had to erase signs of my passing. I backed down the steep hill, erasing tracks with my hands. All the time my neck hairs tingled, with the thought that someone might be watching. I couldn't go back and check my work, but just prayed I had been thorough. To leave a sign of my presence would ruin any chance of catching my quarry here.

When I told Hoss about my finding, he gave me one of those baleful looks, and I avoided the range of his hooves. He had every right to kick me. I cleaned up every sign of my little fire, and we returned the way we had come. After a couple of miles, we turned left and climbed the east hill out of the valley. We turned north when out of sight of the valley to the place I guessed we were opposite the shelter. With Hoss picketed out of sight, I crept to the top of the slope into the valley and looked over the area with my glasses.

Trees blocked my view of the opposite hill and the shelter. I was not even sure where it was, but I could sweep the ground under the trees. There was no sign that anyone had been in the valley, not one. It convinced me I was looking for people who could be as invisible as they wanted to be. They must be Indians; and the best way to find an Indian was with another Indian. I knew the one I wanted if I could find him.

The people I hunted were nomadic. I mean by that they had several places hidden around the countryside where they stayed a few days at a time, then moved on to another before their presence became known. They were also very, very good at not being seen. The mystery of that was, why the chains? I couldn't figure that out.

It was a tired Hoss and rider that rode into the Sheep Pen Ranch. We had been gone eight days and covered a couple of hundred miles of rough country. Bud Pack saw us coming and met us at the barn. He took Hoss and led him to the trough to drink while he stripped the saddle from him. "Lee, how many of your horses are named Hoss?"

"Just th' one I'm ridin'." I trundled up to the house, where Mollie met me at the door. "Welcome back, stranger. Where have you been?"

"Around the world and back again, Mollie; how about something to eat?"

"Colita is at the stove this minute. You will have time to clean up before the food is ready."

"Good. Thanks, Mollie." I headed to the bedroom. There in the middle of the floor sat the bathtub full of steaming water. Kat stood there, towel, wash rag, and soap in hand. "Hello, we saw you coming, Lee." She hugged and kissed me and said, "Dinner when you finish your bath."

Seems like every time I see that woman, she's wantin' me to take a bath. I heard Bud come in the house and stepped to the door and called, "Bud, ride up to the line shack and tell Tex to get down here as soon as he can."

"Yessir." The screen door banged shut.

"Mollie, catch that boy and tell him to stay up there and help," I yelled.

"Yes, Lee." The screen door banged again, and I heard Mollie calling Bud.

The water became cool before I left that tub. I put on the clean clothes that lay on the bed. When I was dressed, with my hair combed, I sat down to my first hot meal in a week.

Later, Tex clumped across the porch. "Tex, here's a telegram I want you to take to Ratón and send to that agent at Rainy Mountain. Wait for his answer." I gave him a twenty-dollar gold piece for his expenses.

"Sure, Lee." He opened the note and read it. "Hot da . . . ng. Blue Earth is comin', an' we're gonna catch Bill Coe's Ghost."

Kat snorted. "You have been away from good company too long, Tex, and your mouth tells it. I think I need to go up to that camp for a while and clean up the language before those scalawags are allowed back into polite society."

Tex looked sheepish and Mollie giggled. Colita clucked disapproval from the kitchen door and wagged her spoon at Tex. Just before sunup, I heard Tex trot out of the yard.

There were chores and things to catch up on around the place. When I had the hottest ones taken care of, Kat and I drove out for the cove with supplies early the fourth morning. It was warm and sunny, but winter was far from through with us, and we were well aware of how fast the weather could turn.

The fencing was complete, and everyone had pitched in on the shack and shed. They had used up the logs we had cut. Red, Sol, and Blackie had gone to the cedar breaks and gathered the limbs trimmed from the logs and were in the process of building up the roof. They had spanned the vigas with the stronger limbs, then covered them with the boughs of cedar needles. Their last chore would be to cover that with clay, since sod was not so plentiful up here.

"We brought more grub; what else do you need?" I asked and was inundated with suggestions. "Hold on there, let me make a list." I got out my notebook and turned to a blank page. "After cold beer, ladies, a fiddler, and a cook, none of which will be comin', what else?"

"We need heat in th' shack," Pete said. "We didn't think a chimney would be good."

"I'll get F. B. Drew t' order us a monkey stove and flue." There were several other things the fellers had thought of that made sense. All I needed now was the money to buy the stuff with.

The novelty of building had worn thin with the hands, and they were full of questions about what Tex was doing.

"I sent Tex to Ratón with a message to Rainy Mountain to send us a tracker."

"Blue Earth!" Red exclaimed.

"How do you know him?" Kat asked.

"I don't, but I seen his handiwork at Robbers Roost," he replied.

"Admire people butcherin', do you?" Blackie asked.

"Just on murderers an' wimmin abusers." Red grinned at Kat's look of disgust.

Sol looked up from the gate bar he was whittling. "You think Blue can cut th' head off'n a ghost, Red?"

"If anybody can. I'm tryin' t' get him here to track for us, not butcher ghosts," I said.

Talk of Bill Coe's Ghost revived their yen to search. I had to promise they would be in the posse when the search began—and I didn't know how I'd get out of that.

Tex was at the ranch house when we drove into the yard that evening. "Agent didn't know where Blue Earth was, but he's sendin' out people who can find him. He was sure Blue would be coming our way when he got our message."

I thought about Lane Cañon, that narrow cañon I had bypassed up north, and a half dozen places we needed t' search.

"We can't afford to wait for that time to come. Tex, you've already taken th' oath, so consider yourself deputized agin." We gathered our gear, this time with spare horses and a packhorse for our chuck, and set out to explore some more.

My first objective was to explore Lane Cañon. We crossed the Cimarrón at Castle Rock and veered a little east of north to ascend Gallinas Cañon to the mouth of Lane. Most folks tend to think of cañons as deep, dark, and narrow, but that is not the case with these cañons. They tend to be wide, quite open, and the cañon floors are gently rolling or flat with good grass. Most people would not call Sheep Pen and Gallinas cañons because they are so wide and open. Lane Cañon, on the other hand, fitted our image of a narrow, steep-sided cañon that almost comes together at the bottom. In our parlance, it's more likely to be recognized as an arroyo.

The white limestone layer that striped the bluffs in this region was prominent here, and it was in this formation we were most likely to find shelters and caves. I had hopes of locating another camp such as the one me and Hoss found on South Carrizo. If we were lucky, it would be occupied. We found a place to picket the stock and stashed our gear and food high in some cedars before taking on the arroyo. It was lucky for us that the little stream was dry, for that was the only place to walk for a long ways into the arroyo. The gully climbed steadily toward the mesa top, sometimes steeply, sometimes with a gentle slope.

The bottom of the cañon climbed to the level of the limestone layer, where it had eroded the formation into the shape of a horizontal V running along both walls of the cañon. When we approached that outcropping, we slowed and studied the rock carefully. The hillside had worn back a little ways from the more resistant limestone, with the result that there was a natural path along the top of the layer.

"I'll go left along the path, and you walk the right side back out toward the mouth of the arroyo, Tex."

From this vantage, we could see any shelters or caves not visible from the bottom of the arroyo and any sign of human passage on the paths we walked.

"Hold your hand out, Lee. I think we could touch." Tex stretched out his arm at a narrow place.

"We could, couldn't we? But I don't want t' find us leanin' out too far t' get our balance back. If they found our bodies at th' bottom of this arroyo, they might call it Lover's Leap. *That's* a chance I ain't takin'." We were never more than a stone's throw apart.

There were no signs of human passage, but plenty of animal activity. "I got a panther track here as big as the span of my hand, Tex. You don't see any sign of him around th' corner—or over my head, do you?" I had no desire to make his acquaintance.

"Nope, don't see anything but bees an' bugs," he replied.

Nevertheless, I made a hasty retreat.

"On to the top?" Tex asked as we met back in the arroyo.

"Might as well. I could be putting too much store in finding something in this limestone layer." There was nothing of interest in the rest of the climb.

We found ourselves on top of the mesa with a good view of the surrounding country. To the south, this tableland we stood on was cut up and irregular, with gullies that cut deep into the mesa. In places, the top looked to be not more than a hundred yards wide.

"We could look over an awful lot of territory just by walkin' along th' rim, Lee," Tex observed.

"Which side do you want t' take, an' I'll take t'other."

Tex studied the land a moment. "I'll take the west side an' you take th' east."

"Good enough for me," I said. "Let's try to stay within sight of each other, but where that is not possible, if you run into trouble, fire a shot, count to five, and fire again. I'll find you."

"More likely, you'll be th' one firin' shots." He chuckled.

We took our sides, and it wasn't ten minutes before the gentle rise of the mesa hid Tex from me.

The bluffs were steep, sometimes a sheer drop to the detritus banked against the base of the butte. From above, the animal trails were easy to see. They converged on an arroyo south of me a ways. From the head of that arroyo, I caught the glint of sun on water. There must be a spring at the base of the cliff there, which would be incentive for a camp somewhere nearby. About a mile south, the trails showed the location of another spring. Two springs meant twice the possibility of a hideaway nearby. Another mile south, and the bluffs turned abruptly back northwest along the north edge of Bingaman Cañon. It came to a head where the mesa was not a hundred fifty yards wide. I found Tex there, sitting in the shade of a cedar. He turned his canteen upside down, indicating it was empty—as empty as mine.

"Know a good place t' get down?" he asked.

"None better than right here," I said, indicating the slope before us.

Tex grunted himself up. "No time better than now."

We started walking down and found it was easier to trot, lope, and run down the slope than to try a slow descent. Our momentum carried us down and out on the flat a ways. We walked near three miles down Bingaman Cañon and around the north point of the bluff. Another mile brought us to the first stream from a spring. We drank, washed off dust, and rested a few minutes before moving on toward the horses.

The second spring was stronger, and the water flowed farther into the cañon before sinking. "Can you think of a better place to locate a camp, Tex?"

"No. I would be pretty close around here," he replied.

"Me too. I wonder if we're being watched right now."

Tex grinned. "Got that crawly feelin' on th' back o' your neck?"

"Not yet, but it may not be far away. We can turn from the hunters to the hunted in th' blink of an eye and never know it."

"Bet our horses are gettin' thirsty, don't you?" He stood, dusted off his seat, and we went to the horses.

We reloaded our gear and led the horses to water. "There's a likely lookin' box cañon on th' point between Bingaman and Gallinas cañons," I said. "We could turn the stock loose in there and not have to worry about them straying if we strung rope across th' mouth."

"I noticed that too. Let's go." Tex wasn't one t' sit around when there was something t' do. The horses were glad to be free. It took all our rope to span that cañon mouth. A few dead cholla sticks and some prairie coal made a good fire for our coffee and fixin's for supper.

"Got any ideas for tomorrow, Lee?"

"I got a strong feelin' we missed something here. This is just too good an area for a hideout."

"Maybe so, but not any better than a hundred other places we could think of," he replied. "We could hunt a week an' not find anything. It's gonna take as much luck t' find our ghost as searchin'."

"Let's give this another look tomorrow. We'll go somewhere else if we don't find anything."

"There's lots of places at the top of the scree where someone could hide an' we can't see from down here. We could walk up there and at th' same time keep our eyes on th' bottoms down here."

After a few more minutes when it was good and dark, we picked up our bedrolls, moved apart, and made our beds.

A second look did no more good than the first, and we moved around the point into Bingaman Cañon. It didn't look very promising—and it continued that way prior to the time we got around on the west side where a butte stood alone out from the cañon a ways. Tex scrambled up to go between the bluff and the little butte while I rode around the other side. He hadn't appeared by the time I got to the cañon wall, and I rode up the gully a ways to see if he had found something. His horse stood ground-tied, but no Tex was in sight.

"Tex, where are you?"

"In here," came a muffled call that seemed to originate in some bushes growing against the near-vertical side of the butte. When I finally got through those cedar bushes, I found a little clearing where there was a hollow in the side of the butte. In the back, Tex sat on a natural limestone bench beside a stack of folded blankets and some cooking ware. A rock-lined pool had been dug under a seep that dripped from the underside of the limestone layer.

"Found it, Lee." He grinned.

"By what miracle?" I asked.

"I don't know. How many places like this have we passed and never given a glance?" He shook his head, "It was just like I naturally knew it was here, an' it didn't surprise me at all when I found it. Look at the stuff they got stored here—an' they aren't th' first t' live here. Look at those carvings on that wall."

"They call them petroglyphs, Tex." There were the usual images: Kokopelli, deer and buffalo, that spiral circle, a man stalking mountain sheep with a bow and arrow.

"Look, th' man's naked privates hangin' out."

"That's their way of showin' it's a man doin' th' huntin', Tex."

As usual, there was no sign of human presence except for the gear neatly stored. We erased all our signs as we left, even the horse tracks. Down the slope a ways, we found a boulder where someone had been pounding something metal on it. "Our 'ghost' is tryin' t' break outta his bonds."

"Tole yuh he had chains on."

"An' I'm telllin' you no ghost has t' beat on his chains t' get 'em off," I shot back.

"Well, tell me how he can come an' go without leavin' no more sign except rattles and an occasional big-ass footprint."

"I swear I don't know, Tex. He must be leavin' it apurpose for some reason. A foot that big would fit on a man seven feet tall."

"We found two camps. Wonder how many more he has."

"There's one south of town; this one is northeast of town. I would expect he would have one on the northwest and probably west of town. That's where we should look next."

"Let's go. I wanna see if Blue Earth has got here." Tex turned south for Castle Rock and the Cimarrón. He was all set to grab Blue Earth and continue the hunt, but other things would demand our attention first.

Chapter 21
The Posse

It had been a desperate fight for a minute or two. Shooters had come at us from places we hadn't expected. My horse went down, and I ended up on my belly shooting at anything that moved while Bass sat his horse covering my backsides.

We were gathering prisoners and binding up wounds when Bass Reeves started chuckling. "Lee, never stop thinking about a plan and never stop looking at the situation. It's never goin' t' go like yuh planned, an' yo' gotta be able t' adjust."

We refreshed ourselves at Pressley's Saloon. Few people were in town. "People been talkin' about losing cattle—quite a bit in some cases," Pressley informed us. "Seems it's all down th' valley from Folsom to down past th' 101 and OX."

"Sounds like th' spring rustlers is migratin' back from th' south," Tex said.

"If you Texians'd keep them home, we would appreciate it." Pressley sniffed.

We picked up the mail for our neck of the range and headed for home. We weren't two miles out of town when we were met by a crowd of riders. By th' way they spread out when they saw us, they were not making a friendly visit.

"Gives you a real hankerin' t' turn around an' run, don't it?" Tex asked.

"Just what they'd like us t' do," I replied, "an' hopin' we think we could outrun their bullets."

"Bet they're lookin' for some vanished cattle." Tex moved his .44 to his belt under his coat, just inches from where his hands rested on the horn.

I flipped the loop off my pistol and loosened it in the holster. "Stay cool, Tex. If something starts out of this, make 'em pay. Just know if somethin' starts you and I won't be walkin' away."

Tex grinned and turned his horse left a little to face the riders on that side of the arc. "You fellers know it's not healthy t' shoot at someone in th' middle of your circle, don't you?"

"We don't plan on our bullets goin past th' center," a man with a single-shot Spencer growled.

"Any of you boys in charge of this mob?" I asked. I fought the urge to get mad.

A young man in the center of the arc spoke. "I'm Union County Deputy Sheriff Dan Handlin."

"Seems t' me, Deputy, you don't have much control of your posse here," I said. "How many innocent travelers on th' road have they strung up?"

"We ain't met any travelers afore you," the man next to Deputy Dan said.

"Well, Deputy, state your business. We have some pressing business ourselves an' can't spend th' whole day visitin' with you friendly folks." I stared at the speaker until his eyes faltered.

"We're after cattle thieves," the deputy said.

"If you're on their trail, you must have noticed we were going in th' *opposite* direction they're goin'. 'Course, we might be the two those thieves sent back t' stop you." The deputy opened his mouth to reply and I continued, "You should know that you are out of Union County by a few hundred yards, and that means you are in No Man's Land. You should also know that I am Lee Sowell, Deputy United States Marshal *at large,* which means I can represent any federal court available. This is not a posse, this is a mob, and if you don't get these men under control, they're gonna get innocent men hurt and over nothing more than a few missing cows."

"Them cows ain't nothin'," someone growled.

"Them cows ain't worth th' life of one innocent man ridin' a road an' tendin' to his own business. I say again, Deputy, *get your men under control or go home*—and let those hardcases that stole their cattle handle them."

Deputy Dan suddenly grinned. "You know, Marshal, I think I'll just take your advice and turn this horse around and get the hell out of here." A murmur went through the crowd as the man turned his horse. "You men are relieved of your responsibilities as a deputized posse of Union County."

Tex and I heeled our horses through the circle and followed the deputy, leaving the men standing. "I ain't gonna look back," Tex said, grinning, "but I shore wish I had a mirror."

"Why? These hills are full of asses, an' you can see them any time you want to."

"Yeah, but never in a big bunch like that." Tex laughed like young men do when they pass through danger. Older men just get mad.

We caught up with the deputy. "Deputy Handlin, we've been off chasin' ghosts. Tell us what's goin' on with this cattle stealin'," I asked.

"Emory's Ranch over east of Folsom lost a few head last fall. The trail led north and ended at the Las Animas shipping pens at the rails. The pens were empty, and the broker who bought them had left for the season.

"I guess the thieves were just lookin' over th' country an' makin' their plans. They came back the first of March, an' they're makin' a clean sweep of th' valley, pickin' up whole herds as they go. Looks like they are going clear to the 101, OX, and ZH ranches over east of Florence."

"How many cattle have they gotten?"

"Should be somewhere between eight hundred and a thousand."

"That trail shouldn't be too hard to follow," Tex observed.

"Why weren't you following it when we met?" I asked.

"We figgered to save time coming by th' road, maybe get ahead of them instead of stayin' in th' rough with the herd's tracks."

"How many men in th' bunch?" Tex asked.

"We thought there were ten, but they've been pickin' up help as they came. Th' new help all had cattle with them. Looks like they planned it thataway. They're on th' north side of th' river, and we expect them t' turn up Easley or Gallinas cañons and head for the railroad."

"You don't think they'll turn around th' point of Black Mesa?"

"I guess they could." Deputy Dan pushed back his sombrero and scratched his head. "Any place they go, they're gonna have t' stop and rest; they've pushed that herd pretty hard."

"Go back to that mob an' pick out a couple of fellers with level heads. Then meet us at Castle Rock Crossing where th' Cimarrón runs south a ways. We have to have fresh horses, and we'll check out the trail around the end of Black Mesa as we come," I said.

Handlin grinned and turned his horse. "Sure thing, Marshal. See you at th' river."

We were not three quarters of an hour at the ranch—just long enough to trade horses, gather some more grub, and go, much to the disgust of Kat, who had a tub of water cooling in th' middle of her bedroom floor, and Buck, who would have given an eyetooth t' go with us.

From the size of the herd's trail, I would not have put the head count above five hundred. They were being pushed hard, and it might be that some of the slower ones had dropped out.

A herd on the move like this one didn't bother with the drag.

"They can't go at this pace very long," Tex the trailman said. "Cattle, horses, and men have got to rest."

We could see that the herd had watered at the river. "They won't be goin' much farther," Trailman said.

A young feller built like a brick outhouse who introduced himself as Bear Webb met us at the ford. "Dan's gone ahead to see which cañon the thieves has gone into."

By the time we had gone two miles, we also knew which cañon they had taken for they bypassed Easley. My plan was to go up the cañon the cattle had *not* taken and come down on them from a direction they would not expect. Now we would have to wait for Dan and his man to reappear or go after them. Either way was an unnecessary delay or use of horseflesh.

"Bear, go find Dan, and you-all come up Easley Cañon. We'll go as high as daylight will let us and camp. I want to get ahead of the herd and come down on those men as unexpected as we can."

He nodded and turned to go, when we saw Dan and his partner returning. We rode up Easley. Just before it was too dark to travel we made a dry camp. Before we slept, I swore the three men into the posse.

Lant North was a lanky feller, his arms longer than his shirtsleeves. With wrist bones showing at one end and bare ankles above his moccasins at the other, he looked like he had outgrown his clothes. His gun belt was well worn, but the gun it held was clean, as was the rifle hung from the horn of his old kack of a saddle. The stirrups had been let out as far as they could go and still needed more length to fit Lant's long legs. The saddle was fastened to a good horse, and the boy gave him special attention. North didn't say much, but he was always where he should be and ahead of his companions.

I woke the posse up before four o'clock, and we rode on up the cañon.

"It's just as dark now as when we went to bed, Lee. How're we gonna see any better on this end of th' night?" Tex grumbled.

"Maybe it's a little early, but I don't want to end up behind those thieves agin."

Hoss must have agreed with Tex, for he had complained when I threw the saddle over him. It must have felt cold clear through th' blanket. We fumbled our way up the mountainside to the mesa top and had to wait for more daylight to single-file down an arroyo into Gallinas Cañon.

"Horses smell th' herd," Lant said softly.

"They're straight ahead of us," Dan whispered.

I could see the dark form of the bedded cattle out in the middle of Gallinas. When we cleared the arroyo, I made a sharp left and followed the base of the bluff northward. Hidden in the cedars, we surveyed the layout.

"Where's their camp?" Bear asked.

"There may be more than one," I opined. "Ten or fifteen men wouldn't bunch up, especially with no chuck wagon along."

"Five agin fifteen ain't bad odds." Lant spat a long stream of brown juice at an anthill.

"It may be longer odds than that if it makes you happier," Dan whispered. "Here comes enough cattle t' double that herd an' maybe th' men."

Light from the early dawn reflected on a cloud of dust far down the cañon. By the size of it, Dan's estimate was about right.

"How's six t' one odds strike you, Lant?" Tex chuckled.

"Strikes me, we just had a change of attention from outlaws to cattle," I said. "Th' only way I see out of this is to run this herd into that one and hope they keep runnin' clear to th' river."

"It's for sure some of those fellers are gonna show fight,"

Dan asserted.

"Let's hope they'll be so busy runnin' or tryin' t' stop a stampede that they won't have much time t' send lead our way." It was a nice idea, but I had my doubts even as I spoke.

'Sa-a-ay, isn't that their cavvyard over there by th' far side?" Tex pointed to our left at a dark spot in the shadow of the eastern bluffs of the cañon.

Lant spat again. "Yup."

"All right, Tex," I said, "you go jump those horses. Dan, you and Bear split up th' left side of th' herd after we start 'em runnin', an' Lant and I will split to th' right. Don't let anyone get to th' head of th' run an' start a mill. We want those cows t' run a long ways. Watch, an' don't let yourself get ambushed or cornered. These fellers are gonna be mad as red wasps in August."

We all got down and tightened chinches and added th' last shell to our guns.

I had learned to never stop thinking about a plan and to never stop looking at the lay of the land, meaning the situation you were in. I got everything adjusted and rode out of the trees a step or two. It was light enough to see individual animals in the herds.

"All ready, Lee. Let's git 'em." Tex turned to go after the cavvyard.

"Hold on, Tex, somethin's wrong." All motion stopped and the men looked around.

Lant had to spit before he said, "Ain't no riders."

"Tex, do you see any nighthawk with the cavvy?" I asked.

"N-o-o, can't say that I do."

"The cows are beginning to stir, but there's not a man with them," Dan observed.

"Saddled horse over there without a rider." Lant pointed to a horse standing on the left of the herd. He seemed to be waiting for the herd to get organized for the day's drive, with or without his rider.

"Here comes another saddled horse out of the trees over there." Bear pointed to the trees on the right side of the herd. The horse stood there a moment as if unsure what to do, then walked a few steps and began grazing. It didn't look like he had a bridle on.

It was quiet while we looked the situation over and over. "What the hell is goin' on?" Dan said, more to himself than to anybody.

"Somethin's happened to those men, an' we gotta find out before that other herd gits here. Dan, take your men and go through th' brush over there to th' left. Tex an' I will go right. If you don't find anyone, come to th' herd, and we'll start them moving north. Maybe we can get close enough to catch those fellers with th' other herd." I turned and trotted across to the edge of the cedars with Tex.

"I hate brush poppin'," he said as he pushed into the thick cedars.

I looped my reins over the horn, and with my rifle cocked and in my hands, kneed Hoss along the outside of the trees. When we got close to the grazing horse, I could see dark stains on his saddle. It looked like blood. We had gone another hundred feet or more when Tex cautioned from behind, "Coming out."

Hoss turned about, and Tex rode into the open. "Three men in there on the long sleep. Fire's cold. Gear for about a dozen men layin' around."

"That other herd's gettin' too close. Let's git this one moving and drop back to th' drag an' catch a thief or two. We'll have t' look into that camp later."

"Sure thing, Lee."

His lips were tight and I could see his jaw muscles clamped.

It must have been pretty bad in that camp. He rode with his rifle pointed toward the tree line. Dan and Lant were across the herd chousing cattle, and I could see Bear riding for the lead steer. We had the herd lined out and moving when the second herd came into sight. Dan signaled, and Bear turned the leaders into a mill while the other herd blended in. We all drifted to the back, and it was no trouble to catch five of the new thieves unawares. The drag man and nighthawk saw what was happening and flew back the way they had come. "Let 'im go, Lant; we got our hands full here," I hollered.

We got our prisoners dismounted and shackled together while I told the whole bunch what Tex had found in the campsite.

"We found a body in the edge of the trees, but no camp on the east side of the cañon," Dan said.

"Let the herd go; they'll take care of themselves. We have more pressing business." I looked at the prisoners, "Any of you men good at trackin'?"

"Don't bother with them, Lee. Bear's half Injun an' half bloodhound," Dan said.

"Good; let's get these men secured in th' trees, an' we'll put Bear t' work sniffin' out what went on here last night."

Tex produced a chain from his saddlebag, and we chained one end of our prisoner chain to a stout cedar and left Tex guarding them—and mad. I sent Lant to bring in the other cavvyard.

Bear Webb began tracking from where we were standing. He walked along the edge of the trees in the morning sunrise, stopping occasionally to study the ground and the limbs of the cedars. Angling away from the trees into open ground, he walked slower, occasionally squatting down to study tracks. Dan and I followed some distance behind, spread out and alert. There were still several thieves unaccounted for.

Eventually, Bear turned back to the tree line and waited for us to catch up. "The tracks all converge here." He pointed to a faint path through the trees.

"All right," I said. "I'm going down that path. You two go through the trees ten or twelve yards either side of me. If there is anyone layin' for us, one of you can get him. I'll go real slow so you can keep up without making too much noise. Be careful."

When they were in place, I started down the path, bending low to avoid as many branches as I could. Sweat gathered on my eyebrows and stung my eyes. It dripped from my nose, and my shirt stuck to my back. I sure needed a drink of water.

We had only gone thirty yards or so when the brush opened up and revealed a flat space against the rock bluff. There was a seep spring dripping from the bottom of that limestone layer into a rock-lined pool. It was an ideal campsite. The fire pit was old, probably ancient.

I counted ten bedrolls scattered around. Two of them held bodies. A third body sprawled in the middle of the clearing. He held a broken bridle in his hand. I stopped at the edge and motioned to Bear. He stepped out while Dan and I guarded him.

In a quiet voice, Bear carried on a running commentary on what he found. "Lots of tracks, boots, and moccasins." He moved to one of the bodies in a bedroll. "Died in his sleep. Never knew what hit him." He continued his search, eventually reaching the other man on top of his bedroll. "Neck's broken. Came up behind him when he was sitting up."

"*Who* came up behind him?" Dan asked.

"Big man, very strong."

A ghostly vision in chains floated through my mind. "I need a drink bad, Bear."

"I'll look first."

He studied the ground across to the seep. I thought he would never get there. Things were beginning to look swimmy, and it seemed I was looking at the world through a tunnel.

"Here's your drink, Lee." Dan was handing me a canteen. I don't know how long he had been standing there. I drank it all. Bear rolled the man with the bridle over on his back. "Choked him." His head had a long gash and he had bled a lot. There were marks of chain links around his neck. "Must have crushed his windpipe, and it swelled shut as he was trying to get on his horse. The throatlatch strap on the bridle is broken." Dan looked up and shrugged. "That's all. There are five men rode out of here in a hurry."

"All the saddles are missing," I said. "They must have had night horses nearby, and the horses of the two dead men must have left with the others."

We dipped our canteens full and sat over under the cedars. The sun was warming the rock cliff, and it was hot.

"What signs of the killers did you see, Bear?" Dan asked.

"Didn't see none."

"Nothing?" I asked, then nodded.

"What, Lee?" Dan asked.

"We've had a sneak thief around here. Steals food and things like pots and blankets. Folks hear chains rattle, don't see anything, but we sometimes find a big bare footprint. Sure got people spooked."

"He was up the river a while, but people didn't catch on. Thought it was Injuns pilferin' 'round." Dan took another long drag on his canteen. "I found two barefoot tracks. That feller must be seven feet tall."

We heard Lant's cavvy trot up, and I said, "If you're through, Bear, we better get everyone together here. I imagine they're all gettin' pretty thirsty by now."

Bear led the way down the path. I nearly bumped into him when he stopped short of the edge of the trees. Without a word, he pointed to the now familiar imprint of a huge foot, toes pointing away from the bluff.

I swore and Dan whistled low. "That's some big footprint."

"Bear, I'll swear that wasn't there when I came in here."

Bear nodded and pointed to the heel of one of my footprints peeking out from under the giant toe prints. The heel of my next step was just beyond the heel of that footprint: it was that long.

"He may be *ten* feet tall," Bear opined. He measured his foot against the print.

Lant North stuck his head in the pathway. "You fellers kill a snake?"

"No, Lant, we're trackin' a midget thief," Bear retorted and pointed to the footprint.

"How many midgets did he steal?" Lant's mind was also quick. "Nighthawk's dead."

"That makes five dead, and five on th' run." I hurried down the valley to collect Tex and his prisoners and the saddled horses. We preserved the big footprint and showed it to our prisoners to help prove that we had not killed their partners in crime. They were convinced we didn't kill them when they saw the bodies at the camp.

"Looks like we're gonna eat off your chuck wagon," Tex said to the prisoners.

"Our chuck is out there still on th' hoof," one of them shot back.

"Beef without no biscuits?" Lant asked. "I'd as well do without."

"You can for a day or two," another prisoner allowed.

"Tex, you and Bear get these prisoners watered. We're gonna chouse all this stock down the cañon to the river, then come back and start a cemetery somewhere. Get the names of the dead and collect their things. There may be letters or addresses of next of kin. If you fellers know them, help us out a little," I said to the prisoners.

CHAPTER 22
WHERE BULLETS DON'T STOP

We didn't move the stock too far down Gallinas, just far enough that they could smell water and get to the river when they wanted to. Their main interest seemed to be grass, and we were content to let them have their way.

On the way back to camp, Dan pointed out a likely cemetery site a little east of the north-south trail on what was named the Red Cañon Trail. The ground didn't look too rocky. There was a nice view down the slope to the creek.

Tex and Bear had been busy while we were gone and, in addition to identifying the deceased, had rolled up all the bedrolls except those of the dead men and stacked them in the open where we could get to them easily.

Noon came and we ate the rest of our grub. Our stay wouldn't last much longer without food.

"This grave-diggin's gonna be awful tedious with one little shovel, five graves, an' no food t' keep us goin'." Tex said out loud what the rest of us were thinking.

"Heat don't help diggin' or breathin'," Bear allowed, looking at the five bodies laid out in the hot sun. Even with them rolled in their beds, there was the heavy odor of death if you happened downwind of them.

"It's fifteen miles t' town. Takin' time t' get a wagon, load it with grub, an' headed back, a man couldn't be here any sooner than this time tomorrow," I said.

"Looks like Lant's gonna have his steak without biscuits

tonight." Tex dodged a dirt clod from the lanky cowhand.

"Why is it that those prisoners git t' sit in th' shade fannin' their selves while we're out here in th' sun diggin' graves for *their* friends?" Bear asked.

"Any of you fellers want to volunteer t' dig awhile an' be off those shackles?" I asked.

"I'll dig," one of the younger boys in the middle of the line replied.

Tex wasted no time turning him loose, and Lant handed him the shovel. "Handle's hot," he remarked.

"Any heat in that handle is left from when I used it," Tex declared. "You ain't done enough with it t' keep it warm."

Lant spat a stream and said, "Company's comin'."

We could see riders among the horses and cattle down the valley. They were looking over the stock, probably reading brands and looking for their particular one. Gradually, they rode our way.

"101 outfit," Lant said without spitting.

One of the riders separated from the others and loped our way. "Looks like Henry Jones," Dan said. "He's boss of the 101, Lee."

I knew Henry from previous acquaintance.

"Howdy, Dan," the man spoke as he rode up. "Looks like you're in the middle of a funeral."

"Lighten that horse's load, Henry. We could use a hand here," Dan replied.

The man stepped down from his horse and left him ground-tied. He shook Dan's hand. "This is Tex Shipley and I think you know Lant and Bear. And this is U.S. Deputy Lee Sowell. He is ranching in Sheep Pen Cañon."

"Heard about that," Jones said. "Welcome to No Man's Land, Sowell." His smile was genuine and his hand was firm.

"It's good to be here," I replied. "We heard news from the

101 when we passed through Liberal."

"Looks like you've had a little trouble here." Jones looked around at the five bundles.

"We found them scattered around the night herd, all dead," Dan explained.

"That so? Who killed 'em?"

"We think they were all killed by one man—with his hands—busted heads, broken necks, choked with a chain," I explained. "It looks like it was a big man who has been hangin' around town and pilfering things and food."

"You're meanin' that big-footed feller?" Henry Jones asked.

"Looks thataway. We found his track at the camp the thieves were using."

"Well, Lee, maybe we got more to thank th' feller for than t' condemn him. If these thieves had kept on going, we would not have caught them before the cattle were on a train headed for Kansas City or Chicago."

I nodded, "You're probably right. This is the first time he has harmed anyone around here, and we haven't figured out why, unless he had a hideout somewhere near and didn't want any neighbors."

Cap Leslie and several other 101 hands were riding up. Lant grinned when he saw a covered wagon turn up the valley.

"Ha." Bear laughed. "Looks like Lant's gonna have biscuits with his steak after all."

"Can't eat steak without 'em, myself." Cap grinned.

"There'll be a shovel or two on the wagon," Henry said. "We'll have these folks in their graves in no time. You fellers mind if I take a look at 'em? I might know one or two."

"We got names on 'em, but they may not have been th' ones they wore when you might have known them," Tex said.

"It might be good to wait for all your men to gather and look at them all at one time," I said. "They're gettin' awful ripe."

"We can sure do that," Henry said. Cap was already trotting down to the chuck wagon for the shovels. "Tell Cookie t' turn around an' find a place along th' river. We're goin' t' need to be near water," he shouted.

It wasn't long before three shovels were working. Not much later, they were scraping on solid rock only about three feet down. "That's as deep as you're goin', boys. Might as well get on those other two graves, an' th' rest of us will start gatherin' rocks," Henry Jones said.

There was a stir among our prisoners. We looked up to see another group of riders approachin'.

Tex cursed softly, "It's your former posse, Dan. Tell them th' hotel's full an' they better ride back to town."

The riders pulled up in a bunch and looked the crowd over. "Damn, looks like we missed the fun," a man who acted as spokesman for the bunch announced.

"We don't call killin' people 'fun' on this end of th' valley," I said. "This job's almost finished. Why don't you all ride back to Florence? We'll call you when it's time t' sort out the herd."

"Oh, I think we'll stick around. Work's not finished here. There's some crooks still standin'." He nodded toward the prisoners.

"They'll still be on th' green side of grass when they leave here. They are my prisoners. Part of their crimes were committed in New Mexico Territory, and I will deliver them to the law there for prosecution." My hand was resting on my gunstock for emphasis.

"He's right, men. This is now a matter for the proper authorities to handle." Henry Jones and the rest of the 101 men spread a little around the mounted men, hands near or on their guns.

"You know it as well as we do, Henry, that there's no law in No Man's Land 'cept what we make ourselves. This here *U-S* deputy may not know that."

"I know it, all right," I said, "and I know that you came here from New Mexico, where there *is* law. These men are not going to answer to your lead-and-hemp law."

"That hasn't been determined yet. Your high-handed lawin' just might git you in th' same situation these crooks are in."

"I give every man who makes personal threats to me the opportunity to stand by his word or prove that he's a liar. Why don't you step down from there and keep your word right here in front of everybody? Braggin' rights ain't near so impressive if a job is done when no one's watchin'."

The man had talked himself into a corner. It was either take up my challenge, or prove he was a cowardly bully not worthy of leadership. He stepped down from his horse and faced me across the ten yards separating us. "What'll it be?" I asked. "Guns, knives, or fists?"

He was a big man, and it only took him a moment to decide. "Fists."

Just what I wanted, I thought. I nodded and unbuckled my gun belt, even laying my pocketknife aside, and sat down. "Take off your boots, too."

This wasn't to his liking, but I still held the upper hand. Being heavier, the gravelly ground might bother him enough to make up for my bum leg. It also had the effect of removing his boot knife from the action.

I would like t' say the fight didn't last long and I gave the man a good whippin', and I would like t' give you a blow-by-blow accounting. But that would take too long, and you would know how many times I got knocked down. The outcome was that I whipped the man, but not by much. His buddies had to help him on his horse, and he rode away to lick his wounds. I didn't have that luxury; I had a funeral to conduct.

Even though we hurried some, by th' time we were ready for the sermon, my lips were too swollen to talk. Tex had to read the "Outlaw's Sermon" from my book. I think it was his first time, and he did pretty good.

When they viewed the bodies, the congregation gave different names for three of them, and Tex wrote them down. We found family information on only two of the men. Later, at Sheep Pen, I wrote letters to the families.

That three-mile ride to the river for supper was an ordeal. Hoss sensed I was hurting, but I never got him to tiptoe. I don't know why I even rode down there; I couldn't eat. Bear followed the mob back toward Florence until it was too dark to see them. When he rode back, we were ready to go.

"Go where?" he asked. "I just got here, ain't had a bite t' eat."

"We're makin' a run for Colorado," Dan informed the boy.

"First thing I'm gonna do is eat."

Tex took up Bear's reins. "Hurry an' feed your face while I catch up a fresh mount for you. Any preference for brands?"

Bear was too occupied with eating to answer.

Henry Jones had been busy seeing that everything was in order. He sent riders out to inform area ranchers where the herd was. The roundup was complete, but the next week would be spent sorting and branding and herding cattle back to their home ranges. He came over and squatted beside me. "Lee, I could spare a couple of men if you need them."

"Don' phink I need 'ny more poss. Could use a guide," I lisped.

"Cap Leslie knows this country better than anybody. I'll send him with you. Good luck." He was off, seeing to business. In a few minutes, Cap walked up. "Ready to go when you are, Lee." He looked to be about thirty years old, a slim and tough vaquero.

"Wha'sh besh way t' Col'rad'?"

Leslie squatted and drew in the sand. "Best way is straight up Gallinas. That's th' way that mob would expect us t' go. They'll backtrack an' go up by my place, expectin' t' meet us when we come out of Gallinas Cañon about sunrise. I recommend us to cut over to Red Cañon and outflank 'em."

I nodded agreement, " 'Esh go." Tex read Leslie the posse pledge, and we swore him in.

It took a few minutes to get the prisoners mounted and secured on their horses. We rode one guard per prisoner, Leslie leading alone.

Now, don't think those prisoners went like lambs to the shearing. We had to keep constant watch for their tricks. The closer we got to the state line, the more they tried to get away. When I got tired of the struggle with my man, I buffaloed him and he slumped over the horn. He was tied on, so he couldn't fall off. We crossed the state line just at sunrise.

Cap stopped a hundred yards beyond the boundary monuments, and I formally arrested the prisoners.

I whispered instructions to Tex, and he spoke to the men. "You men have stolen cattle and horses in the Territory of New Mexico, and we intend to return you to the authorities there—if Colorado does not have an interest in keeping you here."

"Tessh, I did'n shay 'ny phing 'bou' Col'rad'."

"Throws a little more scare on 'em."

I glared at him; it hurt too much to talk. There was little chance that my arrest would hold up because I had captured them in No Man's Land, but with luck, lawmen could arrest them legally before they were released on the world again. At the very least, the men would be known as thieves, and lawmen could keep an eye on them. I was determined they would reach the courts safely.

Cap led us west along the border. We got to the Gallinas Cañon Road before the New Mexico mob. We could see them about a mile below the border.

"May ash well wait f' 'um catssh up; cannu' ou'run 'um," I

slurred. My leg was throbbing.

We put the prisoners and horses safely out of sight, with Cap Leslie guarding them. I sent Dan Handlin scooting for Springfield to telegraph his boss that we would meet him with the prisoners at the mouth of Sheep Pen Cañon. Tex found an old buffalo wallow about fifty yards north of the boundary monuments, and the four of us stood on the lip waiting. The mob approached the monuments and spread out in a line along the south side of the border. Knowledge that I could legally arrest them in Colorado kept them there.

"We want those thieves, Dep'ty, and we aim to get them." The gang had a new spokesman. I didn't see my old opponent in the crowd.

A man on the end of the line yelled, "You oughta know that bullets don't stop at th' border, Deputy." He raised his rifle to his shoulder, and at the boom of a .50 from behind us, the would-be shooter's sombrero flew off.

"Now he knows bullets can go *both* ways across that line." Cap Leslie spoke softly so only we could hear.

"Shoph, Less'y," I slurred.

Resolve faltered in the mob, and several men half-turned their mounts as if to leave.

"Ask yourselves if gettin' these cow thieves is worth gittin' shot," Tex yelled.

"I know ever' one of 'em." It was Leslie again.

"We have your names, and if you persist, we can turn them over to th' law—or notify your widow." Tex shouted. As Leslie quietly prompted, Tex began calling the roll. Now they were not a mob anymore, they were individuals; men who would have to stand alone before authorities or public opinion. All resolve melted away, and single riders and pairs turned back.

We waited for them to get a mile or more down the valley. Cap Leslie stepped from behind the cut bank. "Just hate t' be left out o' th' action" was his only concession to an apology.

I could only grin—and that hurt. "Phine us water, Cap, lesh resh."

Our guide led us to Carrizo Creek and turned up a side cañon to a rock shelter in the east cliff. Inside, there were crumbling rock walls of an old Indian house. A trickle of water ran down the little branch.

"We can rest here safely," Leslie said. And we did, the rest of the afternoon and night.

I awoke in the morning gloom with a splitting headache. My teeth felt like they were on the verge of falling out.

"Here, Lee, swish this around in your mouth." Tex handed me a cup of warm water.

It took only one sip and swish to set my mouth on fire, and I spat out bloody water, "Whash 'at?"

"Warm saltwater. It'll clean out your mouth and toughen it up," Tex informed. "Swish the whole cup." He stood and watched my torture and took the empty cup. "If you do that two or three times a day, you'll heal faster and not get an infection."

"Yesh, doc'or." I had a very urgent need and hurried to the brush.

We waited for late afternoon to leave our hideout, even though we were out of food. It was out of the question to cross over Black Mesa, and the trip around the west end was more than forty miles. Our most direct route would be around the east end of the mesa in No Man's Land and the neighborhood of Florence. It would have to be done at night. In spite of the night travel, the trip was easier, because not one prisoner struggled to be free while in No Man's Land or New Mexico, where they were in danger of a rope-stretching.

Cap Leslie led us safely around the foot of the mesa to Sheep Pen, where we found the Union County sheriff and his posse waiting for us. A chuck wagon also waited for them about halfway to Clayton, so he took the prisoners without waiting for them to be fed. It was a trip that a man needed to start with a little fat reserve.

Tex rode ahead to warn Colita that we were coming in hungry. Not long after we arrived, she called us in to a midmorning meal fit for a king. Those saltwater gargles were helping, but my loose teeth kept me on a soft diet for some time.

It took the Union County prosecutor a few days to determine that the prisoners had been illegally captured in No Man's Land, and, therefore, could not be successfully prosecuted. His delay was just long enough that when the men walked out of the jail, sheriffs from three counties in New Mexico and Colorado were standing there to arrest every one of them on a variety of other charges, which resulted in convictions and prison time for some. I was satisfied.

A week later, several men from the posse drove eleven head of cattle with Kat's brand on them into the yard. It was the closest they ever came to apologizing for their behavior, and we accepted their apology in the same manner. We corralled the cattle and treated the men to supper. They were our neighbors up and down the valley, and over time we became friends.

The five escaped cattle thieves rode out of Gallinas Cañon into obscurity, the mystery of who they were never revealed. Likely, they simply dispersed, resumed their former occupations, and waited for the next opportunity to get a quick stake. You certainly couldn't say stealing cattle was an easy job; but for some it was really habit-forming.

I loafed around the house, taking the salt cure and healing cracked ribs, until I could talk without a lisp, eat real food, and walk without a limp—well, *almost* without a limp.

Chapter 23
A Sheep Pen Christmas

Our only help for the summer were Tex and Rockin' R Bill Wylie. Both were proving up on homestead property and had to stay around to develop the land in accordance with homestead law requirements. Bud Pack got a letter that told of his father's sudden death and that his mother needed him to run the farm. He left the first of June. Pete, Red, Sol, Spider, and Blackie took up their annual harvest of wild hay, and we didn't see them until frost.

It was one of the many times I considered quitting the marshal business; and when I look back on it, probably the time I came nearest to doing it. Hearing that this big-footed man had killed five men really got people stirred up. It put all night activity out of business. When the sun went down, it was as if it took all light with it. Candles and kerosene were very slow-selling items at Fairchild Drew's store.

The interesting thing about it all was that visitations by the prowler totally stopped. Not one item disappeared from a clothesline or a smokehouse all summer long; not one chain-rattle was heard. Still, almost the only subject of discussion was about that ominous threat. I sure got tired of it.

Some noise in the yard brought me out of the barn one forenoon to see what looked like half the Kiowa nation invading us. Blue Earth rode at the head of the procession. Kat and Mollie stood on the porch watching. Colita was peering from the doorway, the heavy wooden door closing more and more as the cavalcade approached. Should any threat come from these visitors, I'm sure the two on the porch would have found the door closed and barred from inside, and they would have been left to their own devices—outside.

"Hello, Blue Earth. Welcome," I greeted.

"Hello, Leesowell. Is all well with you?"

"It is, my friend."

The man dismounted at my invitation. A young girl, not more than sixteen or seventeen, came forward leading her horse and took the reins of Blue Earth's horse.

"This is Antelope."

The girl smiled and bowed slightly. She led the horses to the water trough. An older woman followed after Antelope with two more horses. True to Kiowa practice, Blue Earth would not mention the name of the deceased. I learned that Antelope was the sister of Snow Flower. Snow Flower had been a young Kiowa girl kidnapped from the Rainy Mountain School by the murderer A.B. Chew. Blue Earth joined our posse in our search for Chew and the girl. We found the murdered girl, and Blue Earth helped us track down and capture Chew at Bill Coe's old Robbers Roost. One morning we awoke to find Blue Earth gone, and Chew's head with him. He took it back to Snow Flower's parents as proof that he had gotten their daughter's killer. I never did ask what they had done with the head.

I believe that Blue was married to Antelope at the time we first knew him. It is probable that the family's intention was for him to also marry Snow Flower, in spite of the fact that the Anglos were discouraging multiple marriages.

A very old man limped forward. "This is Two Calf, my father," Blue Earth said, though in reality, he was Blue Earth's father-in-law. Two Calf and his wife, White Rabbit, were the parents of Antelope and Snow Flower. Two Calf was several years older than his wife. Quite possibly, he had married a younger White Rabbit to help his ailing first wife run the household.

The old man offered his hand and we shook. He murmured something to Blue, which he translated. "Two Calf wishes to thank you for welcoming us to your village."

"You are welcome," I repeated. The two women returned, and Blue introduced his mother-in-law as his mother. Antelope said something to Blue and nodded to the packhorses waiting patiently.

"Oh, I am sorry, Antelope," I said. "Blue, they may set up their tipi there by the trees." I pointed to the cottonwoods on the west side of the yard. The Kiowa's entrance, which always faced east, would be so they could see the front door of the house to their left and the west-facing door of the bunkhouse.

The women hurried away and soon *two* tipis were erected under the trees.

Two Calf was an old warrior. He was battle-scarred, crippled, and very bow-legged. Ten or fifteen years ago, he might have been after my scalp instead of setting up house peacefully in my front yard. The buffalo hides of his tipi were worn and tattered and would not serve much longer. It was a sad thing, even to us Anglos, that there would be no new replacement hides. Buffalo hides were the only hides sturdy enough to serve as tipi covers. Blue Earth's tipi was canvas.

Two Calf's shield stood proudly on its stand in front of his tipi. The several Anglo and Pawnee scalps that would have normally hung from the shield were stored away in deference to his host.

Kat and Mollie had been sitting on the porch watching. As the Kiowa women seemed to have finished setting up house, Kat spoke through the screen door to Colita. Presently, the housekeeper appeared with a stack of cups and a large coffee pot on a tray. She would not come out of the door, so Mollie had to go in and get the tray.

"We have coffee for our guests," Kat said as she poured steaming cups for the three of us. She motioned for the two women to join us on the porch, and they enjoyed rocking and drinking the coffee. White Rabbit knew enough English to converse with Kat and Mollie.

Our two vaqueros rode into the yard. Tex hollered, "Hello there, Blue Earth." He jumped down from his horse and greeted Blue warmly. "This here's Bill Wylie, formerly of the Rockin' R and now of No Man's Land," he said by way of introduction.

"This is my father, Two Calf."

The old man rose and shook hands with both men.

"Did Lee tell you we are looking for a spirit?" Tex asked.

"We have not talked of that," Blue answered. He glanced at me and interpreted to Two Calf. The old man shook his head.

"No, no, it is not a spirit, Blue Earth," I added quickly. "It is a man who is very good at hiding. I would not ask my friend to chase a spirit."

Two Calf nodded at the interpretation. "Lee knows we do not chase after spirits," Blue Earth said with a smile.

"This man is very, very good at hiding, Blue Earth, and no one has seen him. I believe you are the only one who can find him," I said.

Blue was pleased. "We will see."

"Trouble is, he hasn't been around for a while, and we don't know when he'll come back this way," Wylie added.

"Lee, we passed a maverick up the way without burn or notch, and it looks like we're gonna be needin' fresh meat. You want us t' go drive him in?" Tex asked.

"That would be good," I replied. All our cattle were reserved for breeding and expansion. What beef we needed came from a purchase or the occasional maverick that wandered by.

Tex and Bill drove the bull in, and before they could kill him, the two Kiowa women showed up with knives and pans. After Tex shot him, the women took over the butchering.

"Got everything but hooves and holler, Lee," Wylie said.

"All I hope is that bull didn't introduce himself to any of our heifers."

"Don't think he got th' chance; but you know how sneaky those old boys can be." Tex grinned.

Blue Earth and his family stayed with us all summer waiting for Bigfoot to show. In the good old-fashioned way, we men were not supposed to notice that Antelope was with child, but it became very obvious that her time was near as fall approached. They would not be moving before the child was born.

Pete, Red, Sol, Spider, and Blackie showed up one blustery fall day. Their pockets were jingling, and they were anxious to talk to Kat. She held court on the front porch in her favorite rocking chair. "And what can the Sheep Pen Queen do for you scamps?"

Pete had been short-strawed into the spokesman position. "We're done hayin' for th' year, Mrs. Sowell—"

"Call me Kat or Your Highness."

"And we ain't likely—"

"Are not."

"Huh?"

"Use proper English when addressing the queen."

"Yes, ma'am. We are not likely to find any payin' work before th'—the—grass turns green next spring. We were wonderin'—wondering—if we could . . . wondering if you would—"

"You want to stay here for the winter?" The queen was drawing short on patience, but her subjects could see the twinkle in her eyes.

"Yes, ma'am, but we would pay—"

"There would be no charge for staying in the bunkhouse."

"Yes, ma'am, but we would like to pay you for two meals a day if we could—in advance."

"What two meals would that be?"

"We ai—are not used to eating at noon, ma'am."

"So you would eat breakfast and supper with us."

"Yes, ma'am, an' we would be willing to pay for them."

"In advance," Red added.

"How long do you plan for this arrangement to run?" Her Highness smoothed the apron in her lap.

"We figger—"

"Four months, a hunnert twenty days, two hunnert forty meals." Blackie injected himself into the negotiations.

Pete shrugged. "We figger fifty cents a meal would—"

"Be a little too much," Kat interrupted. She thought a moment. "I suppose six bits a day would cover the meals, but that wouldn't account for the gallons of coffee you scalawags would drink up at the bunkhouse. How about six bits a day and a one-time charge of two bits a month for coffee?"

That was satisfactory with the boys. Some time was spent figgering up the amount they owed. Sol wrote figures in the sand, and with three mathematicians looking over his shoulder, he came up with the total. "Comes to ninety-one dollars a man," he said, rubbing out his ciphers with his foot.

"That will be fine," Kat said, rising to retreat into the warmth of the house. "You'll have to make arrangements for your bunkhouse accommodations with Lee."

"Wait a minute; we're gonna pay you now," a couple of voices implored.

"That won't be necessary—"

"If we don't pay up now, we won't have it when we come back," Pete explained.

It took some digging and change-exchanging to come up with the right amounts. They left a bemused Kat holding an apron full of cash as she watched them lope down the lane to the road. The last she saw of them was a cloud of dust on the Ratón and Trinidad road.

It was the middle of November, when they came back with empty pockets and aching heads, before we saw them again. They had not met Blue Earth, just seen his handiwork, and they readily made acquaintance with him. The boys spent their time visiting Mollie (until Kat or Colita would run them out of the house), riding the range on good days, or running up a tab at one of the three saloons in town.

We all got an added diversion when Antelope appeared one morning with a little black-eyed bundle she named Sunflower, and we became victims of the spell cast by all infant girls on unsuspecting males. White Rabbit had her hands full trying to keep the young men from spoiling the child, a task she largely failed to accomplish.

Tex and Wylie took turns staying at the line shack a week at a time, and usually one or two of the boarders would keep them company. Our herd was small enough that they could be comfortable in the pen, so they got the habit of coming in there to bed down. I found a stout wagon, and we kept the manure picked up. Later on, the extra green on the range where we spread it attracted the cattle. When I could afford it, I got a Kemp and Burpee manure spreader, in spite of the salesman's joke about Kemp not "standing behind it."

Christmas Eve morning, Tex and Spider rode into the yard with a cedar tree tied to the packhorse. We spent the afternoon and evening making decorations for the tree. Blue and Antelope were intrigued with the doings. We had oyster stew and crackers for supper. I think it was the first time the Kiowas had eaten it, and they all four seemed to enjoy it.

"I wonder if they would eat the oysters if they saw where they came from," Kat whispered to me.

"It wouldn't bother them near as much now that they have tasted it," I replied.

"Time to light the tree," Tex announced. With three helpers, he had the candles going in no time.

Kat sat close to me. "I'm not sure who is more entranced, the boys or the Indians," she whispered. It would have been hard to decide. We all tried to explain to our Indian guests what the occasion was. It was when I got my Bible out and read the story—with ample interpretation from the Anglo audience—that Blue Earth and his family seemed to understand. "It is for the birth of the child," he said.

Antelope, who had attended Rainy Mountain School some, nodded and patted Blue's hand. It was an unusual act of affection for the Kiowa. The four soon retired with the sleeping Sunflower to the warmth of their tipis, and Kat hustled the vaqueros out soon after. "We have much to do before bedtime and we don't need you fellows under foot," she said.

They left in a cloud of good-natured banter. Kat retrieved a box from under our bed, and we distributed gifts around the tree. She had gotten something for every one of us. When she wasn't looking, I snuck a gift for her on the tree. We had a great first Christmas at the ranch. After a feast of *two* turkeys and trimmings, we enjoyed the afternoon with neighbors and friends who dropped by.

We celebrated New Year's by putting up a new calendar. That's all we had time for.

Chapter 24
Blue Earth Searches

1889

In March, I hired Pete and Sol to help with the spring branding. We shut the herd up in the cove and worked through them, branding and marking new calves and tending to any cow with problems. A kid rode up to the pen one forenoon, horse and rider well lathered.

"He's back," he yelled from the fence even before he dismounted.

"Who is that?" Tex asked.

"A bearer of bad news," I said. "I'll go see what it's all about." I walked over to the fence.

"Mr. Sowell, Pa sent me to—"

"Just a minute, son, first things first. Take the saddle off your horse and rub him down with the blanket. When he has caught his breath a little, *walk* him over to that tank and give him a drink while you count to fifty—you can count to fifty, can't you?"

He nodded.

"At fifty, bring him back this way. When you get back, we'll talk."

"Yes, sir."

While the boy tended his horse I walked to the gate and waited for him to return. "How is he?"

"He's all right, Mr. Sowell. Pa sent me t' tell you that—"

"Big-footed rascal is back in th' country." I finished for him.

He nodded, "He stole a whole quarter of beef out of the smokehouse."

"Are you sure it was Mr. Bigfoot?"

"Pa said no man could carry that off and not leave sign."

"No footprints?"

"No . . . sir."

"Where do you live?"

"T'other side of Florence 'bout four mile. He run th' cows over our roof."

"Did any fall through?"

"No, but we got a good shower o' dirt. Ma's madder'n a hatter."

"I can imagine," I said, trying to hide my grin. "You walk that horse back to the tank for another short drink and bring him back here. We'll put him in the shed and get you a fresh horse. I'll send a tracker back with you to look things over."

"Yes, sir." He turned to walk the horse to water.

I walked over to where the boys were working over a calf. "JD, saddle up and go find Blue. You two go with that boy to where Bigfoot visited last night and see if they's enough sign left after everyone has stomped around for Blue to pick up something."

Tex threw a couple of fries into the bucket and wiped his hands on his pants, "What 'bout me?"

"You can get to th' house an' make us an outfit. We'll need grub for four or five days. I'll ride that bay, and you choose somethin' with bottom for yourself." I shouted after JD, "Take your bedroll. You're liable t' be gone a few days. Get th' lady at that ranch t' fix you up some grub, and don't waste time.

"Pete, we're almost done here, think you an' Sol can finish up?"

"Sure, Lee, what you want done with them then?"

"You might haze them to th' top of th' cañon. They'll follow water back down as th' creek dries."

"All right, Lee. I'll boss this outfit till th' first cuttin' or you git back." He grinned as Sol snorted and questioned his ancestry.

"Sol, keep him straight an' out o' trouble." I stepped into my saddle and followed Tex's dust to the house. I heard hammer music coming from the blacksmith shed and found Red sweating over the fire while Spider pumped the bellows. Blackie was wrestling with a wheel on the sickle. They had brought their haying outfit up to get into shape for the season.

"If it don't rain soon, you may have only one cuttin' this year," I hollered over the hammer.

Red answered between blows, "Ain't . . . had th' usual . . . spring blizzard . . . yet. We'll be set . . . up after that."

"Spider, better water down that hammer user afore he falls out."

"I think you're right, Lee. Do I pour it over him or stick his head in th' bucket?"

"Either way works, just be sure that hammer ain't in reach when you do it." I turned to the house. Slipping off my boots on the kitchen stoop, I searched through the house. "Kat, Mollie, Colita, anybody here?"

"We're all here, Lee, trying to get something done without someone running through the house yelling." Mollie smiled, set a sad iron on the stove, and picked up the hot one with a rag around the handle. She was red-faced, and her hair was frazzled from wiping her eyes with her forearm. I opened the front door and let in some cool air.

"That cools the irons too quick," the girl protested.

"Don't matter how hot th' irons are if'n you're laid out on th' floor," I retorted.

"What is all this clatter about, Lee Sowell? Can't we get our work done without you makin' all this fuss?" Kat stood in the doorway, hands on hips.

"Bigfoot's back in town, Kat. Where's Colita?"

"Colita's minding her house. If you need grub, grab some air-tights out of the pantry and don't bother her. Where's your gunnysack?"

"Don't sass me, woman, time's-a-wasting." I hugged her and kissed her forehead, which always evoked her protest, "Lips are for—"

"I know, Kat, but the kid's watchin'."

Mollie snorted. "Kid my eye, Lee Sowell."

"Gotta go. We'll be back when we get back."

"More likely when the food runs out," Kat retorted to my back. "You be careful, Lee—" her admonition was cut off by the slamming of the screen door. "He left the door open again."

Just then, the kitchen door banged shut, drawn by the breeze blowing through the house. Mollie hurried and shut the front door.

"I better not hear him compare someone to a retired fire horse any time soon." Kat couldn't help smiling, and Mollie giggled as she heated both irons.

I gathered the trail gear out of the storage room and had it laid out when Tex led up the packhorse. "Git your bedroll, an' I'll load this stuff, Tex."

"Where we going, Lee?"

"Depends on where Blue heads when he finds a trail. I suspect our man has been south for the winter, and he's coming back to spend th' summer with us."

"I guess he'll prob'ly be headin' for his northern haunts."

"I'm thinkin' that too, but we'll go where Blue points us." I tied the bedrolls to either side of the pack and mounted. Kat and Mollie were standing on the porch. "I don't know when we will be back, Kat, but I need to be here when the first trail herds come through to keep them off our pastures and maybe buy a few head of feeders."

"Can we do some of that if you're not back?" she asked.

"Yes. Tell Pete and Sol to look at the drags and pick out some likely to fatten if they don't have to travel every day. We only need fifty to seventy-five head, and it may take lookin' at several herds t' get what we want. Don't pay more'n eight or ten dollars a head, and be sure t' get a bill of sale."

"We will. You two be careful."

"Yeah, we don't want t' have Juana come all the way up here to take care of you again," Mollie added as we turned toward the road.

I shuddered and they must have seen, for both women laughed.

"It wasn't all that bad, was it, Lee?" Tex grinned.

"No-o-o, Juana was really good to me, but the whole experience made me sensitive to lead.

"As soon as we know which direction Blue has taken, I want to go ahead of him and look at possible hideouts we know of in that direction. We'll have t' circle around t' stay away from any signs of his passing."

It would take Blue a little time to get started on his hunt, so we took our time getting there. As we approached the settler's dugout, we saw JD and Blue Earth a quarter mile south, both walking and JD off to one side with the horses and the kid. I stopped and surveyed the layout.

"Kinda hard t' think he went south, ain't it, Lee?"

"It is."

"Suppose Blue's on the back trail?"

"No more sign than this feller leaves, it could be, but I think Blue would discover that before long."

"It's almost like this ghost can fly, an' his trail blows away in th' wind."

"Now you're havin' dreams, Tex. This yahoo is good, but he

don't have wings." I couldn't get over my feeling that this thief had gone north from the house. It just didn't make sense that he had gone north for the winter, though I had to admit that winter on the Llano was just as fierce as here or north of here. But once below the caprock, the weather was much milder. Wintering there would be easy.

"Learn to listen to your hunches, Lee. You'll find them to be pretty reliable."

The message was so clear; I almost looked around to see if Bass Reeves was standing there. We were only half a mile south of the Cimarrón, and I could see the entry to Easley Cañon, but the butte to our east hid Castle Rock and Gallinas Cañon from us.

"Blue seems to be going up Mesquite Draw. Our thief would have some pretty rough country to cross, over to South Carrizo," Tex observed.

"It'd be pretty rough *without* a beef quarter on his shoulder, wouldn't it?"

"If th' feller's as big as we think he is, he could *throw* that beef over the mountain an' not have to lug it around." Tex chuckled.

"On the other hand, if he went north, he would have a good ford at the river and flat land to cross up to Bingaman Cañon and his hideaway. Let's look up that way, Tex."

"Up Easley and down from above like b'fore?"

"Yeah, that's a plan." I turned Hoss an' sloped for Easley Cañon.

The sun was halfway on the downside of noon when we topped out of Easley and began to work our way down the slope of Bingaman Cañon. I searched the lone butte for any activity around the hideaway, and just as I expected, there was none. Far down the cañon, two men walking rounded the point of the hill.

"We got Blue and JD comin' from th' south an' th" hideaway between us."

"Problem is, they don't know where th' place is," Tex observed.

"If they stay on th' trail, it'll lead them to it."

"But that's not likely to be a straight line. They may even end up on the north side just like us." Tex broke off a grass stem and chewed it.

"We'll find that out eventually," I said, and led the way down the hill in an arroyo out of sight of the hideaway. We rode into the open and ran for the hideaway as fast as the tired horses could run. When we got to the rocks, we left the horses and scrambled up the scree through the brush. Now caution tempered our pace, and we crept through the undergrowth, Tex about ten yards to my right.

I paused at the edge of the little clearing and looked around. There was a wisp of smoke rising from the fire pit! A portion of a beef quarter hung from a tree limb. Nothing moved. Tex looked at me for directions. I motioned him to circle around to the bluff beyond the cave opening. As quietly as I could, I approached the mouth of the shelter. I could see a blanket spread on the floor and as I got closer, I saw a foot—a small foot. The ankle was encased in an iron cuff with a small length of chain dangling from it.

With my finger to my lips, I signed to Tex that I saw one person inside. He raised his gun and waited. Step by cautious step, my toes felt their way over the ground, my eyes never leaving that person's foot. It was discolored and slightly swollen; the leg above it was that of a very dark person. Strain as I might, I saw only that one person in the gloom of the cave. I stepped into the little room and Tex moved closer. The sleeper was a small person with wild, bushy hair. I could see no facial features for the hair.

I picked up a small stone and tossed it against the rock wall. The sleeper sat up at the sound, and we realized it was a woman. Seeing me, she gave a little scream and backed up against the cave wall in a ball. She covered herself with a blanket and stared.

"Well, I'll be . . ." Tex was too surprised for words.

"Don't be afraid, ma'am, we won't hurt you," I said, putting my gun away.

She didn't seem to comprehend and sat shivering in fear. She had the large flat nose, black eyes, and large protruding lips of the Negro race. I saw that both ankles were cuffed tightly. In spite of all our attempts to talk to her, it was obvious she did not understand.

"Well, it's for sure this ain't Bigfoot," Tex declared.

"No, but she's gonna be *no* foot if those cuffs don't come off." I sat down and scooted a little closer to the woman. She drew herself into a tighter ball and whimpered. I pointed to my foot, then to hers, and motioned for her to show me her foot. It took several minutes for her to agree to let me look at one of her feet. She extended one, and with more persuasion, let me touch her. The cuffs had been branded on and the resulting burns on her ankles had left red and angry-looking scars.

Tex cursed softly. Here was a Texas Southerner, maybe for the first time recognizing that the suffering of a black person was a human emotion—maybe, just maybe—she was mortal flesh with a soul, in his eyes.

"May not be so hard after all, Tex, this brad is brass. A hacksaw or file will go right through it. There's a file in my horseshoe kit. I don't think I have a saw."

The woman gave a little cry and withdrew her foot. We turned to see Blue Earth standing in the entryway.

"Blue, where is JD?" I asked.

"Right here, Lee." He stepped up beside Blue Earth.

"Run back to the packhorse and dig out my horseshoe kit. I

need the file in it and a hacksaw if there is one." He turned and hurried off.

Tex got up and followed. "Feller's gonna git hisself kilt without some protection," he muttered.

Blue squatted beside me, studying the woman. "Buffalo woman not ghost." He grinned.

I motioned for the girl's foot. She extended it tentatively because of Blue. No telling what she thought of him, but she was definitely scared.

Blue stared at the iron cuffs and chain.

"No spirit, but once someone's prisoner, Blue."

In a few minutes, the two men returned, JD with the file, a pair of pliers, and Vermont's Original Bag Balm from the kit; and Tex with his white shirt and a spare work shirt. The woman did not seem uncomfortable that she was bare above the waist, but she accepted the warm shirt and put it on. The way she fumbled with the buttons showed that she was not familiar with their use. Tex showed her how to button the shirt by unbuttoning his shirt and fastening it back a time or two.

"White one's for bandages, Lee."

"Hold off rippin' it up until we see if we need them." I took the file and motioned to the girl what I was going to do. She nodded tentatively, but her leg tensed a time or two like she was about to pull it back. I ran my fingernail up her sole, and she didn't flinch. "No feeling in that foot," I murmured.

JD clamped the pliers on the end of the pin to keep it from turning, and I began filing with the triangular file. It was slow going, and in spite of our care, the cuff rubbed and her ankle bled some. A half hour later, the pin was cut in two, and we carefully opened the cuff. The return of circulation must have been painful, for the girl cried. Rubbing her foot gently seemed to help. She could eventually wiggle her toes, but even that was somewhat painful.

The cuff on the other ankle was off in another half hour, and we applied the balm to both ankles. Tex was at the fire boiling meat into a broth. Blue had disappeared and returned with a handful of several plants. He stripped leaves from them and dropped them into the broth. When the root from another plant was added, he sat back and said, "Good medicine."

Meanwhile, JD and I worked with the girl's feet, massaging lightly and flexing ankles and toes. At first it was painful to the girl, but as we worked, she relaxed more and more.

"Look at the soles of her feet, Lee," JD said.

"They're soft as a baby's, aren't they?"

"It's for sure she hasn't walked on them for a while. She was carried here."

"And not on horseback, as much as we can tell."

JD sat back and looked at the girl. "Doesn't speak a language we know, chains on her legs, but not her arms, has lived where the women go bare atop. She's a mystery, Lee."

"Blue, come here and see if this woman can speak any of the Indian languages you know," I murmured.

Blue Earth squatted before the girl and spoke several languages with no response. Then he stumbled over a few words in another language, and the girl nodded and smiled and replied with a long speech.

"What language is that, Blue?" I asked.

"Seminole. I do not know it much."

"So she's a Black Seminole, probably from Indian Territory down by the Red River," I guessed.

Blue struggled with a few words, and the girl vigorously shook her head and made another long speech. Blue shrugged, "I not know much she say except she come from Mexico where she was slave."

"But she doesn't know Spanish." I was puzzled by that.

"Not need Spanish if she work in mines," Blue explained.

"Women work in the mines?" Tex asked. He had a steaming cup of beef broth and handed it to the girl. She took it in both hands and drank eagerly as it cooled.

"Live in mines," Blue said.

"And someone *carried* her all the way up here?" JD wondered.

"Not likely all the way, or they would have been caught by the soldiers sent to catch them," Tex said. "They had to start out on horses."

"Well he's carryin' her around now, an' I wouldn't want t' meet up with this feller when his dander was up," avowed JD.

"I don't think she's a prisoner. It would be too much trouble to keep someone a prisoner all this time and distance. Bigfoot must care for her a whole lot," I said.

"I wouldn't want to take her away from here and have that feller follow me. Could be tellin' on your health," Tex observed.

"Yup, I don't see her packin' her bags," JD said.

Blue stumbled through some more words with the girl, who shrugged her shoulders, palms up. "She not know where he go," he said.

"And she 'not know' when he comes back, either," I said. "You know, the last time anyone got near these two, a bunch of 'em died. I think we might be in the same danger."

"Just how do you propose to git out of this, Lee?" Tex was back from refilling the woman's cup.

"We could run like scalded cats."

"You gotta do better than that, Lee," JD scolded.

It was a problem we had never thought about. We had come here thinking we might trap our ghost in this cave. Instead, we found this woman that our quarry valued so much, he had carried her all over the country. Now, we could be trapped here with our stalker out there somewhere, waiting for his chance to get us.

"There's one thing sure about this place," Tex said. "I'll never close my eyes so long as I'm here."

"I chuckled. "Wouldn't pay, would it?"

"We should either leave before dark or light a fire and crawl in th' back of that cave with all the weapons we got," Tex said.

"Maybe we should do both," I said.

"O-o-oh no, here it comes," JD groaned.

I waited, letting them squirm a little.

"Well, take all afternoon, Lee, but you'll be talkin' to th' breeze of me leavin' afore sundown," Tex growled.

"Well then, here's what we'll do. You three leave, and I'll stay here with the girl. Take these cuffs with you. If Bigfoot shows up, show them to him. Maybe he'll not harm you—"

"An' maybe he'll not harm you sittin' here with his girl?" Tex asked. "That ain't gonna work, Lee. We done seen what he does when men are just *near* her. What you think he's gonna do when he finds you *with* her?"

"You got a better idea?"

"Yeah," JD put in. "*All* of us just leave. Let this gal talk to her man an' convince him we mean no harm. Maybe he will show up somewhere lookin' for us—without blood in his eye."

"You stay here, some-ones die," Blue added.

"Well that gets us back to runnin' like scalded cats," I said.

"I'm all for it," Tex declared. He began gathering up things and banking the fire to last.

"Blue, tell the girl we are leaving, that we are friends and want them both to come to Sheep Pen. We'll give them food and clothing, and they won't have to steal it anywhere else."

There followed a long, broken conversation between Indian and slave. Blue drew a map in the sand for the girl to see. She nodded and seemed to understand what we wanted.

"All right," I said. "We're gonna walk outta here two-by-two and get our horses and leave. Bigfoot may or may not be around. If we run into him, show him the cuffs. That may stave him off.

If not, we may have to kill him. One bullet ain't likely to stop him, so be ready."

We left without attempting to be quiet about it and got to our horses without incident. At Florence, we put out the word about the ghost, then returned to the ranch.

Some time later, I had need of a file and went through my horseshoe kit bag without finding it.

"JD, have you seen my rattail file?" I hollered.

"Look in th' horseshoe bag," he shouted back.

"I did, an' it ain't there."

"You had it last when we cut those cuffs off Littlefoot."

"I looked for it and it wasn't there. You or Tex must have picked it up."

"I didn't pick it up," he returned.

"I didn't either," Tex agreed from the bunkhouse roof where he was nailing down loose shingles.

I dumped the bag out on the porch, "I don't see those pliers, either."

"Ha!" Tex laughed. "That Littlefoot stole 'em both!"

Chapter 25
Billy Hill and the Vigilantes

Blue Earth and family packed up and left early one morning, returning to the reservation around Rainy Mountain. His visit was the first of many; his "tribe" growing almost yearly. They had four children, from nine years to papoose in carrying board. The in-laws came until age prevented them from traveling.

There wasn't any waiting around for our ghost to show up. The hay crew disappeared for the summer, Rockin' R Bill with them. JD, Tex, and I were the only ones left for the spring roundup. Tine Arnold came by just in time to help. Folks said he had been around the valley forever, seeming to have been there before anyone else showed up. Some folks said he rode the chuck line, but he always paid his way in some way or other. With us that time, he worked hard at the branding, and when day was done, he could cook the best of all of us.

Tine was a man happy with his freedom; never owned more than his little bay horse could carry, and he was contented with that. He could fix anything mechanical and was the best fence-builder in the country. He would just show up one day, and he might stay the night or a few weeks, so long as he felt useful. Then one day he would be gone, just like he came. He stayed that way as long as he had his health, contented with life, and his freedom, his most treasured possession.

We stayed at the line shack, which was just as well for me, 'cause I would be staying in the bunkhouse or taking a bath every night at the house. Toward the end, we went in Saturday nights, rode right on by the house to the river, and washed. We rested up Sundays, gathered supplies, and went back to the line shack Sunday night.

Still not wanting to butcher one of our own beeves, we had been relying on venison and antelope for our meat. When those wild critters left the area, it took too much time to hunt them. Our best opportunity for fresh meat was rabbit. We worked on the cottontail population pretty heavy there at the last.

"I've eaten so much rabbit, I'm gittin' afraid o' dogs," JD complained one evening.

"Two more days an' we'll be finished till fall," Tex opined.

"Make it three. We got the manure wagon loaded an' another load on th' ground," I said.

"Never heered o' pickin' up droppin's afore they was dried 'nough t' burn," Tine said.

"Did you notice those patches of greener grass comin' up th' valley, Tine?"

"I shore did, Lee, an' those cows did too."

"Those are places we spread manure last fall."

"Ya don't say . . . maybe somethin' other folks might need t' consider." He rubbed his chin in thought.

"What's next, Lee?" Tex was always eager to get on to the next project.

"I have a lot of work around the ranch house, and you two need to be doing work on your claims t' prove up."

"Pitchin' manure or plowin'. Can't decide which I love th' most," JD said.

"T'ain't right, bustin' up sod t' plant stuff that ain't gonna grow," Tine said.

"You wouldn't question th' wisdom of some fat-assed senator or gover'ment man sittin' up there in Washington, *D.C.*, would you?" JD asked.

"Them folks don't need a pitchfork t' throw manure." Tine's

opinion matched the opinions of most men on the range.

The pounding of hooves came from down the valley. We looked up to see a man running toward us as fast as his winded horse could go. "Looks like Billy Hill's in trouble again." Tine chuckled. We could see a cloud of dust rising from eight or ten horses coming our way a half-mile behind Billy.

The boy slid to a stop where our horses were tied and grabbed his rifle out of its boot. He turned to face three .45's pointed at him. "Whoa, there, boys. I ain't atter you, but I gotta have fresh horseflesh. Mine's fagged out. I'm borryin' this'n; bring it back in a few days." He grabbed the reins of Tex's horse, which happened to be nearest.

"Hey, that's *my* horse," Tex yelled.

"Bring him back to th' dugout when I can, Tex. You can have mine. He's a better horse than this'n—when he's rested." He turned and spurred on up the cañon.

Not three minutes later, the vigilantes rode into the yard. The leader waved his posse on to the chase and surveyed us with a critical eye, "I see he has *stolen* another horse," he said, sarcasm dripping from his mouth.

I boiled inside. This man knew I was a U.S. marshal, but didn't hesitate to cast doubt on our honesty.

"Naw, sir," Tex drawled. "I insisted he take my horse b'fore he rode his'n t' death."

The man leaned to pick up the reins of the panting horse. "I'll take this horse to bring that feller's body back on."

He froze when he heard the sound of three guns cocking. "That's my horse now, mister, an' he's stayin' here." Tex held his gun in his left hand and reached for the horse's reins, jerking them out of the vigilante's hand.

"Looks like you're abetting a horse thief, feller. Consider yourself under arrest, and don't leave before we get back."

That was more than I could stand. "You have no authority to

arrest anyone, much less a U.S. marshal's sworn posse member. I'll remind you of two things: You are in the U.S. Territory of New Mexico. And you are trespassing on private property. Go get your men and get out of this cañon—without any prisoners. If that man is harmed in any way, I'll arrest you and everyone else who had a part in this. It's a long ways to Santa Fe—might take all summer to see the court there, an' I hear that *federal* judge has special feelings for vigilantes who take the law into their own hands."

The man sat there and glared. He sure had gall. "Depity—"

"So you know I'm a U.S. deputy marshal, and cast doubt on me and my posse's honesty?" I took a step or two toward the man.

"It's not that I—"

"Shut up. Go get your men out of here before I get *really* mad." I slapped his horse with the rope I held in my hand, the end slapping the man's leg with a satisfying pop. The horse jumped and trotted on up the hill. Gunshots echoed from the cañon walls.

"Tine, let Tex borrow your horse, I don't want you exposin' yourself to this mess."

"Never shied from trouble, Lee."

"I know that, but the way you travel around here, you don't want to make more enemies than you have to. We can take care of this so you won't expose your shoulder blades to lead poisonin' some day. Take care of Billy's horse, and we will be back soon."

Tine could see the logic of what I said and reluctantly gave in. The three of us loped up the hill. There were no more shots echoing down.

The vigilantes were scattered among the rocks at the base of the hillside. One horse lay dead. A few splatters of blood indicated his rider had not gotten by unscathed. I motioned for

Tex to cover the left flank of the crowd and for JD to go to the right side of the men.

"Don't hesitate to shoot any man who resists, and keep us out of your line of fire." I rode through the vigilantes and up the hill a ways.

"Don't come past that red boulder, Lee, I promised to shoot anyone who did," Hill shouted from somewhere among the rocks above.

"Consider yourself under *federal* arrest, Billy Hill, and stay where you are," I ordered. I turned to the men hiding among the rocks before me. "Men, I am a United States deputy marshal, as most of you already know. Billy Hill is now my prisoner, and it is a federal offense for you to harm him while in my custody. Your president has been instructed to remove you from this place and from private property you have trespassed upon.

"Stand down. I have instructed my deputies to shoot any man who raises his gun. I have arrested Billy Hill, and he will answer to the federal judge in Denver or Santa Fe if he has committed any crimes. You must leave *now.*"

One by one, the men began to rise, their pistols holstered, their rifles pointing to the ground. One man stood with help, his leg tied off above his bloody pant leg.

"One of you men bring a horse up for that man. Someone strip the gear off that dead horse, and *all* of you skedaddle down the cañon, back to where you belong. There's a doctor at Florence."

Tex rode a couple of hundred yards behind the departing group. JD and I watched them disappear around a bend in the cañon wall. Hill came down, leading his borrowed horse.

"What's this all about, Billy?" I asked.

"I was sittin' by th' river drinkin' my breakfast coffee when these fellers rode up. They was lookin' for some horse thief named Smith. Said I looked a lot like him. *El Presidente* sent men to find a tall tree and a man to escort me to my horse. Somehow, my escort ran into my gun barrel and fell out. I fired a few shots at the bunch to scatter them and left my coffee simmering on the fire for them. They chased me all the way up here. I couldn't get on up the mountain without exposin' Tex's horse to lead poisonin'." He grinned at us. "Either one of you got water, I'm dry."

JD tossed him a canteen, and he drained it.

"Mount up, Hill, and come with us. We'll get to the bottom of this." We didn't take his gun or put manacles on him. He wasn't going to run away from us.

"Sorry, ol' hoss," he muttered when we rode past the dead horse.

"Where were you when those men arrested you, Billy?"

Billy lifted the brim of his hat with his thumb and forefinger and scratched his head with the three free fingers. "Up by the river north of Florence, Lee."

"My gosh, Billy. A man in your business? How can you sleep that close to tall cottonwoods?" JD asked.

Billy chuckled. "Better a tree limb than a wagon tongue or telegraph pole. Don't want t' be laid to rest with splinters in my ass."

"Did you have horses with you?" I asked.

"Jist me an' ol' Solomon there." He nodded toward his horse. Tine had stripped his saddle off and was rubbing him down with the blanket. "Much obliged, Tine." He eyed the blanket and the amount of hair it was picking up, thinking about the next time he had to sleep under it.

I eyed the boy closely. "Not any more horses?"

"Nary a one, Lee—look, can I hep it if horses love me an' want t' foller me ever'where I go?"

"I know. It's a blessing and a curse, Billy."

"Shore is." Tine chuckled. "All I gits follerin' me is graybacks an' bedbugs."

"They's places, Tine, bringin' 'em with you would git you hung," Tex said. He was back from his escort duty and gave me a nod to say everything was in order.

"You'll swear to me that you were in No Man's Land and that you only had ol' Solomon with you?" I asked Billy.

"I swear, Lee. Horse *thieves* don't lie like horse *traders* do—and I don't have my horse-tradin' hat on."

"I don't have any reason to hold you under those conditions. So, Billy Hill, I hereby release you from arrest. Now, go and sin no more."

"Thank you, Lee. You saved my bacon an' I appreciate that. Guess ol' Sol an' me'll go see what's on t'other side o' Black Mesa." He saddled the horse and led him to water, then rode up the cañon.

Tine shook his head. "A good boy pushed over on th' Owl Hoot Trail. He an' his brother got into some trouble over east, an' a posse come after 'em. His brother got killed, and Billy killed every man in the posse. Buried his brother an' left th' rest to th' wolves. He's been workin' for John Brite an' layin' low."

"It's a lucky man who don't get followed by his trouble," I said. We watched the rider climb the mountain. When he got to the top, over two miles away, he waved his hat and disappeared over the rim.

"He goes north, we're liable to see him again—if th' vigilantes don't git to him first," said Tex.

"O-oh, mebbe not," Tine said. "That mesa's mostly flat an' twenty mile long. If you knows which arroyos t' find, it's th' outlet on th' world."

"If I ever need t' go into unknown country 'round here, Tine, I'm lookin' you up fer a guide." I turned Hoss and we all rode for the house.

Chapter 26
An Unexpected Visitation

We were eating Sunday dinner, just Kat and me, when she put her hand over mine and gave it a squeeze. "Honey, we're going to Mary Leslie's tomorrow with Agitha Cook and her children so they can play with the Leslie children. Will you and the boys get the buggy ready for us?"

Well, that certainly wasn't what I had in mind for a Sunday afternoon alone with my wife, but how could I say no? We spent the afternoon getting the buggy cleaned and greased and the mules curried and spotless for the trip. Tine spent his time oiling the harness. We left the shining buggy covered by a sheet, parked in the shed, ready to go.

Kat threw kisses to the boys as they rode out, and I trotted over to collect my kiss in person.

"Thank you so much for getting us ready to go, Lee."

"You're welcome, lady. I'll collect my pay later. I'm just like the devil says: 'Play now and you can pay me later,' only I work now, an' we can play later."

"Mañana, dear. Always *mañana,"* she whispered.

"Be careful, lady. I can make *mañana 'hoy en dia.'* "

She slapped Hoss, and he loped out of the yard.

Morning came early at the ranch house and with much astir: Colita putting together a basket of food for the all-day ride; Mollie dressing in one room and Kat in another.

"Mollie, I can't find my hairbrush."

"Look in your top bureau drawer. Colita, don't forget the salt."

"*Sí,* señorita, *sí, sí,* iss here."

"Kat, can you button my dress?"

"*Sí,* señorita, *sí, sí.*" Kat laughed and buttoned. "Have you packed everything you will need?"

"All but my sanity." Mollie sighed. "I can't find my shoes."

"Here by thee stove, where you polish them," Colita called.

Gradually, "astir" became semi-calm. Breakfast was eaten with only minor fuss, and the three women emerged on the porch to see the coach ready and waiting. There was a flurry of loading and settling; Mollie took the reins and clucked Pet and Tobe into action.

"*Vaya con Dios,*" Colita blessed from the porch.

"*Gracias, Dios.*" Tomas thanked him under his breath as he watched the ladies leave in a swirl of dust, only to slump as he saw the buggy make a wide turn in the field and return to the yard. Colita stood on the porch, hands on hips.

"Colita, I forgot my shawl," Kat said. "It's on the bed—I think."

After a few moments, Colita returned, saying as she crossed the living room, "Iss not on bed, señora . . . a-a-ah, eet iss here by the door." She hurried down the steps and handed it to Mollie, who passed it on to Kat.

"Thank you, Colita. We'll not stop again, even if one of us falls out of the buggy," Kat promised as the mules passed through the yard gate.

Colita looked at Tomas peeking out of the barn. "*Gracias a Dios,*" she said with a shrug of her shoulders, palms up. Tomas grinned and turned to his chores.

As the women drove east, the sun peeked over 101 Hill, a big red ball. "Red sky at morning—"

"Don't even mention it," Kat interrupted.

Three Cook children were in the yard, ready to go. They came bouncing across the yard before Mollie had stopped the buggy, and would have climbed over the tailgate right onto the picnic basket if Kat hadn't hollered at them. One by one they climbed the rear wheels and tumbled into the back seat, jostling for the best place. Agitha appeared at the door, a squalling Cook draped over one forearm and a large bag in the other hand. She struggled to shut the door. After three tries, she gave up and hurried to the buggy. She installed the toddler in the back seat with promises to all four of dire circumstances for misbehavior, and stowed her bag safely in the back. Mollie trotted to the house and closed the door, and they were soon on their way east to Easley Cañon.

Far to the west, a little white cloud appeared over Sierra Grande Mountain, and blew away. In a bit, another little cloud appeared above the mountain. This time it stayed. It stayed, and as the sun-warmed air rose up the sides of Sierra Grande, the little cloud grew. By midmorning it was large enough to cast a shadow across the western side of the mountain and plains.

On the backside of the cloud, it began to rain. At first the drops were large and very cold. Some were slushy when they hit. Gradually the rain spread across the entire bottom of the cloud.

The ladies and children had stopped to picnic on the banks of South Carrizo Creek, where they enjoyed wading in the cool water. They noticed the cloud to the west, but it was far away and posed no immediate threat.

"It would be nice to get a good rain and settle this dust," Aggie said.

"Yes, Lord, but let it rain tonight after we've gotten to shelter," Mollie prayed.

"I agree, Mollie. This buggy has no side curtains, and we'd all get soaked," Kat observed.

Some minor emergency at the creek drew their attention back to earth. The storm loosed its hold on the mountain and drifted east. The travelers didn't think more of the cloud, until well on their way; they were thankful to drive in its cooling shade.

A huge drop of icy cold rain struck Pet's rump. He flinched, then enjoyed the cold moisture running down his backsides. More drops fell, thumping on the buggy's canvas top. Sleeping children stirred as drops of cold rain found their heads and shoulders.

Kat looked behind. "O-o-o-oh no, here it comes. Stop, Mollie, and let's get out the quilts." It only took a moment to fluff out a quilt and spread it from the buggy's canvas top to the tailgate to protect children and cargo. As they were settling in their seat, a chunk of ice struck Tobe on the back. He flinched as if he'd been stung by a horsefly.

"Hail," Aggie exclaimed. "We have to cover the mules or they will bolt." She jumped out the right side of the buggy, removing the blanket from her shoulders and slinging it over Tobe. The mule shook his head vigorously, trying to dislodge the blanket from his ears. Agitha pulled the blanket back and uncovered the mule's head.

In the meantime, Kat had covered Pet with her blanket, while Mollie tried to huddle under the scant canvas top. The women drove on through the hail. Lightning struck a hill nearby, and the mules swerved into a cedar thicket, where they gained some shelter. Mollie slapped reins and the mules pulled the buggy into the shelter of the trees also.

The hail tapered off and the rain came in earnest, so heavy the women were forced to pull their long skirts from under them and over their heads to breathe. The youngest Cook child squalled and scrambled over the seat into his mother's lap. The sodden quilt fell on the remaining children, and they huddled under it. It was a rain to rival Noah's deluge. The canvas sagged under a pool of water that dripped on everyone. Soaked to the skin, the women wilted.

Gradually, the cloud died, its huge anvil spreading over half the sky, its rumbles no longer fearsome. Its soft drenching rain fell on the travelers stuck in a cedar thicket.

"The only way out of this is to back the mules up, Mollie." Kat stood at the heads of the mules and coaxed them backwards one step at a time. When they were almost out of the trees, Tobe, seeing open space to his right, turned, and in spite of instructions otherwise, pulled the buggy over the smaller trees at the edge of the thicket. The buggy tilted on two wheels, dumping the pond in the canvas top on passengers, front and back.

Kat hurried to the waiting buggy, noticing the wheels were sinking into the mud. "We have to be careful, Mollie, or we'll be stuck."

For a while, they drove beside the tracks, avoiding the deeper mud where the road had stirred it. At a narrow place between rocks, they were forced into the road. Before they could get back to firmer ground, the buggy sank hub-deep in the mud, the two mules unable to pull it through. Passengers disembarked into ankle-deep muck, with three children, then four, thrilled at the rare sensation of mud squeezing between toes. Three women, hampered by long, sodden dresses, struggled to push the buggy out of the mud's clutches. It was no use. Pet and Tobe stood exhausted, sunk fetlock-deep.

"It's no use, ladies, this buggy won't budge." Kat looked around in the gathering gloom, "We can't stay here like this. We'll freeze by morning."

"I see a light over there." Mollie pointed to a light far across the plain.

"It must be a homesteader's place," Aggie said. "We can walk over there and find shelter."

"If I'm going to walk that far, I am not dragging these petticoats with me," Kat declared. In a trice, three women had shed their many underskirts.

Agitha smiled. "This is much better. I feel forty pounds lighter."

Mollie giggled. "I feel naked."

They unhitched the mules, and with the three youngest astraddle Pet, they slogged toward that light—until the eldest son, Jackson, stepped on a prickly pear leaf.

"E-e-e yow," he cried and sat down in the mud, holding up his foot, thereby revealing a whole leaf impaled on it. The softly falling rain was not adequate to wash the mud off the foot and reveal the remaining spines.

"He'll have to ride to where we can wash that foot and see the spines," Mollie said.

A fourth rider was too far back on the mule's rounded rump, making the possibility of sliding off almost sure. The only choice was to carry the young Cook, who squalled at being removed from the mule's back. A firm hand applied forcefully to his posterior convinced him of the wisdom of riding in his mother's arms while he wiped his feet clean on her skirt.

Kat soon relieved the tired mother of her burden, and the child finished cleaning his feet. "Is that light moving away from us?" Kat asked.

"Things are always farther away than they look out here," Mollie replied. "What looks like a mile may be three, even more in this rain."

They slogged on and on. When they were near enough, they could tell that the light was a lantern high on a pole above what appeared to be a substantial house. As was the general custom on the plains, the homesteader had raised the light to signal travelers in need of shelter or aid. Still, the light was a mile away.

On they trudged, gaining sticky mud on feet and skirts. Mollie handed Tobe's lead to Kat and took the toddler on her back; the little boy, enjoying his own "horse," spurred poor Mollie with his heels.

"Who do you think lives there, Aggie?" Kat asked.

"I'm not sure, but I think it might be Jim Dacy's place. He's off working on the Fort Worth and Denver Railroad."

The darkness was complete and the little group stumbled on, meeting and detouring around cacti and bushes. If not for the light, they would have been hopelessly lost.

They were within a hundred yards of the house when a mule nickered off to their left. Tobe's ears shot forward and he stopped. "Come on, Tobe, don't get stubborn now." Kat pulled, and Tobe reluctantly followed. Suddenly, Kat stepped off a steep bank and plunged into water over her head. Tobe stopped at the edge of the bank as Kat came to the top of the water, sputtering and coughing.

"Kat, where are you?" Mollie cried. Little Cook lost his mount and sat in the mud, squalling.

"I fell into the well. Get Tobe to back up and pull me out."

"You still have the rope?"

"Yes, yes. Pull me out!"

Groping in the dark, Mollie ran smack into the side of Tobe, and finding his head, was in the process of getting him to walk backwards when the bank she stood on crumbled, and she fell into the water, her skirt billowing up over her head. Alarmed, Tobe backed up and turned to retreat, pulling Kat into the sputtering Mollie, who grabbed the lead. The mule pulled both women out of the hole and across the muddy ground, with Kat hollering, "Whoa, Tobe. Whoa, Tobe," until he finally stopped.

The two women sat up, dripping, cold and confused. "What

was that hole?" Kat asked.

"I don't know, but this is the Dacy place for sure." Aggie's voice came through the darkness.

A voice hailed from the house, "Who's there?"

"It's Agitha Cook and friends, Mrs. Dacy. Please bring us a light."

In a moment, a girl emerged from the house holding a lantern high. A woman lugging a heavy shotgun followed.

"Don't come any closer. You might fall into the pit," Johanna Dacy warned as she approached.

"You're too damned late," Kat muttered under her breath.

Mollie coughed and scooped her hair off her face. She started to rise, felt a tug from the skirt she was standing on, and fell to her knees. She had to turn and sit down to untangle her feet.

Johanna gasped as the lantern light illuminated the bedraggled, muddy visitors. "Oh my stars, we have to get you out of this right now. Come around the pit this way," said Bridget Dacy, James's wife. She led the tribe to the front porch and turned. "Ye can put the mules in the garden with our stock. It's the only thing fenced on the place."

Johanna took Pet's lead when the kids had hopped down, Jackson balancing on his good foot, and led the way to the garden gate. "The hail ruined the garden and the rain filled the pit, so we put the stock here for the night," she explained to Mollie. They removed the harnesses and shooed the mules into the pen.

Kat and Agitha had not been idle in Johanna and Mollie's absence. When they returned, four stripped waifs were standing in the house while the two women on the porch struggled to free themselves from the remnants of their dresses. Bridget hurried into the house and returned with three blankets.

"I think we can find clothes to dress you in after you are in the house," she said.

Three once-nice dresses dripped muddy water from the edge of the porch onto six balls of mud that had once been shoes. The blanket-wrapped women stepped into the warmth of the house.

There followed a time of washing children and pulling cactus needles from feet and legs before they were tucked into pallets laid on a bedroom floor, and the women could turn their attention to their own needs. The women finally got to bed after midnight. Lucy, the Dacys' oldest daughter, had gone to cook for her father and older brothers while they built up roadbed for the FW&D railroad, so Mollie took Lucy's place beside Johanna.

Sunrise found Kat sipping coffee and looking out the kitchen window at the large pond she had found in the night.

"That's Jim's idea of a barn for his mules," Bridget explained. "The Indians won't see them down there. When it's finished, he will roof it so there will be no danger of people stumbling into it in the dark."

Kat smiled, though it was too soon after the event for her to find much humor in it. "I suppose it was good it was filled with water to cushion our falls."

"O-o-oh, but it must have been icy, with all that hail falling in it," Bridget sympathized.

The three younger Dacys awoke to find that four playmates had appeared in the night. It was hard to corral them all for breakfast.

The women were dismayed at the pile of dirty clothes on the porch. Before long, a fire crackled under the wash pot and washday began.

Mary Leslie paced the floor from window to door to window. "They should have been here hours ago, Cap."

"I'm sure they saw the cloud comin' an' holed up somewhere.

Probably didn't get any farther than Cook's. First light, I'll ride thataway an' see where they are." He eyed the pie safe, knowing the goodness that lay within.

Mary sighed. "Oh all right, Cap. One piece of cake, but I'm not cutting any pies until we know where they are and safe."

They sat at the table while Cap savored his slice of yellow layer cake with butter crème icing. "M-m-m-m, Mary, I shore married th' right gal when it comes t' bakin' cakes." He finished and carried the cake back to the safe. "O-ops." He looked at the icing on his finger he'd "accidentally" swiped through the bottom fringe of icing on the cake.

"Cap Leslie, I knew I should have never let you close to that safe."

Cap sucked icing off his finger to hide his grin. "Best we get t' bed so I can get an early start in th' mornin'."

Mary spent a restless night, listening every time the dogs barked, and getting up twice to look and listen. She had the coffee on by four o'clock. Cap caught up his horse and left him at the hitching post by the stoop while the rancher ate his breakfast. Taking a biscuit for himself and one for the horse, he kissed Mary and rode down the track to town.

The approaching storm had chased the boys out of Sheep Pen Cañon before noon, and they sat on the front porch watching the hail and rain. Tex had caught a pan full of hailstones, and they had ice in Colita's tea for a change.

"Reckon th' girls didn't git any farther than Cook's when they saw this a-comin'." JD had to raise his voice to be heard over the drum of the rain.

"That buggy . . . oughta have side . . . curtains," Tex observed between crunches on his ice.

"Side curtains wouldn't do any good in this rain," Lee said. "Those women are gonna need fresh mules t' pull them through that mud. We'll take another span of mules to them in th' morning, wherever they got to."

Colita, knowing the time the ladies left and how preoccupied they would be with children and gabbing, put coffee on the stove before four and made enough noise to rouse Lee. He had gone to bed in his own bed without the mandatory bath and slept well. The housekeeper had sent Tomas to the bunkhouse, and two sleepy vaqueros sipped coffee and waited for the biscuits and gravy. "Cain't no one complain 'bout gittin' up early when Colita's got biscuits an' gravy waitin'," Tex said.

Colita smiled. "*Gracias,* Tex."

It took all three vaqueros to keep two sleek mules lined up with the rising sun. Finally, loops settled over rambunctious necks and they were led. Old man Hubbard was sweeping mud off the front walk when they passed through Florence.

"Did you notice what time our buggy drove through town?" Lee asked in passing.

"Tol'able early, I'd say. They didn't even stop to see the new calico I got in last week," the merchant replied.

No one was home at Cook's, and it was an hour past South Carrizo Creek when they saw the buggy hub deep in the trail. Cap Leslie was sitting atop a boulder watching his horse graze. "Saw you comin' when I rode up an' decided t' wait on followin' th' folks' trail in th' off chance that might be you," he said.

"Where'd they go, you reckon?" Lee asked. There still wasn't need for alarm, but his stomach tightened a little.

Cap pointed with his chin, "Dacys always have their yard light out, an' signs point thataway." He pointed to a pile of clothes in the buggy. "Looks like they lightened their load first." He chuckled.

The "clothes" were all petticoats. "I don't know why they wear that stuff in th' first place," Lee said.

"If women wore pants, they could ride clothespin style," Tex said.

"As likely t' happen as snow in August," JD asserted.

Lee looked in the buggy. "I don't see harness anywhere."

"Must have left them on th' mules." Tex looked under the pile of clothes to no avail.

Lee untied the short-handled shovel from his saddle, and the four men dug the wheels out as best they could. Cap and Tex tied ropes to the front of the wagon while JD and Lee lifted and pushed the back of the buggy. Slowly, it climbed up to within three inches of the mud surface.

"That's as good as it's gonna git today," Cap allowed.

The men tied the tongue up over the buggy and, with ropes from saddles to buggy axle, pulled toward Dacy's place. We left the buggy a quarter mile from the house. A passel of women and kids watched our progress, and we breathed a lot easier when we recognized who they were. At least they were all on their feet.

Tex jogged up beside JD. "I see Johanna, but looks like Lucy's gone with her pa agin."

"I see Nellie and that kid Katie. You better shy away from Johanna. Henry Labrier almost got you last time you tangled. He's liable t' whip you next time he catches you sparkin' his girl."

"That'll never happen, JD, an' you know it. I got th' inside track on that girl. Henry's just jealous."

"Wouldn't surprise me if he had his brand on her b'fore you even got your iron hot."

"No way." Tex rode up to the high end of the porch, and the Dacy girls clustered around him. Looking up at Johanna, he said, "I have something of yours, Jo. You forgot to get it at the Goodson party." He reached into his shirt pocket and brought out a small handkerchief.

"Why, Tex, that party was three weeks ago. Have you been carrying this all that time?" She leaned over and reached out to take the handkerchief. It only took a little nudge from Katie to propel Johanna off the porch and into Tex's arms.

"O-o-oh, oh," she cried, falling against the surprised Tex and his horse. Tex had his hands full, holding the girl with one arm and trying to control his horse with the other. Johanna grasped Tex and held on for dear life. Not only was there danger of being trampled by the frightened horse if she fell, but there was all that mud to consider.

JD grabbed the horse's bridle and held his head close to calm him. Tex kicked his left foot free of the stirrup and asked the girl, "Can you get your foot in the stirrup, Jo?"

The girl struggled and raised her foot to find the stirrup. She got her toe into the stirrup, but could go no further because her skirt was over her toe. She had to withdraw her foot and pull her skirt over her shoe to reinsert it into the stirrup, all the while clinging to Tex. Now she stood on one foot, relieving the pressure on Tex, but still clinging tightly to him.

"Do you want to get up behind me, Jo?" the vaquero asked.

"And ride astrad . . . clothespin?" The girl was shocked at the idea. "I'll ride to the steps right here."

"Well, hang on tight, an' I'll try t' git you there in one piece with no mud." The girl clung to him. It seemed Tex took a little wider circle than necessary to get the horse lined up just right so Johanna could step on the steps without getting into the mud.

"That Katie is really gonna get it when I get back," she hissed in Tex's ear. Her face was crimson. If the whole world hadn't been looking on, she would have enjoyed Tex's embrace much more.

"She really should," Tex agreed. He was pretty sure he had a two-bit piece in his pocket.

Johanna climbed the steps, still red-faced, while the ladies smiled, knowing the event had not been all *that* unpleasant for the girl. In fact, it evoked sweet memories of days gone by when a boy's first embrace was so exciting. Katie was nowhere in sight; she seemed overly shy the rest of the day. Nellie couldn't suppress a giggle and got her toes stepped on by her older sister.

"Is everyone all right?" Lee asked Kat.

"We're just fine—now," Kat replied.

"All of you look nice and fresh and clean."

"We should," Mollie said. "We had a shower, and Kat and I had *two* baths when we got here—one out there." She pointed to the pit and shuddered, seeing things floating in the water she would rather not have seen.

"Sure as Jamie gets home, he'll be buildin' a fence around that . . . that *hole,*" Bridget vowed. "The shame of it all, that it hasn't been built a'ready. Oh, my stars, get down, gen'lemen, get down an' come in. Here it is near noon, an' not a thing on th' stove." She hurried into the house, calling orders to various children as she went.

The rest of the women followed, Kat directing, "Leave your boots on the steps, *gentlemen.*"

JD pulled his boots off, looked at his socks, and dug a clean pair out of his hip pocket.

"Wish I had thought of that," Tex muttered, looking at his bare toe sticking through the end of his sock.

Nellie came through the door with a big coffee pot, and Katie followed with four cups. When she handed Tex his cup, he squeezed her hand and whispered, "Thanks, Katie." He winked and she found a quarter-dollar in her hand. The girl grinned and a pink blush rose from her collar. "She's gonna kill me," she whispered.

"Not if I can help it," he replied.

Dinner was an Irish treat with corned beef and cabbage, and

fried potatoes with the skin on, cut in long crescents like a slice of watermelon. For the men, there was a cup of mead, brewed right there on the farm.

Chapter 27
Fire

Cap Leslie leaned back in his chair. "That was a most satisfyin' meal, Mrs. Dacy, most satisfyin'."

"Shore was, ma'am," Tex agreed, as did the entire population of the table.

Bridget Dacy blushed with pleasure. "Sure, and it was just a common meal here. It would be much better had we known you were comin'."

"Couldn't have been better, I'm thinkin'," Cap reassured her.

Kat looked at Lee and said, "We sit here in borrowed clothes, ours all but ruined, and I think it would be the wiser thing to go back home and make a start another day."

"Robert expects to be home tomorrow, and I would need to be there," Agitha Cook said.

I had figured that would be their desire, so I said, "All right, we will take the fresh mules and bring the buggy here for you, and we'll head for home."

Leslie leaned forward and cleared his throat. "Lee, if I could borry these two boys, I saw a bunch of my cows over by Castle Rock. I need a little help gittin 'em back where they b'long." He didn't mention the pie safe contents until the three men were well on their way.

"Fine by me if it's all right with them." Lee thought a moment. "If we could leave Pet and Tobe here, Mrs. Dacy, the boys could drop back by and pick them up on their way home." Of course, a second visit with the Dacy girls would be just fine—enough incentive to get those two boys to do just about anything. They all rose and, with compliments again to the hostess, went about their businesses; Cap and Tex riding east, and JD planning to join them after the spare mules were hitched and on their way.

"We got about a year's worth of rain yesterday, didn't we?" JD asked as they rode along, mules on tethers.

"Yeah. Too bad it all came in one day," Lee replied.

"Ground's dryin' fast. Shouldn't be too hard drivin' th' buggy now."

"I think you can go on and catch up with Cap and Tex when we get these jackass mules hitched up. I'll drive the orneriness out of them by th' time we get to Dacy's." That said, the two wrestled the mules into place, and with Hoss tied to the tailgate, trotted for Dacy's. When the mules were winded and behaving, JD waved and loped off to catch up with Tex and Cap.

The women gave their leftover picnic goodies to the Dacys and, with a big bundle of clothes in the back, they drove for home. The Cimarrón was up at the ford, and they watched it recede an hour before attempting to cross. Hoss and Lee tied on to the upstream side of the buggy, and Kat drove it across with three waifs sitting backwards on the tailgate and splashing with their feet. The water was a little swift, but not swimming for the animals. The ladies came through it with nothing worse than wet feet.

The sun was just setting when we let the Cook tribe off at their house. Hoss welcomed the opportunity to loaf along behind the buggy, and I drove through Florence toward home.

"Oh, look at the sunset, Kat. Isn't it beautiful?" Mollie exclaimed.

I looked up and saw the redness and bright fiery light where the sun had dropped below the horizon. It was really bright—

too bright, I suddenly realized. "That's not the sun, Mollie." I slapped reins on the mule backs. "Git up there, you lazy mules."

Kat gasped. I looked to see if she was scared of my driving, but she was staring at the bright light. We could see black smoke rising above the light. She gripped my arm. "It's our house, isn't it?"

"Let's hope it's the barn or bunkhouse," I answered.

"No, Lee, it's the house. I know." She stared at the fire, dry-eyed. Mollie's eyes were moist, and she chewed on her handkerchief.

All doubt was removed before we turned off the road and saw fire leaping from the doors and windows of the house. The roof fell in as we galloped up the lane. "Colita! Lee, where is Colita—and Tomas?" Kat searched the area for signs of life.

"There's someone on the bunkhouse roof," Mollie exclaimed, pointing. A woman, who could only have been our Colita, came trotting across the yard carrying two buckets of water.

"Thank you, God," Kat prayed.

Tomas hoisted a bucket to the roof and splashed the water over the shingles. It looked like the barn was out of danger. I handed the reins to Kat and jumped out of the buggy, running for Colita and the buckets.

"Señor Lee, they have burned our house!" Tracks of tears streaked Colita's begrimed face.

"Are you hurt, Colita?" I asked as I grabbed the buckets and ran for the tank.

"No, Señor, but the house . . ."

"Oh, Colita," Kat exclaimed, "the house is just full of *things*. The important news is that you and Tomas are safe."

I caught a glimpse of the three women embracing as I trotted back with two buckets of water sloshing around. I looked at Tomas after I hooked a bucket on the rope. His sombrero was jammed down tight on his head, and a trickle of blood ran down his cheek. "Tomas, are you all right?" I shouted.

"*Sí,* Señor," was all he said as he disappeared. In a moment he was back, and we exchanged buckets. By the time he returned with the empty, I had filled mine and hooked it to the rope before running for the tank.

"Lee, Colita says Tomas is hurt," Mollie yelled as I passed.

It looked like several people were coming up the lane in buggies and on horseback. I dropped the bucket and ran around the back to the ladder leaning against the eave. Tomas was pouring water over the roof. When he saw me, he sat down heavily. His lip was split, and some teeth were missing. One eye was swollen shut, and his hatband was dark with blood. He had been beaten.

"How can we help, Lee?" someone asked from below.

"Come around to the ladder and help me get Tomas down from here." I helped the man up, and we walked to the ladder. I couldn't tell who it was who poked his head over the eave. "Tomas has been hurt. Help him down."

I looked around the roof and saw it had been well soaked. The fire was beginning to die down, and it seemed that the roof was safe for the time being. Tomas was making progress down the ladder, his helper only a step below him, both hands on the rails around the injured man.

"The barn is safe, Lee. No danger there. I turned the horses into the pasture for safety's sake," a voice came from below.

"Thanks," I answered, and started my descent of the ladder. Tomas had made it to the ground and almost collapsed there. Two men held him up. "Take him inside the bunkhouse," I said. "I'll get the women."

There was a yard full of people gathered in little groups or rescuing the small pile of furniture and things Colita and Tomas had been able to remove from the house before being driven off by flames and heat. Lights were being lit in the bunkhouse as I searched for Colita and Kat. There was a general movement toward the lighted room, and Doctor Harris came out of the gloom with his black bag. "Heard someone was hurt." He hurried on to the house.

In the light, I recognized people. Tine Arnold was there, as were E.E. Hubbard and wife. Their daughter, Florence, was comforting Mollie. Pressley and his wife came forward and offered condolences. I saw Billy Hill hanging around at the edge of the light. When he caught my eye, he motioned me to follow him and faded into the dark.

"I'm sorry, Lee." He shook my hand. "I was coming back from Des Moines when I saw the smoke an' came on th' run. Just b'fore I got here, four men ran out of the house and rode up Sheep Pen. I saw that the two Mexicans were safe and followed the four. They rode clear up past the line shack into the back cañon. I came back after I lost them in the dark. They knew I was followin', an' I wasn't in th' mood t' go stumblin' around in there not knowin' where they were. It shore looked like they set th' fire. I guess Tomas an' Colita will know more about that."

Tine had seen me follow Billy and wandered our way. "Might be a good idee if'n me an' Billy stayed at th' shack an' watched th' cañon fer traffic," he offered.

I looked at Billy, and he nodded. "I would surely appreciate that, Tine. Thanks for offering." I knew Tine would stay there as long as he thought he was needed—and I also knew Billy's restless nature would only allow him a day or two of watching before he would be off looking for adventure, as likely to ride up the cañon *toward* the raiders as away from them. He had lived a charmed life so far, but I didn't want him to expose Tine to danger unnecessarily. I would have to follow them pretty soon.

"There should be enough food there for a day or two. I'll bring more when I come up." The two nodded and went for their horses. It was just a moment or two before I heard them ride out. Kat met me as I returned to the bunkhouse. "Lee, Colita says four men came in, beat Tomas, and set the fire. They gave her this note for you."

Someone had lit the yard light, and we walked over to stand under it. I unfolded the paper and read:

> "Mr. Lee Sowell
>
> "My compliments for a good meal. Colita is a great cook, but I think she got the stove too hot. Don't delay a return visit to our new ranch. We now own Sheep Pen Cañon.
>
> "Warmest Regards, Pard Newman."

I looked at Kat, too angry for words. "Do you think it was really Newman?" she asked.

"It doesn't matter who they are. They burned our house after taking advantage of our hospitality and beat up our man, and now they say they will run us out of the cañon. I'll have to go get them."

Further conversation was interrupted by people crowding around us offering condolences and their assistance in rebuilding. More than one person pressed money into my hand when they shook. I had no choice but to accept. Later, when we had time to reflect, we were grateful and touched by their generosity. At that moment, we were too overcome by the situation to think rationally.

Tomas had been badly beaten. His most serious wound had been inflicted on his head by the fireplace poker. It had split his scalp. He had held the skin in place and jammed his hat on to hold it together. Everyone marveled at his fortitude and strength to fight through his pain and do the things he thought he should do to save the place. I hoped we could hold on to the ranch long enough for us to show our gratitude. Doc Harris patched him up and put him to bed there in the bunkhouse.

"I will stay with him tonight and as long as I can tomorrow. If his brain swells, he has little chance of recovering," he told me privately. He instructed Colita and Kat: "It is most important that he remain flat in bed so his brain will have a chance to heal. I won't even lift him to bind his ribs. They will have to heal without binding. Any activity is liable to cause permanent damage or death."

Colita was very pale and in shock. Doc gave her a dose of laudanum and put her to bed in another bunk.

As the fire died down, people began pouring water on it in the hopes that, if a wind came up, it wouldn't spread. It was daylight before the last flame was extinguished; still, the fire smoldered for days. Sparks had fallen on the prairie grass, but the recent rain had kept a big fire from breaking out. Diligent patrolling kept damage to the grass to a minimum.

After our noon meal from the many dishes brought by our far-flung neighbors, I determined it was time to clean the vermin out of Sheep Pen Cañon. I was in the act of saddling Hoss when Kat found me.

"You haven't slept for two nights, and now you're going up to dig outlaws out of the rocks without a posse? No you aren't, Lee Sowell. Not in a pig's eye, are you. If you get a good night's rest tonight, we'll go up tomorrow and see if we can smoke them out. The road up Black Mesa is washed out, so our guests are trapped in a box cañon for now."

I thought a moment and had to agree with the woman. It would be foolish for me to go up there alone, though I had Billy Hill and Tine Arnold to go with me. Billy surmised that four-to-one were about even odds for him, but I warned him sternly that he was not to take on the outlaws alone. He would probably be held by that edict for about two days, then all restraints would come off.

Rockin' R Bill rode in ahead of the rest of the hay crew, and I sent the whole bunch to the line shack to guard the cañon and be sure there were no escapees.

Chapter 28
Unforeseen Undertakings

Bass Reeves told me once, "Lee, we ain't got an endless stock of posse-men, so you have to take care of your men. Treat 'em right, pay 'em right, an' for Lord's sake, don't get 'em killed off by puttin' 'em in foolish and dangerous positions. That job b'longs t' us, an' you won't be a deputy with a posse if you put other men in places only you should be in."

I think I circled those smoldering ruins a dozen times that afternoon. It seemed to be the only thing I could do. There wasn't a usable thing left, and it made me think about how a house of wood burned in this climate. I determined right then that our next house would be adobe with a tile roof. At least it wouldn't burn so readily. Tomas would know who to get to build for us.

A man anxious about his expectant wife summoned Doc Harris away about midafternoon. He left medicine and instructions with the women on how to care for Tomas. Basically, they were to keep him medicated enough that he would sleep most of the time. "It's the best thing for him to do right now. I'll be back some time tomorrow to see him."

I brought the doctor's buggy around, and he was off.

I just picked at my supper and, before the sun was good and down, spread my bed in the hay wagon, leaving the bunkhouse to the women. Sometime in the night, Kat joined me and I held her close. I never saw her cry about the house. Women of her generation were made of stern stuff, and Kat was among the strongest. I never asked her much about her past, knowing it was a dark time for her and best forgotten. Before the children came, she said I was her only family. Her words reminded me of that verse in Genesis: *Therefore shall a man leave his father and his mother, and shall cleave unto his wife and they shall be one flesh.*

Some vague uneasiness woke me, and I noticed that the Big Dipper was in its last quarter. The morning star was just rising. Kat was sleeping soundly. I would have been, too, but for this restlessness in me. It wouldn't let me sleep; it wouldn't let me lie still. I was able to ease out of the bed without waking my girl and dressed on the ground.

A lamp burned dimly in the bunkhouse when I looked in. Colita and Mollie were asleep, as was Tomas. His scalp showed white where it had been shaved around the stitches. He hadn't run much fever, which was a big relief.

A vague urgency kept me moving, and I prowled the grounds. Nothing seemed out of place; the barn was empty and quiet. Still, uneasiness pushed me. I caught up Hoss and saddled him. We circled the place again, and Hoss didn't find anything amiss. At the northwest corner of our patrol, he continued on northward. It seemed his pace was steady and had purpose, so I let him go. The line shack was dark, and there were no horses in the pen. Hoss walked on by, just like he knew where he was going, and he only stopped when he breasted up aginst a rope strung across his path.

"Yuh cain't pass th' rope without th' secret password, Lee." Spider was standing not thirty feet to my left, his rifle cradled in the crook of his arm.

"Hoss don't seem t' think he needs a password. What is it anyway?" I asked.

"Hell, it's so secret even *we* don't know what it is." I turned, and there stood Red behind me. I didn't have to worry about the burners getting out of the cañon this way. "Everyone holdin' th' line?"

"Yeah. Some's grumpy, everone's sleepy 'cept Tine, who's tellin' tall tales both ways, an' Billy, who's gettin' awful antsy. We look fer him to break loose any minnit," Red replied.

"I'm ready to break loose, myself. How 'bout you fellers?"

"We wus jest holdin' off, waitin' for you, Lee," Spider said.

"See if you can retie this rope a little above horse-head high, an' I'll gather the other boys," I said. We were able to get the ropes repositioned in most places, then gathered back at the west end, where I swore them all in as my posse.

"Seems kind of strange bein' on this side o' th' chase," Billy Hill observed.

"Don't worry. You'll git used to it." Blackie seemed to have had the same experience somewhere along the way.

I began, "We don't know where these fellers are or how many there—"

"They's at least five o' them by th' way they was throwin' lead an' insults our way last night," Pete interrupted.

I looked around and didn't see any blood or bandages. "Not good shots, you say?"

"No, Lee, not good *targets,*" Billy corrected. "I winged one of 'em, an' that might've influenced them to slope back up the way they come."

"At least five and probably more," I said. "We need some kind of a plan." I looked up at that Black Mesa caprock brooding over us and would have given a hundred dollars to have a man up there with glasses. The cañon was narrowing here, and the flat tops of the west bluff seemed like a good lookout place. "Tine, you got your Sharps .50 with you, don't you?"

"Never more'n my saddle boot away, Lee."

"There looked like an easy place to climb that west wall back a ways. Why don't you get up there, ride along the rim, and direct us to the hiders down here?"

"I'm on my way." He turned and loped back down the valley.

"Someone could get up th' slope o' Black a ways, but he'd have t' walk, Lee. You want me to try it?" Pete asked.

"Rest of us'll be glad t' stay down here amongst th' lead bees buzzin' 'round our heads while you loaf along up there," Sol growled.

"You got rocks an' holes t' hide in, while I got nothin' up there. Any 'bees' sting you are yore own fault," Pete retorted.

"If you see someone, point your rifle at him. If that don't work, fire a round. Maybe we'll see him when he replies," I said. "The six of us down here will spread out and work our way up the valley."

"Yo're a good target up there, Pete, so don't let any o' them fellers git ahind us." Sol finally had his say.

"*You* wouldn't shoot me, would you?" Pete asked.

"It all depends on the provocation."

Red looked at Sol. "You inventin' words agin?"

"Th' word belongs to Mr. Webster."

In a few minutes, Tine waved from the mesa top, and Pete had scrambled up the scree to the base of the solid wall of Black Mesa. "All right, let's spread out even spaced along th' rope an' start walkin' in. I'll be in th' middle. Hold your position even if you hear firing along the line. We don't want a one of these rats t' escape. If you need help, give the long yell. If this really is Pard Newman, he has broken jail, and he'll sure be against returning."

I looked at the men spread along the line and at the brush and boulders we had to pass through. Even with the cañon narrower, our line was too thin to catch men if they wished to avoid us—or pick us off one by one. I recalled the men back to me.

"This isn't gonna work, fellers. We're spread too thin. The next best thing I can think of is for us to get closer together and depend on Tine and Pete to spot those men and direct us to them. It's doubtful they will be too far away from each other."

We spread out enough to put a few yards between us and proceeded up the hill, flanking the trail on both sides. Tine moved along ahead of us, back from the edge far enough to avoid being a target. Occasionally he would crawl to the rim and search, then move back and on along the mesa. Red was to my right, and he kept an eye on Pete for us. "Lee, Pete's stopped."

I looked. Pete was squatted down, looking at something a little ahead of us. "May be lookin' at the foot of the slope?"

"Whatever he sees is behind that big boulder over there," Rockin' R said.

"Or on top of it," Spider amended.

Pete stood and walked along the slope, his gun held ready.

"Must be seein' snakes or possums," Red guessed.

"Shore not somethin' he's too afeered of, is it?" Spider observed.

When Pete got directly over the boulder, he held up one finger and pointed down at the big rock. "Bill, you and Spider go look at what he's found. It must not be a danger, or he wouldn't be standing there like that. Surround the rock an' see what it is."

We watched as the two men separated and went around both sides of the boulder, then disappeared behind it. We could tell they were having some kind of sign conversation with Pete. Then they returned to us. "Dead man, Lee. Looks like he ain't been dead long," Spider told us.

"His head was in a funny position like it wasn't attached under the skin," Bill said.

"Did it look like he fell off'n th' rock?" Blackie asked.

"No-o, I don't think he ever got up there, his rifle was propped up agin' th' rock."

"What did th' sign look like?"

"Jest his tracks, Lee. Nothin' else."

"No sign of a horse, I guess."

"Nope. It looked like he come from thataway," Spider pointed up the cañon. "Angled in from th' trail, looked like."

"Let's go 'thataway' an' see what's there," I said. "I hope Pete gets more cautious."

"Don't worry 'bout him, Lee. A long shot'd just bounce off'n that hard head." Sol grinned.

We proceeded, a little more cautiously. It seemed Pete was more cautious, also. I looked for Tine and saw his head appear over the rim. He looked right for a moment, then looked to his left up the valley. Something caught his attention, and he stared for some moments, then disappeared. The next time I saw him, he was not more than a couple hundred yards farther along the rim. He stared straight down a long time, then stood up and signaled us, pointing straight below where he stood. When we were closer, he laid his head over on his hands, then pointed down below.

"He's saying they're asleep?" Red asked. "That ain't likely. Must be a trap."

"I'm thinkin' he's meanin' th' *long sleep,*" I answered.

"Somethin' like what you an' Tex found up Gallinas?" Blackie asked.

"Could be, but let's don't take any chances. Spread out around that point, and we'll go in slow an' easy." Lever actions jacked shells into chambers, and we spread and crept forward. Tine stood openly on the rim and watched. Any movement below would be immediately apparent to him.

When Blackie got to the cliff face, we waited for Bill to get there on the right side and we had circled the area. I glanced up, and Tine was watchin' behind us. Blackie and Bill reached the clearing before the rest of us, and Blackie hollered, "All's clear."

Three bodies lay in different places around the clearing. One leaned against a rock, his rifle across his lap. Another sprawled by the dead fire, and one lay in his bedroll, his head crushed. *This is just like Bingaman Cañon.* I looked to see if the man beside the fire held a bridle.

"Holy crow," Red said softly.

"Nobody move," I said. "Don't mess up any sign that might be here."

"There ain't gonna be any sign, Lee—more'n this." Spider was pointing at the ground in front of him. There in the dust was that big footprint we had grown used to seeing.

"I knowed it," Rockin' R Bill said.

"That's all we'll find, but be careful and look close just th' same. He may have left somethin' he didn't intend to."

"Like what, Lee? A feather er two from his wings?" Spider asked.

I didn't get a chance to reply before the echo of a shot bounced off the bluff, and we turned to see what Pete was doing. He waved his rifle high above his head, then aimed at something up the valley.

"Tine, do you see any horses?" I shouted.

He cupped his hands and yelled back. "No. I'll ride up there a little farther and look."

It seemed that Pete was pointing to a lone stunted piñon tree up the valley a ways, so we headed that way. As we neared, we could see a body dangling from a limb of the tree, his heels dragging the ground.

"Well, I'll be . . . would you look at that!" Red exclaimed.

Around the body's neck was an iron band about three inches wide with a chain about eight feet long tied to the limb. The band was hinged in the back at the chain, and in the front there were two staples welded where it could be fastened. Two pieces of a broken rattail file were jammed into the hasps, holding them together.

"Found your file, Lee," Bill whispered.

"Fellers, meet Pard Newman," I said. "I guessed the outlaws had been killed in the night after their skirmish with the posse or this morning." Papers on them identified Loftis McCoy, Lin Huie, and Moon Adams. The body by the fire had no identification on it, but examination of one of the "possibles" bags revealed a wanted circular that described a man named Arlie Marsh, along with a half dozen aliases. We could only guess that was the name of the unidentified man. I recognized Huie, McCoy, and Adams. We found the contents of that third bag of loot from the train robbery. The loot was divided into two saddlebags, with the pouch it had been in piled on top of the contents of one bag.

While we were laying out the bodies and identifying them, we heard horses coming. It was Tine Arnold driving down a bunch of horses, some of which were mine. Tine paused as the horses loped by. "Found another body up there. Had the horses penned without water. I'll see they get to the water and come on back."

We moved their bodies to the campsite and buried them against the bluff. We dug the graves and marked them by carving crosses in the rock wall at their heads.

"Why couldn't they have died by a gully where we could just cave off th' bank on them, 'stead o' out here in th' flats?" Bill complained.

"We could ask Bigfoot when we meet him." Blackie wiped his muddy face on his shirttail.

"Let's just ask him why he don't clean up his own messes an' make his own cemeteries," Red drawled.

Tine came back and took Spider back up the valley to bury

the body up there. They rode back a couple of hours later. "Rolled him into that gully by the old sheep pen and caved th' sides off on him," Tine said.

"Dammit," was all Red said.

Just as we were adding the final touches to the graves, Kat and Mollie drove up in the buggy. Kat had the shotgun across her lap.

"Yer too late, battle's over," Blackie hailed, his red hair dark with sweat and plastered to his neck.

"What happened? We only heard one shot," Kat said.

"Oh, that was Pete. Only way he knows t' empty his gun is through th' barrel," Red explained. "These others give up an' died on their own."

"All except one man who said he wasn't dead yet, but we knew how fellers like him lie an' buried him anyway," Sol added.

Mollie gasped, then giggled. "You are all too ghastly."

"We brought food with us. It's at the line shack when you are ready," Kat said. "Are you through here?"

Blackie smacked a grave with the shovel. "Just about, if this feller quits tryin' t' dig his self out."

"One more crack like that, and we're taking the food back with us," Kat warned. Without another word, she turned and drove back down the valley.

"Let's go eat, boys, while we got th' chance. We can look around here later," I said.

The return of Bigfoot was a mixed blessing. His dispatching of the Newman gang at least saved my posse from being shot up, but I worried that this killing business might become a matter of course for him. Our only perceived reason for the first murders was that the cattle thieves had come too close to his hideaway—and that might be the same reason in Sheep Pen Cañon. The fact that the gang had burned a house and were willfully destructive might have influenced his resolve to eliminate them the only way he knew how. The young woman must still be with him. That's the only way I could justify his killings.

At least he was free of that collar he'd wore. Later, I took the collar into Florence and hung it from the eave of Hubbard's store. It caused quite a stir when people realized what it was. It also changed some attitudes about the "ghost" who wore it, and made it safer for Bigfoot to pass through the country. From that time on, there was no more pilfering.

I didn't hunt for the two fugitives in our cañon—just let 'em be. There were a hundred places they could have been—and Bigfoot might be a real danger to the person who found them. That piñon tree became our post office. Whenever we butchered, I would see that meat and other food was left there for them. Kat would occasionally bundle up some clothes for Littlefoot, and they always disappeared promptly. The couple stayed in the cañon six years, and the appearance of tiny footprints at the tree told us there were now three of them.

Bigfoot looked after our cattle when they were in the upper end of the cañon and sometimes even down close to the ranch. He never butchered any of them, though occasionally the neighbors lost one, which made me suspect him. The third spring they were here, I registered a new branding iron made in the form of a footprint. It made a large brand that was impossible to alter. At the roundup and the next two spring roundups, I had every tenth heifer branded with the new brand. In our herd they only amounted to sixty-one calves that first year. My phantom vaquero deserved them.

Right from the start, those Bigfoot yearlings showed a marked tameness, and I knew my unseen friend was handling them in a special way. When we started the fall gather for market at the end of their sixth year in the valley, my Bigfoot branding iron couldn't be found. There was not a single Bigfoot cow in the herd. Our neighbors had left.

Chapter 29
Pata Grande

That house fire had nearly wiped us out. In the parlance of the Cimarrón Valley, we were "land rich and cash poor." Tomas and Colita stayed with us in their little cottage, and Kat, Mollie, and I moved into the bunkhouse. Mollie was soon swept off her feet and kidnapped by a young man who had a small spread over near Folsom. We see them often.

It turned out that Tomas was proficient at making adobe bricks, and we were soon laying walls, even though I could not afford lumber for completing the house. The cattle market stayed good for several years. When it was low, we sold to cattlemen up north in Wyoming, the Dakotas, and Nebraska. Gradually, we pulled out of the hole we had been burned into, and our finished adobe house was better than the first one.

Tomas kept making bricks, so we rebuilt the bunkhouse with their cottage attached on one end and the bunkhouse kitchen on the other. The aging couple was now more comfortable and lived nearer to us, so we could look after them if need be.

I resigned my U.S. deputy marshal job and, except for a couple of terms as deputy sheriff in our corner of New Mexico, retired from the law enforcement business. We were blessed with a covey of kids: three ol' boys and three of the sweetest daughters a man could have. A man must be born with more than one heart, for mine was stolen three times, not counting the first big theft by Kat.

★ ★ ★ ★ ★

I had been hearing of a ranch down south of the border that had an improved herd of whiteface cattle. When we needed an infusion of fresh blood in the herd, I determined to visit to see if I could purchase a few bulls. Tomas and I drove over to Ratón and rode the train to El Paso. From there, we took the El Paso and Southwestern Railroad to Douglas, Arizona. We rented horses and rode south to Fronteras, Mexico, where the ranch was said to be. There, we learned the ranch headquarters was at Esqueda, a few miles farther south. Soon, we began to encounter some fine-looking whiteface cattle.

We came upon a bunch of cattle under mesquite trees a little ways from the trail and rode over to look at them. "Señor Lee, look at that brand!" Tomas exclaimed.

He hadn't needed to point it out; I had already seen the Bigfoot brand on the steer. "I think I know where he got his start with whiteface cattle, Tomas."

"*Sí.* Now we go home?" Tomas had no desire to meet Bigfoot.

"I still want to see about some bulls, Tomas. If you want to, you can wait for me at Fronteras."

Tomas sighed and shrugged his shoulders, "No, Señor Lee. Eef you go, I go."

"I wouldn't go if I expected any danger. We helped these people, and they appreciated us enough to kill our enemies. I don't think we have anything to worry about."

We rode into the little village and were directed to a road that led to the ranch headquarters. It was a five-mile ride. A tall vaquero met us as we rode through the gates in the wall surrounding the compound. "*Bienvenido,* Señores." He clapped his hands, and two small boys came running and led our horses away. "I am Sebas Orrites, the foreman of Pata Grande." He extended his hand.

"This is Tomas Florrera, and I am Lee Sowell. We are from

Sheep Pen Ranch in *Nuevo Mexico.*"

The man nodded. "I have heard about the Sheep Pen Ranch and you, Señor Lee. Our first cattle came to us from your ranch, and we are very grateful." He led us to chairs on the porch, and a young girl handed us glasses of cool water. She set the olla on a little table between the chairs.

"I see you have kept up the breed, and they seem improved over those first cattle," I said.

"*Sí*—yes, we have been careful to keep the breed from being diluted by common cattle and have improved them as we can."

"You have done a good job of that. We had heard of your cattle without knowing they came from the same stock as ours. I had hoped to buy some bulls to improve my stock."

"I am sure that is possible without inbreeding. We have bulls that have no relationship with those first cattle," he said.

"I have never met your *patrón,* Señor Orrites."

"He is a very private man, Señor Lee; few people have seen him. He lives far up in the Sierra Madre with his family. I will relay your request, but I do not think it will be possible for you to see him."

"I understand," I said. "Please do not disturb him. If we can conduct our business quickly, we should be getting back before winter sets in at our ranch. I will perhaps arrange a return trip when it is convenient to see your *patrón.*"

"You will always be welcome at Pata Grande, Señor Lee." Sebas Orrites went on to explain that they kept several ages of bulls on the ranch. I decided I would like three young mature bulls and four yearlings for our future needs. Sebas nodded and said, "We will go to the pastures tomorrow, and you can choose the ones you want. I will have them driven to the hacienda tomorrow, and you may leave the day after if you wish. Please be assured you may stay as long as you wish, but I know the press of running a ranch, and I understand your haste."

A young woman appeared at the door and announced that dinner was ready, so we retired to the dining room. Sebas's wife, Susano, young and quite accomplished, presided over the table. "We have heard so much about you from our *patrón,* Señor Lee. It is a great pleasure to finally meet you."

"I had no idea we would be finding the Bigfoot Ranch when we began this trip," I said.

"Oh, but there is much more of you here than you would imagine," she said.

I wondered what she meant, but she didn't explain, being distracted by instructions to the servants—and that by design, I thought. Tomas was uncomfortable at the table, and afterward excused himself to go visit with the groundskeeper and others. I didn't see him until the next morning.

I was impressed by the organization of the ranch and how the cattle were kept. They must have had nearly two hundred mature bulls in the pasture and twice that many yearlings in another pasture. All the cattle were reasonably tame, and that spoke of their handling. On most ranches north of the border, the cattle were not at all used to human interaction and strongly disapproved of their presence.

It was obvious these animals had been carefully chosen. Their conformity was quite uniform, such that I didn't worry about choosing specific animals. I told Sebas to bring out the number I requested, and I would be satisfied. I would have gladly paid a premium for the bunch, but Sebas asked a much lower price. We finally agreed to pay the market value, and the transaction was complete.

The ranch contained many thousands of leagues, and I wondered how my friend Bigfoot had come by such a large holding. "He has a silver mine in the Madre, which has made him very wealthy," Sebas said with a little smile that told far more than his words. *A mine bought by many graves,* I thought.

Our visit, though short, was very pleasant, and we were a little reluctant to leave so soon, but the late season dictated our departure. I was worried that the bulls would have trouble with the colder climate and wanted to get them back into it before it got any colder, so they might become somewhat acclimatized. Even at that, I planned to keep them in the barn for the winter.

Sebas sent two vaqueros to help us get the herd to the railroad. We stopped at a tank early and allowed the cattle to graze before herding them into a corral. The two vaqueros rode back to the hacienda for the night, promising to be back early the next morning. Tomas turned in early, and I sat watching the stars as the fire died. I must have dozed off. A female voice nearby spoke softly, "Señor Lee, may we come in?"

"Yes," I said, even before my eyes were fully open. I threw sticks on the fire to give us light. A young woman stepped into the light with a huge man close behind her. I could see his white teeth beneath the shadow of his sombrero. Both were grinning because they had caught me napping.

The girl was young, not yet twenty years, I would guess, and the boy looked to be some younger. Both were dressed in the fashionable upper-class Mexican manner, with much silver ornamentation. The girl's *rebozo* draped over her shoulders and beneath her hair in back, indicating she did not use it to cover her head. She was small, confident, and attractive, but not beautiful. Her hands and their movements were familiar to me.

The boy towered over her, well above six feet tall and still growing. The way he carried himself spoke of great strength. I was sure he could bend iron bars and carry horses. Without a word, he slipped off his boot, and with his foot, began drawing a big bare footprint in the sand.

"My name is Katherine, and my brother's name is Lee. I am the oldest daughter of the man you call Bigfoot, who told us to draw this footprint for you."

"Yes," I said. "I can see your parents in both of you. Though I have never seen your father, I have seen your mother. We named her Littlefoot—*and,* young lady, I have seen *your* footprints many times."

Her eyes widened in surprise. "I did not know that, but Father says he has heard you call my mother Littlefoot. He teases her about it."

He *heard* me? Now it was my turn for surprise; yet I knew that for him, it was entirely possible.

"My father says that you were a friend at a very dark time for them." The boy spoke for the first time. His voice was that deep, mellow, soft voice you hear from time to time in men of his race.

"They do not talk much about those times, and I remember very little of them. We thought perhaps you would know something of our parents and tell us," the girl named Katherine said.

"I know little enough myself, but I will tell you what I know, and you can tell me about them now." I wondered if their parents had sent the children to me because the things they experienced were too painful for them to talk about. I didn't know; but with a mental shrug, I began from the start of my acquaintance with the ghostly big man's activities and told them what I knew. I did not mention any killings. Those things were not for me to relate. We talked well into the morning hours, and I learned as much as I gave.

A shadowy figure appeared, holding horses at the ready, and I knew it was time for the young people to depart. "I suppose we should call you Big Lee and me Little Lee," I told the boy as we shook hands. "You must come to Sheep Pen some day, the both of you. Give your parents my regards, and thank them for thinking of us. They have paid us a great compliment in naming you." I listened to them mount up and heard the soft pad of hooves in the sand as they left.

There was no use lying down. The eastern horizon was already a gray streak. I made a fresh pot of coffee and set it in the coals. Then I went out and watered the horses and gave them a little grain. When I heard the vaqueros approaching, I hurried to the fire. As I reached for the coffee pot, something familiar caught my eye. There in the sand by the fire was a large footprint that had not been there before.

Addendum: The Hay Crew

I thought the book was finished with the end of Chapter 29, but upon review by my chief editor, Mrs. Katherine Sowell, I was made aware that I had neglected to properly introduce the men we christened the Hay Crew (that's about the only printable name for the group). Therefore, I now take pen in hand to tell you about those five amigos *in this addendum, since there is no place to properly insert this chapter within the book. –Lee*

I first met the Hay Crew in Marrs's saloon. They were playing poker with matchstick currency, known among them as the wood common medium (as opposed to the silver and gold common mediums). True to their reputation for nonconformity, they invited an obvious *lawman* to join their game, which I did. As I became better acquainted with the men, I found them to be fairly honest, mostly responsible, ordinarily straightforward young men. After I tell you what I learned about these individuals by long association with them, I will relate some of the activities and adventures they experienced in and around the west end of No Man's Land.

"Red" Crow was not quite twenty years old when we first met. He has been accused of taking the bird's name when the XIT bookkeeper asked whom his paycheck should be made out to. It had never occurred to him that some outfits didn't pay in hard cash. He was dark complexioned with black hair and beard. Naturally, the outfit, in its perversity, would name him

Red. He was a man of few words, but seldom without opinion. Some people thought he was too free in giving it.

Rumor was that he came into the Llano Estacado with Charlie Goodnight's outfit and drifted north out of that featureless plain to "find land with some variety to it." The Cimarrón Valley was agreeable to him. No Man's Land freed him.

"Solomon" (Sol) Barlowe was another one of those fellows who took his name on the spur of the moment; in this case from the style of knife he carried in his pocket. No one ever used his last name, and he was given his first name because of the wisdom he disbursed when he occasionally spoke. He lived by the philosophy that there was seldom much crime in minding one's own business.

"Blackie" Barnes was a redhead with blue eyes, freckles and all. He was christened with the same humor that let Joe Don Jones believe Kat Ingram was a man; in fact their sense of humor was like a disease that had infected all five of the Hay Crew. They got much entertainment from the confusion caused by Red and Blackie's names.

Blackie loved poker, as witnessed by the fact that he was always broke and had to borrow matches when he lit up. His greatest interest was trying to figure out how the cardsharps cheated when he played with them.

"Spider" Spivey's name descended from his last name. In fact, his is one of the few names that rode into the country with its owner. It was a long time before anyone heard his last name. He seemed to have some education above the average man. There were whispers from time to time that he had left a carpetbagger corpse or two on his back trail. Texas was ever a sort of fragrance in his memory, but forbidden fruit for Spider.

Pete Harden came late to the crew, but survived his initiation. He was only the second one of the bunch with the same name he was born to. Still, his residency in No Man's Land had a lot to do with the fact that no one could arrest him there.

All of these men were in the lower half of their twenties when I first knew them. They subscribed to the cowboy philosophy that to shoot an unarmed man, change a brand, steal a horse, cheat at cards, run sheep in cow country, or build a fence were the only *real* crimes. All together, they fit the description Frederic Remington gave: "The cow-men are good friends, virulent haters and if justified in their own minds, would shoot a man instantly, and regret the necessity, but not the shooting, afterwards."

They found out early in their vaquero careers that range outfits did not carry their men over the winter, cow-work being basically a seasonal occupation. That left a feller with up to six months without pay and not enough working-month pay to carry him over. A man faced the necessity of finding an off-season job, the occupation of grub-line rider having already been taken in the region. With few such jobs available and a half dozen men vying for each one, the boys had to think of other forms of employment. That's when they saw the advantages of summer haying. It would be a nine- or ten-month job and profitable enough to carry them through the three or four idle months until the hay was ready for cutting again.

Pooling their saved wages, they spent one winter rounding up used mowers and rakes and discarded pitchforks and other equipment and repairing them. Pete and Sol visited the different ranches and got agreements to provide hay or harvest the hayfields set aside on the different ranges. Ranch foremen gladly agreed to contract haying. It eliminated the unpleasant task of coercing vaqueros into working on the ground in the hayfields.

They did very well in their new profession, and it took some convincing, sometimes with fists, to get other ranch hands to agree that the hay crew was just as important and as much a part of ranching as anyone who hair-pinned a horse.

For a couple of years, they wintered in an old abandoned nester's shack until one evening when Red was cooking supper. "An' *I say* President Cleveland has no right telling United States citizens they can't settle land that ain't assigned to any Injun tribe, even if it is in the Indian Territory," Red declared, wagging his spatula at Sol.

"But you don't have any problem with Ol' Grover tellin' ranchers where they can't build fences." Sol's reply was a restatement of previous Red-crafted assertions, not a question.

" 'Bob war' is th' devil's own invention," Pete declared for the tenth time that afternoon.

A soft whoosh from the stove drew Red's attention. His pan of grease had ignited and sent flames reaching for the low rafters.

"Good gosh a-mighty, now look what you gone an' made me do with yore Yankee talk." He grabbed the skillet handle and had whirled toward the door before his hands could get the signal to his brain that he had forgotten the potholders. "Ye-e-eow!" The pan clattered to the floor, spreading burning grease over floor and Red's pant legs.

At the sight of Red's intentions, Sol had jumped to open the door for him. When he turned back, he saw Pete with the water bucket, intent on putting out the fire. "Pete, no! Don't pour water on a grease—" Too late to stop the man, he turned to exit the house when the grease-water combination exploded and propelled him into the yard, slamming the door behind him. Rising to his hands and knees and spitting dust, Sol turned in time to see the roof settle back down on the walls. A cloud of dust roiled out from the eaves.

"Help, help! Open the door," came from inside, and Sol hurried to push the door open. It was stuck, and he had to lay his shoulder to it to open it a crack. The bottom of the door scraped across the floorboards for the first time in its life. Hands pulled and jerked on the door to make space for Red and Pete to crawl out beneath the thick cloud of smoke and steam. A goodly portion of the dirt roof had fallen and effectively extinguished the fire.

As they watched, the end wall folded and collapsed, bringing down the ridgepole and roof with it.

"Well, I'll be . . ." Pete was at a loss for words. All of his facial hair was gone, singed off as slick as if it had been shaved. His pant legs still smoldered.

Red had plunged his hands into the water trough. He, too, had been to the same "barber."

"What in the world is going on?" They turned to see that Blackie and Spider had ridden into the yard and were sitting looking at the ruins.

"Red cooked supper," Sol said.

The Hay Crew was up on the headwaters of Corrumpa Creek cutting hay in one of their favorite hayfields when a large flock of sheep appeared and happily began grazing, on both cut and standing hay.

"Hey, git those sheep outta our hayfield," Spider stopped his mower and yelled—in Spanish—at the shepherds.

Pretending ignorance, the herders shrugged and continued watching their sheep, rifles across their laps or propped within reach.

"Git 'em out!" Spider yelled, "Git, you range maggots, git!"

He tried chasing the sheep with the mower, but they just ran out of the way, and one of the shepherds shot over his head. Somewhat sobered, Spider assessed his situation. A half dozen or more shepherds were in a big arc, and he was the center. There wasn't anything more to do than die or retreat. Even if he had his rifle, they would get him before he got more than two or three of them. Spider was about to choose retreat when he heard the wagon. From the corner of his eye, he saw the company wagon, full of the rest of the gang.

Red turned the wagon broadside to the circle, and the boys sat down behind the sideboards, nothing but heads and rifle barrels showing. "What's goin' on, Spider?" Red shouted.

"These boys showed up with them maggots an' took possession of our hayfield."

"You try t' talk to 'em?" Pete asked.

"I tole 'em t' git, that this was our field, but they only rattled their sabers at me."

"These ain't Baca's men, are they?" Blackie asked.

"Let's find out," Pete said, and jumped out of the wagon. He walked toward the central man in the arc, hands up and open. They talked for a few moments, and Pete came back shaking his head. "They're not Baca's sheep. They belong to someone named Romero, and those men say they are here to stay. The only way they'll leave is if Romero says so—or an army runs them off."

"We ain't got an army, but I got a good night horse and a long whip. That would git mutton *and* men movin'," Red said.

"That could also git you kilt." Spider enlarged on the subject.

Sol was looking at the sun setting behind Capulin. "Let's get back to camp. I've got an idea or two." He slapped reins on horses and gathered a dirty look from Red the driver. Pete ran to catch the tailgate and hop in.

Horses and supper were the main chores before they were lounging on their rolls watching the purple of night rise across the sky. La Carreta, the Big Dipper, blinked on and began its nightly march around the polestar, and the evening star chased the sun.

"What's this big idea you got, Sol?" Spider asked. He was stung by not handling the situation, and yenned for revenge.

"Bet I know," Red said. "He's gonna set a fire."

"Shore, Red, an' when they're gone, we can go right on an' harvest th' ashes. Cows love it," Blackie drawled.

"Well, whatever it is had better be done quick. Two more days, an' that hayfield'll be ruined."

"Might not take that long, Red," Pete muttered, his eyes closed and mind drifting. "Come on, Sol, out with it afore I'm plumb gone."

"Oh, I was lookin' at th' sundown an' thinkin', 'It's gonna take a volcano t' root these sheep outta here.' " He lay back on his bed. It was only a moment before the thought took root. Pete bolted upright, "Say, that's a great idea, Sol, an' I'm in."

"In what—a muddle?" Red asked. "Lay back down, Pete. You had a dream."

"No-o-o, I think it was Sol's dream, Red." Spider lit his pipe and blew out a plume of smoke. "What you think them ignorant sheep jockeys would think if ol' Capulin started smokin' an' belchin'?"

"Why, those superstitious ignoramuses would hightail it outta here so fast they'd forget everything, an' th' dogs'd hafta herd their sheep," Pete declared.

"It's gonna take time t' set all that up. There ain't nothin' t' burn up there, an' we can't drag enough stuff up there in a week."

"Them little volcanoes like that one northeast of Capulin're easy t' git to, and it's got plenty o' fuel around, Blackie." Spider's pipe glowed.

"Say, there's one that's still got its hole in th' middle where a fire couldn't be seen." Pete pointed to a small hill named Horseshoe Crater south of the big mountain, not two miles from camp.

"An' lookee all them cedars 'round th' bottom of it. Lots o' dry wood t' make a big fire, an' some green thrown on top'll make a purty white smoke," Blackie observed.

"Moon risin' 'ud help," Sol reckoned.

Pete reached for his hat and put it on, pulled on his britches, and stomped into his boots. "Whatcha waitin' on? Let's git."

"You four go load that cauldron with wood an' git started buildin' for a daylight show. I'm gonna go over on Sierra Grande an' git somethin' we'll need. Think I can be back afore sunrise."

"Think I know what yo're after, Sol. Gonna need a packhorse, ain't you?" Red was stompin' his left boot on his foot without a sock.

"And a lo-o-ong lead." Sol chuckled.

Within ten minutes, the five men rode out, four west and one east. It isn't necessary to describe the feverish work that went on the entire night. By the time Sol returned just before dawn, that little caldera brimmed with firewood.

"Say, is that a box o' Little Giant Dyn-o-*mite*?" Pete hailed.

"Half full, with caps an' fuse," Sol replied.

"Fire's hot es th' pits o' hell," Blackie remarked.

"Hope it don't draw up that fire b'low," Sol said.

"Ya think it could?" Spider looked concerned.

Sol grinned.

"Some day, Sol, some day . . ." Spider backhanded his shoulder as Sol spun away.

"Here, Spider, throw this on the fire." Sol handed him a stick of dynamite with a short fuse.

Spider dug in his overalls. "Yuh don't need a match, there's your light." Blackie pointed to the fire.

The man threw the stick into the fire, and they ducked below the rim of the caldera. The boom of the explosion rolled across the prairie and sent a shower of sparks and burning debris into the air. "Time to warn the sheep men," Sol said as he mounted up. "Ride with me, Pete, an' let's have some fun. The rest of you get ready to throw that green stuff on the fire at my signal."

"What's th' signal?" Blackie asked as he prepared another

stick of Little Giant.

"You'll know," Sol shouted as he rode after Pete. They stopped at a little cinder cone within a quarter mile of the sheep camp, and Sol lit a long fuse that led into the cinders. They loped on to the camp, where they could see men moving around the fire and preparing to move their flocks out into the field.

Pete gave the long yell and Sol bawled, "Run! Run! Th' volcano's blowin' up!"

The sheep men stared in disbelief. As they stood there, the little cinder mound blew up with a mighty boom, sending cinders of all sizes high into the air.

"My gosh, Sol, how many st—"

"Three." Sol was trying to huddle under his sombrero as they were peppered with cinders and gravel. The cinder cone was no more.

"Probably a hole in th' ground," Pete grumbled. The shower of rock died away, and he brushed dust from his hat and shoulders. A long roll of Little Giant thunder rumbled across the plain, and a large white cloud rose from Horseshoe Crater. Shepherds no longer stood and stared; they were running for the flocks, whistling for their dogs. The two camp keepers were far ahead of the flocks, running north to get away from the volcano. There wasn't any need for Sol and Pete to run any farther. They rescued the mutton and biscuits from the fire and made a feast. More explosions rolled over them.

"If they blow up Horseshoe, there'll be th' devil t' pay," Pete said through a biscuit stuffed with a mutton chop.

"M-m-m-m," was all his companion could respond.

"Reckon he'll want t' play again?" Pete asked Spider as they rode along toward the 101 Ranch.

"Shore he will, so long as he can make a nickel out'n it."

"Can't wait t' see his face when we shoot." Pete grinned at

the thought.

"Don't show you're anxious t' shoot. It'd be best if they brought th' subject up."

"Who's that comin'?" Pete pointed with his chin at a cowboy riding to meet them at the river.

Spider squinted at the approaching rider. "Looks like ol' Cap Leslie, don't it?"

"Think you're right," Pete said and waved.

"Howdy, boys. Yuh come t' make a visit?" Cap greeted.

"Right after we water these horses," Sol said. The three rode to the river and down the bank to a long pool of water.

"Shore 'nuf, Cap, how're you makin' it?" Pete asked.

"Doin' fine, doin' fine."

Sol lit his pipe, "Other boys well and whole?"

"Was when I left 'em, but you know how they git without any supervision—say, we got ol' Jep t' sing after you boys left last month."

"How'd yuh do that?" Spider eased his horse down the riverbank.

"Gave him a plug o' tobaccer."

Pete grinned. "For a whole plug, *I'd* sing. Can he sing?"

"Oh, could he ever sing. Sang ever song I ever knowed an' some I never heard afore. Sang at th' table, sang in th' barn, sang in th' bunkhouse, sang in th' outhouse." Cap's horse pushed in between the two drinking horses and shoved them over.

Pete's horse struggled to keep out of the water. "Sang all th' time, did he?"

"Wouldn't shut up." Cap's horse shouldered for more room and drank.

Spider backed his horse up the steep bank and stood behind the two horses at the water. "How'd you git him t' shut up?"

Cap snorted. "Give him two plugs. Sentiments is, we ain't

gonna ask him agin." He paused a moment as his rude horse continued nudging Pete's horse. Some horses are jealous of the spot other horses are drinking. They must think the water's better there. Cap didn't try to control his horse. "This is th' deepest hole on th' river," he said. "Ain't found th' bottom out there in th' middle." His horse pushed hard against Pete's so that the horse had to scramble up the bank or fall into the river.

Pete turned and pulled his rope off the horn. Raising it high, he slapped it down on the rump of Cap's drinking horse. In an instant, the horse raised his head and leaped as far as he could into the river. Horse and rider disappeared while Cap's hat bobbed serenely in the current.

The horse popped up, swimming, with Cap holding on to his tail and sputtering.

"Did yuh find th' bottom, Cap?" Spider asked.

"Dam yore hide, Pete. I'm agonna kill you when I get outta here!" The rude horse swam for the ford where he knew there was shallow water, towing Cap along behind him.

"See you at th' ford, Cap," Pete said as they loped ahead. They hardly got their stirrups wet as they crossed. Cap and horse made it to standing water. As the man waded out of the river, he pulled his gun and fired at the waiting men. The gun fired, but only half the powder fired, the rest being wet. Water squirted out of the barrel with a pop. The bullet traveled fifty feet and gave up with a splash.

"Cain't kill anyone with a water pistol, Cap." Pete hollered. They turned and loped off, leaving the 101 hand to dry as best he could. "When I git dry powder, Pete, when I'm dry . . ." he promised.

They rode up to the 101 bunkhouse as a half dozen men were lounging on the porch watching Nigger Bill finish his third plate of beans. "Empty those saddles, boys, an' come see if Bill's left anythin' in th' kitchen," Henry Jones, the 101 foreman, invited. "You see anything of Cap Leslie when you come through?"

"Seen him hanging 'round th' Deep Hole, talkin' 'bout findin' th' bottom of it," Spider replied, eyeing Nigger Bill's plate. The two found enough food left by Bill to get by, and sat on the porch eating and talking.

"Say," one of the hands said. "Is that th' stock of a new rifle in your boot, Pete, or is it a new stock on your old gun?"

"New gun, Jep. Take a look at it."

Jep looked the gun over. "Got a good heft an' balance to it. How's she shoot?"

"Shoots good," Spider said. "Has a higher muzzle velocity, too."

"Why, you both got one, didn't you?" one of the men asked.

"Yup. Couldn't let Pete git th' jump on me thataway. I'd'a never heard th' end of it."

Bill eyed the guns. "Still ain't faster'n me, I bet." The men paid him scant attention, talking about the new rifles. "I say, they's not es fast es me. Ain't a gun borned yit can catch me."

Henry looked at the black cowhand. "You thinkin' t' challenge them, Bill?"

"Shore, I will," he replied.

Now, Bill wasn't talking about outrunning a bullet; he was talking about out-*dodging* a bullet. The game was played this way: Bill stood behind the corner of the house and stuck his head around the edge. His challenger stood two hundred feet away and had the choice of rifle or pistol. For a nickel a shot, Bill would let the men shoot at his head. Two things were in Bill's favor: the smoke of the black powder appeared before the bullet with its slow muzzle speed got to the corner. When he saw the smoke, Bill ducked. The fact that he was sitting there bragging was ample evidence he had never lost. He grinned; it was a sure thing.

"Nah," Pete said, "I ain't payin' you for th' privilege of you seeing me shoot my new gun, Bill."

"An' I ain't lettin' *no-o-o body* shoot at my noggin fer nothin'," Bill replied.

Pete had his rifle halfway into its boot when Spider said, "Hold on there a minute. Bill, how much money you got in your pocket?"

"I got sixty cent."

"I'll bet you sixty cents that my bullet gets to you before you can duck."

"I takes you up on that. Nothin' like doublin' yore money on one shot." Bill laughed.

There was a shuffle for guns as Bill marked the two-hundred-foot line and gathered thirty cents from six hopeful men.

"Let these fellers go first t' be sure you're warmed up good, and we'll go last," Spider said to Bill.

"Sho 'nough." Bill trotted off to the corner. Six men toed the line and six men heard the taunts of the target after their shot. Now was the time for Pete and Spider to demonstrate their new guns.

"How much money's in your pocket now, Bill?" Spider asked.

"Ninety cent."

"I'll bet you ninety cents my bullet gets there before you duck."

"Hey, wait a minute," Pete interjected. "Where's that leave me? I ain't shootin' fer nothin'."

Bill couldn't pass up a sure thing, "I covers your ninety cent, too," he said.

"You got it?"

"Shore."

"How we gonna collect with two bullet holes in your head?" Spider asked.

"Ninety's in my pocket, an' you can have ninety outta my possibles."

"Good enough. Here goes," Pete said. Lower, to Spider, he said, "You shoot high, an' I'll shoot low." To Bill; "We're gonna both shoot at once, Bill."

"All right, go 'head."

The two shooters toed the line, aimed, and on the count, fired together. Splinters flew from the corner just above Bill's head and barely below his fingers peeking around the corner below. The target's eyes widened, and his knees were suddenly very weak. *Something's wrong. They shot and there was no smoke.* He backed against the wall and slid down until he was sitting. Eight anxious hands rounded the corner. "You get hurt, Bill?"

Nigger Bill had time to gather his thoughts. "Beat you. Tole you I could."

"Beat us? Yore head never moved," Spider exclaimed.

"I'se still alive, ain't I? You both missed, an' I won yore money."

"The bet wasn't that they would hit you, Bill. It was that their bullets would get to you before you could move," Henry Jones said.

"Well, I ducked 'em, so I wins," Bill persisted.

"Hey, Bill, is that blood runnin' down yore neck?" Jep asked.

"Shore it is," one of the others said. He moved Bill's head aside and found a splinter imbedded at the base of his skull. "Splinter says yore head was stickin out when th' bullet hit th' wall."

"They wasn't no smoke," Bill said as much to himself as to anyone else.

"We got some of them new smokeless powder bullets, Bill." Pete grinned at the man.

" 'Tain't fair. Bet's off," Bill almost begged.

"Th' bet was fair, Bill. Pay up or walk." Henry was short of patience with pikers.

Reluctantly, Bill dug out his ninety cents and handed them to Spider. "I got your money in th' house, Pete." He had almost reached the door when it slammed open and Cap stomped out, "*Now,* my powder's dry, an' I'm after you, Pete. Where are you?"

Pete jumped and blanched slightly. "Swapping horses with you for a while, Henry," he whispered and trotted off behind the bunkhouse for the corral. In a moment, he was out on a horse bareback. Cap got one shot off before he ran for his horse. It was quite a race for a while, and Pete stayed out of Cap's sight for some time before Cap cooled off. But he never let Pete get behind him again.

Bill never paid off on Pete's bet.

REAL CHARACTERS

Lee's journey from Liberty Springs, Arkansas, to northeast New Mexico Territory involved contact with an amazing number of real characters of that time. The following is a list of those people in the approximate order they appeared in the story:

Bass Reeves, Ol' Baz, Deputy U.S. Marshal.

Judge Isaac Charles Parker, judge for the U.S. District Court for the Western District of Arkansas.

John Carroll, U.S. Marshal.

Edward (Dirty Face) Jones, founded Jones and Plummer Trail with Joe Plummer.

Jim Lane, Beaver Road Ranch.

William Waddle, Ernest Reiman, Beaver Townsite Co.

D.R. Healey, Jim Donnelly, Beaver City men.

O.P. Bennett, Frank Thompson, Road Trotters (Claim Jumpers).

Billy Olive, Print Olive's son.

Bill Henderson, barkeeper.

Addison Mundel, first Beaver marshal.

Charles Siringo, Pinkerton man.

Asa Soule, Hop Bitters owner.

Tom & Jim Masterson, Bill Tilghman, Neal Brown, Dodge Peace Commission members.

I.W. English, casualty of war.

Juan Cortina, Mexican bandit.

Colonel Jack Hardesty and his brother, John.

Ludwig Kramer, rancher.

John Durfee, Half Circle S manager.

Joe Cruse (Cruze) and common law wife.

Mr. and Mrs. E.E. Hubbard, Florence merchant and postmistress.

Florence Hubbard, daughter.

George Marrs-Florence (Kenton) lunch counter and saloon owner.

Pressley-Kenton saloon owner.

Frank Pierce Tipton, Springfield, Colorado, merchant.

S.W. Harman, lawyer, wrote *Hell on the Border.*

Joe Ferguson, Club Saloon owner at Joplin, Missouri.

Bill Coe's Ghost.

Henry Jones, 101 Ranch boss.

Albert Easley, early settler and 101 Ranch hand, and his wife, Molly.

Judge L.M. Hubbard, nee Sutter, No Man's Land distiller, lawyer.

Tine Arnold, chuck-line rider, cook, fence builder; came to No Man's Land in 1848.

Billy Hill, horse thief.

John Brite.

James and Bridget Dacy and their children: Lucy, Johanna, Nellie, Katie, James.

Doctor Harris.

Henry Labrier, married Johanna Dacy.

ABOUT THE AUTHOR

James Crownover began his third career as a writer after retiring from his engineering career. His lifelong interest in history and, more particularly, the history of the western migration of early American pioneers, led him to write about those people and their times. Too little is told about the unnoticed people who struggled to bring order to their lives and, in so doing, brought order and peace to a whole land.

Jim lives in a small community in northwest Arkansas where he enjoys raising laying hens, and watching the wildlife of the area crossing his meadow. He enjoys traveling the western highways, but has lately found, as Somerset Maugham found, that the best journeys are the ones you take at your own fireside.

The employees of Five Star Publishing hope you have enjoyed this book.

Our Five Star novels explore little-known chapters from America's history, stories told from unique perspectives that will entertain a broad range of readers.

Other Five Star books are available at your local library, bookstore, all major book distributors, and directly from Five Star/Gale.

<u>Connect with Five Star Publishing</u>

Visit us on Facebook:
https://www.facebook.com/FiveStarCengage

Email:
FiveStar@cengage.com

For information about titles and placing orders:
(800) 223-1244
gale.orders@cengage.com

To share your comments, write to us:
Five Star Publishing
Attn: Publisher
10 Water St., Suite 310
Waterville, ME 04901